# THE ALIBI

# SANDRA BROWN

# THE ALIBI

WARNER BOOKS

A Time Warner Company

Copyright © 1999 by Sandra Brown Management, Ltd.

Warner Books, Inc., 1271 Avenue of the Americas,
New York, NY 10020

Visit our Web site at www.warnerbooks.com

 A Time Warner Company

Printed in the United States of America

ISBN 0-446-51980-4

# THE ALIBI

# SATURDAY

# PROLOGUE

THE SCREAM RENT THE AIR-CONDITIONED SILENCE of the hotel corridor.

Having entered the suite only seconds earlier, the chambermaid stumbled from the room crying for help, sobbing, and randomly banging on the doors of other guest rooms. Later, her supervisor would chastise her for this hysterical reaction, but at that point in time she was in the throes of hysteria.

Unfortunately for her, few guests were in their rooms that afternoon. Most were out enjoying the unique charms of Charleston's historic district. But finally she managed to rouse one guest, a man from Michigan, who, wilted from the unaccustomed heat, had returned to his room to take a nap.

Though groggy from being abruptly awakened, he immediately determined that only a major catastrophe could cause the level of panic the chambermaid was experiencing. Before he could even make sense of her blubbering, he called the front desk and alerted hotel personnel to an emergency on the top floor.

Two Charleston policemen, whose beat included the newly opened Charles Towne Plaza, promptly responded to the summons. A flustered hotel security guard led them to the penthouse suite, where the maid had gone in for early turndown service, only to find that it wouldn't be needed. The occupant was sprawled on the suite's parlor floor, dead.

The police officer knelt down near the body. "Holy . . . that looks like—"

"It's him all right," said his partner in an equally awestruck voice. "Is this gonna stir up a shitstorm or what?"

CHAPTER | 1

HE NOTICED HER THE MOMENT she stepped into the pavilion.

Even in a crowd of other women dressed, for the most part, in skimpy summer clothing, she was definitely a standout. Surprisingly, she was alone.

As she paused to get her bearings, her gaze stopped briefly on the dais, where the band was performing, before moving to the dance floor, then to the haphazard arrangement of chairs and tables surrounding it. Spotting a vacant table, she moved to it and sat down.

The pavilion was round in shape, about thirty yards in diameter. Although it was an open-air structure with a conical roof, the underside of which was strung with clear Christmas lights, the pitched ceiling trapped the noise inside, making the din incredible.

What the band lacked in musical talent they made up for with volume, obviously of the opinion that decibels would make their missed notes less discernible. They did, however, play with raucous enthusiasm and showmanship. On the keyboard and guitar, the musicians seemed to be pounding the notes out of their instruments. The harmonica player's braided beard bounced with every jerking motion of his head. As the fiddler sawed his bow across the strings, he danced an energetic jig that showed off his yellow cowboy boots. The drummer seemed to know only one cadence, but he applied himself to it with verve.

The crowd didn't seem to mind the discordant sound. For that matter, neither did Hammond Cross. Ironically, the racket of the county fair was somehow soothing. He absorbed the noise—the squeals coming from the midway, catcalls from rowdy teenage boys at the top of the Ferris wheel, the crying of babies grown tired, the bells and whistles and horns, the shouts and laughter inherent to a carnival.

Going to a county fair hadn't been on his agenda today. Although there had probably been some advance publicity about it in the local newspaper and on TV, it had escaped his notice.

He'd happened on the fair by accident about a half hour outside of Charleston. What had compelled him to stop, he would never know. It wasn't like he was an avid carnival-goer. His parents certainly had never taken him to one. They had avoided general-public attractions like this at all costs. Not exactly their crowd. Not their kind of people.

Ordinarily Hammond probably would have avoided it, too. Not because he was a snob, but because he worked such long, hard hours, he was selfish with his leisure time and selective about how he spent it. A round of golf, a couple hours of fishing, a movie, a quiet dinner at a good restaurant. But a county fair? That wouldn't have topped his list of pleasurable pursuits.

But this afternoon in particular the crowd and the noise appealed to him. Left alone, he only would have brooded over his troubles. He would have reflected himself into despondency, and who needed that on one of the few remaining weekends of the summer?

So when his highway speed was reduced to a crawl and he got trapped in the traffic inching into the temporary parking lot—actually a cow pasture turned parking lot by an enterprising farmer—he had remained in line with the other cars and vans and SUVs.

He paid two bucks to the tobacco-chewing youth who was collecting for the farmer and was fortunate enough to find a spot for his car beneath a shade tree. Before getting out, he removed his suit jacket and tie, and rolled up his shirtsleeves. As he picked his way carefully around cow patties, he wished for blue jeans and boots instead of dress slacks and loafers, but already he felt his spirits rising. Nobody here knew him. He didn't have to talk to anyone if he didn't want to. There were no obligations to be met, no meetings to attend, no telephone messages to return. Out here he wasn't a professional, or a colleague. Or a son. Tension, anger, and the weight of responsibility began to melt off him. The sense of freedom was heady.

The fairgrounds were demarcated by a plastic rope strung with multi-colored pennants that hung still and limp in the heat. The dense air was redolent with the tantalizing aromas of cooking food—junk food. From a distance, the music didn't sound half bad. Hammond was immediately glad he had stopped. He needed this . . . isolation.

Because despite the people streaming through the turnstile, he was, in a very real sense, isolated. Being absorbed by a large, noisy crowd suddenly seemed preferable to spending a solitary evening in his cabin, which had been his original plan upon leaving Charleston.

The band had played two songs since the auburn-haired woman had sat down across the pavilion from where he was seated. Hammond had continued to watch her, and to speculate. Most likely she was waiting for someone to join her, probably a husband and assorted children. She appeared to be not quite as old as he, maybe early thirties. About the age of the carpool-driving set. Cub Scout den mothers. PTA officers. The homemakers concerned with DPT booster shots, orthodontia, and getting their laundry whites white and their colors bright. What he knew of such women he had learned from TV commercials, but she seemed to fit that general demographic.

Except that she was a little too . . . too . . . edgy.

She didn't look like a mother of young children who was enjoying a few minutes' respite while Daddy took the kids for a ride on the carousel. She didn't have the cool, competent air of his acquaintances' wives who were members of Junior League and other civic clubs, who went to salad luncheons and hosted birthday parties for their kids and dinner parties for their husbands' business associates, and who played golf or tennis at their respective country clubs once or twice a week between their aerobics classes and Bible study circles.

She didn't have the soft, settled body of a woman who had borne two or three offspring, either. Her figure was compact and athletic. She had good—no, *great*—legs that were muscled, sleek, and tan, shown off by a short skirt and low-heeled sandals. Her sleeveless top had a scooped neck, like a tank top, and a matching cardigan which had been knotted loosely around her neck before she had removed it. The outfit was smart and chic, a cut above what most of this shorts-and-sneakers crowd was wearing.

Her handbag, which she'd placed on the table, was big enough only for a key ring, a tissue, and possibly a lipstick, but nowhere near large enough for a young mother whose purse was packed with bottled water and Handi Wipes and natural snacks and enough equipment to survive days in the wilderness should an emergency situation arise.

Hammond had an analytical mind. Deductive reasoning was his forte. So he concluded, with what he felt was a fair degree of accuracy, that it was unlikely this woman was a mom.

That did not mean that she wasn't married, or otherwise attached, and waiting to be joined by a significant other, whoever he might be and whatever the nature of their relationship. She could be a woman devoted to a career. A mover and a shaker in the business community. A successful salesperson. A savvy entrepreneur. A stockbroker. A loan officer.

Sipping his beer, which was growing tepid in the heat, Hammond continued to stare at her with interest.

Then suddenly he realized that his stare was being returned.

When their eyes met, his heart lurched, perhaps from embarrassment for having been caught staring. But he didn't look away. Despite the dancers that passed between them, intermittently blocking their line of sight, they maintained eye contact for several seconds.

Then she abruptly broke it, as though she might also be embarrassed for having picked him out of the crowd. Chagrined over having such a juvenile reaction to something as insignificant as making eye contact, Hammond relinquished his table to two couples who'd been hovering nearby waiting for one to become available. He weaved his way through the press of people toward the temporary bar. It had been set up during the fair to accommodate the thirsty dancers.

It was a popular spot. Personnel from the various military bases in the area were standing three deep at the bar. Even if not in uniform, they were identifiable by their sheared heads. They were drinking, scoping out the girls, weighing their chances of getting lucky, wagering on who would and who wouldn't, playing one-upmanship.

The bartenders were dispensing beer as fast as they could, but they couldn't keep up with the demand. Hammond tried several times to flag one's attention but finally gave up and decided to wait until the crowd had thinned out before ordering another.

Feeling a little less pathetic than he had no doubt looked sitting alone at his table, he glanced across the dance floor toward her table. His spirits drooped. Three men now occupied the extra chairs at her table. In fact, the wide shoulders of one were blocking her from Hammond's view. The trio weren't in uniform, but judging by the severity of their haircuts and their cockiness he guessed they were marines.

Well, he wasn't surprised. Disappointed, but not surprised.

She was too good-looking to be alone on a Saturday night. She'd been merely biding her time until her date showed up.

Even if she had come to the fair alone, she wouldn't have remained dateless for long. Not at a meat market like this. An unattached serviceman with a weekend pass had the instincts and singlemindedness of a shark. He had one purpose in mind, and that was to secure a female companion for the evening. Even without trying, this one would have attracted attention.

Not that *he* had been thinking about picking her up, Hammond told himself. He was too old for that. He wouldn't regress to a frat-rat mentality, for crying out loud. Besides, it really wouldn't be proper, would it? He wasn't exactly committed, but he wasn't exactly *un*committed, either.

Suddenly she stood up, grabbed her cardigan, slung the strap of her small purse over her shoulder, and turned to leave. Instantly the three men seated with her were on their feet, crowding around her. One, who appeared to be hammered, placed his arm across her shoulders and lowered his face close to hers. Hammond could see his lips moving; whatever he was saying to her made his companions laugh uproariously.

She didn't think it was funny. She averted her head, and it appeared to Hammond that she was trying to extricate herself from an awkward situation without causing a scene. She took the serviceman's arm and removed it from around her neck and, smiling stiffly, said something to him before once again turning as though to leave.

Not to be put off, and goaded by his two friends, the spurned one went after her. When he reached for her arm and pulled her around again, Hammond acted.

Later, he didn't remember crossing the dance floor, although he must have practically plowed his way through the couples now swaying to a slow dance, because within seconds he was reaching between two of the muscle-bound, hard-bellied marines, shoving the persistent one aside, and hearing himself say, "Sorry about that, honey. I ran into Norm Blanchard and you know how that son-of-a-gun can talk. Lucky for me, they're playing our song."

Curving his arm around her waist, he drew her out with him onto the dance floor.

"You got my instructions?"

"Yes, sir, Detective. No one else comes in, no one leaves. We've sealed off all the exits."

"That includes everybody. No exceptions."

"Yes, sir."

Having made his orders emphatic, Detective Rory Smilow nodded to the uniformed officer and entered the Charles Towne Plaza through the hotel's main doors. The staircase had been touted by numerous design magazines to be an architectural triumph. Already it had become the signature feature of the new complex. Epitomizing southern hospitality, two arms of wide steps swept up from the lobby floor. They seemed to be embracing the incredible crystal chandelier, before merging forty feet above the lobby to form the second-story gallery.

On both levels of the lobby policemen were mingling with hotel guests and employees, all of whom had heard by now that there had been what appeared to be a murder on the fifth floor.

Nothing created this kind of expectant atmosphere like a killing, Smilow thought as he assessed the scene.

Sunburned, perspiring, camera-toting tourists milled around, asking questions of anyone in authority, talking among themselves, speculating on the identity of the victim and what had provoked the murder.

In his well-tailored suit and French cuff shirt, Smilow was conspicuously overdressed. Despite the sweltering heat outside, his clothing was fresh and dry, not even moist. An irritated subordinate had once asked beneath his breath if Smilow ever sweated. "Hell, no," a fellow policeman had replied. "Everybody knows that aliens don't have sweat glands."

Smilow moved purposefully toward the bank of elevators. The officer he'd spoken with at the entrance must have communicated his arrival because another officer was standing in the elevator, holding the door open for him. Without acknowledging the courtesy, Smilow stepped in.

"Shine holding up, Mr. Smilow?"

Smilow turned. "Oh yeah, Smitty. Thanks."

The man everyone knew only by his first name operated three shoeshine chairs in an alcove off the hotel lobby. For decades he had been a fixture at another hotel downtown. Recently he had been lured to the Charles Towne Plaza, and his clientele had followed him. Even from out-of-towners he received excellent tips because Smitty knew more than the hotel concierge about what to do, and where to go, and where to find whatever you were looking for in Charleston.

Rory Smilow was one of Smitty's regulars. Ordinarily he would have paused to exchange pleasantries, but he was in a hurry now and actually resented being detained. Curtly he said, "Catch you later, Smitty." The elevator doors slid closed.

He and the uniformed cop rode up to the top floor in silence. Smilow never fraternized with fellow officers, not even those of equal ranking, but certainly not with those of lower rank. He never initiated conversation unless it pertained to a case he was working on. Men in the department who were fearless enough to try chitchatting with him soon discovered that such attempts were futile. His bearing discouraged comradeship. Even his natty appearance was as effective as concertina wire when it came to approachability.

When the elevator doors opened on the fifth floor, Smilow experienced a thrill he recognized. He had visited countless murder scenes, some rather tame and unspectacular, others remarkably grisly. Some were forgettable and routine. Others he would remember forever, either because of the imaginative flair of the killer, the strange surroundings in which the body had been discovered, the bizarre method of execution, the uniqueness of the weapon, or the age and circumstance of the victim.

But his first visit to a crime scene never failed to give him a rush of adrenaline, which he refused to be ashamed of. This was what he had been born to do. He relished his work.

When he stepped out of the elevator, the conversation among the plain-clothes officers in the hallway subsided. Respectfully, or fearfully, they stepped aside for him as he made his way to the open door of the hotel suite where a man had died today.

He made note of the room number, then peered inside. He was glad to see that the seven officers comprising the Crime Scene Unit were already there, going about their various duties.

Satisfied that they were doing a thorough job, he turned back to the three detectives who'd been dispatched by the Criminal Investigation Division. One who'd been smoking a cigarette hastily crushed it out in a smoking stand. Smilow treated him to a cold, unblinking stare. "I hope that sand didn't contain a crucial piece of evidence, Collins."

The detective stuffed his hands into his pockets like a third-grader who'd been reprimanded for not washing after using the rest room.

"Listen up," Smilow said, addressing the group at large. He never raised his voice. He never had to. "I will not tolerate a single mistake. If there's any contamination of this crime scene, if there's the slightest breach of proper procedure, if the merest speck of evidence is overlooked or compromised by someone's carelessness, the offender's ass will be shredded. By me. Personally."

He made eye contact with each man. Then he said, "Okay, let's go." As they filed into the room they pulled on plastic gloves. Each man had a specific task; each went to it, treading lightly, touching nothing that they weren't supposed to.

Smilow approached the two officers who had been first on the scene. Without preamble, he asked, "Did you touch him?"

"No, sir."

"Touch anything?"

"No, sir."

"The doorknob?"

"The door was standing open when we got here. The maid who found him had left it open. The hotel security guard might have touched it. We asked, he said no, but . . ." He raised his shoulders in a shrug.

"Telephone?" Smilow asked.

"No, sir. I used my cellular. But again, the security guy might have used it before we got here."

"Who have you talked to so far?"

"Only him. He's the one who called us."

"And what did he say?"

"That a chambermaid found the body." He indicated the corpse. "Just like this. Face down, two gunshot wounds in his back beneath the left shoulder blade."

"Have you questioned the maid?"

"Tried. She's carryin' on so bad we didn't get much out of her. Besides, she's foreign. Don't know where she's from," the cop replied to Smilow's inquiring raised eyebrow. "Can't tell by the accent. She just keeps saying over and over, 'Dead man,' and boo-hooing into her hankie. Scared her shitless."

"Did you feel for a pulse?"

The officer glanced at his partner, who spoke for the first time. "I did. Just to make sure he was dead."

"So you *did* touch him."

"Well, yeah. But only for that."

"I take it you didn't feel one."

"A pulse?" The cop shook his head. "No. He was dead. No doubt."

Up to this point, Smilow had ignored the body. Now he moved toward it. "Anybody heard from the M.E.?"

"On his way."

The answer registered with Smilow, but he was intently gazing at the dead man. Until he saw it with his own eyes, he had been unable to believe that the reported murder victim was none other than Lute Pettijohn. A local celebrity of sorts, a man of renown, Pettijohn was, among other things, CEO of the development company that had converted the derelict cotton warehouse into the spectacular new Charles Towne Plaza.

He had also been Rory Smilow's brother-in-law.

# CHAPTER | 2

$S$HE SAID, "THANK YOU."

Hammond replied, "You're welcome."

"It was becoming a sticky situation."

"I'm just glad that my ruse worked. If it hadn't, I'd have three of the few and the proud after me."

"I commend your bravery."

"Or stupidity. They could have whipped my ass."

She smiled at that, and when she did, Hammond was doubly glad he had acted on his idiotic, chivalrous impulse to rescue her. He had been attracted to her the moment he spotted her, but seeing her from across the dance floor was nothing compared to the up-close and unrestricted view. She averted her eyes from his intense stare to gaze at a nonspecific point beyond his shoulder. She was cool under pressure. No doubt of that.

"What about your friend?" she asked.

"My friend?"

"Mr. Blanchard. Norm, wasn't it?"

"Oh," he said, laughing softly. "Never heard of him."

"You made him up?"

"Yep, and I have no idea where the name came from. It just popped into my head."

"Very creative."

"I had to say something plausible. Something to make it look like we were together. Familiar. Something that would, at the very least, get you out on the dance floor with me."

"You could have simply asked me to dance."

"Yeah, but that would have been boring. It also would have left an opening for you to turn me down."

"Well, thank you again."

"You're welcome again." He shuffled her around another couple. "Are you from around here?"

"Not originally."

"Southern accent."

"I grew up in Tennessee," she said. "Near Nashville."

"Nice area."

"Yes."

"Pretty terrain."

"Hmm."

"Good music, too."

*Brilliant conversation, Cross,* he thought. *Scintillating.*

She didn't even honor the last inane statement with a response, and he didn't blame her. If he kept this up, she'd be out of here before the song ended. He maneuvered them around another couple who were executing an intricate turn, then, in a deadpan voice, he asked the lamest of all lame pick-up lines. "Do you come here often?"

She caught the joke and smiled the smile that might reduce him to a total fool if he wasn't careful. "Actually, I haven't been to a fair like this since I was a teenager."

"Me, too. I remember going to one with some buddies. We must've been about fifteen and were on a quest to buy beer."

"Any success?"

"None."

"That was your last one?"

"No. I went to another with a date. I took her into the House of Fright specifically for the purpose of making out."

"And how successful was that?"

"It went about like the attempt to buy beer. God knows I tried. But I always seemed to be with the one girl who . . ." His voice trailed off when he felt her tense up.

"They don't give up easily, do they?"

Sure enough, the trio of troopers were standing just beyond the edge of the dance floor, nursing fresh beers and glowering at them.

"Well, if they were quick to surrender, our national security would be at risk." Giving the young men a smug smile, he tightened his arm around her waist and waltzed past them.

"You don't have to protect me," she said. "I could have handled the situation myself."

"I'm sure you could have. Fending off unwanted male attention is a skill every attractive woman must acquire. But you're also a lady who was reluctant to cause a scene."

She gazed up at him. "Very perceptive."

"So, since it's a done deal, we had just as well enjoy the dance, hadn't we?"

"I suppose."

But agreeing to continue the dance didn't reduce her tension. She wasn't exactly taking hasty glances over her shoulder, but Hammond sensed that she wanted to.

Which left him wondering what she would do when this dance ended. He expected a brush-off. A polite one, but a brush-off just the same. Fortunately the band was playing a sad, syrupy ballad. The singer's voice was unrefined and tinny, but he knew the words to all the verses. As far as Hammond was concerned, the longer the dance lasted, the better.

His partner fit him well. The top of her head was even with his chin. He hadn't breached the imaginary boundary she had set between them the moment he pulled her into his arms, although the thought of holding her flush against him was tantalizing.

For the time being he was okay with this, with having the inside of his forearm resting on the narrow small of her back, her hand—absent a wedding ring—resting on his shoulder, their feet staggered as they moved in time to the slow dance.

Occasionally their thighs made glancing contact and he experienced a fluttering of lust, but it was controllable. He had a bird's-eye view down the scooped neckline of her top but was gentleman enough not to look. His imagination, however, was running rampant, flitting here and there, ricocheting off the walls of his mind like a horsefly made crazy by the heat.

"They're gone."

Her voice drew Hammond from his daze. When he realized what she had said, he looked around and saw that the marines were no longer there. In fact, the song had ended, the musicians were laying down their instruments, and the bandleader was asking everybody to "stay right where you're at" and promising they would return with more music after taking a short break. Other couples were making their way back to tables or heading for the bar.

She had lowered her arms to her sides. Hammond, realizing that his arm was still around her, had no choice but to release her. When he did, she stepped back, away from him. "Well . . . never let it be said that chivalry is dead."

He grinned. "But if dragon-slaying ever comes back into vogue, forget it."

Smiling, she stuck out her hand. "I appreciate what you did."

"My pleasure. Thanks for the dance." He shook her hand. She turned to go. "Uh . . ." Hammond plunged through the crowd behind her.

When they reached the perimeter of the raised pavilion, he stepped to the ground, then took her hand to assist her down, an unnecessary and courtly gesture since it was no more than a foot and a half below. He fell into step with her. "Can I buy you a beer?"

"No, thank you."

"The corn on the cob smells good."

She smiled, but shook her head no.

"A ride on the Ferris wheel?"

She didn't slow down, but she shot him a wounded look. "Not the House of Fright?"

"Don't want to press my luck," he said, grinning now because he sensed a thaw. But his optimism was short-lived.

"Thanks, but I really need to go now."

"You just got here."

She stopped abruptly and turned to him. Tilting her head back, she looked at him sharply. The setting sun shot streaks of light through green irises. She squinted slightly, screening her eyes with lashes much darker than her hair. Wonderful eyes, he thought. Direct and candid, but sexy. And right now, piercingly inquisitive, wanting to know how he had known when she arrived.

"I noticed you as soon as you entered the pavilion," he confessed.

She held his gaze for several beats, then self-consciously lowered her head. The crowd eddied around them. A group of young boys ran past, dodging them by inches and kicking up a cloud of choking dust that swirled around them. A toddler set up a howl when her helium-filled balloon escaped her tiny fist and floated toward the treetops. A pair of tattooed teenage girls making a big production of lighting their cigarettes sauntered past talking loudly and profanely.

They reacted to none of it. The cacophony of the fair seemed not to penetrate a private silence.

"I thought you noticed me, too."

Miraculously she had no difficulty hearing Hammond's softly spoken words above the carnival noise. She didn't look at him, but he saw her smile, heard her light laugh of embarrassment.

"So you did? Notice me?"

She raised one shoulder in a small shrug of concession.

"Well, good," he said on a gust of breath that overstated his relief. "In that case I don't see why we're limiting our entire county fair experience to a single dance. Not that it wasn't great. It was. It's been ages since I enjoyed a dance that much."

She raised her head and gave him a retiring look.

"Hmm," he said. "I'm dorking out, right?"

"Totally."

He broke a wide grin just because she was so goddamn attractive and because it was okay with her that he was flirting like he hadn't flirted in twenty years. "Then how's this? I'm sorta footloose this evening, and I haven't been this unscheduled—"

"Is that a word?"

"It suffices."

"That's a fifty-cent word."

"All this to say that unless you have dinner plans . . . ?"

She indicated with a shake of her head that she didn't.

"Why don't we enjoy the rest of the fair together?"

Rory Smilow, staring into Lute Pettijohn's dead eyes, asked, "What killed him?"

The coroner, a slightly built, thoughtful man with a sensitive face and soft-spoken manner, had earned something extremely hard to come by—Smilow's respect.

Dr. John Madison was a southern black who had earned authority and position in a consummately southern city. Smilow held in high regard anyone who accomplished that kind of personal achievement in the face of adversity.

Meticulously Madison had studied the corpse as it had been found, face down. It had been outlined, then photographed from various angles. He had inspected the victim's hands and fingers, particularly beneath the nails. He had tested the wrists for rigidity. He had used a tweezers to pull an unidentifiable particle from Pettijohn's coat sleeve, then carefully placed the speck in an evidence bag.

It wasn't until he had completed the initial examination and asked assistance in turning the victim over that they uncovered their first surprise—a nasty wound on Pettijohn's temple at the hairline.

"Did the perp hit him, you think?" Smilow asked, squatting down for a better look at the wound. "Or was he shot first, and this happened when he fell?"

Madison adjusted his eyeglasses and said uneasily, "If it's difficult for you to talk about this, we can discuss it in detail later."

"You mean because he was once my brother-in-law?" When the medical examiner gave a small nod, Smilow said, "I never let my private life cross over into my professional life, and vice versa. Tell me what you think, John, and don't spare me any of the gory details."

"I'll have to examine the wound more closely, of course," Madison said, without further comment on the relationship between the victim and the detective. "However, my first guess would be that he sustained this head wound before he died, not postmortem. Although it's certainly ugly. It could have caused brain trauma of several sorts, any one of which could have been fatal."

"But you don't think so."

"Truly, Rory, I don't. It doesn't appear that traumatic. The swelling is on the outside, which usually indicates that there's little or none on the inside. Sometimes I'm surprised, though."

Smilow could appreciate the coroner's hesitancy to commit to one theory or another before an autopsy. "At this point, is it safe to say that he died of the gunshots?"

Madison nodded. "But that's only a first guess. Looks to me like he fell, or was pushed or struck before he died."

"How long before?"

"The timing will be harder to determine."

"Hmm."

Smilow gave the surrounding area a quick survey. Carpet. Sofa. Easy chairs. Soft surfaces except for the glass top on the coffee table. He duck-walked over to the table and angled his head down until he was eye-level with the surface. A drinking glass and bottle from the minibar had been found on the table. They had already been collected and bagged by the CSU.

From this perspective, Smilow could see several moisture rings, now dried, where Pettijohn had set down his drinking glass without a coaster beneath it. His eyes moved slowly across the glass surface, taking it an inch at a time. The fingerprint tech had discovered what appeared to be a handprint on the edge of the table.

Smilow came to his feet and tried to mentally reconstruct what could have happened. He backed up to the far side of the table, then moved toward it. "Let's suppose Lute was about to pick up his drink," he said, surmising out loud, "and pitched forward."

"Accidentally?" one of the detectives asked. Smilow was feared, generally disliked, but no one in the Criminal Investigation Division quarreled with his talent for re-creating a crime. Everyone in the room paused to listen attentively.

"Not necessarily," Smilow answered thoughtfully. "Somebody could have pushed him from behind, caused him to lose his balance. He went over."

He acted it out, being careful not to touch anything, especially the body. "He tried to break his fall by catching the edge of the table, but maybe his head struck the floor so hard he was knocked unconscious." He glanced up at Madison, his eyebrows raised inquisitively.

"Possibly," the medical examiner replied.

"It's fair to say he was at least dazed, right? He would have landed right here." He spread his hands to indicate the outline on the floor that traced the position in which the body had been found.

"Then whoever pushed him popped him with two bullets in the back," said one of the detectives.

"He was definitely shot in the back while lying face down," Smilow said, then looked to Madison for confirmation.

"It appears so," the M.E. said.

Detective Mike Collins whistled softly. "That's cold, man. To shoot a guy in the back when he's already down. Somebody was pissed."

"That's what Lute was most famous for—pissing off people," Smilow said. "All we've got to do is narrow it down to one."

"It was somebody he knew."

He looked at the detective who had spoken and indicated for him to continue. The detective said, "No sign of forced entry. No indication that the door lock was jimmied. So either the perp had a key or Pettijohn opened the door for him."

"Pettijohn's room key was in his pocket," one of the others reported. "Robbery wasn't a motive, unless it was thwarted. His wallet was found in a front pocket, beneath the body, and it appears intact. Nothing missing."

"Okay, so we've got something to work with here," Smilow said, "but we've still got a long way to go. What we don't have are a weapon and a suspect. This complex is crawling with people, employees as well as guests. Somebody saw something. Let's get started with the questioning. Round them up."

As he trudged toward the door, one of the detectives grumbled, "We're headed toward suppertime. They ain't going to like it."

To which Smilow retorted, "I don't care." And no one who had worked with him doubted that. "What about the security cameras?" he asked. Everything in Charles Towne Plaza was touted as state of the art. "Where's the videotape?"

"There seems to be some confusion with that."

He turned to the detective who had been dispatched earlier to check out the hotel security system. "What kind of confusion?"

"You know, confusion. General screwup. The tape is temporarily unaccounted for."

"Missing?"

"They wouldn't commit that far."

Smilow muttered a curse.

"The guy in charge promises we'll have it soon. But, you know . . ." The detective raised his shoulders as though to say with deprecation, *Civilians.*

"Let me know. I want to see it ASAP." Smilow addressed them as a group. "This is going to be a high-profile murder. Nobody talks to the media except me. Keep your mouths shut, got that? The perp's trail gets cooler with each minute, so get started."

The detectives filed out to begin the questioning of hotel guests and employees. People automatically resented being questioned because it implied guilt, so it would be an unpleasant and tiresome task. And Smilow, they knew from experience, was an unrelenting and merciless taskmaster.

He now turned to Dr. Madison again. "Can you get this done quickly?"

"A couple of days."

"Monday?"

"It'll mean my weekend's shot to hell."

"So's mine," Smilow said unapologetically. "I want toxicology, everything."

"You always do," Madison said with a good-natured smile. "I'll do my best."

"You always do."

After the body had been removed, Smilow addressed one of the CSU techs. "How is it?"

"It's in our favor that the hotel is new. Not that many fingerprints, so most of them will probably be Pettijohn's."

"Or the perp's."

"I wouldn't count on that," the technician said, frowning. "It's as clean a site as I've ever seen."

When the suite was empty, Smilow walked through it himself. He personally checked everything, opening every drawer, checking the closet and the built-in safe, looking between the mattresses, underneath the bed, inside the bathroom medicine cabinet, the tank of the toilet, looking for anything that Lute Pettijohn might have left behind that hinted at his killer's identity.

The sum total of Smilow's find was a Gideon Bible and the Charleston telephone directory. He found nothing personal belonging to Lute Pettijohn, no date book, receipts, tickets, scribbled notes, food wrappers, nothing.

Smilow counted two bottles of scotch missing from the minibar, but only one glass had been used, unless the murderer had been smart enough to take the one he'd used with him when he left. But Smilow learned after checking with housekeeping that the standard number of highball glasses stocked in a suite was four, and three clean ones remained.

As crime scenes go, it was virtually sterile—except for the bloodstain on the sitting room carpet.

"Detective?"

Smilow, who'd been thoughtfully staring at the blood-soaked carpet, raised his head.

The officer standing in the open doorway hitched his thumb toward the corridor. "She insisted on coming in."

"She?"

"Me." A woman nudged aside the patrol officer as though he were of no significance whatsoever, removed the crime scene tape from the doorway, and stepped inside. Quick, dark eyes swept the room. When she saw the dark bloodstain, she expelled a breath of disappointment and disgust. "Madison has already got the body? Damn!"

Smilow, crooking his arm in order to read the face of his wristwatch, said, "Congratulations, Steffi. You've broken your own speed record."

## CHAPTER 3

I THOUGHT YOU MIGHT BE WAITING on the husband and kids."

"When?"

"When you came into the pavilion."

"Oh."

She didn't take Hammond's bait, but only continued licking her ice-cream bar. Not until the wooden stick was clean did she say, "Is that your way of asking if I'm married?"

He made a pained face. "And here I thought I was being so subtle."

"Thanks for the chocolate nut bar."

"Is that your way of avoiding an answer?"

Laughing, they approached a set of uneven wooden steps leading down to a pier. The platform stood about three feet above the surface of the water and was about ten yards square. Water lapped gently against the pilings beneath the weathered planks. Wooden benches formed the perimeter, their backs serving as a safety railing. Hammond took her ice-cream stick and wrapper and discarded them along with his in a trash can, then motioned her toward one of the benches.

At each corner of the deck was a light pole, but the bulbs were dim and unobtrusive. Clear Christmas lights like those on the ceiling of the pavilion had been strung between the light poles. They softened the rusticity, making the ordinary, unattractive pier a romantic setting.

The breeze was soft, but strong enough to give one a fighting chance against mosquitoes. Frogs croaked in the dense undergrowth lining the riverbank. Cicadas sang from the low-hanging, moss-strewn branches of the sheltering live oak trees.

"Nice out here," Hammond remarked.

"Hmm. I'm surprised no one else has discovered it."

"I reserved it so we could have it all to ourselves."

She laughed. They had laughed a lot in the last couple hours while sampling the high-caloric fares of the food vendors and walking aimlessly from booth to booth. They had admired home-canned peaches and string beans, got a lesson on the latest in workout equipment, and tried out the cushioned seats of high-tech tractors. He had won a miniature teddy bear for her at a baseball toss. She had declined to try on a wig, although the saleswoman had been very persuasive.

They had taken a ride on the Ferris wheel. When their car stopped at the summit and swayed precariously, Hammond had felt downright giddy. It was one of the most carefree moments he could remember since . . .

He couldn't remember a more carefree moment.

The tethers that kept him grounded so securely—people, work, obligations—seemed to have been snipped. For a few minutes he had been floating free. He had felt free to enjoy the thrill of being suspended high above the fairgrounds. Free to enjoy a lightheartedness he rarely experienced anymore. Free to enjoy the company of a woman he had met less than two hours ago.

Spontaneously he turned to her now and asked, "*Are* you married?"

She laughed and ducked her head even as she shook it. "So much for subtlety."

"Subtlety wasn't doing it for me."

"No, I'm not married. Are you?"

"No." Then, "Whew! I'm glad we got that clarified."

Raising her head, she looked across at him, smiling. "So am I."

Then they stopped smiling and just looked at each other. The stare stretched into seconds, then moments, long, still, quiet moments on the outside, but clamorous where emotions were housed.

For Hammond it was one of those once-in-a-lifetime-if-you're-lucky moments. The kind that even the most talented movie directors and actors can't quite capture on film. The kind of connecting moment that poets and songwriters try to describe in their compositions, but never quite nail. Up till now, Hammond had been under the misconception that they'd done a fair job of it. Only now did he realize how miserably they had failed.

How could one, anyone, describe the instant when it all comes together? How to describe that burst of clarity when one knows that his life has only just now begun, that everything that's happened before was rot compared to this, and that nothing will ever be the same again? The elusive answers to all the questions ceased to matter, and he realized that the only truth he really needed to know was right here, right now. This moment.

He had never felt like this in his life.

Nobody had ever felt like this.

He was still rocking on the top car of the Ferris wheel and he never wanted to come down.

Just as he said, "Will you dance with me again?" she said, "I really need to go."

"Go?" "Dance?"

They spoke at the same time again, but Hammond overrode her. "Dance with me again. I wasn't in top form last time, what with the Marine Corps watching my every step."

She turned her head and looked in the direction of the parking lot on the far side of the fairgrounds.

He didn't want to press her. Any attempt at coercion probably would send her running. But he couldn't let her go. Not yet. "Please?"

Her expression full of uncertainty, she looked back at him, then gave him a small smile. "All right. One dance."

They stood up. She started for the steps, but he reached for her hand and brought her around. "What's wrong with here?"

She pulled in a breath, released it slowly, shakily. "Nothing, I guess."

He hadn't touched her since their last dance, short of placing his hand lightly on the small of her back to guide her around a bottleneck in the crowd. He'd offered her his hand when they stepped into and out of the Ferris wheel car. They'd been elbow to elbow and hip to hip for the duration of the ride. But other than those few exceptions, he had curbed every temptation to touch her, not wanting to scare her off, or come across as a creep, or insult her.

Now he pulled her forward gently, but firmly, until they were standing toe to toe. Then he curved his arm around her waist and drew her close. Closer than before. Against him. She went hesitantly, but she didn't try to angle away. She raised her arm to his shoulder. He felt the imprint of her hand at the base of his neck.

The band had called it a night. Music was now being provided by a DJ who had been playing a variety ranging from Creedence Clearwater to Streisand. Because it was growing late and the mood of the dancers had turned more mellow, he was playing slower songs.

Hammond recognized the tune, but couldn't name the singer or the song currently coming from the pavilion. It didn't matter. The ballad was slow and sweet and romantic. At first he tried to get his feet to execute the sequence of steps that he had learned as a youth reluctantly attending cotillions his mother roped him into. But the longer he held her, the more impossible it became to concentrate on anything except her.

One song segued into another, but they never missed a beat, despite her agreeing to only one dance. In fact, neither noticed when the music changed. Their eyes and minds were locked on each other.

He brought their clasped hands up to his chest and pressed hers palm down, then covered it with his. She tipped her head forward and down until her forehead was resting on his collarbone. He rubbed his cheek against her hair. He felt rather than actually heard the small sound of want that vibrated in her throat. His own desire echoed it.

Their feet shuffled to a decreasing tempo until eventually they stopped moving altogether. They were still except for the strands of her hair that the breeze brushed against his face. The heat emanating from every point of contact seemed to forge them together. Hammond dipped his head for the kiss that he believed was inevitable.

"I must go." She broke away and turned abruptly toward the bench where she'd left her handbag and cardigan.

For several seconds he was too stunned to react. After taking up her things, she made to move past him with a rushed, "Thanks for everything. It was lovely. Truly."

"Wait a minute."

She eluded his touch and quickly went up the steps, tripping once in her haste. "I have to go."

"Why now?"

"I can't . . . can't do this."

She tossed the words over her shoulder as she hurriedly made her way toward the parking area. She followed the string of pennants, avoiding the midway, the pavilion, and the waning activity in the booths. Some of the attractions already had closed. Exhibitioners were tearing down their booths and packing up their arts and crafts. Families loaded down with souvenirs and prizes trudged toward their vans. The noises weren't so joyful or so loud as earlier. The music in the pavilion now sounded more forlorn than romantic.

Hammond stayed even with her. "I don't understand."

"What's not to understand? I've told you I must go. That's all there is to it."

"I don't believe that." Desperate to detain her, he reached for her arm. She stopped, took several deep breaths, and turned to face him, although she didn't look at him directly.

"I had a lovely time." She spoke in a flat voice with little inflection, as though these were lines she had memorized. "But now the evening is over and I have to leave."

"But—"

"I don't owe you an explanation. I don't owe you anything." Her eyes made brief contact with his before skittering away again. "Now please, don't try and stop me again."

Hammond released her arm and stepped back, raising his hands as though in surrender.

"Goodbye," was all she said before turning away from him and picking her way over the rough ground toward the designated parking area.

Stefanie Mundell tossed Smilow the keys to her Acura. "You drive while I change." They had left the hotel by the East Bay Street entrance and were moving briskly down the sidewalk, which was congested not only with the usual Saturday night crowd, but with curiosity-seekers drawn to the new complex by the emergency vehicles parked along the street.

They moved through the curious onlookers without drawing notice because neither's appearance denoted "public official." Smilow's suit was still unwrinkled, his French cuffs unsoiled. Despite the hullabaloo surrounding Pettijohn's murder, he hadn't broken a sweat.

No one would suspect Steffi of being an assistant county solicitor, either. She was dressed in running shorts and sports bra, both still damp with perspiration that even the hotel's air-conditioning system couldn't dry. Her stiff nipples, along with her lean and muscled legs, attracted several male passersby, but she wasn't even aware of their appreciative glances as she motioned Smilow toward her car, which was illegally parked in a tow-away zone.

He depressed the keyless entry button but didn't go around to open the passenger door for her. She would have rebuffed the gesture if he had. She climbed into the back seat. Smilow got behind the wheel. As he started the car and waited to pull into traffic, Steffi asked, "Was that the truth? What you told those cops as we came out?"

"Which part?"

"Ah, so some of it was bullshit?"

"Not the part about us having no apparent motive, no weapon, and no suspect at this time." He had told them to keep their mouths shut when reporters started showing up asking questions. Already he had called a press conference for eleven o'clock. By scheduling it at that time, he ensured the local stations going live with it during their late newscasts and consequently maximizing his TV exposure.

Impatient with the endless line of cars crawling down the thoroughfare, he poked Steffi's car into the narrow lane and earned a loud horn blast from an oncoming vehicle.

Showing the same level of impatience that Smilow exhibited with his driving, Steffi whipped the sports bra over her head. "Okay, Smilow, no one can overhear you now. Talk. This is me."

"So I see," he remarked, glancing at her in the rearview mirror.

Unabashed, she wiped her underarms with a hand towel she took from her gym bag. "Two parents, nine children, one bathroom. In our house if you were timid or prissy, you stayed dirty and constipated."

For someone who disclaimed her blue-collar roots, Steffi frequently referred to them, usually to justify her crass behavior.

"Well, hurry and dress. We'll be there in a few minutes. Although you don't even need to be there. I can do this alone," Smilow said.

"I *want* to be there."

"All right, but I'd like not to get arrested on the way, so stay low where no one can see you like that."

"Why, Rory, you're a prude," she said, playing the coquette.

"And you're bloodthirsty. How'd you smell out a fresh kill so fast?"

"I was running. When I passed the hotel and saw all the police cars, I stopped to ask one of the cops what was going on."

"So much for orders not to talk."

"I have my persuasive ways. Besides, he recognized me. When he told me, I couldn't believe my ears."

"Same here."

Steffi put on a conventional bra, then peeled off her shorts and reached into the bag for a pair of panties. "Stop changing the subject. What have you got?"

"About the cleanest crime scene I've had in a long time. Maybe the cleanest I've ever seen."

"Seriously?" she asked with apparent disappointment.

"Whoever did him knew what he was doing."

"Shot in the back while lying face down on the floor."

"That's it."

"Hmm."

He glanced at her again. She was buttoning up a sleeveless dress, but her mind wasn't on the task. She was staring into near space, and he could practically see the wheels of her clever brain turning.

Stefanie Mundell had been with the County Solicitor's Office a little more than two years, but during her tenure she had made quite an impression—not always a good one. Some regarded her as a royal bitch, and she could be. She had a rapacious tongue and wasn't averse to using it. She never, ever backed down during an argument, which made her an excellent trial lawyer and a scourge to defense attorneys, but it didn't endear her to co-workers.

But at least half the men, and perhaps some of the women, who worked in and around the police department and county judicial building had the hots for her. Fantasy alliances with her were often discussed in crude detail over drinks after work. Not within her hearing, of course, because no one wished on himself a sexual harassment rap filed by Stefanie Mundell.

If she was aware of all the closet lusting for her, she pretended not to be. Not because it would bother her or make her uneasy to know that men were applying the lewdest terms to her. She would simply look upon it as something too juvenile, silly, and trivial on which to waste time and energy.

Secretly Rory watched her in the mirror now, as she buckled a slim leather belt around her waist and then pushed her hands through her hair as a means of grooming it. He wasn't physically attracted to her. Watching her operate didn't spark in him any mad, carnal desire, only a deep appreciation for her keen intelligence and the ambition that drove her. These qualities reminded him of himself.

"That was a very meaningful 'hmm,' Steffi. What are you thinking?"

"How furious the perp must've been."

"One of my detectives commented on that. It was a cold-blooded killing. The M.E. thinks Lute might have been unconscious when he was shot. In any case, he was posing no threat. The killer merely wanted him dead."

"If you made up a list of all the people who wanted Lute Pettijohn dead—"

"We don't have that much paper and ink."

She met his eyes in the mirror and smiled. "Right. So, any guesses?"

"Not now."

"Or you just aren't saying?"

"Steffi, you know I don't bring anything to your office before I'm ready."

"Just promise me—"

"No promises."

"Promise no one else will get first shot."

"No pun intended."

"You know what I mean," she said crossly.

"Mason will assign the case," he said, referring to Monroe Mason, Charleston County solicitor. "It'll be up to you to see that you get it."

But looking at her in the mirror and seeing the fire in her eyes, he had no doubt that she would make that a priority. He brought the car to a halt at the curb. "Here we are."

They alighted in front of Lute Pettijohn's mansion. Its grandiose exterior, befitting its prestigious South Battery address, was a layering of architecture. The original Georgian had given way to Federal touches following the Revolutionary War. There followed the addition of Greek Revival columns when they were the antebellum rage. The imposing structure was later updated with splashes of Victorian gingerbread. This patchwork of architecture was typical of the Historic District, and, ironically, made Charleston all the more picturesque.

The three-story house had deep double balconies lined with stately pillars and graceful arches. A cupola crowned its gabled roof. For two centuries it had withstood wars, crippling economic lulls, and hurricane winds, before sustaining the latest assault on it—Lute Pettijohn.

His well-documented restoration had taken years. The first architect overseeing the project had resigned to have a nervous breakdown. The second had suffered a heart attack; his cardiologist had forced him to retire from the project. The third had seen the restoration to completion, but it had cost him his marriage.

From the elaborate ironwork front gate with its historically registered lantern standards, down to the reproduction hinges on the back doors, Lute had spared no expense to make his house the most talked about in Charleston.

*That* he had achieved. It wasn't necessarily the most admired restoration, but it was certainly the most talked about.

He had battled with the Preservation Society of Charleston, the Historic Charleston Foundation, and the Board of Architectural Review over his proposal to convert the ancient and crumbling warehouse into what was now the Charles Towne Plaza. These organizations, whose purpose was to zealously preserve Charleston's uniqueness, control zoning, and limit commercial expansion, initially had vetoed his proposal. He didn't receive permits until all were assured that the integrity of the building's original brick exterior would not be drastically altered or compromised, that its well-earned scars would not be camouflaged, and that it would never be defaced with marquees or other contemporary signposts that designated it for what it was.

The preservation societies had harbored similar reservations about his house renovation, although they were pleased that the property, which had fallen into a sad state of disrepair, had been purchased by someone with the means to refurbish it in a fashion it deserved.

Pettijohn had abided by the rigid guidelines because he had no choice. But the general consensus was that his redo of the house, particularly the interior, was a prime example of how vulgar one can be when he has more money than taste. It was unanimously agreed, however, that the gardens were not to be rivaled anywhere in the city.

Smilow noticed how lush and well groomed the front garden was as he depressed the button on the intercom panel at the front gate.

Steffi looked over at him. "What are you going to say to her?"

Waiting for the bell to be answered from inside the house, he thoughtfully replied, "Congratulations."

## CHAPTER 4

$B$UT EVEN RORY SMILOW wasn't that heartless and cynical.

When Davee Pettijohn gazed down the curving staircase to the foyer below, the detective was standing with his hands clasped behind his back, staring either at his highly polished shoes or at the imported Italian tile flooring beneath them. In any case, he appeared totally focused on the area surrounding his feet.

The last time Davee had seen her husband's former brother-in-law, they were attending a social function honoring the police department. Smilow had been presented an award that night. Following the ceremony, Lute had sought him out to congratulate him. Smilow had shaken Lute's hand, but only because Lute had forced it. He had been civil to them, but Davee surmised that the detective would rather rip out Lute's throat with his teeth than shake his hand.

Rory Smilow appeared as rigidly controlled tonight as he had been on that last occasion. His bearing and appearance were military crisp. His hair was thinning on the crown of his head, but that was noticeable only because of her bird's-eye view.

The woman with him was a stranger to her. Davee had a lifetime habit of sizing up any other woman with whom she came into contact, so she would have remembered if she had met Smilow's companion.

While Smilow never looked up, the woman seemed avidly curious. Her head was in constant motion, swiveling about, taking in all the appoint-

THE ALIBI | 31

ments of the entryway. She didn't miss a single European import. Her eyes were quick and predatory. Davee disliked her on sight.

Nothing short of a catastrophe would have brought Smilow into Lute's house, but Davee chose to deny that as long as possible. She drained her highball glass and, making certain not to rattle the ice cubes, set it on a console table. Only then did she make her presence known.

"Y'all wanted to see me?"

Following the sound of her voice, they turned in unison and spotted her up above on the gallery. She waited until their eyes were fixed on her before starting her descent. She was barefoot and slightly disheveled, but she came down the staircase, her hand trailing along the railing, as though she were dressed in a ball gown, the princess of the evening, with humble subjects adoring her and paying homage. She had been born into a family at the epicenter of Charleston society. From both sides, she was of the *noblesse oblige*. She never forgot it, and she made certain no one else did, either.

"Hello, Mrs. Pettijohn."

"We don't have to stand on ceremony, do we, Rory?" She came to stand within touching distance and, tilting her head to one side, smiled up at him. "After all, we're practically kinfolk."

She extended him her hand. His was dry and warm. Hers was slightly damp and very cold, and she wondered if he guessed that came from holding a tumbler of vodka.

He released her hand and indicated the woman with him. "This is Stefanie Mundell."

"Steffi," the woman said, aggressively thrusting her hand at Davee.

She was petite, with short dark hair and dark eyes. Eager eyes. Hungry eyes. She wasn't wearing stockings even though she had on high-heeled pumps. To Davee that was a breach of etiquette more offensive than her own bare feet.

"How do you do?" Davee shook Steffi Mundell's hand but released it quickly. "Are y'all selling tickets to the Policemen's Ball, or what?"

"Is there someplace we can talk?"

Concealing her uneasiness with a bright smile, she said, "Sure," and led them into the formal living room. The housekeeper, who had admitted the two before notifying Davee that she had guests, was moving about the room switching on lamps. "Thank you, Sarah." The woman, who was as large and dark as a mahogany armoire, acknowledged Davee's thanks, then left through a side door. "Can I fix y'all a drink?"

"No, thank you," Smilow replied.

Steffi Mundell also declined. "What a beautiful room," she said. "Such a wonderful color."

"You think so?" Davee looked around as though assessing the room for the first time. "Actually, this is my least favorite room in the whole house, even though it does offer a lovely view of the Battery, and that's nice. My husband insisted on painting the walls this color. It's called terra-cotta and is supposed to be reminiscent of the villas on the Italian Riviera. Instead, it makes me think of football jerseys." Looking directly at Steffi and smiling sweetly, she added, "My mama always said that orange was a color for the common and coarse."

Steffi's cheeks flamed with anger. "Where were you this afternoon, Mrs. Pettijohn?"

"None of your goddamn business," Davee retorted without a blink.

"Ladies." Smilow shot Steffi a stern look with a silent command behind it for her to shut up.

"What's going on, Rory?" Davee demanded. "What are ya'll doing here?"

Coolly, calmly, and deferentially, he said, "I suggest we all sit down."

Davee held his gaze for several seconds, gave the woman a withering glance, then with a brusque gesture indicated the sofa nearest them. She sat down in an adjacent armchair.

He began by telling her that this wasn't a casual call. "I'm afraid I have some bad news."

She stared at him, waiting him out.

"Lute was found dead late this afternoon. In the penthouse suite at the Charles Towne Plaza. It appears he was murdered."

Davee kept her features carefully schooled.

One never displayed too much emotion in public.

It simply wasn't done.

Holding emotions intact was a skill one naturally acquired when Daddy was a womanizer, and Mama was a drunk, and everybody knew the reason she drank, but everybody also pretended that there wasn't a problem. Not in *their* family.

Maxine and Clive Burton had been a perfect couple. Both descended from elite Charleston families. Both were utterly gorgeous to look at. Both attended exclusive schools. Their wedding was a standard by which all others were compared, even to this day. They were a sublime match.

Their three adorable daughters had been given boys' names, either because Maxine was drunk when she went into labor each time, or because she was so far gone she was confused about the gender of her newborn, or because she wanted to spite the wayward Clive, who yearned for male offspring and blamed her for producing only females. Never mind the absence of Y chromosomes.

So little Clancy, Jerri, and Davee grew up in a household where serious domestic problems were swept beneath priceless Persian rugs. The girls learned at an early age to keep their reactions to any situation, no matter how upsetting, to themselves. It was safer that way. The atmosphere at home was unreliable and tricky to gauge when both parents were volatile and given to temper tantrums, resulting in fights that shattered any semblance of peace and tranquillity.

Consequently the sisters bore emotional scars.

Clancy had healed hers by dying in her early thirties of cervical cancer, which the most vicious gossips claimed had been brought on by too many bouts of venereal disease.

Jerri had gone in the opposite direction, becoming a convert to a fundamentalist Christian group her freshman year in college. She had dedicated herself to a life of hardship and abstinence from anything pleasurable, particularly alcohol and sex. She grew root vegetables and preached the gospel on an Indian reservation in South Dakota.

Davee, the youngest, was the only one who remained in Charleston, defying shame and gossip, even after Clive died of cardiac arrest in his current mistress's bed between his board meeting in the morning and his tee time that afternoon, and following Maxine's being committed to a nursing home with "Alzheimer's" when everybody knew the truth was that her brain had been pickled by vodka.

Davee, who looked as soft and malleable as warm taffy, was actually tough as nails. Tough enough to stick it out. She could survive anything. She had proved it.

"Well," she said, coming to her feet, "even if y'all declined a drink, I believe I'll have one."

At the liquor cart, she dropped a few ice cubes into a crystal tumbler and poured vodka over them. She drank almost half of it in one swallow, then refilled the glass before turning back to them. "Who was she?"

"Pardon?"

"Come on, Rory. I'm not going to have vapors. If Lute was shot in his fancy new hotel suite, he must've been entertaining a lady friend. I figure that either she or her jealous husband killed him."

"Who said he was shot?" Steffi Mundell asked.

"What?"

"Smilow didn't say your husband had been shot. He said he'd been murdered."

Davee took another drink. "I assumed he was shot. Isn't that a safe guess?"

"Was it a guess?"

Davee flung her arms wide, sloshing some of her drink onto the rug. "Who the hell are you, anyway?"

Steffi stood. "I represent the D.A.'s office. Or, as it's known in South Carolina, the county solicitor."

"I know what it's known as in South Carolina," Davee returned drolly.

"I'll be prosecuting your husband's murder case. That's why I insisted on coming along with Smilow."

"Ahh, I get it. To gauge my reaction to the news."

"Precisely. I must say you didn't seem very surprised by it. So back to my original question: Where were you this afternoon? And don't say that it isn't any of my goddamn business because, you see, Mrs. Pettijohn, it very much is."

Davee, curbing her anger, calmly raised her glass to her lips once again and took her time answering. "You want to know if I can establish an alibi, is that it?"

"We didn't come here to interrogate you, Davee," Smilow said.

"It's okay, Rory. I've got nothing to hide. I just think it's insensitive of her"—she gave Steffi a scathing once-over—"to come into my house and start firing insulting and insinuating questions at me seconds after I've been informed that my husband was murdered."

"That's my job, Mrs. Pettijohn, whether you like it or not."

"Well, I don't like it." Then, dismissing her as no one of significance, she turned to Smilow. "I'm happy to answer your questions. What do you want to know?"

"Where were you this afternoon between five and six o'clock?"

"Here."

"Alone?"

"Yes."

"Can anyone vouch for that?"

She moved to an end table and depressed a single button on a desk telephone. The housekeeper's voice came through the speaker. "Yes, Miss Davee?"

"Sarah, will you come in here, please? Thank you."

The three waited in silence. Fixing the prosecutor with a cool, contemptuous gaze, Davee fiddled with the single strand of perfectly matched pearls that she wore around her neck. They had been a coming-out gift from her father, whom she both loved and hated. Her therapist had suggested that they were a symbol of her mistrust of people, due to her father's unfaithfulness to his wife and daughters. Davee didn't know if that was true or if she just liked the pearls. Whatever the case, she wore them with everything, including the short shorts and oversize white cotton shirt she had on this evening.

Davee had inherited her live-in housekeeper from her mother. Sarah had been working for the family before Clancy was born and had seen them through all their tribulations. When she came into the room, she shot Smilow and Steffi Mundell a hostile glance.

Davee formally introduced her. "Ms. Sarah Birch, this is Detective Smilow and a person from the County Solicitor's Office. They came to tell me that Mr. Pettijohn was found murdered this afternoon."

Sarah's reaction was no more visible than Davee's had been.

Davee continued, "I told them that I was here in the house between five and six o'clock and that you would back me up. Isn't that right?"

Steffi Mundell nearly blew a gasket. "You can't—"

"Steffi."

"But she's just compromised the interrogation," she shouted at Smilow.

Davee looked at him innocently. "I thought you said I wasn't being interrogated, Rory."

His eyes were frosty, but he turned to the housekeeper and said politely, "Ms. Birch, to your knowledge was Mrs. Pettijohn at home at that time?"

"Yes, sir. She's been in her room resting nearly all day."

"Oh, brother," Steffi muttered beneath her breath.

Ignoring her, Smilow thanked the housekeeper. Sarah Birch moved to Davee and enveloped her hands between her own. "I'm sorry."

"Thank you, Sarah."

"You all right, baby?"

"I'm fine."

"Anything I can get you?"

"Not now."

"You need anything, you just let me know."

Davee smiled up at her, and Sarah ran her hand affectionately over Davee's tousled blond hair, then turned and left the room. Davee finished her drink, smugly eyeing Steffi over the rim of her glass. When she lowered it, she said, "Satisfied?"

Steffi was seething and didn't deign to respond.

Crossing to the liquor cart again, Davee asked, "Where is the . . . where was he taken?"

"The medical examiner will perform an autopsy."

"So funeral arrangements will have to wait—"

"Until the body is released," Smilow said, finishing for her.

She poured herself another drink, then when she came back around asked, "How did he die?"

"He was shot in the back. Two bullets. We think he died instantly, and may even have been unconscious when the shots were fired."

"Was he in bed?"

Of course Smilow knew the circumstances of her father's death. Everybody in Charleston was well apprised of the scandalous details. She appreciated Smilow for looking a little pained and embarrassed as he answered her question. "Lute was found on the floor in the sitting room, fully dressed. The bed hadn't been used. There was no sign of a romantic rendezvous."

"Well, that's a change, at least." She drained her glass.

"When did you last see Lute?"

"Last night? This morning? I can't remember. This morning, I think." Davee ignored Steffi Mundell's harrumph of disbelief and kept her eyes on Smilow. "Sometimes we went for days without seeing one another."

"You didn't sleep together?" Steffi asked.

Davee turned to her. "Where up North are you from?"

"Why?"

"Because you are obviously ill-bred and very rude."

Smilow intervened again. "We'll invade the Pettijohns' private life only if we need to, Steffi. At this juncture it isn't necessary." Back to Davee, he asked, "You didn't know Lute's schedule today?"

"Not today or any day."

"He hadn't indicated to you that he was meeting someone?"

"Hardly." She set her empty glass on the coffee table, and when she straightened, she squared her shoulders. "Am I a suspect?"

"Right now everyone in Charleston is a suspect."

Davee locked eyes with him. "Lots of people had good reason to kill Lute." Under her penetrating stare, he looked away.

Steffi Mundell stepped forward as though to remind Davee that she was still there, and that she was somebody important, somebody to be reckoned with. "I'm sorry if I came on a little too strong, Mrs. Pettijohn."

She paused, but Davee wasn't about to forgive her for her many infractions of the unwritten rules of decorum. Davee kept her expression impassive.

"Your husband was a prominent figure," Steffi continued. "His business concerns generated a lot of revenue for the city, the county, and the state. His participation in civic affairs—"

"Is all this leading somewhere?"

She didn't like Davee's interruption, but she persisted undaunted. "This murder will impact the entire community and beyond. My office will give this top priority until the culprit is captured, tried, and convicted. You have my personal guarantee that justice will be swift and sure."

Davee smiled her prettiest, most beguiling smile. "Ms. Mundell, your personal guarantee isn't worth warm spit to me. And I've got unhappy news for you. You will not be prosecuting my husband's murder case. I never settle for bargain-basement goods." She gave Steffi's dress a look of blatant distaste.

Then, turning to Smilow, the former debutante mandated how things were going to be. "I want the top guns on this. See to it, Rory. Or I, Lute Pettijohn's widow, will."

$\mathbf{A}$ HUNERD BIG ONES, RIGHT HERE." The man slapped the stained green felt, flashing a beery and obnoxious grin that made Bobby Trimble shudder with revulsion.

Pinching his wallet from the back pocket of his trousers, Bobby removed two fifties and passed them to the stupid bastard, a cracker if he'd ever seen one. "Good game," he said laconically.

The man pocketed the bills, then eagerly rubbed his hands together. "Ready to rack 'em up again?"

"Not right now."

"You pissed? Come on, don't be pissed," he said in a wheedling voice.

"I'm not pissed," Bobby said, sounding pissed. "Maybe later."

"Double or nothing?"

"Later." Winking, he fired a fake pistol into the other guy's expansive gut, then ambled off, taking his drink with him.

Actually he would love to try and win back his losses, but the sad fact of the matter was, he was strapped for cash. The last series of games, all of which he'd lost, had left him several hundred dollars poorer. Until his cash flow problem abated, he couldn't afford to gamble.

Nor could he indulge in the finer things of life. That last hundred would have gone a long way toward taking the edge off his nerves. Nothing fancy. Just a few lines. Or a pill or two. Oh, well . . .

It was a good thing he still had the counterfeit credit card. He could cover his living expenses with that, but for extras he needed cash. That was a little harder to come by. Not impossible. It just required more work.

And Bobby had his heart set on less work and more relaxation. "It won't be long now," he told himself, smiling into his highball glass. When his investment paid off, there would be years of recreation to look forward to.

But his smile was short-lived. A cloud of uncertainty moved across the fantasy of his sunny future. Unfortunately, the success of his money-making scheme depended on his partner, and he was beginning to doubt her trustworthiness. In fact, doubt was burning his gut as fiercely as the cheap whiskey he'd been drinking all evening. When it came right down to it, he didn't trust her any farther than he could throw her.

He sat down on a stool at the end of the bar and ordered another drink. The maroon vinyl seat had once borne a leather grain imprint, but it had been worn almost slick from supporting decades of hard drinkers. Except for needing to keep a low profile, he wouldn't have patronized a low-class tavern like this. He had come a long way since hanging out in joints of this caliber. He had moved up from where he'd started. Way up. Upwardly mobile, that was Bobby Trimble.

Bobby had cultivated a new image for himself, and he wasn't about to give it up. One couldn't help what he'd been born into, but if he didn't like it, if he knew instinctively that he was destined for bigger and better things, he could sure as hell shake one image and create another. That's what he had done.

It was this acquired urbane appeal that had landed him the cushy job in Miami. The nightclub owner had needed a guy with Bobby's talents to act as host and emcee. He looked good and his line of bullshit drew the ladies in. He took to the job like a duck to water. Business increased significantly. Soon the Cock'n'Bull was one of the most happening nightspots in Miami, a city famous for happening nightspots.

The nightclub had been packed every night with women who knew how to have a good time. Bobby had cultivated and then nurtured its raunchy reputation to compete with the other ladies' entertainment clubs.

The Cock'n'Bull made no apology for having a down-and-dirty floor show that appealed to *women*, not ladies, who weren't afraid to really let their hair down. On most nights, the dancers went all the way down to the skin. Bobby kept his tuxedo on, but he talked the talk that whipped the women into a sexual frenzy. His verbal come-ons were more effective than the thrusting pelvises of the dancers. They adored his dirty dialogue.

Then one night a particularly enthusiastic fan climbed up on the stage with one of the dancers, dropped to her knees, and started doing the nasty thing on him. The crowd went wild. They loved it.

But the vice squad working undercover didn't.

They secretly called for backup, and before anyone realized what was happening, the place was lousy with cops. He had been able to sneak out the back door—but not before helping himself to all the cash in the office safe.

Because of a fondness for the racetrack, and a recent streak of very bad luck, he had been in debt to a loan shark, who wouldn't have understood that the club's closing amounted to a temporary cessation of income, which would have been reversed soon. "Soon" wasn't in a loan shark's vocabulary.

So, with the club owner, the cops, and the loan shark on his tail, he had fled the Sunshine State, with nearly ten thousand dollars lining the pockets of his tuxedo. He had his Mercedes convertible painted a different color and switched the license plates on it. For a time, he traveled leisurely up the coast, living well off stolen money.

But it hadn't lasted forever. He'd had to go to work, plying the only trade he knew. Passing himself off as a guest of the luxury hotels, he hung out at the swimming pools, where he worked his charm on lonely women tourists. The money he stole from them he considered a fair exchange for the happiness he gave them in bed.

Then, one night, while sipping champagne and sweet-talking a reluctant divorcee out of her room key, he spotted an acquaintance from Miami across the dining room. Excusing himself to go to the men's room, Bobby had returned to his hotel, hurriedly packed his belongings into the Mercedes, and got the hell out of town.

He laid low for several weeks, forgoing even the hustling. His reserve cash dwindled to a piddling amount. For all his affectations and polished mannerisms, when Bobby looked in the mirror, he saw himself as he'd been years ago—a brash, small-time hustler running second-rate cons. That self-doubt was never so strong as when he was broke, when it set in with a vengeance. One night, feeling desperate and a little afraid, he got drunk in a bar and wound up in a fight with another customer.

It was the best thing that could have happened. That barroom brawl had been observed by the right person. It had set him on his present course. The culmination was in sight. If it worked out the way he planned, he would make a fortune. He would have the wealth that befitted the Bobby Trimble he was now. There would be no going back to the loser he had been.

However—and this was a huge "however"—his success rested with his partner. As he had earlier established, women were not to be trusted to be anything other than women.

He drained his drink and raised his hand to the bartender. "I need a refill."

But the bartender was engrossed in the TV set. The picture was snowy, but even from where he sat Bobby could make out a guy talking into the microphones pointed at him. He wasn't anybody Bobby recognized. He was an unsmiling cuss, that was for sure. All business, like the welfare agents who used to come nosing around Bobby's house when he was a kid, asking personal questions about him and his family, butting into his private business.

The guy on TV was one cool dude, even with a dozen reporters stepping over each other to crowd around him. He was saying, "The body was discovered this evening shortly after six o'clock. It has been positively identified."

"Do you have—"

"What about a weapon?"

"Are there any suspects?"

"Mr. Smilow, can you tell us—"

Bobby, losing interest, said louder, "I need a drink here."

"I heard ya," the bartender replied querulously.

"Your service could stand some improve—"

The complaint died on Bobby's lips when the picture on the TV screen switched from the guy with the cold eyes to a face that Bobby recognized and knew well. Lute Pettijohn. He strained to catch every word.

"There was no sign of forced entry into Mr. Pettijohn's suite. Robbery has been ruled out as a motive. At this time we have no suspects." The live special report ended and they returned to the eleven o'clock news anchor desk.

Confidence once more intact, grinning from ear to ear, Bobby raised his fresh drink in a silent salute to his partner. Evidently she had come through for him.

"That's all I have to tell you at this time."

Smilow turned away from the microphones, only to discover more behind him. "Excuse me," he said, nudging his way through the media throng.

He ignored the questions shouted after him and continued wedging a path through the reporters until it became evident to them that they were going to get nothing further from him and they began to disperse.

Smilow pretended to hate media attention, but the truth was that he actually enjoyed doing live press conferences like this one. Not because of the lights and cameras, although he knew he looked intimidating when photographed. Not even for the attention and publicity they generated. His job was secure and he didn't need public approval to keep it.

What he liked was the sense of power that being filmed and quoted evoked.

But as he approached the team of detectives who had gathered near the registration desk in the lobby of the hotel, he grumbled, "I'm glad that's over. Now what've you got for me?"

"Zilch."

The others nodded agreement to Mike Collins's summation.

Smilow had timed his return to Charles Towne Plaza from the Pettijohns' home to coincide with the eleven o'clock news. As he had predicted, all the local stations, as well as others from as far away as Savannah and Charlotte, had led with a live telecast from the hotel lobby, where he imparted the rudimentary facts to the reporters and viewers at home. He didn't embellish. Primarily because all he knew were the rudimentary facts. For once he wasn't being coy when he had declined to give them more information.

He was as anxious for information as the media. That's why the detective's terse summation of their success took him aback. "What do you mean, zilch?"

"Just that." Mike Collins was a veteran. He was less intimidated by Smilow than the others, so by tacit agreement he was generally the spokesperson. "We've got nothing so far. We—"

"That's impossible, Detective."

Collins had dark rings around his sunken eyes, proof of just how tough his night had been. He turned to Steffi Mundell, who had interrupted him, and looked at her like he would like to strangle her, then pointedly ignored her and continued his verbal report to Smilow.

"As I was saying, we've put these folks through the ringer." Guests and employees were still being detained in the hotel's main ballroom. "At first they kinda enjoyed it, you know. It was exciting. Like a movie. But the new wore off hours ago. They've given the same answers to the same questions several times over, so now they're getting surly. We're not getting much out of them except a lot of bellyaching about why they can't leave."

"I find it hard to believe—"

"Who invited you, anyway?" Collins fired at Steffi when she interrupted again.

"That out of all those people," she said, speaking over him, "somebody didn't see something."

Smilow held up his hand to squelch a full-fledged quarrel between his discouraged detective and the outspoken prosecutor. "Okay, you two. We're all tired. Steffi, I see no reason for you to hang around. When we've got something, you'll be notified."

"Fat chance." She folded her arms across her chest and glared defiantly at Collins. "I'm staying."

Reluctantly, Smilow gave the go-ahead for the hotel guests to be allowed to return to their rooms. He then assembled his detectives in one of the meeting rooms on the mezzanine level and ordered pizzas to be delivered. While they decimated the pizzas, he reviewed the scanty amount of information they had gleaned after hours of exhaustive interrogation.

"Pettijohn had a massage in the spa?" he asked, reviewing the notes.

"Yeah." One of the detectives swallowed a large mouthful of pizza. "Right after he got here."

"Did you question the masseur?"

The man nodded. "Said Pettijohn asked for the deluxe massage, a full ninety minutes. Pettijohn showered in the locker room, that's why the bathroom in the suite was dry."

"Was this guy suspicious?"

"Not that I could see," the detective mumbled around another bite. "Hired from a spa in California. New to Charleston. Met Pettijohn for the first time today."

Smilow studied the hastily compiled breakdown of registered guests. All appeared above suspicion. All claimed never to have met Lute Pettijohn, although a few knew of him through the media blitz given the opening of Charles Towne Plaza a few months earlier.

Most were just plain folks on vacation with their families. Three couples were honeymooning. Several others pretended to be, when it was obvious that they were secret lovers on an illicit weekend getaway to a romantic city. These answered the detectives' questions nervously, but not because they were guilty of murder, only adultery.

All but three rooms on the fourth floor were occupied by a group of lady schoolteachers from Florida. Two suites were overfilled with a boys' basketball team who had graduated high school in the spring and were having one last fling together before scattering to their respective universities. Their only crime was underage drinking. To the consternation of his buddies, one voluntarily turned over a nickel bag of marijuana to the interrogating officer.

The consensus was that if Lute Pettijohn hadn't been murdered the previous afternoon, it would have been a routine summer Saturday.

"Long, hot, and sticky," remarked one of the detectives, yawning hugely.

"You talking about the day, or my dick?" another joked.

"You wish."

"What about the security video?" Smilow asked, bringing the banter to a halt. The detectives smirked at what was obviously an inside joke. "What?" Smilow demanded.

"You want to see it?" Collins asked.

"Is there something to see?"

After another round of snickers, Collins suggested that Smilow take a look, and even invited Steffi to watch the video with them. "You might learn something," he said to her.

Smilow and Steffi followed the detectives across the wide mezzanine lobby and into one of the smaller conference rooms, where a VCR machine was cued up and ready to play on a color monitor.

With unnecessary fanfare, Collins introduced the video. "At first the guy monitoring the security cameras yesterday afternoon told me that the video from the camera on that floor had been misplaced."

Smilow knew from experience that surveillance cameras were usually attached to time-lapse recorders that exposed one frame of video every five to ten seconds, depending on the user's discretion. That's why they appeared jumpy when replayed. Typically they recorded for days before automatically rewinding.

"What was the tape doing out of the machine? Aren't the tapes generally left in the recorders and recycled unless there's a need to view them?"

"That was my first tip-off that he was lying," Collins said. "So I kept after him. Finally he coughed up this video. Ready?"

Getting a nod from Smilow, he pushed the play button on the VCR. Even if there had been no accompanying video, the sound track was unmistakably that of a triple-X-rated film. The sighs and moans were background for a grainy moving picture of a couple engaged in a sexual act.

"This scene runs for about fifteen minutes," Collins explained. "After the come shot, it switches to two broads in a bathtub getting each other off. Then it's got your basic domination scene with—"

"I get it," Smilow snapped. "Turn it off." He ignored the boos and hisses from the other men in the room. "Sorry, Steffi."

"Don't be. Detective Collins's little joke at my expense merely supports my theory that the phrase 'adult male' is a contradiction in terms."

The other men laughed, but Collins harrumphed, unfazed by the put-down. "Here's the kicker," he told them. "Pettijohn's boast about state-of-the-art security was so much hot air. The cameras on the guest room floors are bogus. Dummies."

"What?" Steffi exclaimed.

"The only working camera in the entire complex is in the accounting department. Pettijohn didn't want anybody stealing from him, but I guess he didn't care if his guests got robbed or bumped off. The joke's on him, huh?"

Smilow asked, "Why did the kid lie?"

"That's what he'd been told to do. By big bad Pettijohn himself. We're not talking about a rocket scientist here, so he held tough even after we assured him that Pettijohn was dead and that the only thing he had to fear was lying to us. He finally cracked. We checked it out. The cameras are shills."

"How many people know that?"

"My guess would be not too many."

"Check it out. Start with people in managerial positions."

"Will do."

Addressing the group at large, Smilow said, "First thing in the morning, we start on Pettijohn's enemies. We'll compile a list—"

"Or we could save ourselves the trouble and just use the phone book," one of the men quipped. "Everybody I know will be glad the son of a bitch is dead."

Smilow shot him a hard look.

"Oh, sorry," he mumbled, his smile vanishing. "I forgot you two were kin."

"We weren't kin. He was married to my sister. For a while. That's it. I probably had less liking for him than anyone."

Steffi leaned forward. "You didn't pop him, did you, Smilow?"

Everyone laughed, but Smilow's terse, "No, I didn't," spoken as though he'd taken her question seriously, ended the laughter as abruptly as it had started.

"Excuse me, Mr. Smilow?"

Standing in the open doorway was Smitty. Smilow checked his wristwatch. It was after midnight. "I thought you'd be anxious to get home," he said to the shoeshine man.

"They only just now told us we could go home, Mr. Smilow."

"Oh, yeah." He hadn't thought of hotel fixtures like Smitty being detained for long hours of questioning, although he had mandated it himself. "Sorry about that."

"Never mind, Mr. Smilow. I was just wonderin', did anybody 'round here tell y'all about those folks that were taken to the hospital yeste'day?"

"Hospital?"

CHAPTER | 6

THE CAPITAL LETTER E ON THE INSTRUMENT PANEL of her car flashed red.

She groaned with frustration. The last thing she wanted to do was stop and pump gasoline, but she knew from experience that when the gauge on this car said empty, it was dangerously accurate.

Service stations were scarce on this stretch of rural highway, so when she came upon one only a few miles after seeing the warning light, she pulled in and lethargically got out of her car.

Ordinarily when she pumped her own gas she paid by credit card at the pump. But technology hadn't stretched this far into the boonies. As a matter of principle, she disliked having to pay in advance. So she removed the nozzle from the pump and flipped down the lever. She twisted off her gas cap and set it on the roof of her car, inserted the nozzle in the tank, then waved at the attendant in the booth, motioning for him to engage the pump.

He was watching a wrestling match on his black and white TV. She could barely see him through the neon beer signs and the posters taped to the window announcing outdated events and lost pets. Either he hadn't noticed her or he was standing on his own principle of not turning on the pump until the customer paid in advance, especially after dark.

"Damn." She relented, walked to the office, and slid a bill into the dirty tray beneath an even dirtier window.

"Twenty dollars' worth? Anything else?" he asked, his eyes remaining glued to the TV screen.

"No, thanks."

The rate of flow was a trickle, but the pump finally clicked off. She removed the nozzle and replaced it on the pump. As she was reaching for the gas tank cap, another car pulled off the road and into the station. She was caught in the bright headlights and squinted against the glare.

The car rolled to a stop only a few feet from her rear bumper. The driver turned off the headlights but didn't kill the engine before opening the door and stepping out.

Her lips parted in wordless surprise. But she didn't move or speak. She didn't berate him for following her. Or demand to know why he had. Or insist that he get lost and leave her alone. She didn't do anything but look at him.

His hair looked darker now that the sun had gone down, not as tawny as it appeared in daylight. She knew his eyes were grayish blue, although now they were deeply shadowed. One eyebrow was slightly higher and more arched than the other, but this asymmetric quirk added interest. His chin had a shallow vertical cleft. He cast a long shadow because he was tall. Weight would never be a problem; he didn't have the frame to carry much extra poundage.

For several seconds they stared at each other across the hood of his car, then he stepped around the open door. Her eyes followed his progress as he came toward her. The determination with which his jaw was set said a lot about his character. He wasn't easily discouraged, and he wasn't afraid to go after something he wanted.

He didn't stop until he was standing directly in front of her. Then he cupped her face between his hands and lifted it toward his as he bent down and kissed her.

And she thought, *Oh, God.*

His lips were full and sensual, and they delivered what they suggested. His kiss was warm and sweet and earnest. He applied the perfect amount of pressure, leaving no question that she was being soundly kissed, but without making her feel overpowered or threatened. It was such a perfect kiss that her lips parted naturally. When his tongue touched hers, her heart expanded and her arms encircled his waist.

He lowered his hands, so that one arm was free to go around her shoulders while the other curved to fit the small of her back and to draw her against him full-length. He angled his head. Hers made a countermove. The kiss deepened, his tongue probing. The longer they kissed, the more ardent it became.

Then suddenly he broke away. He was breathing hard. His hands resumed their previous position on either side of her face. "That's what I had to know. It wasn't just me."

She shook her head as much as his hands would allow it to move. "No," she said, surprised by the huskiness of her own voice. "It wasn't just you."

"Follow me?"

Protests died on her lips before she could even speak them.

"I have a cabin not far from here. Two, three miles."

"I—"

"Don't say no." His whispered voice was ragged, impassioned. His hands pressed tighter. "Don't say no."

Her eyes searched his, then she made a small, assenting motion with her head. He released her immediately, turned, and strode back to his car. She dropped the gas cap in her haste to screw it back in. Finally getting it secured, she rounded her car and got in. She started her motor; his car pulled up beside hers.

He looked at her as though to make certain that she was as resolute as he, that she wasn't going to bolt and disappear the first chance she got.

Which she knew was what she should do. But she knew with just as much certainty that she wouldn't. Not now.

Hammond didn't take an easy breath until her car came to a full stop beside his. He got out and went to open her door for her. "Watch your step, it's dark." Taking her hand, he led her up a crushed-shell path toward the cabin. A small porch fixture provided just enough light for him to see to open the lock with the key he had brought with him from Charleston.

He pushed the door open and ushered her inside. A local lady cleaned the place whenever needed. He had scheduled her to come earlier that day. Rather than smelling musty, like an empty, infrequently used dwelling, the cabin smelled clean, like freshly laundered linens. Per Hammond's request, the air conditioner had also been left on, so it was pleasantly cool.

He closed the front door, separating them from the porch light and plunging them into complete darkness. He had every intention of being a good host and gentleman, of showing her around the cabin, of offering her something to drink, of telling her more about himself and giving her time to adjust to being alone with him only hours after their meeting. Instead, he reached for her.

She came willingly into his arms, seemingly as eager for his kiss as he was for hers. Her mouth responded warmly to the thrusts of his tongue that stroked and tested and tasted her until he had to pause to catch his breath. Lowering his head, he pressed his face into her neck, while her hands closed around the back of his head and her fingers combed through his hair.

He kissed his way up to her ear. "This is crazy," he whispered.

"Very."

"Are you afraid?"

"Yes."

"Of me?"

"No."

"You should be."

"I know, but I'm not."

His lips rubbed against hers in a not-quite kiss. "Afraid of the situation?"

"Terrified," she said as her mouth dissolved against his.

Finally ending the kiss, he said, "This is rash and reckless and—"

"Totally irresponsible."

"But I can't help it."

"Neither can I."

"I want so much to—"

"I want you to," she sighed as his hands slipped beneath her top and covered her breasts.

Any misgivings he had that the desire was one-sided vanished when her head fell back, offering her throat to his lips while he caressed her. Her breath caught and held when he fumbled with the front clasp of her brassiere, but she released a soft murmur of pleasure when his fingertips brushed her bare skin.

Her hands moved over his back. He felt all ten of her fingers kneading muscle and exploring ribs and spine. Her palms skimmed over his belt, settled on his butt, pulled him into her.

They kissed once more, a long, deep, provocative kiss.

Then he took her hand again and pulled her along behind him as he felt his way across the living area into the bedroom. The cabin wasn't luxurious by any means, but he hadn't sacrificed all creature comforts. Into a room too small for one, he had crammed a king-size bed.

It was across this that they fell, coming together in its center and twining around one another with the blind, mindless craving of new lovers.

She lay on her side facing away from him.

Hammond tried to think of something appropriate to say, but he discarded possibilities before they were fully formed. Everything that came to mind sounded either false, corny, clichéd, or a combination thereof. He even thought about telling her the truth.

*My God, that was incredible.*

*You are incredible.*

*I've never felt like this in my life.*

*I don't want this night ever to end.*

But he knew she wouldn't believe any of it, so he said none of it. The long, strained silence became even longer and more strained. Eventually he rolled to his side and switched on the nightstand lamp. She reacted to the light by pulling her knees up closer to her chest, if anything becoming more withdrawn and untouchable.

Discouraged, he sat up. His shirt was twisted and unbuttoned, his pants unzipped, but he was still wearing both. Getting up, he removed everything except his boxers. When he looked up again toward the bed, she had rolled onto her back and was watching him, her eyes wide and apprehensive.

"This is an awkward moment. That's fair to say, isn't it?"

Hammond gingerly sat down on the edge of the bed. "It's fair, yes."

She wet her lips, rolled them inward, averted her eyes from his, and nodded. "Are you trying to think of a graceful way to get rid of me now?"

"What?" he exclaimed softly. "No. *No.*" He extended his hand to touch her hair, but let it fall before it reached her. "I was trying to think of a way to get you to stay the night without making a complete fool of myself."

He could tell that pleased her. Her eyes found his again. She smiled shyly. Still sex-flushed, her lips slightly swollen from hard kissing, her hair tousled around her face, clothes in more disarray than his had been, she looked incredibly seductive. Her breasts, freed from her brassiere, lay softly against her chest beneath her top. But her nipples were distinct against the weave. He started getting hard again.

"I'm a mess." Self-consciously she tugged her skirt down over her thighs. Both of them ignored the pair of panties lying on top of the bedspread at the foot of the bed. "May I use your bathroom?"

"Right through that door." He stood to leave so she would have more privacy. "I'll get us something to drink. Are you hungry?"

"After eating all that junk food at the fair?"

He returned her smile. "How about some water? Juice? Tea? Soft drink? Beer?"

"Water's fine."

He hitched his chin toward the connecting bathroom door. "If you need anything, just ask."

"Thank you."

She seemed reluctant to get off the bed while he was still in the room, so he smiled at her again and left her alone. Thankfully the cleaning lady had stocked the fridge with bottled drinks, including water. While there, he took an inventory of staples. A half dozen eggs. A pound of bacon. English muffins. Coffee. Cream? No. He hoped she drank her coffee black. Orange juice? Yes. A six-ounce can of concentrate in the freezer.

He rarely ate breakfast unless it was a business meeting. But in the country, where the weekend mornings were longer and lazier, he liked to indulge in a hearty late breakfast. He was an okay cook, especially something as basic as bacon and eggs. Maybe they would cook breakfast together, dividing the chores, bumping into one another as they went about them. Laughing. Kissing. Then they could carry their plates out onto the porch to eat. He smiled at the thought of tomorrow morning.

"This morning," he corrected, checking the clock and realizing that it was well after midnight.

Yesterday had been a bitch. He had left Charleston upset and angry, frustrated on many levels. Nothing in his life had been right. Never in a million years would he have guessed that such a sour day would end with his making love to a woman he hadn't known existed a few hours ago. Nor that it would be such a meaningful experience.

He continued marveling over the caprice of fate until he heard the water in the bathroom shut off. He forced himself to wait two minutes more, not wanting to reappear too quickly or at an inopportune time. Then he grabbed two bottles of water and made his way back to the bedroom.

"By the way," he said as he pushed open the door with his bare foot, "I think it's time we properly introduced—"

He stopped when she turned quickly from the dresser, the telephone receiver in her hand. She hung up immediately and blurted out, "I hope you don't mind."

Actually, he did mind. He minded one hell of a lot. Not that she had used his telephone without asking first. But that she had someone in her life who was important enough to call in the wee hours of the morning within minutes of making love to him. It stunned him how much he minded.

He'd dallied in the kitchen, fantasizing about having breakfast with her, counting the minutes until he could return with propriety. Now he was standing here with a dumb expression on his face and a semi-erection poking against his undershorts. And all this while she was placing a phone call to somebody else. He set the bottles of water on the nightstand.

He felt stupid and ridiculous, alien feelings for Hammond Cross. Usually self-confident and on top of any given situation, he felt like a real dumb-ass, and he disliked the feeling intensely.

"Would you like some privacy?" he asked woodenly.

"No, it's all right." She replaced the receiver. "I couldn't get through."

"Sorry."

"It wasn't important." She folded her arms across her waist, then nervously dropped them to her sides.

*If it wasn't important, then why in hell were you trying to place a call at this time of night?* he wanted to ask, but didn't.

"Is it okay if I wear this?"

"What?" he asked distractedly.

She ran her hand down the front of the old, faded T-shirt. He recognized it as a fraternity party shirt from college days; it caught her midthigh. "Oh. Sure. It's fine."

"I found it in the chest of drawers in the bathroom. I wasn't snooping. I just—"

"Don't mention it." His curt tone spoke volumes.

Her hands formed fists at her sides, then she shook them loose. "Look, maybe it would be better if I left now. We both got a little carried away. Maybe the ride on the Ferris wheel went to our heads." Her stab at humor fell flat. "Anyway, this was . . ." Her words trailed off as she glanced at the bed.

Her gaze lingered there probably longer than she intended it to. The jumbled linens were a poignant reminder of what had taken place on them, and how involving and satisfying it had been. Words whispered with unrestraint seemed to echo back to them now.

While in the bathroom, she had washed. Hammond could smell soap and water on her skin. But he hadn't washed. He smelled like sex. He smelled like her.

So when she said hastily, "I'll just change back into my clothes and be on my way," and made to move past him, his arm shot out and caught her waist.

She came to a standstill, but she didn't turn toward him. She stared straight ahead. "Whatever else you may think about me, I want you to know that . . . that this isn't something I do casually or routinely."

Softly he said, "It doesn't matter."

She looked at him then, turning only her head. "It matters to *me*. It matters to me that you know that."

Moving carefully, he rested his hands on her shoulders and brought her around to face him. "Do you honestly think it was just a ride on the Ferris wheel that brought us to this?"

As though to keep her lower lip from trembling, she pulled it through her teeth and shook her head no.

Placing his arms around her, he drew her close and hugged her. Just that. And he held her for a long time, with his cheek resting on the crown of her head, toes touching, sharing body heat. Barefoot, swaddled in his T-shirt, she seemed smaller and daintier than before. Embracing her like this made him feel virile and protective. In fact, since meeting her, he had felt like goddamn Conan.

He chuckled at the thought. She raised her head from his chest and looked up at him. "What?"

"Nothing. Just thinking how good you make me feel." Then his smile was replaced by a worried frown. "What about you? Are you all right?"

She tilted her head in puzzlement. "Yes."

"I mean . . . with . . . you know."

"Oh." Her gaze dropped to his Adam's apple. "Yes. Thank you for doing the responsible thing."

He kept a box of condoms in the nightstand drawer. But never had one been so difficult to open and put on. Embarrassed now by his clumsy wrestling match with the stubborn thing, at a time when he had wanted to be at his suavest, he muttered, "In the nick of time."

Surprising him, she rested her hands on his chest and stroked it lightly. Hardly above a whisper, she said, "For me, too."

Desire was manifested in a low moan as he cupped her chin in his hand and tilted her head back for his kiss. Passions sparked again. Ignited. Burned. Hotter than before.

The whispers intensified the intimacy.

"You like this."

"Yes."

"Too hard?"

"No."

"I didn't realize."

"Neither did I."

"I'm sorry."

"It didn't matter."

"But if I hurt you—"

"You didn't. You won't."

"Do you mind if . . ."

"No."

"Jesus. Look at you. Beautiful. You're already—"

"Yes."

"So—"

"Oh . . ."

"Wet."

"I'm sorry, sorry."

"Sorry?"

"Well, I mean . . . you . . ."

"Don't be sorry."

"Let me touch you."

"No, let *me* touch *you*."

# CHAPTER | 7

Wᴵᴛʜ Sᴛᴇꜰꜰɪ ᴅʀɪᴠɪɴɢ, ꜱʜᴇ ᴀɴᴅ Sᴍɪʟᴏᴡ reached Roper Hospital in record time.

"How many did they say?" she asked as they jogged across the emergency room parking lot toward the building. She had missed the details when she left the hotel conference room to retrieve her car. She had picked up Smilow at the main entrance to Charles Towne Plaza.

"Sixteen. Seven adults, nine children. They belong to a touring church choir from Macon, Georgia. They ate lunch early in the hotel restaurant before setting out on an afternoon walking tour of downtown. They returned a couple hours later, after the kids began getting sick."

"Stomach cramps? Vomiting? Diarrhea?"

"All of the above."

"You don't forget food poisoning if you've ever had it. I did once. Cream of mushroom soup from a reputable deli."

"They traced this back to a marinara meat sauce that was used on the pizza the kids ate. It was also on the pasta special."

Almost at a run, they entered the hospital emergency room. For a Saturday night, the waiting room was relatively calm, but there were a few patients. A uniformed cop was guarding a man in handcuffs. The man had a bloody bath towel wrapped around his head like a turban. His eyes were closed and he was moaning, while his wife provided laconic answers to a nurse's standard questions regarding medical history. A young mother and father were trying in vain to pacify their crying infant. An elderly man was sitting alone, sobbing into a handkerchief for no apparent reason. A woman sat bent almost double in her chair, her head nearly in her lap. She appeared to be asleep.

It was a little early yet for the real emergencies to start streaming in.

Neither Smilow nor Steffi paid any attention to the people in the waiting room, but walked directly to the admissions desk, where Smilow introduced himself to the nurse, showed her his badge, and asked if the people transported from Charles Towne Plaza were still in the emergency room or if they'd been admitted to rooms.

"They're still here," the nurse told him.

"I need to see them right away."

"Well, I . . . Let me page the doctor. Have a seat."

Neither sat. Steffi paced. "What I don't get is how your guys missed the discrepancy. Weren't they supposed to check the number of guests registered against the number they interrogated?"

"Cut them some slack, Steffi. People straggled in over the course of hours, after being away from the hotel for hours. We're talking hundreds of registered guests in addition to employees changing shifts. It would have been nearly impossible to get an accurate head count."

"I know, I know," she said impatiently. "But after midnight? When everyone is more or less tucked in? I would have expected one of them to think of doing another head count. Or were they too engrossed in their movie?"

"They had their hands full," he said stiffly.

"Yeah, getting jack."

Smilow was the first to criticize if a criminal investigation officer screwed up. It was something else if the criticism came from an outsider. His lips turned hard and thin with anger.

"Look, I'm sorry," Steffi said in a much mollified tone. "I didn't mean to say that."

"Yeah, you did. But let me worry about evidence gathering, okay?"

Steffi knew when to back off. It wouldn't be wise to alienate Smilow. Despite the new widow's directive, she had every intention of going to County Solicitor Monroe Mason and asking to be named the chief prosecutor of this case. When she did, she needed the police department's support. Specifically Smilow's.

She gave him a few moments to cool down before saying, "I'm afraid that these people with food poisoning won't know jack, either. They were brought to the hospital earlier than the estimated time of Pettijohn's murder."

"The symptoms didn't strike some of them until later," he argued. "The hotel manager confessed to sneaking them out as late as eight o'clock this evening."

"Why didn't he tell you about it?"

"Bad P.R. He seemed to be more worried about the food-poisoning outbreak and what it says about his shiny new kitchen than he was about the discovery of Pettijohn's body in the penthouse suite."

"You wanted to see me?"

Both turned. The doctor was young enough to have acne, but the eyes behind his wire-framed glasses looked old, tired, and sleep-deprived. His green scrubs and white lab coat were wrinkled and sweat-stained. His photo ID read RODNEY C. ARNOLD.

Smilow flashed his badge again. "I need to question the people brought in with food poisoning from Charles Towne Plaza."

"Question them about what?"

"They could be material witnesses to a murder that took place in the hotel this afternoon."

"The new hotel? You're kidding."

"I'm afraid not."

"This afternoon? Like yesterday?"

"Until the M.E. can give us a more definite time, we're estimating the victim died anywhere between four and six P.M."

The resident smiled grimly. "Detective, at that time last evening these folks were either having acute diarrhea or puking their guts up, or both. The only thing they were eyewitness to was the bottom of the commode bowl. If they were lucky enough to get to a commode in time, which I heard some of them weren't."

"I understand they were very sick—"

"Not were. Are."

Steffi stepped forward and identified herself. "Dr. Arnold, I don't think you understand the importance of our questioning these people. Some were occupying rooms on the fifth floor where the murder took place. One could have vital information and not even be aware of it. The only way to find out is to question them."

"Okay," he said with a shrug. "Check in with the main admissions desk tomorrow. I'm sure some of them will still be here, but by then they'll have been assigned to rooms." He turned to go.

"Wait a minute," Steffi said. "We need to see them now."

"Now?" Dr. Arnold divided an incredulous glance between them. "Sorry. No can do. Some of these folks are still in extreme gastrointestinal distress. Extreme. Distress," he repeated, separating the words for emphasis.

"We're giving them fluids through IVs. The ones lucky enough to have passed the crisis are resting, and after the ordeal their intestines have put them through, they need it. Come back tomorrow. Possibly early afternoon. Preferably evening. By then—"

"That's not soon enough."

"It'll have to be," the doctor stated. "Because nobody's talking to any of them tonight. Now please excuse me. I've got patients waiting." With that he turned and pushed through the doors separating the lobby from the examination rooms.

"Dammit," Steffi swore. "Are you going to let him get by with that?"

"You want me to storm the emergency room and start hassling patients in extreme . . . et cetera? Talk about bad P.R." Returning to the desk nurse, Smilow asked her to give Dr. Arnold his business card. "If any of the patients begin feeling better, tell him to call me. Any hour."

"I don't have any confidence in the doctor's willingness to help," Steffi remarked when Smilow rejoined her.

"Me either. He seems to enjoy being ruler of his small domain."

Steffi looked at him with an arch smile. "To which you can relate."

"And you can't?" he returned. "Don't you think I know why you want this case so badly?"

Smilow was an excellent detective because of his insight. But sometimes that perception made him uncomfortable to be around. "Can we take five? I need some caffeine." She moved to a vending machine and fed coins into it. "Buy you a Coke?"

"No, thanks."

She peeled the tab off the top of the soft drink can. "Well, look at it this way. If these Macon people are that sick, you probably wouldn't have got anything useful or reliable from them anyway. Afflicted with food poisoning, how observant could they have been yesterday afternoon? It won't hurt to come back tomorrow and talk to them, but I think it'll wind up being a dead end for you."

"Maybe." He sat down in a vacant chair, propped his elbows on his knees, and tapped his lips with steepled index fingers. Steffi sat down in the chair next to him. He waved off an offer to take a sip of her drink. "One of the rules of crime detection—somebody saw something."

"You think people are withholding information?"

"No. They just don't know that what they saw is important."

Both were quiet for a moment, each lost in his own thoughts. Finally Steffi asked, "What do you think happened in that penthouse suite?"

"I try not to develop a theory. Not this early on, anyway. If I did, it could color the investigation. I'd be looking for clues to support my guess, and overlooking the clues that led to the actual solution."

"I thought all cops relied on hunches."

"Hunches, yeah. But hunches are based on clues. They get stronger or weaker as you go along, depending on the clues you gather, which either support your hunch or dispel it." He leaned back and sighed deeply, uncharacteristically letting his fatigue show. "All I really have at this point is a man who many would enjoy seeing dead."

"Including you."

His eyes turned hard. "I'd be lying if I said no. I hated the bastard and made no secret of it. You, on the other hand—"

"*Me?*"

"Pettijohn wielded a lot of influence in local politics. The County Solicitor's Office is no exception. With Mason about to retire—"

"That's not public knowledge yet."

"But it soon will be. With him declining to run for reelection and his second in command battling prostate cancer—"

"Wallis has been given about six weeks."

"So, come November, the office is up for grabs. Pettijohn has been known to dangle carrots like that in front of the ambitious and corruptible. Think what a boon it would be for a swindler like him to have a sweet young thing like you serving as D.A."

"I'm not sweet. As for young, forty is looming terribly close."

"Strange that you should address that and not the ambitious and corruptible part."

"I admit to the former and deny the latter. Besides, if Pettijohn were the red carpet ushering me into the solicitor's office, why would I kill him?"

"Good question," he said, studying her with one eye closed.

"You're so full of shit, Smilow." Shaking her head, she laughed. "I see what you're getting at, though. Considering all of Pettijohn's machinations, the list of suspects grows endless."

"Which doesn't make my job easy."

"Maybe you're trying too hard." She sipped her drink thoughtfully. "What are the two most common motivations for murder?"

He knew the answer, and it pointed to one person. "Mrs. Pettijohn?"

"The shoe fits, doesn't it?" Steffi held up her index finger. "She got fed up with her husband's flagrant cheating. Even if she didn't love him, his womanizing humiliated her."

"Her daddy did the same thing to her mother."

"Which could explain the second shot when the first probably killed him." She raised her second finger. "Tubs of money come her way if Lute Pettijohn is dead. One of those motives would be sufficient. Combined . . ." She raised her shoulders as though the conclusion spoke for itself.

After considering it for a moment, he frowned. "It's almost too obvious, isn't it? Besides, she's got an alibi."

Steffi scoffed. "The loyal family servant? Yes, Miss Scarlett. No, Miss Scarlett. Why don't you slap me again, Miss Scarlett?"

"Sarcasm doesn't flatter you, Steffi."

"I'm not being sarcastic. Their relationship reflects an archaic attitude."

"Not to Mrs. Pettijohn. I'm sure not to Sarah Birch, either. They're devoted to one another."

"As long as Miss Davee is boss."

He shook his head. "You'd have had to grow up here to understand."

"Thank God I didn't. In the Midwest—"

"Where people are more enlightened and all men are created equal?"

"You said it, Smilow, not me."

"Not just sarcastic, but condescending and self-righteous, too. If you have so much bloody scorn for us and what you perceive to be our archaic attitudes, why'd you move down here?"

"For the opportunity it afforded."

"To right all our wrongs? To enlighten us poor, backward-thinking southern folk?"

She scowled at him.

"Or do you find our way of life enviable?" Further baiting her, he added, "Are you sure you're not jealous of Davee Pettijohn?"

She mouthed, *Fuck you, Smilow.*

Then she finished her soft drink and stood up to toss the empty can into a metal trash receptacle. The clatter it made roused everyone in the waiting room except the sleeping woman.

Steffi said, "I can hardly stomach women like Davee Pettijohn. That all too obvious southern belle affectation of hers makes me want to throw up."

He motioned her toward the door. They stepped out into the warm, humid air. The eastern sky was turning a grayish pink, harbinger of dawn. Upon reflection he said, "I'll grant you that Mrs. Pettijohn has it down to an art."

"What I'm thinking is that she's artful enough to use it to get away with murder."

"You've got a cold heart, Steffi."

"You're a fine one to talk. If you were an Indian your name would be Ice Flows in Veins."

"True enough," he said, taking no offense. "But I'm not so sure about you."

She had reached the driver's door, but didn't get in. Instead she paused and looked at him across the roof of her car. "What about me?"

"No one questions your ambition, Steffi. But I've heard that work isn't all that's keeping your blood hot these days."

"What have you heard?"

"Rumors," he said.

"What kind of rumors?"

Smiling his chilly smile, he said again, "Just rumors."

Loretta Boothe raised her head from her sagging position and watched Rory Smilow and Stefanie Mundell make their way across the parking lot to a car where they paused to chat before getting in and driving away.

They had entered the emergency room with a burst of energy and purpose, which Loretta knew both possessed in abundance. They seemed to suck all the oxygen out of the atmosphere. She disliked them equally. But for different reasons.

She carried a personal grudge against Rory Smilow that went back several years. As for Steffi Mundell, she knew her by reputation only. The assistant D.A. was universally regarded as an unmitigated bitch who thought her shit didn't stink.

Loretta couldn't say why she hadn't spoken to them or made her presence known. Something had compelled her to keep her head lowered, her face down, pretending to be asleep. Not that either would have given a flip about her one way or the other. Smilow would have looked at her with disdain. Steffi Mundell probably wouldn't have recognized her, or if she had, she wouldn't remember her name. More than likely they would have said something passably civil, then ignored her.

So why hadn't she said something? Maybe it had given her a sense of superiority to be unseen and unobserved while she eavesdropped on their conversation, first with the doctor, then with each other.

Earlier in the evening, before she had started feeling sick and had to drive herself to the emergency room, she had heard about the Lute Pettijohn murder on TV. She'd watched Smilow's press conference. He had conducted it in his typically efficient and unflappable manner. Steffi Mundell was already horning in where she wasn't wanted or needed, overstepping her bounds, which it was said she was good at.

Loretta chuckled. It did her old heart good to see them grappling for clues and following dead-end leads. The investigation couldn't be going very well if their only possible witnesses were people sick with food poisoning. One thing was certain: Smilow didn't have a viable suspect or he wouldn't be chasing down emergency room patients.

Loretta glanced at the wall clock. She had been waiting for over two hours and was feeling worse by the minute. She hoped help would be coming soon.

To pass the time and keep her mind off her personal miseries, she stared through the plate-glass window at the spot, now empty, where their car had been parked. Rory Smilow and Steffi Mundell. Jesus, what a dangerous combination. God help the luckless murderer when they did catch him.

"What are you doing here?"

At the sound of her daughter's voice, Loretta turned. Bev was standing over her, fists on hips, eyes judgmental, not at all happy to see her. She tried smiling, but felt her dry lips crack when she stretched them across her teeth. "Hi, Bev. Did they just now tell you I was down here?"

"No, but I was busy and couldn't get away until now."

Bev was an ICU nurse, but Loretta figured she could have asked someone to cover for her for five minutes if she had wanted to. Of course, she hadn't wanted to.

Nervously she wet her scaly lips with her tongue. "I thought I would come by and see . . . Maybe we could have breakfast together."

"When my shift ends at seven, I will have put in twelve hours. I'm going home to bed."

"Oh." This wasn't going even as well as Loretta had hoped, and she hadn't held out much hope that it would go well. She picked at the buttons on the front of her dirty blouse.

"You didn't come here so we could have breakfast together, did you?" Bev's voice had an imperious tone that grabbed the attention of the admitting nurse. Loretta noticed her glance at them curiously. "You ran out of money, so you couldn't buy your booze, so you came begging to me."

Loretta lowered her head to avoid her daughter's angry, unmerciful glare. "I haven't had a drink in days, Bev. I swear I haven't."

"I smell it on you."

"I'm sick. Truly. I—"

"Oh, save it." Bev opened her pocketbook and took out a ten-dollar bill. But she didn't hand it to Loretta; she forced her to reach for it, adding to her humiliation. "Don't bother me at work again. If you do, I'll have hospital security escort you off the premises. Understand?"

Loretta nodded, swallowing her pride and her shame. The rubber soles of Bev's shoes squeaked on the tiles as she turned to go. When Loretta heard the elevator doors open, she raised her head and called plaintively, "Bev, don't—"

The doors closed before she could finish, but not before she could see that Bev's eyes were averted, as though she couldn't bear the sight of her own mother.

# SUNDAY

## CHAPTER 8

IT JUST DIDN'T MAKE SENSE.

Unexpectedly, out of the blue, you meet someone. It's like getting a gift for no particular reason. The attraction is instantaneous, strong, and mutual. You enjoy each other's company. You laugh, you dance, you eat corn on the cob and ice cream. You have sex that makes you feel like you've never known what it was all about before. You fall asleep in each other's arms and feel more content than you can remember feeling, ever.

Then you wake up alone.

She's gone. No so long, no goodbye. No *hasta la vista,* baby. No nothing.

Hammond thumped the steering wheel of his car, angry at her, but angrier at himself for giving a damn. Why should he care that she had run out? Hey, he had had a terrific Saturday night. He'd had great sex with a gorgeous stranger who had accommodated him in bed, then, being even more accommodating, had disappeared, leaving no strings attached. The dream date, right? It didn't get much better than that. Ask any single male his number one, primo fantasy, and that would be it.

*So accept it for what it was, you jerk,* he reprimanded himself. *Don't make too much out of it. And don't remember it better than it actually was.*

But he wasn't making it out better than it was. It had been fantastic, and that's exactly how he was remembering it.

Cursing, he swerved around a motorist who was testing his patience by driving too slow. Everything was an irritant today. Since waking up this morning, he had been taking out his disappointment and frustration on inanimate objects. First on the bureau on which he had rammed his big toe as he had bolted from the bed and run into the living area of the cabin, frantically hoping to see her puttering around in the kitchen looking for a cereal bowl, or thumbing through a magazine in the living area, or sitting in the porch rocking chair watching the river flow languidly past as she sipped coffee and waited for him to wake up.

His fantasies had taken on the soft-focus glow of greeting card commercials.

But that's all they had been—fantasies.

Because the living room and kitchen were empty, her car was gone, and the only occupant of the front porch rocking chair had been a spider busily spinning a web that spanned the seat from one armrest to the other.

Uncaring that he was bare-assed, he had brushed the spider aside and sat down in the rocker, pushing back his hair with all ten fingers, the gesture of a desperate man on the brink of losing all self-control.

What time had she left? What time was it now? How long had she been gone?

Maybe she was coming back. Maybe he was getting upset over nothing.

For half an hour, he had deluded himself into believing that she had gone in search of donuts and danish. Or cream for her coffee. Or a Sunday newspaper.

But she didn't come back.

Eventually he had relinquished the rocking chair to the spider and went indoors. In his attempt to make coffee, he had spilled grounds on the countertop. Angry over that, he had cracked the glass carafe and wound up throwing the whole damn machine onto the floor, breaking it apart and dumping the water with which he'd filled the tank.

He had searched the cabin, looking for something she might have left behind, wishing for a business card . . . or, better yet, a note. He found nothing. In the bathroom, he had inspected the wastepaper basket beneath the sink, but there was nothing in it except the disposable plastic liner. When he came back up, he bumped his head on the open door of the storage cabinet. Furiously he slammed the door, but cursed with even more ferocity when he slammed it shut on his finger.

Finally, although the bed was the most poignant reminder of her, he had returned to it, flinging himself down onto it and placing his forearm across his eyes, willing himself to get it together.

What the hell was wrong with him? he had asked himself. No one who knew him would have recognized him this morning, prowling around naked and unshaven and not giving a damn, looking and behaving like a wild man, like a dangerously unbalanced lunatic. Hammond Cross, acting like a chump, like a lovesick calf. *Our* Hammond Cross? You gotta be kidding!

Wait a minute, did you say *lovesick*?

Slowly he had lowered his arm and turned his head toward her pillow. He touched it, placing his hand in the depression left by her head. Gradually he had rolled onto his side, drew the pillow against his chest, and buried his face in it, breathing deeply of her scent.

Desire engulfed him, but this wasn't about sex.

Okay, it was, but not entirely.

This wasn't ordinary lust. He'd experienced that lots of times. He would recognize that. This was different. Deeper. More involving. He was in the grip of a . . . yearning.

"Shit," he had whispered. *Would you listen to yourself? Yearning?*

Rolling onto his back again, he had gazed up at the ceiling and dismally conceded that he didn't know the term for what he felt. It was foreign to him. He had never experienced it before, so how could he put a name to it? He only knew that it was encompassing and debilitating, that he had never felt like this before even though he had been with a lot of beautiful, captivating, sexy women.

From there his thoughts had wandered from his sexual history to hers. And that's when he had remembered the telephone call. Frowning, he had looked at the telephone on the table across the room. When he had caught her using it, she had looked startled and guilty. Who could she have been calling?

Suddenly he had sprung off the bed. Heart racing, he bent over the telephone and ran his finger along the rubberized buttons on the panel. He wasn't even sure that this particular model had the feature he sought, but then, *yes!*, there it was.

Auto Redial.

Hesitating only a second, he depressed the button. Beeping a series of tones, the telephone automatically dialed the number, which simultaneously appeared on the LED. He grabbed a pencil and the only paper within reach—last season's *Sports Illustrated* swimsuit edition. He scribbled the telephone number across the cover girl's abdomen.

"Dr. Ladd."

He didn't know what he had expected, but after two rings when his call was answered by a clipped, professional, female voice, it caught him off guard.

"Pardon?"

"Were you calling Dr. Ladd?"

"Uh . . . I'm . . . I might have the wrong number." He repeated the number he had jotted down.

"That's correct. This is an answering service. Were you trying to reach the doctor?"

At a loss, he said, "Uh, yeah."

"Your name and a number where you can be reached, please."

"You know, on second thought, I'll wait and call during office hours."

He had hung up quickly, but for a long time afterward, he had sat on the edge of the bed and pondered who the hell Dr. Ladd could be, and why she had been calling him in the middle of the night.

He had run through a roster of names and faces in his memory bank. He mixed socially with a number of physicians. He was a member of two country clubs that were jam-packed with doctors of every specialty. But he couldn't recall ever having met a Dr. Ladd.

But had he met Dr. Ladd's wife? Did he know Dr. Ladd's wife intimately?

Annoyed by that grim but very real possibility, he had forced himself to get up and shower. Not that a hot shower was indicative of anything. Not that he felt guilty and in need of cleansing. If she was married and had lied about it, he was blameless. Right? Right.

After dressing, he had trudged into the kitchen, where he settled for two cups of decaf freeze-dried coffee. He even forced down half an English muffin, chewing and ruminating in sync. She had told him she wasn't married, but hell, how could he believe a woman who hadn't even told him her name?

He didn't even know her name, for chrissake!

She had told him a lot of things. For instance, that she didn't habitually go to bed with men she had only just met. Casually or routinely. Weren't those her exact words? But how did he know if that was true?

How did he know that she wasn't a compulsive liar and slut, who happened to be married to a poor schmuck with a medical degree? She could be a wayward wife who had cheated on Dr. Ladd so much that he was no longer surprised by telephone calls in the middle of the night.

The more Hammond thought about it, the more morose he became.

As he straightened up the kitchen, he had checked the wall clock and was surprised to see that it was already midafternoon. How could he have slept so late? Easy. They hadn't stopped making love. . . . They hadn't drifted off to sleep until nearly six.

He hadn't intended to return to Charleston until dark. He had planned on spending a leisurely Sunday fishing, or sitting on the porch and taking in the scenery, basically doing nothing that required him to think too much.

But staying in the cabin hadn't held much appeal. Nor had thinking. So he had locked up the place and headed back ahead of schedule. Now as he crossed Memorial Bridge into the city, he wondered if she was a Charlestonian who had taken a similar route home.

What if they bumped into each other some night at a cocktail party? Would they acknowledge their night together, or would they greet one another like polite strangers and pretend they had never met?

It would probably depend on whether or not they were with other people at the time. How would he feel if he was introduced to the seemingly happy couple, Dr. and Mrs. Ladd, and was required to look her husband in the eye and shake his hand and make small talk and act like he hadn't had carnal knowledge of the woman standing beside him?

He hoped for many reasons that he would never be faced with a situation like that, but that if he was, he would handle it with a reasonable degree of aplomb. He hoped he wouldn't look like a sap. He hoped he would be able to turn his back on her and walk away.

He wasn't sure he could. That's what worried him most.

When faced with a moral dilemma, Hammond usually chose on the side of right. Beyond normal childhood pranks, high school mischief, and college debauchery, his conduct was unimpeachable. Whether he was cursed with an extra measure of virtue or merely cowardice, he customarily abided by the rules.

It hadn't always been easy. In fact, his unshakable sense of right and wrong had been at the crux of most of his conflicts with friends and colleagues, even his parents. Especially his father. His father and he didn't abide by the same rules of behavior. Preston Cross would consider this quandary over a woman amusing.

Turning into the condo complex where he lived, Hammond asked himself what would have happened if he had walked in on her moments earlier last night and had heard her say into the telephone something to the effect of, "Darling, since it's so late, I've decided to stay over with my friend [insert feminine name here]. That is if you don't mind. I thought it might be dangerous to drive back alone this late. All right then, see you in the morning. Love you, too."

When the automated door opened, Hammond guided his car into his narrow garage. But for several moments after he had turned off the engine, he sat there and stared into near space, pondering whether or not he would have passed or failed that particular test of his moral fiber.

Finally, annoyed with himself for engaging in such pointless speculation, he got out of his car and let himself into his townhouse through the door connecting the garage to the kitchen. Out of habit, he headed for the telephone to check his voice mail. On second thought, he ignored it. There was bound to be at least one message from his father. He wasn't in the mood to rehash yesterday's confrontation. He wasn't in the mood to talk to anyone.

Maybe he would go for a quick sail. There were a few hours of daylight remaining. The sixteen-foot craft, a gift from his parents when he passed the bar, was moored across the street at City Marina. That's why he'd bought a condo in this complex; it was a short walk to the marina.

Today was a perfect day to take the boat out. It might help clear his mind.

Quickening his pace, he went through the kitchen, into the hall, past the living room, and was headed for the stairs when he heard a key being inserted in the front door lock. He barely had time to turn before Steffi Mundell came in, a cell phone held to her ear.

She was saying, "I can't believe they're being such hard-asses about this." Juggling keys, phone, briefcase, and handbag, she waggled her fingers in a hello wave. "I mean, food poisoning isn't exactly bone cancer. . . . Well, let me know. . . . I know I don't have to be there, but I want to be. You have the number of my cell, right? . . . Okay, 'bye." She clicked the phone off and looked at Hammond with exasperation. "Where the hell have you been?"

"What happened to hello?"

His colleague never stopped working. In an oversize briefcase, she carried around with her what amounted to a miniature desk. Upon joining the Charleston County Solicitor's Office, she'd had a police scanner installed in her car, and she listened to it like other motorists listened to music or talk radio. It was a standing joke among the other attorneys and police officers that Steffi was the prosecution's equivalent of an ambulance-chasing defense attorney.

She dumped her plethora of belongings into a chair, stepped out of her high heels, and pulled her shirttail from her skirt waistband. She fanned her midriff with the loose blouse. "God, it's stifling outside. I'm smothering. Why haven't you answered your phone?"

"I told you I was going to be at my cabin."

"I called there. About a million times."

"I turned off the ringer."

"For heaven's sake why?"

*Because I was totally involved in a woman and didn't want to be disturbed,* he thought. But he said, "You must have the radar of a bat. I just came in through the back door. How'd you know I was here?"

"I didn't. Your place is closer to CPD than mine. I figured you wouldn't mind me waiting here until I heard something."

"About what? Who were you talking to? What's so urgent?"

"Urgent? Hammond?" Facing him, hands on hips, she appeared at first to be mystified. Then her expression changed to one of profound amazement. "Oh, my God, you don't know."

"Apparently not." Her dramatics didn't impress him. Steffi was always dramatic.

So much for sailing. He didn't want to invite Steffi to come along, and she wasn't easy to shake, especially when her spirits were running this high. He suddenly felt very tired. "I need something to drink. What can I get you?"

He retraced his steps into the kitchen and opened the refrigerator. "Water or beer?"

She padded along behind him. "I can't believe it. You honestly don't know. You haven't heard. Where is that cabin of yours, Outer Mongolia? Doesn't it have a TV?"

"Okay, beer." He took two bottles from the refrigerator, opened the first one, and extended it to her. She took it, but she continued staring at him as though his face had just broken out in oozing sores. He opened the second beer and tipped the bottle toward his mouth. "The suspense is killing me. What's got you so hyped?"

"Somebody murdered Lute Pettijohn yesterday afternoon in his Charles Towne Plaza penthouse."

The beer bottle never made it to Hammond's mouth. He lowered it slowly, staring at her with total disbelief. Seconds ticked by. Gruffly, he said, "That's impossible."

"It's true."

"Can't be."

"Why would I lie?"

At first immobilized by shock, he eventually moved. He ran his hand around the back of his neck where tension had already gathered. Operating on autopilot, he set his beer on the small bistro table, pulled a chair away from it, and lowered himself into it. When Steffi sat down across from him, he blinked her into focus. "You did say *murdered*?"

"Murdered."

"How?" he asked, in that same dry voice. "How did he die?"

"Are you okay?"

He gazed at her as though he no longer understood the language, then he nodded absently. "Yeah, I'm fine. I'm just . . ." He spread his hands.

"Speechless."

"Flabbergasted." He cleared his throat. "How'd he die?"

"Gunshot. Two bullets in the back."

He lowered his eyes to the granite tabletop, staring sightlessly at the condensation forming on the cold beer bottle while he assimilated the staggering news. "When? What time?"

"He was found by a hotel housekeeper a little after six."

"Last evening."

"Hammond, I'm not stuttering. Yes. Yesterday."

"I'm sorry."

He listened as she described what the chambermaid had discovered. "The head injury was more than a bump, but John Madison thinks the bullets killed him. Naturally he can't officially rule cause of death until he's completed the autopsy. All the particulars won't be known until then."

"You talked to the M.E.?"

"Not personally. Smilow filled me in."

"So he's on it?"

"Are you serious?"

"Of course he's on it," Hammond muttered. "What does he think happened?"

For the next five minutes, Hammond listened while she gave him the known details of the case. "I thought the office should be in on this one from the beginning, so I spent the night with Smilow—in a manner of speaking." Her impish smile seemed grossly inappropriate. Hammond merely nodded and gestured impatiently for her to continue. "I was with him as he followed up on some leads, precious few that they are."

"Hotel security?"

"Pettijohn died without a whimper. No sign of forced entry. No sign of a struggle. And we can eliminate camera surveillance. All we've got on videotape is a monotonous sound track and writhing naked people."

"Huh?"

When she told him about the bogus security cameras, he shook his head with dismay. "Jesus. He made such a big deal of that system and how much it had cost. The gall of the man."

Hammond was well acquainted with the unsavory personality traits and unscrupulous business dealings of Lute Pettijohn. He had been covertly investigating him for the attorney general for six months. The more he had learned about Pettijohn, the more there was to disdain and dislike. "Any witnesses?"

"None so far. The only person in the hotel who had any real contact with him was a masseur in the spa, and he's a dead end." She then told him about the outbreak of food poisoning. "Discounting the kids, there are seven adults Smilow wants to question. Neither of us is very optimistic about the outcome, but he's promised to call as soon as the doctor gives him the green light. I want to be there."

"You're becoming very personally involved, aren't you?"

"It'll be a huge case."

The statement lay between them like a thrown gauntlet. The rivalry was unspoken, but it was always there. Hammond humbly conceded that he usually held the advantage over her, and not because he was smarter than she. He'd ranked second in his law school class, but Steffi had been first in hers. Their personalities were what distinguished them. His served him in good stead, but Steffi's worked against her. People didn't respond well to her abrasiveness and aggressive approach.

His distinct advantage, he admitted, was Monroe Mason's blatant favoritism of him. A position had come open soon after Steffi joined the office. Both were qualified. Both were considered. But there was never really any contest as to who would be promoted. Hammond now served as special assistant solicitor.

Steffi's disappointment had been plain, although she had handled it with aplomb. She wasn't a sore loser and hadn't carried a grudge. Their working relationship continued to be more cooperative than adversarial.

Even so, like now, silent challenges were sometimes issued. For the time being neither picked it up.

Hammond changed the subject. "What about Davee Pettijohn?"

"In what regard? Do you mean, What about Davee Pettijohn as a suspect? Or as the bereaved widow?"

"Suspect?" Hammond repeated with surprise. "Does someone think she killed Lute?"

"I do." Steffi proceeded to tell him about accompanying Smilow to the Pettijohn mansion and why she considered the widow a likely suspect.

After hearing her out, Hammond refuted her theory. "First of all, Davee doesn't need Lute's money. She never did. Her family—"

"I've done my research. The Burtons had money out the kazoo."

Her snide tone didn't escape him. "What's bugging you?"

"Nothing," she snapped. Then she took a deep breath and blew it out slowly. "Okay, maybe I am bugged. I get bugged when men, who are supposedly adult, professional, and intelligent, turn to quivering towers of jelly when they get around a woman like her."

"'A woman like her'?"

"Come on, Hammond," she said, with even more vexation than before. "Fluffy kitten on the outside, panther on the inside. You know the type I'm talking about."

"You typed Davee after meeting her only once?"

"See? You're defending her."

"I'm not defending anybody."

"First Smilow goes ga-ga over her, if you can believe that. Now you."

"I'm hardly 'ga-ga.' I just fail to see how you could draw a complete personality profile on Davee after—"

"All right! I don't care," she said impatiently. "I don't want to talk about

Lute Pettijohn and the murder and motives. It's all I've thought about for almost twenty-four hours. I need a break from it."

She left her chair, put her fists into the small of her back and stretched luxuriously, then came around the table to sit on Hammond's lap. Looping her arms around his neck, she kissed him.

## CHAPTER 9

After several quick kisses, Steffi sat back and ruffled his hair. "I forgot to ask. How was your night away?"

"It was great," Hammond replied truthfully.

"Do anything special?"

Special? Very. Even their silly conversations had been extraordinary.

"I played football in the NFL, you know."

"You did?"

"Yeah, but after winning my second Super Bowl, I went to work for the CIA."

"Dangerous work?"

"The routine cloak-and-dagger stuff."

"Wow."

"Actually, it was a yawn. So I enlisted in the Peace Corps."

"Fascinating."

"It was okay. To a point. But after I was awarded the Nobel prize for feeding all the starving children in Africa and Asia, I started looking around for something else."

"Something more challenging?"

"Right. I narrowed my choices down to becoming president and serving my country, or finding a cure for cancer."

"Self-sacrifice must be your middle name."

"No, it's Greer."

*"I like it."*

*"You know I'm lying."*

*"Your middle name's not Greer?"*

*"That much is true. The rest, all lies."*

*"No!"*

*"I wanted to impress you."*

*"Guess what?"*

*"What?"*

*"I'm impressed."*

Hammond recalled the touch of her hand, the sensation of swelling . . .

"Hmm," Steffi purred. "Just as I thought. You missed me."

He was hard, and it wasn't for the woman sitting on his lap and fondling him through his trousers. He brushed her hand aside. "Steffi—"

She bent forward and kissed him aggressively. Hiking her skirt up around her hips, she straddled his thighs and continued kissing him while her hands attacked his belt buckle.

"I hate to rush," she said breathlessly between kisses. "But when Smilow calls, I'll need to dash. This will have to be quick, I'm afraid."

Hammond reached for her busy hands and clasped them between his. "Steffi. We need to—"

"Go upstairs? Fine. But we can't dawdle, Hammond."

Agile and energetic, she hopped off his lap and headed for the door, unbuttoning her blouse as she went.

"Steffi."

She turned and watched with bafflement as Hammond stood up and rezipped his trousers. She laughed lightly. "I'm willing to try just about anything, but it's going to be a little tricky if you don't take it out of your pants."

He moved to the other side of the room and braced his arms on the edge of the granite counter. He stared down into the spotless kitchen sink for several moments before turning to face her again.

"This isn't working for me any longer, Steffi."

Once the words were out, he felt hugely relieved. He had left town yesterday afternoon burdened for several reasons. One of them—the least of them, actually—was indecision over his affair with Steffi. He was unsure he wanted to put an end to it. They had a comfortable arrangement. Neither made unreasonable demands on the other. They shared many of the same interests. They were sexually compatible.

However, the topic of cohabitation had never come up, and Hammond was glad. If it had, he would have compiled a list of appropriate excuses as to why living at the same address would be a bad idea, but the real reason was that Steffi's energy level would have worn thin very quickly. Apparently she hadn't wanted him around her constantly, either. They kept their affair private. They saw each other regularly and when they wanted to. For almost a year it had been a perfect setup.

But lately, he had come to feel that it wasn't so perfect after all. He disliked secrecy and subterfuge, especially when it came to personal relationships, where he clung to the outdated belief that honesty should be a requisite component.

He was dissatisfied with their level of intimacy, too. More to the point, there was no intimacy. Not really. Although Steffi was an ardent and capable lover, they were no closer emotionally than they had been the first time she had invited him over for dinner and they had wound up wrestling out of their clothes on her living room sofa.

After weighing all the pluses and minuses, brooding over it for weeks, Hammond had resolved that the relationship had reached a plateau that left him wanting and needing more. Instead of anticipating their evenings together, he had begun to dread them. He was returning her calls later rather than sooner. Even in bed when they were having sex, he found himself distracted and thinking about other things, performing adequately but routinely, physically but unemotionally. Before indifference festered into resentment, it was better to break it off.

What he wanted and needed from a relationship, he wasn't sure. But he was certain that whatever it was, he wasn't going to find it in Stefanie Mundell. He had come closer to finding it last night, with a woman whose name he didn't even know. That was a sad commentary on his relationship with Steffi, but sound confirmation that it was time to end it.

Reaching that decision was only half the problem. He was now faced with actually doing it. He wished to end the affair as gracefully as possible, preferably avoiding the temperamental equivalent of the Hundred Years War. The best he could hope for was that it would end with no more fireworks than it had started.

The likelihood of that was nil. A scene was virtually guaranteed. He had dreaded it, and now he saw it coming.

It took a moment for his meaning to sink in. When it did, Steffi swallowed, folded her arms over her open blouse, then, in a defiant motion, uncrossed them and let them hang at her sides. "By 'this,' I take it you mean—"

"Us."

"Oh?" She cocked her head to one side and raised her eyebrows in a manner that was all too familiar. It was the expression she assumed when she was pissed off, when she was about to tear into somebody, usually an intern or clerk who hadn't done a good job preparing a brief for her, or a

cop who had failed to include an integral fact of a case in his report, or anyone who dared cross her when she was determined to have her way. "Since
when hasn't it been 'working' for you?"

"For a while now. I feel like we're moving in different directions."

She smiled, shrugged. "We've both been distracted lately, but that's easily fixed. We have enough in common to salvage—"

He was shaking his head. "Not just different directions, Steffi. Opposing directions."

"Could you be a little bit more specific?"

"Okay." He spoke evenly, although he resented her tone because it implied that he wasn't quite as smart as she. "Eventually I would like to
marry. Have kids. You've made it plain to me on numerous occasions that
you're not interested in having a family."

"That *you* are comes as a surprise."

He smiled wryly. "Actually it surprises me, too."

"You said you didn't want to be to any unsuspecting kid what your father had been to you."

"And I won't be," he said tightly.

"Isn't this a recent change of heart?"

"Recent but gradual. Our relationship was perfect for a while, but then—"

"The novelty wore off?"

"No."

"Then what? It's not exciting anymore? Sleeping with the hot number in
the County Solicitor's Office has lost its appeal? Being Steffi Mundell's secret lover doesn't excite you any longer?"

He hung his head and shook it. "Please don't do this, Steffi."

"I'm not doing anything," she retorted, her voice going shrill. "This conversation was your idea." Her dark eyes narrowed. "Do you have any idea
how many men would love to fuck me?"

"Yes," he said, raising his voice to the angry level of hers. "I hear the
locker room gossip about you."

"It used to give you a thrill when they wagered on who the mystery man
in my bed was, when all along it was you. We used to laugh about it."

"I guess it stopped being funny."

Left with nothing to say to that, she stood there and fumed in silence.

He continued in a calmer voice. "In any case, I went away this weekend
to reassess our relationship—"

"Without even talking about it first? It never occurred to you to invite
me to go away and reassess it with you?"

"I didn't see the point."

"So your mind was made up even before you went to your precious
cabin in the woods to *reassess*," she said, hissing the word.

"No, Steffi. My mind was not made up. While I was away, I looked at it from every angle and always reached the same conclusion."

"That you wanted to dump me."

"Not—"

"Dump? What word would you use?"

"This is precisely the kind of scene I hoped to avoid," he said, finally shouting over her. "Because I knew you would argue. I knew you would beat it to death as though you were in court pleading your case to a jury. You would refute everything I said simply for the sake of argument and not give an inch, because with you every goddamn thing comes down to a contest. Well, this isn't a competition, Steffi. And it isn't a trial. It's our lives."

"Oh, God, spare me the melodrama."

He snuffled a short laugh. "That's just it. I need a little melodrama. Our relationship is totally devoid of melodrama. Melodrama is human. It's—"

"Hammond, what in the hell are you talking about?"

"Everything in life can't be summed up in a brief. All the answers aren't found in law books." Frustrated with his own inability to explain, he swore beneath his breath before making another stab at it. "You're brilliant, but you never stop. The arguing, the besting, they're constant. Incessant. There's no down time with you."

"Forgive the pun, but I didn't know that being with me had been such a trial for you."

"Look," he said curtly. "I'll spare you the melodrama if you'll spare me the phony wounded-party act. You're angry, but you're not hurt."

"Will you stop telling me what I am and what I am not? You don't know what I'm feeling."

"I know it isn't love. You don't love me. Do you? Given a choice right now, what would you take: Your career? Or me?"

"What?" she cried. "I can't believe that you would issue such a ridiculous and juvenile ultimatum. 'Given a choice'? What kind of sexist bullshit is that? Why must I make a choice? You don't have to choose. Why can't I have you and my career?"

"You can. But in order for it to work, it takes two people who are willing to make a few sacrifices. Two people who love each other very much and are dedicated to the relationship and one another's happiness. What we do together," he said, pointing upstairs toward the bedroom, "isn't love. It's recreation."

"Well, we've gotten to be damn good at keeping each other entertained."

"I don't deny that. But entertainment is all it ever was, and it's pointless to suspect it was something else." He paused to catch his breath. She continued to stare at him stormily.

He moved to the table, picked up his beer, and took a long drink. Finally he looked over at her. "Don't pretend that you disagree. I know you agree."

"We get along so well."

"We did. We do. We had some great times. No one's to blame for this. There's no right side or wrong side. It's simply a matter of our wanting different futures."

She thought on that for a moment. "I made no secret of what I wanted, Hammond. If I had wanted hearth and home, I would have stayed in my hometown, obeyed my father, and married immediately after high school—if not before—and started having babies like my sisters did. I would have spared myself their scorn and his sermons. I wouldn't have struggled to get where I am. I've still got a long way to go to get where I want to be. From the beginning you knew what my priorities were."

"I admire you for them."

"Correction. What my priorities *are*."

"I hope you surpass all the goals you've set for yourself. I mean that sincerely. It's just that your personal goals leave no room for anything else. They're incompatible with the commitment I want from a life partner."

"You really want a Holly Homemaker?"

"God, no," he said, laughing and shaking his head. He stared into near space for a moment, then said, "I'm not sure what I want."

"You're just sure you don't want me."

Again, he knew that she was more miffed than hurt. Nevertheless, no woman liked being rejected. He respected her enough to let her down gently. "It's not you, Steffi. It's me. I want to be with someone who's at least willing to compromise on a few points."

"I never compromise."

Softly, he said, "You're slipping. You just made my case for me."

"No, I gave you that one."

"Thanks, I'll take it."

Then they smiled at each other, because beyond their physical attraction they had always admired one another's shrewdness. She said, "You're very smart, Hammond. I like smart and admire intellect. You have a sharp wit. You're tough when toughness is called for. You can even be mean when you have to be, and mean really gets me off. You're indisputably good-looking."

"Please. I'm blushing."

"Don't be coy. You know you set hearts aflutter and jump-start hormones."

"Thank you."

"You're generous and thoughtful in bed, never taking more than you give in return. In short, all the things I desire in a man."

He placed his hand over his heart. "It would take much longer for me to enumerate all the qualities that I admire in you."

"I'm not fishing for compliments. I'll leave that kind of feminine wiliness to the Davee Pettijohns of the world."

He chuckled.

"What I am leading to is . . ." She drew in a deep breath. "I don't suppose you'd consider carrying on as we have been until—"

He stopped her with a firm shake of his head. "That wouldn't be good, or fair, for either of us."

"There's no option B?"

"I think a clean break would be best, don't you?"

She smiled sourly. "It's a little late to be soliciting my opinion, Hammond. But yes, I suppose if that's the way you feel, I don't want you sleeping with me out of pity."

He gave a full-blown laugh then. "The very last thing you are is an object of pity."

Placated, she said, "You'll miss me, you know."

"Very much."

Curling the tip of her tongue up to the center of her upper lip, she opened her blouse. It didn't surprise him that her nipples were tight and dark with arousal. Steffi's biggest turn-on was an argument. Nothing stimulated her better than a shouting match. Typically their rowdiest sex had followed a confrontation of one sort or another. He realized now that she had guaranteed herself an ultimate win for every dispute. His climax had always been her victory. That, if nothing else, validated his decision.

She flashed him a mischievous grin. "One last time? For old times' sake? Or are you too high-minded and principled to fuck a woman you've just dumped?"

"Not exactly a romantic lead-in, Steffi."

"So now you want melodrama *and* romance? What's got into you, Hammond?"

He was tempted to take her up on her offer, not because he had any desire for her, but because sleeping with her might help blur the clear and sweetly painful memory of last night. To have another woman now might ease the weighty sense of loss.

While still considering it, his telephone rang.

Steffi laughed without humor as she closed her blouse and rebuttoned it. "You lucky bastard. Fortune just continues to smile on you, Hammond. You've been saved by the bell." She turned on her heel and went into the living room to retrieve her things.

Hammond reached for the telephone. "Hello?"

"It's Monroe."

Not that County Solicitor Monroe Mason needed to identify himself. He knew only one pitch of voice, and that was booming. The man's vocal cords seemed to have come equipped with a built-in megaphone. Hammond immediately adjusted the volume on the telephone receiver.

"Hey, Monroe, what gives? I spend one night away from Charleston and all hell breaks loose."

"So you've heard?"

"Steffi told me."

"I understand she's already in the thick of it."

Hammond glanced into the living room, where Steffi was stepping into her shoes and tucking in her blouse. Hammond put his back to the door and lowered his voice. "She seems to think she's got the case."

"Do you want her to have it?"

Hammond realized that his shirt was sticking to his torso. When had he begun to sweat? He rubbed his forehead, and discovered that it was damp, too. There was a reason for this uncustomary perspiration: He had met with Lute Pettijohn yesterday afternoon in his suite at the Charles Towne Plaza.

Monroe Mason should know that. Now was the time to tell him.

But why make an issue of it?

It didn't relate to Pettijohn's murder. Their meeting had been brief. It had occurred before the estimated time of death. Shortly before, but nevertheless . . .

He saw no reason to tell Mason about it, any more than he had deemed it necessary to tell Steffi when she broke the startling news of the homicide to him. There was nothing to be gained by informing them of this coincidence, and much to be lost.

Wiping his forehead on his shirtsleeve, he said, "*I* want the case."

His mentor chuckled. "Well, you've got it, boy."

"Thank you."

"Don't thank me. You had it even before you asked."

"I appreciate the vote of confidence."

"Stop sucking up, Hammond. I didn't make the decision independently. You got the case because the Widow Pettijohn has been calling me every hour on the hour since about ten o'clock last night."

"What for?"

"She's requested—make that demanded—that you be the one to put her husband's killer on trial."

"I'm grateful for her—"

"Cut the bullshit, Hammond. I can smell it a mile off. Hell, I'm so goddamn old, I think I invented it. Where was I?"

"The widow."

"Oh, yeah. Lute's dead, but it appears that Davee's going to take over where he left off when it comes to throwing weight around. She can make noise in this county. So, to spare our office a lot of grief and bad press, I agreed to assign you to the case."

This case would impact his career as no other case could. A high-profile murder victim. Media saturation. It had all the elements that cause ambitious prosecutors to salivate. Of course, he would feel better if Mason had assigned it to him without Davee's intervention, but he wasn't going to dwell on a minor detail like that. No matter how it had come about, the case was his.

He wanted it, needed it, and he was definitely the man for the job. He had tried five murder cases before and won convictions in all except one, when the accused had plea-bargained. From the day he had joined the prosecuting side of the law, he had been preparing himself for a case of this magnitude. He had the appetite for it, and he had the know-how to come out the winner. The Lute Pettijohn murder trial was going to catapult his career right where he wanted it to go . . . the County Solicitor's Office.

Since he already had the case, the confidence of his superior, and the backing of the widow, he reconsidered telling Mason about his meeting with Pettijohn. He hated to go into a project of this caliber with even the slightest disadvantage. A negligible ambiguity like this could become critically damaging if discovered later rather than sooner.

"Monroe?"

"Don't thank me, boy. You're in for a lot of sleepless nights."

"I welcome the challenge. It's something else. I . . ."

"What?"

Following the small hesitation, he said, "Nothing. Nothing, Monroe. I can't wait to get started."

"Fine, fine," he said, then launched into his next point. "You'll be working with Rory Smilow. Is that gonna be a problem?"

"No."

"Liar."

"We don't have to swap spit. All I want is a guarantee that he'll cooperate with our office."

"He drew first blood."

"What does that mean?"

"I got a call from Chief Crane this afternoon. Smilow lobbied for Steffi Mundell to prosecute the case. But I told Crane about the widow's preference."

"And?"

He chuckled. Monroe Mason thrived on politics more than he did the law. Hammond disliked the necessary politics associated with working for the county government, but it was the part of the job that Mason reveled in.

"Davee had already given our chief of police an earful, too. She told him she wanted Smilow to find the killer and she wanted you to put him away. So this is how we worked it out."

Hammond winced as he did when the dentist approached with the anesthetizing shot and told him to expect a slight sting.

"You and Smilow will lay your differences aside until this thing's over. Got that?"

"We're both professionals." He was making no promises where Rory Smilow was concerned, but a cease-fire truce was an easy enough concession. Then Mason added the second condition.

"And I'm putting Steffi in there to act as referee."

"What?" Trying to hide his anger and keep his voice down, Hammond said, "That's a shitty deal point, Monroe. I don't need a monitor."

"That's the trade-off, Hammond, take it or leave it."

Hammond could hear Steffi conversing on her cell phone in the other room. "Have you told her about this arrangement yet?" he asked.

"Tomorrow morning will be soon enough. You got it straight, boy?"

"I've got it straight."

Even so, Monroe Mason shouted it one more time. "Steffi's assisting you and acting as a buffer between you and Smilow. Hopefully, she can keep one of you from killing the other before we get Lute's murderer tried and convicted."

## CHAPTER 10

Her lungs felt ready to burst. Muscles were on fire. Joints were screaming for her to let up. But rather than slowing down, she increased her pace, running faster than she ever had, running harder than was healthy. She had several hundred calories of carnival food to burn off.

And a guilty conscience to try and outrun.

Sweat dripped into her eyes, causing them to blur and sting. Her breathing was loud and harsh; her mouth was dry. Heartbeats drummed in time to her rapid footfalls. Even when she didn't think she could go one step farther, she stubbornly pushed on. Surely she had surpassed her previous best speed and level of endurance.

Even so, she could never run away from what she had done last night.

Running was her favorite form of aerobic exercise. She ran several times a week. She frequently participated in fund-raising races. She had helped organize one to raise money for breast cancer research. This evening, however, she wasn't doing it altruistically, or for the fitness benefits derived from it, or to relieve workday tension.

This evening's run was self-flagellation.

Of course, it was unreasonable to presume that today's physical exertion would atone for yesterday's transgressions. Atonement could only come to one who was genuinely and deeply remorseful. While she regretted that their meeting had been calculated, not capricious; while it hadn't been the random encounter that he believed it to be; while a twinge of conscience had caused her to try and end it before it culminated in lovemaking, she had no remorse that it had evolved as it had.

Not for one moment did she regret the night she had spent with him.

"On your left."

Courteously she edged to her right to allow the other runner to go past. Pedestrian traffic on the Battery was heavy this evening. It was a popular promenade, appealing to joggers, in-line skaters, or those out for a leisurely stroll.

This historically significant tip of the peninsula where the Ashley and Cooper rivers converged and emptied into the Atlantic was on every tourist's agenda when visiting Charleston.

The Battery—comprised of White Point Gardens and the seawall—bore battle scars from wars, woes, and weather, as did all of Charleston. Once the site of public hangings, later a strategic defense post, the Battery's main function today was to provide scenery and pleasure.

In the park across the street from the seawall, the ancient and proud live oak trees which had defied vicious storms, even Hurricane Hugo, shaded monuments, Confederate cannons, and couples pushing baby strollers.

There had been no break from the oppressive heat and humidity, but at least on the seawall overlooking Charleston Harbor and Fort Sumter in the distance, there was a breeze which made it almost balmy for the people who were out to grab the remnants of a beautiful dusk that spelled the end of the weekend.

Slowing to a more prudent pace, she decided it was time to turn back. As she retraced her course, each impact with the pavement drove a splinter of pain up her shins and thighs into her lower back, but at least it was manageable now. Her lungs still labored, but the burning sensation in her muscles abated.

Her conscience, however, continued to prick her.

Thoughts of him and their night together had been launching surprise attacks on her all day. She hadn't allowed herself to entertain these recollections for long, because doing so seemed somehow to compound the original offense, like an intruder who not only invaded his victim's property, but also violated his most personal belongings.

But she couldn't stave off the thoughts any longer. As she wound down her workout, she invited them in and let them linger. She tasted again the food they had shared at the fair, smiled when she remembered his telling a silly joke, imagined his breath in her ear, his fingertips against her skin.

He had been sleeping so soundly, he hadn't awakened when she slipped from the bed and dressed in the dim room. At the bedroom door she had paused to look back at him. He was lying on his back. One leg had been thrust outside the covers; the sheet caught him at his waist.

He had wonderful hands. They looked strong and manly, but well tended. One had a loose grip on the sheet. The other rested on her pillow. The fingers were curled slightly inward toward his palm and until moments ago had been nestled in her hair.

Watching his chest rise and fall with peaceful breathing, she had struggled with the temptation to wake him and confess everything. Would he have understood? Would he have thanked her for being honest with him? Maybe he would have told her that it didn't matter, and drawn her back down beside him, and kissed her again. Would he have thought more or less of her for admitting what she had done?

What *had* he thought when he woke up and found her gone?

No doubt he had panicked at first, thinking that he'd been robbed. Straight out of bed, he had probably checked to see if his wallet was still on the bureau. Had he fanned out his credit cards like a poker hand to make certain that none were missing? Had he been surprised to find all his cash present and accounted for? Had he then felt tremendous relief?

Following the relief, had he become puzzled by her disappearance? Or angry? Probably angry. He might have taken her sneaking out as an affront.

At the very least she hoped that, having awakened and noticed her gone, he hadn't simply shrugged, rolled over, and gone back to sleep. That was a sad but distinct possibility which caused her to wonder whether or not he had even thought of her today. Had he replayed the entire evening in his head just as she had, taking it from the instant their eyes had locked across the dance floor until that last time . . . ?

*His lips brushed kisses across her face. He whispered, "Why does this feel so good?"*

*"It's supposed to feel good, isn't it?"*

*"Yes. But not like this. Not this good."*

*"It's . . ."*

*"What?" Angling his head back, his eyes probed hers.*

*"It's almost better."*

*"Being still, you mean?"*

*She closed her thighs around his hips, hugging him tighter, securing him. "Like this. Just having you . . ."*

*"Hmm." He buried his face in her neck. But after a long moment, he groaned. "I'm sorry. I can't be still."*

*Lifting her hips, she gasped, "Neither can I."*

Suddenly, lest she stumble, she stopped running and bent from the waist, resting her hands on her knees as she sucked in the sultry, insufficient air. She blinked salty sweat out of her eyes and tried to dry them with the back of her hand, only to realize that it was dripping, too.

She must stop thinking about it. Their evening together, while being wildly romantic to her, probably had been nothing out of the ordinary for him, regardless of all the poetic things he had said.

Not that it mattered one way or the other, she reminded herself. It made no difference what he thought of her, or if he thought of her at all. They could never see each other again.

After a time she regained her breath and her heart rate slowed, then she jogged down the steps of the seawall. More than the exhausting run, the certainty of never seeing him again sapped her of energy. She lived only a few blocks from the Battery, but walking those seemed longer than the entire distance she had run.

She was still lost in despondent thought as she unlatched her front iron gate. The rude bleat of a car horn startled her, and she spun around just as a Mercedes convertible screeched to a halt at the curb.

The driver tipped down his sunglasses, looking at her over the frames. "Good evening," Bobby Trimble drawled. "I've been calling you all day and was about to give you up for lost."

"What are you doing here?"

His chiding smile made her skin crawl.

"Get away from my house and leave me alone."

"It wouldn't be a good idea to get me riled. Especially not now. Where have you been all day?"

She refused to answer.

He grinned, seemingly amused by her stubbornness. "Never mind. Get in."

Leaning across the seat, he opened the passenger door. As it swung open, she had to leap back to keep it from striking her shin. "If you think I'm going anywhere with you, you're crazy."

He reached for the ignition key. "Fine, then I'll come in."

"No!"

He chuckled. "I didn't think so." Patting the passenger seat, he said, "Put your sweet little tush right here. Right now."

She knew he wouldn't give up easily and go away. Sooner or later she must confront this, so she might just as well get it over with. She climbed into the car and angrily slammed the door.

Hammond decided not to postpone offering his condolences to Lute Pettijohn's widow. After concluding his conversation with Mason and seeing Steffi off, he showered and changed. Within minutes, he was in his car and on his way to the Pettijohn mansion.

Waiting for the bell at the gate to be answered, he mindlessly observed the people enjoying their Sunday evening at the Battery. Two tourists across the street in the park were taking photographs of the Pettijohns' mansion, despite his presence in the foreground. The usual number of joggers and walkers showed up as moving silhouettes along the seawall.

He was let in by Sarah Birch. The housekeeper asked him to wait in the foyer while she announced him. Returning shortly, she said, "Miss Davee says for you to come on up, Mr. Cross."

The massive woman led him upstairs, across the gallery, and down a wide corridor, then through an enormous bedroom into a bathroom that was unlike any Hammond had ever seen. Beneath a stained-glass skylight was a sunken whirlpool tub large enough for a volleyball team. It was filled with water, but the jets weren't on. Creamy magnolia blossoms as large as dinner plates floated on the still surface.

What seemed to be acres of mirrored walls reflected scented candles that flickered on elaborate candlesticks scattered throughout the room. A silk-upholstered chaise piled with decorative pillows stood in one corner. The gold sink was as large as a washtub. The fixtures were crystal, matching the countless vanity jars and perfume bottles arrayed on the counter.

Hammond realized now that the gossips were probably conservative in their estimate of what Lute had spent on the house's refurbishing. Although he had been inside many times for various social functions, this was the first time he had ever been upstairs. He had heard rumors of its opulence, but he hadn't expected anything quite this lavish.

Nor had he expected to find the recent widow naked and cooing pleasurably as a beefy masseur stroked the back of her thigh.

"You don't mind, do you, Hammond?" Davee Pettijohn asked as the masseur draped a sheet over her to cover everything except her shoulders and the leg he was presently massaging.

Hammond took the hand she extended him and squeezed it. "Not if you don't."

She gave him a wicked smile. "You know me better than that. Not an ounce of modesty to my name. A flaw that liked to have driven my mama crazy. Of course, she was crazy anyway."

Propping her chin on her stacked hands, she sighed as the masseur kneaded her buttock. "We're right in the middle of the ninety-minute session, and it's so divine I just couldn't bring myself to ask Sandro to stop."

"I don't blame you. Funny, though."

"What?"

"Lute had a massage in the hotel spa yesterday."

"Before or after he got himself murdered?" His frown caused her to laugh. "Just kidding. Pour yourself some champagne, why don't you?" With an indolent wave, she indicated the silver wine cooler standing near the vanity. The cork had already been popped, but on the silver tray near the cooler was an extra flute that hadn't been used. It flitted through his mind that Davee might have been expecting him tonight. It was an unsettling thought.

"Thanks, but I'd better not," he said.

"Oh, for goodness' sake," she said impatiently. "Don't be such a stick-in-the-mud. You and I have never stood on ceremony, so why start now? Besides, I think champagne is the perfect drink for when your husband gets blown away in the penthouse suite of his own freaking hotel. While you're at it, pour me another, too."

Her champagne flute was sitting on the floor beside the massage table. Knowing it was usually futile to argue with Davee, Hammond refilled her glass, then poured half a flute for himself. When he brought hers back to her, she clinked their glasses together.

"Cheers. To funerals and other fun times."

"I don't exactly share your sentiment," he said after taking a sip.

She ran her tongue over her lips to savor the taste of the wine. "You may be right. Maybe champagne should only be drunk at weddings."

When she lifted her gaze to him, Hammond felt his face turn warm. Discerning exactly what he was thinking, she laughed.

It was the same laugh he remembered her laughing on a July night years before when both had been attendants in a mutual friend's wedding. Gardenias, Casa Blanca lilies, peonies, and other fragrant flowers had been used to decorate the garden of the bride's home where the reception had been held. The heady scent of the flowers was pervasive and as intoxicating as the champagne he had guzzled in a vain effort to keep cool within the constraints of his tuxedo.

As though they'd been cast by a talent agency, all eight bridesmaids had been gorgeous, matching blondes. In the frothy pink floor-length gown with a deep décolletage, Davee had been even more dazzling than the others.

"You look good enough to eat," he had told her outside the chapel moments before the wedding. "Or drink, maybe. You look like you should have a paper umbrella sticking out the top of your head."

"A paper umbrella is all this getup needs to be thoroughly revolting."

"You don't like it?" he asked, egging her on.

She flipped him the finger.

Later at the reception, when they came off the dance floor after a rousing dance to Otis Day and the Knights' "Shout," she fanned her face, complaining, "Not only is this dress too foofy to be believed, it's the hottest fucking garment I've ever had on my body."

"So take it off."

The Burtons and the Crosses had been friends before either Davee or Hammond was born. Consequently, his first memories of Christmas parties and beach cookouts included Davee. When the kids were shuttled upstairs to bed while the adults continued partying, he and Davee played tricks on the babysitters unlucky enough to be in charge of them.

They'd smoked their first cigarettes together. With an air of superiority she had confided to him when she started menstruating. The first time she got drunk, it was his car she threw up in. The night she lost her virginity, she had called Hammond as soon as she got home to give him a detailed account of the event.

From the time they were kids sharing their vocabulary of nasty words, all the way into adolescence, they had talked dirty to each other. First because it was fun, and they could get away with it. Neither would tattle on the other or take offense. As they progressed into young adulthood, their banter became more sexually oriented and flirtatious, but it was still meaningless and therefore safe.

But leading up to that July wedding, they had been away at their respective universities—he at Clemson and she at Vanderbilt—and hadn't seen each other in a long while. They were more than a little drunk on champagne and caught up in the romanticism of the occasion. So when Hammond issued that naughty challenge, Davee had looked at him through smoky eyes and replied, "Maybe I will."

While everyone else gathered around to watch the cutting of the bridal cake, Hammond stole a bottle of champagne from one of the bars and grabbed Davee's hand. They sneaked into the neighbor's backyard, knowing that the neighbor was at the reception. The lawns of the two houses were divided by a dense, tall hedge that had been cultivated for decades to guarantee the kind of privacy Hammond and Davee were seeking.

The popping champagne cork sounded like a cannon blast when Hammond opened the bottle. That caused them to giggle hysterically. He poured them each a glass and they drank it down. Then a second.

At some point into the third, Davee asked him to help her with the back buttons on her bridesmaid dress, and off it came, along with her strapless bra, garter belt, and stockings.

She hesitated when she hooked her thumbs into the elastic waist of her underpants, but he whispered, "Dare you, Davee," which was a familiar refrain from their childhood and youth. Never had she backed down from a dare. That night was no exception.

She removed her panties and allowed him to stare his fill, then backed down the swimming pool steps into the cool water. Hammond shed his tuxedo in a fraction of the time it had taken him to get into it, scattering studs that were never seen again—at least not by him.

As he stood on the edge of the pool, Davee's eyes widened in astonishment and appreciation. "Hammond, honey, you've come along nicely since that time we got caught playing doctor."

He dove in.

Beyond some experimental kissing as youngsters when they had agreed that it was too "totally gross" to even consider opening mouths and touching tongues, they had never kissed. They didn't that night, either. They didn't take the time. The danger of getting caught had heightened their excitement to a point where foreplay was unnecessary. The moment he reached her, he pulled her onto his thighs and thrust into her.

It was slippery. It was quick. They laughed through the whole thing.

After that night, he didn't see her for a couple of years. When he did, he pretended that the escapade in the swimming pool had never happened, and she did likewise. Probably neither had wanted that one sexual experiment to jeopardize a lifetime friendship.

They had never mentioned it until now. He didn't even remember how they had got back into their clothes that night, or how they had explained themselves to the other people attending the wedding reception, or if they were even required to explain themselves.

But he vividly remembered Davee's laugh—gutsy and lusty, seductive and sexy. Her laugh hadn't changed.

But her smile was almost sad when she said, "We had fun as kids, didn't we?"

"Yes, we did."

Then she lowered her eyes to the bubbles in her glass, watching them for a moment before drinking them down. "Unfortunately, we had to become grown-ups and life started to suck."

Her arm dropped listlessly over the side of the table. Hammond took the flute from her hand before she dropped it and shattered it on the marble floor. "I'm sorry about Lute, Davee. That's why I came, to let you know that I think what happened is terrible. I'm sure my parents will call or come over to see you tomorrow."

"Oh, there'll be a parade of sympathizers marching through here tomorrow. I refused to receive anyone today, but tomorrow I won't be able to fend them off. Bringing their chicken casseroles and lime gelatin salads, they'll crowd in here to see how I'm taking it."

"How are you taking it?"

Noticing the subtle change in his tone, she rolled to her side, pulled the sheet against her front, and sat up, swinging her bare legs over the edge of the table. "Are you asking as my friend, or as the heir apparent to the D.A.'s office?"

"I could argue that point, but I'm here as your friend. I shouldn't have to tell you that."

She pulled in a deep breath. "Well, don't expect sackcloth and ashes, or hair shirts. None of that Bible stuff. I'm not going to cut off a finger or anything like the Indian widows in the movies do. No, I'll behave appropriately. Thanks to Lute, the gossips will have enough to keep them in material without me showing how I really feel."

"And how's that?"

She smiled as brilliantly as she had the night she took her bow at her debutante ball. "I'm positively delighted that the son of a bitch is dead." Her honey-colored eyes challenged Hammond to say something to that. When he didn't, she just laughed and then addressed the masseur over her shoulder. "Sandro, be a love and do my neck and shoulders, please."

From the time she sat up, he had been standing against the mirrored wall with his arms folded over his meaty chest. Sandro was handsome and heavily muscled. Straight black hair was combed away from his face and held there with thick gel. His eyes were as dark as ripe olives.

As he moved in behind Davee and placed his hands on her bare shoulders, his intense, Mediterranean eyes stayed fixed on Hammond as though he were sizing up a competitor. Obviously his services extended beyond the massage. Hammond wanted to tell him to relax, that he and Davee were old friends, nothing more, and that he need not be jealous of him.

At the same time he wanted to warn Davee that now was not the time to flout convention by screwing her masseur. For once in her life she should exercise discretion. Unless Hammond missed his guess, and taking into account Steffi's remarks, her name would top Rory Smilow's list of suspects. Everything she did would be closely scrutinized.

"I admire your candor, Davee, but—"

"Why lie? Did you like Lute?"

"Not at all," he replied honestly and without hesitation. "He was a crook, a scoundrel, and a ruthless opportunist. He hurt people who would let him, and he used those he couldn't hurt."

"You're equally candid, Hammond. Most people shared that sentiment. I'm not alone in despising him."

"No, but you are his widow."

"I am his widow," she said wryly. "I am a lot of things. But one thing I am not is a hypocrite. I won't grieve for the bastard."

"Davee, if the wrong people heard you saying things like that, it could mean trouble for you."

"Like Rory Smilow and that bitch he brought here with him last night?"

"Exactly."

"That Steffi person works with you, right?" When he nodded, she said, "Well, I thought she was positively horrid."

He smiled. "Few people like Steffi. She's very ambitious. She rubs people the wrong way, but she doesn't care. She's not out to win any personality contests."

"Good, because she would lose."

"She's really quite congenial once you get to know her."

"I'll pass."

"You have to understand where she's coming from."

"Up North someplace."

He chuckled. "I wasn't referring to a region, Davee. I meant her drive. She's had some career disappointments. She overcompensates for those setbacks and comes on a little too strong sometimes."

"If you don't stop defending her, I'm liable to get grumpy."

Placing one arm behind her head, she lifted her hair off her neck so Sandro would have easier access. It was a very provocative pose, exposing her underarm and part of her breast. Hammond figured she knew it was provocative, and wondered if she was deliberately trying to distract him.

"Do you honestly think they'll suspect me of murder?" she asked.

"You'll inherit a lot of money now."

"There's that, yes," she conceded thoughtfully. "And then there's the common knowledge that my late husband's main goal in life was to pork as many of my friends—and I use the term loosely—as possible.

"I don't know if he was working his way through them because they are, generally speaking, the most desirable women in Charleston, or if they were desirable to him only because they were my friends. Probably the latter, because Georgia Arendale's ass is bigger than a battleship, but that didn't stop him from taking her over to Kiawah for a day at the beach. I bet she got a serious burn because it would take a whole tube of Coppertone to cover that much cellulite.

"Emily Southerland has a complexion that would stop a clock, despite countless chemical peels, but Lute balled her anyway, in that ghastly downstairs powder room of hers—it has a faux fur toilet seat cover—at her New Year's Eve party."

Hammond laughed although Davee wasn't trying to be funny. "While you, of course, were entirely faithful to your marriage vows."

"Of course." Letting the sheet slip an inch or two, she batted her eyelashes at him to underscore her lie.

"Yours wasn't exactly a marriage made in heaven, Davee."

"I never claimed to love Lute. In fact, he knew I didn't. But that was okay because he didn't love me, either. The marriage still served its purpose. He wanted me for boasting rights. He was the one man in Charleston with balls big enough to bag Davee Burton. In return, I . . ." She paused, looking pained. "I had my reason for marrying him, but it wasn't the pursuit of happiness."

She lowered her arm and shook her hair free while Sandro went to work on her lower spine. "You're wincing, Hammond. What's the matter?"

"Everything you say sounds like motive to commit murder."

She laughed scornfully. "If I was going to kill Lute, I wouldn't have gone about it like that. I wouldn't have trotted myself downtown on a hot Saturday afternoon, when this city is crawling with stinky, sweaty Yankee tourists, toting a handgun like white trash, and shooting him in the back."

"That's what you would want the police to surmise, anyway."

"Reverse psychology? I'm not that clever, Hammond."

He looked at her in a way that said, *Oh, yes, you are.*

"Okay," she said, accurately interpreting his expression. "I am. But I would also have to be industrious, and no one has ever accused me of inconveniencing myself, or sacrificing creature comfort, no matter what the reason. I'm just not that passionate about anything."

"I believe you," he told her, meaning it. "But I don't think there's any legal precedent for basing a defense on laziness."

"Defense? Do you truly think I'll need one? Will Detective Smilow seriously consider me a suspect? That's crazy!" she exclaimed. "Why, *he* would come closer to killing Lute than *I* would. Smilow never forgave Lute for what happened with his sister."

Hammond's brow furrowed.

"Remember? Smilow's sister Margaret was Lute's first wife. Probably she was an undiagnosed manic-depressive, but marrying Lute was her undoing. One day she went over the edge and ate a bottle of pills for lunch. When she killed herself, Smilow blamed Lute, saying he'd been neglectful and emotionally abusive, never sensitive to poor Margaret's special needs. Anyway, at her funeral, they exchanged bitter words that caused a huge scandal. Don't you remember?"

"Now that you've reminded me, I do."

"Smilow has hated Lute ever since. So I'm not going to worry about him," she said, repositioning her hips on the table under Sandro's guidance. "If he accuses me of killing Lute, I'll just turn the tables by reminding him how many death threats he's issued."

"I'd pay to see that," Hammond told her.

Returning his smile, she said, "You've finished your champagne. More?"

"No, thanks."

"I'll have some." While he was pouring, she asked, "Monroe Mason contacted you, I suppose? You'll be prosecuting when they capture the killer?"

"That's the program. Thanks for the recommendation."

She drank from the flute he handed her. "For whatever else I am, Hammond, I'm a loyal friend. Never doubt that."

He wished she hadn't said that. County Solicitor Mason had informed his staff of his pending retirement. Deputy Solicitor Wallis was terminally ill; he wouldn't seek the top office in the upcoming November election. Hammond was third in the pecking order. He was virtually guaranteed Mason's endorsement as his successor.

But Davee's speaking to Mason on his behalf made Hammond uneasy. While he appreciated her recommendation, it could later turn out to be a conflict of interest if she was the one put on trial for her husband's murder.

"Davee, it's my duty to ask . . . how good is your alibi?"

"I believe the term is 'ironclad.' "

"Good."

Throwing back her head, she laughed. "Hammond, darlin', you are just too cute! You're actually afraid you'll have to charge me with murder, aren't you?"

She slid off the massage table and moved toward him, holding the sheet against her front and trailing it behind her. Coming up on tiptoes, she kissed his cheek. "Lay your worries to rest. If I was going to shoot Lute, it wouldn't have been in the back. What fun would there be in that? I would want to be looking the bastard in the eye when I pulled the trigger."

"That's no better a defense than laziness, Davee."

"I won't need a defense. I cross my heart I did not kill Lute." Putting her words into action, she drew an invisible X on her chest. "I would never kill anybody."

He was relieved to hear her deny it with such conviction.

Then she spoiled it by adding, "Those prison uniforms are just too dowdy for words."

Davee lay on her back, eyes closed, replete and relaxed from Sandro's massage, followed by sex that had required no participation from her except to enjoy her orgasm. She felt the pressure of his unappeased arousal against her thigh, but she was ignoring it. He lightly stroked her nipple with his tongue. "Strange," he murmured in accented English.

"What?"

"That your friend made his hints, but he never asked you if you had killed your husband."

Pushing him away, she looked up at him. "What do you mean?"

He shrugged. "Because he's your friend, he doesn't want to know for sure that you did it."

Davee's eyes moved to an empty spot just beyond his shoulder and involuntarily spoke her thought aloud. "Or maybe he already knows for sure that I didn't."

# CHAPTER | 11

As HAMMOND PULLED AWAY from the Pettijohn mansion, he hoped to God that he never would have to cross-examine Davee on the witness stand, for two very good reasons.

First, he and Davee were friends. He liked her. She was hardly a pillar of virtue, but he respected her for not pretending to be. When she claimed not to be a hypocrite, it wasn't an empty boast.

He knew dozens of women who gossiped viciously about her but who were no more moral than she. The difference was that they sinned in secret. Davee sinned flamboyantly. She was considered vain and selfish, and she was. But it was a reputation she herself cultivated. She deliberately spoon-fed her critics reasons to shudder over her behavior. None realized that the persona they censured wasn't the real Davee.

The finer aspects of her personality Davee kept concealed. Hammond reasoned the charade was her self-defensive mechanism against getting hurt even more than her childhood already had hurt her. She turned people away before they had an opportunity to reject her.

Maxine Burton had been a lousy mother. Davee and her sisters had been deprived of Maxine's attention and affection. She had done nothing to earn their love or devotion. Nevertheless, Davee visited her mother faithfully each week at the elite nursing facility where she was confined.

Not only did Davee finance and oversee her mother's care, she was di-rectly involved with it, taking care of Maxine's personal needs herself during her routine visits. Probably he was the only person who knew that, and he wouldn't have known had Sarah Birch not confided it to him.

The second reason he wouldn't want to cross-examine Davee at trial was because she lied so beguilingly. Listening to her was such a delight, one ceased to care whether or not she was telling the truth.

Jurors found witnesses like her entertaining. If she were called to testify, she would arrive at court dressed fit to kill. Her appearance alone would make the jury sit up and take notice. While they might doze through the testimony of other witnesses, they would listen to and anticipate every sugar-coated word dripping from Davee's lips.

If she testified that, while she hadn't killed Lute, she wasn't sorry he was dead, that he had been an unfaithful husband who cheated on her too many times to count, that he was basically wicked and cruel and deserved to die, jurors of both sexes would probably agree. She would have persuaded them that the son of a bitch's character and misdeeds justified his murder.

No, he wouldn't want to put Davee on trial for her husband's murder. But if it came down to that, he would.

Being awarded this case was the best thing that could have happened to his career. He hoped that Smilow's team would provide him plenty to work with, that the accused wouldn't plead out, that the case would actually go to jury trial.

This was a case he could sink his teeth into. Certainly it would be challenging. It would require his total focus. But it also would be an excellent proving ground. He fully intended to run for county solicitor in November. He wanted to win. But he didn't want to win because he was more attractive, or had a better pedigree, or was better funded than the other candidate or candidates. He wanted to merit the office.

Only rarely did a muscle-flexing case like the Lute Pettijohn murder come along. That's why he needed it. That's why he had omitted telling Monroe Mason about his meeting with Pettijohn. He simply had to have this case, and he was unwilling to let anything stand in his way of taking it to trial. It was the perfect vehicle to give him the public exposure he needed before November.

It was also the perfect vehicle to spite his father.

That was the most compelling reason of all. Several years before, Hammond had made a career decision to move from defender to prosecutor. Preston Cross had vociferously opposed that decision, citing the differences in earning potential and telling Hammond he was crazy to settle for a public servant's salary. Not long ago Hammond had learned that a prosecutor's income level wasn't his father's major hang-up.

The switch had placed them in opposite camps. Because Preston was partners with Lute Pettijohn in some unscrupulous land deals, he had feared being prosecuted by his own son. Only recently had Hammond made that discovery. It had sickened him. Their confrontation over it had been bitter, adding a new dimension to the enmity between them.

But he couldn't think about that right now. Whenever he dwelled on his father, he became mentally bogged down. Peeling away the layers of their relationship for closer examination was time-consuming, emotionally draining, and ultimately unproductive. He held out little hope for a complete reconciliation.

For the time being, he shelved that problem and focused on what had immediately become his priority—the case.

The timing of his breakup with Steffi had been fortuitous. He was free of an encumbrance that was making him unhappy and might have hindered his concentration. She would be pissed to learn that she'd been assigned the copilot's seat, but he could deal with her peevishness as the need arose.

For Hammond Cross, today spelled a new start—which actually had begun last night.

Steering his car away from the Pettijohn mansion with one hand, he reached into his breast pocket for the slip of paper he had tucked there earlier and consulted the address he'd written down.

Breathlessly, Steffi barged into the hospital room. "I got here as fast as I could. What've I missed?"

Smilow had reached her on her cell phone shortly before she left Hammond's place. As promised, he had called when the attending physician granted permission for his patients to be questioned.

"I want in on this, Smilow," she had told him over the phone.

"I can't wait on you. The doctor might rescind the offer if I don't jump on it."

"Okay, but go slow. I'm on my way."

Hammond's condominium neighborhood wasn't far from the hospital complex. Even so, she had exceeded every speed limit to get here. She was very anxious to know if the food poisoning patients had seen anyone near the penthouse suite of Pettijohn's hotel.

Following her abrupt arrival, she paused in the doorway for a moment, then crossed the tile floor toward the hospital bed. The patient in it was a man about fifty years old, whose face was the color of bread dough and whose eyes were sunken into his skull and rimmed with dark circles. His right hand was hooked up to an IV drip. A bedpan and a kidney-bean-shaped basin were within easy reach on the bedside table.

A woman that Steffi presumed was his wife was seated in a chair beside the bed. She didn't look sick, just exhausted. She was still dressed for sight-seeing, wearing sneakers, walking shorts, and a T-shirt on which was spelled out in glittering letters: GIRLS RAISED IN THE SOUTH.

Smilow, who was standing beside the bed, made the introductions. "Mr. and Mrs. Daniels, Steffi Mundell. Ms. Mundell is from the district attorney's office. She's closely involved with the investigation."

"Hello, Mr. Daniels."

"Hi."

"Are you feeling better?"

"I've stopped praying for death."

"I guess that indicates some improvement." She looked across him at his wife. "You didn't get sick, Mrs. Daniels?"

"I had the she-crab soup," she replied with a wan smile.

"The Daniels are the last ones I've talked to," Smilow said. "The others in their group couldn't help us."

"Can they?"

"Mr. Daniels is a definite maybe."

Seeming none too happy about it, the man in the bed grumbled, "I might have seen somebody."

Failing to curb her impatience, Steffi pressed him for accuracy. "Either you saw somebody or you didn't."

Mrs. Daniels came to her feet. "He's very tired. Couldn't this wait until tomorrow? After he's had another night's rest?"

Instantly Steffi saw her mistake and forced herself to relent. "I'm sorry. Forgive me for being so abrasive. I'm afraid I've picked up a few bad habits from the people I prosecute. I'm accustomed to dealing with killers, thieves, and rapists, usually repeat offenders, not nice folks like you. It's not too often I get to interact with tax-paying, law-abiding, God-fearing people." After that speech, she didn't dare look at Smilow, knowing that she would see derision in his expression.

Gnawing her lower lip, Mrs. Daniels consulted her husband. "It's up to you, honey. Do you feel like doing this now?"

Steffi had sized them up and immediately concluded that there would be no contest between her I.Q. and theirs. She took advantage of their indecision to do some more manipulating. "Of course if you want to wait until morning for our questions, that's fine, Mr. Daniels. But please understand our position. A leader in our community has been murdered in cold blood. He was shot in the back with no provocation. None that we've determined, anyway." She let that sink in, then added, "We hope to catch this brutal killer before he has another opportunity to strike."

"Then I can't help you."

All were taken aback by Mr. Daniels's unexpected declaration. Smilow was the first to find his voice. "How do you know you can't help?"

"Because Ms. Mundell here said the killer was a 'he,' and the person I saw was a woman."

Steffi and Smilow exchanged a glance. "I used the pronoun generically," she explained.

"Oh, well, it was a woman I saw," Daniels said, settling back against his pillow. "She didn't look like a killer, though."

"Could you elaborate on that?" Steffi asked.

"You mean what she looked like?"

"Start at the beginning and talk us through," Smilow suggested.

"Well, we—that is, our choir group—left the hotel directly after lunch. About an hour into our tour, I started feeling queasy. At first I thought it was the heat. But a couple of the kids with us had already got sick with upset stomachs, so I suspected it was more than that. I got to feeling worse by the minute. Finally, I told my wife that I was going back to the hotel, take some Pepto or something, and would catch up later."

Mrs. Daniels confirmed all this with a solemn nod.

"By the time I'd walked back, I was on the verge of . . . of being real sick. I was afraid I wasn't going to make it to my room in time."

"When did you see the woman?" Steffi asked, wishing he would get to the point sooner rather than later.

"When I got to our room."

"Which was on the fifth floor," Smilow verified.

"Five oh six," Daniels said. "I noticed another person at the end of the hall and glanced in that direction. She was standing outside another door."

"Doing what?" Smilow asked.

"Doing nothing. Just facing the door, like she had knocked and was waiting for somebody to answer."

"How far away from you was she?"

"Hmm, not far. But pretty far. I didn't think twice about it. You know how awkward it is when you make eye contact with a stranger and you're the only two around? It was like that. You don't want to seem either too standoffish or too friendly. Got to be careful of folks these days."

"Did you speak to her?"

"No, no, nothing like that. I just glanced her way. Truth is, I wasn't thinking of anything except getting to the bathroom."

"But you got a good look at her?"

"Not that good."

"Good enough to determine her age?"

"She wasn't old. But not a girl, either. About your age," he said to Steffi.

"Ethnic?"

"No."

"Tall, short?"

Daniels winced and rubbed a spot on his lower abdomen. "Honey?" his wife said, anxiously picking up the basin and tucking it under his chin.

He pushed it aside. "Just a mild cramp."

"Want some Sprite?"

"A sip." Mrs. Daniels brought the covered cup to his lips and he sucked through the bent straw. When he was finished, he looked at Smilow again. "What'd you ask . . . oh, her height?" He shook his head. "Didn't notice. Not too extreme one way or the other. I guess about average."

"Hair color? Was she blond?" Steffi asked.

"Not too."

"Not too?" Smilow repeated.

"Not too blond. It didn't strike me that she was a Marilyn Monroe type, know what I mean? But her hair wasn't dark, either. Sorta medium."

"Mr. Daniels, could you give us a general body description?"

"You mean was she . . . like fat?"

"Was she?"

"No."

"Thin?"

"Yeah. More thin. Well, sorta thin, I guess you could say. See, I really didn't pay her much mind. I was just trying to keep from having a god-awful accident out there in the hall."

"I think that's all he can tell you," Mrs. Daniels said to them. "If you think of something else to ask, you can come back tomorrow."

"One final question, please," Smilow said. "Did you actually see this woman go into Mr. Pettijohn's room?"

"Nope. Quick as I could, I unlocked my door with that credit-card-looking thing and went inside." He rubbed the stubble on his cheek. "For that matter, I don't know if it was the room where the guy got killed or not. It could have been any room down the hallway from mine."

"It was the penthouse suite. The door is slightly recessed," Steffi said. "It's different from the others. If we pointed out Mr. Pettijohn's suite to you, would you be able to determine if that was the door you saw the woman standing in front of?"

"I seriously doubt it. As I told you before, I only glanced down the hall. It registered with me that there was a woman standing at a door waiting for it to be opened. That's all."

"You're sure she wasn't stepping out of it, leaving it?"

"No, I'm not sure." Daniels was beginning to sound querulous. "But that wasn't the impression I got. There was nothing unusual about her or the situation. Honestly, if you folks hadn't asked, I never would have thought of her again. You asked did I see anybody in the hallway yesterday afternoon, and that's who I saw."

Mrs. Daniels intervened again. Steffi and Smilow apologized for having to bother him, thanked him for the information, wished him a speedy recovery, and left.

Out in the hospital corridor, Smilow was glum. "Great. We have an eyewitness who saw a woman standing not too far away from him, but pretty far, who may or may not have been standing outside Pettijohn's suite. She was neither old nor young. She was average height. 'Sorta medium' hair and 'sorta thin.'"

"I'm disappointed but not surprised," Steffi said. "I doubted he would remember anything given his preoccupation at the time."

"Shit," Smilow swore.

"Precisely."

Then they looked at one another and laughed, and were still laughing when Mrs. Daniels emerged from her husband's room. "He's finally talked me into returning to the hotel. I haven't been back since the ambulance brought us here. Are you going down?" she asked politely as the elevator arrived.

"Not just yet," Steffi told her. "I've got other business to discuss with Detective Smilow."

"Good luck with solving the mystery."

They thanked her for her cooperation and willingness to help, then Steffi motioned Smilow toward the waiting room, which was presently empty. When they were seated in facing armchairs, he bluntly informed her that Hammond Cross would be prosecuting the Pettijohn case.

"Mason awarded it to his golden boy."

Making no effort to mask her disappointment or resentment, she asked when he had learned this.

"Earlier this evening. Chief Crane called and told me because I had campaigned for you."

"Thanks. For all the good it did me," she said bitterly. "When was I supposed to be told of this development?"

"Tomorrow, I guess."

Hammond hadn't known about Pettijohn's murder until she told him. It must have been Mason's call he had received while she was still there. It was doubly galling that moments after ending their affair, he had beat her out of a career-making case.

Smilow said, "Davee Pettijohn pulled strings."

"Just as she promised."

"She said she never settles for second best. Apparently she thinks you are."

"That's not it. Not entirely, anyway. She would much rather have a man working on her behalf than another woman."

"Good point. Better chemistry. Besides, her family and the Crosses have been friends for decades."

"It's not what you know, but who."

After a moment of silent reflection, Steffi stood up and slipped the strap of her heavy valise over her shoulder. "Since I'm no longer—"

Smilow waved her back into her chair. "Mason threw you a bone. Act surprised when he gives you official notice in the morning."

"What kind of bone?"

"You're to assist Hammond."

"No surprise there. A case like this requires at least two good heads." Sensing there was more, she queried Smilow with a raised eyebrow. "And?"

"And it's your responsibility to serve as a barrier between us and keep the interaction friendly. Failing that, you're to try and prevent bloodshed."

"Mason's words to your chief?"

"I'm paraphrasing." He smiled grimly. "But don't worry overmuch. I doubt it'll come to bloodshed."

"I'm not so sure. I've seen you two on the verge of what appeared to be mortal combat. What's that about, anyway?"

"We hate the sight of each other."

"That much I know, Smilow. What brought it on?"

"Long story."

"For another time?"

"Maybe."

It frustrated her that he didn't commit to telling her. She would like to know the circumstances behind his and Hammond's virulent dislike for one another. They were entirely different personality types, of course. Smilow's aloofness repelled people, and unless she was way off base, that was by design. Hammond was charismatic. Close friendships with him were earned, but he was friendly and approachable. Smilow was fastidious and impeccably groomed, while Hammond's attractiveness was natural and effortless. In college Smilow would have been the one guy in class who aced the exam and ruined the grading curve for everyone else. Hammond's grades were excellent, too, but he also had been a popular student leader and star athlete. Both were overachievers, but one's accomplishments were hard-earned, while to the other they came easily.

Steffi could identify more closely with Smilow. She understood and could relate to his resentment of Hammond, a resentment compounded by Hammond's own attitude toward his advantages. He did not exploit them. Moreover, he rejected them. Spurning his trust fund, he lived on what he earned. His condo was nice, but he could have afforded much better. His only extravagances were his sailboat and his cabin, but he never advertised that he owned either.

He would be much easier to hate if he flaunted his privileges.

It would be interesting, to say nothing of useful, to know the source of the antipathy between him and Smilow. They were on the same side of the law, working toward a common goal, and yet they seemed more disdainful of each other than they were of unredeemable criminals.

"Must be hard," Smilow said, drawing her out of her musings.

"What?"

"Constantly competing with Hammond on a professional level, but sleeping with him at night. Or is it that competitive edge that makes the affair so exciting?"

For once Steffi was taken completely off guard. She stared at him with mute astonishment.

"You're wondering how I know?" His smile was so cold it sent chills up her spine. "Process of elimination. He's the only man around the judicial building who hasn't boasted of getting there." He looked pointedly at her lap. "I put two and two together, and your stunned reaction to my lucky guess just confirmed it."

His smugness was insufferable, but she refused to act angry or upset, which would have pleased him immensely. Instead she kept her features expressionless and her voice cool. "Why so interested in my love life, Smilow? Jealous?"

He actually laughed. "Flirtation doesn't flatter you, Steffi."

"Go to hell."

Unfazed, he continued. "Deductive reasoning is my business. I'm good at it."

"What do you intend to do with this juicy tidbit of information?"

"Nothing," he said with a negligent shrug. "It just amuses me that the golden boy has compromised his professional ethics. Is his armor beginning to tarnish? Just a little?"

"Sleeping with a colleague isn't exactly a hanging offense. As transgressions go, it's a hand-slapper."

"True. But for Hammond Cross, it's practically a mortal sin. Otherwise, why keep it a secret?"

"Well, you can stop your gloating. There's no longer a secret to keep. The affair is over. True," she said when he gave her a sharply suspicious look.

"As of when?"

She consulted her wristwatch. "Two hours and eighteen minutes ago."

"Really? Before or after Mason gave him the case?"

"One had nothing to do with the other," she said testily.

A corner of his thin lips twitched with a near smile. "You're sure of that?"

"Positive. You might as well know the truth, the whole truth, and nothing but the truth, Detective. Hammond dumped me. Flat. End of discussion."

"Why?"

"I got the standard 'we're moving in opposing directions' speech, which usually translates to 'been there, done that, and I'm ready to try a new vacation spot.'"

"Hmm. Do you know of any *resorts* he plans to visit?"

"None. And a woman can usually tell."

"So can a man."

His tone conveyed more than the four words. Steffi regarded him closely. "Why, Rory! It is even remotely possible that Mr. Ice in Veins was once in l-o-v-e?"

"Excuse me?" They hadn't noticed the nurse's approach until she spoke to them. "My patient . . ." She hitched a thumb over her shoulder indicating Mr. Daniels's room. "He wanted to know if you had left. When I told him you were out here, he asked me to tell you that he remembered something that might help you."

Before she had finished speaking, they were on their feet.

# CHAPTER | 1 2

Hammond consulted the street address he had jotted down and tucked into his shirt pocket before leaving his place to visit Davee.

Uncertain that the telephone number for Dr. Ladd's answering service was a Charleston exchange, Hammond had anxiously run his finger down a listing of physicians in the Yellow Pages until he found one Dr. A. E. Ladd. He knew immediately he had the right one because the after-hours number listed matched the one he had called from the cabin that morning.

Dr. Ladd was his only link to the woman he'd been with last night. Of course, talking to him was out of the question. Hammond's short-term goal was only to locate his office and see what, if anything, he could learn from it. Later he would try and figure out how to go about approaching him.

Despite being preoccupied with his breakup with Steffi, and his disturbing conversation with Davee, and the Pettijohn murder and all that it implied, thoughts of the woman he had followed from the county fair and kissed at a gas station wouldn't leave him alone.

It would be useless to try and ignore them. Hammond Cross did not accept unanswered questions. Even as a boy, he couldn't be pacified with pat answers. He nagged his parents until they provided him with an explanation that satisfied his curiosity.

He'd carried the trait into adulthood. That desire to know not only the generalities, but the particulars, benefitted him in his work. He dug and continued to dig until he got to the truth, sometimes to the supreme frustration of his colleagues. Sometimes even he was frustrated by his doggedness.

Thoughts of her would persist until he learned who she was and why, after the incredible night they had spent together, she had walked out of his cabin and, consequently, out of his life.

Locating Dr. Ladd was an attempt, albeit a juvenile, pathetic, and desperate one, to find out something about her. Specifically, whether or not she was Mrs. Ladd. If so, that's where it must end. If not . . .

He didn't allow himself to consider the various if nots.

Having grown up in Charleston, Hammond knew the street's general location, and it was only blocks away from Davee's mansion. He reached it within minutes.

It was a short and narrow lane, where the buildings were shrouded in vines and history. It was one of several such streets within easy walking distance of the bustling commercial district, while seemingly a world apart. Most of the structures in this area between Broad Street and the Battery boasted historical markers. Some house numbers ended with a 1/2, indicating that an outbuilding to the main structure, such as a coach house or detached kitchen, had since been converted into a separate residence. Real estate was at a premium. It was a pricey neighborhood. The acronym for anyone living south of Broad was S.O.B.

It wasn't surprising to Hammond that the doctor's practice was located in a basically residential section. Many noncommercial professionals had converted older houses into businesses, often living in the top stories, which had been a Charleston tradition for centuries.

He left his car parked on a wider thoroughfare and entered the cobblestone lane on foot. Darkness had fallen. The weekend was over; people had retreated inside. He was the only pedestrian out. The street was shadowed and quiet, but overall friendly and hospitable. Open window shutters revealed lighted rooms that looked inviting. Without exception, the properties were upscale and well maintained. Apparently Dr. Ladd did very well.

The evening air was heavy and dense. It was as tangible as a cotton flannel blanket wrapping around him claustrophobically. In a matter of minutes his shirt was sticking to him. Even a slow stroll was enervating, especially when nervousness was also a factor.

He was forced to breathe deeply, drawing into his nostrils exotic floral scents and the salty-seminal tang of seawater from off the harbor a few blocks away. He smelled the remnants of charcoal smoke on which somebody had cooked Sunday supper. The aroma made his mouth water, reminding him that he had eaten nothing all day except the English muffin at his cabin.

The walk gave him time to think about how he was going to make contact with the doctor. What if he simply went up to the door and rang the bell? If Dr. Ladd answered, he could pretend that he obviously had been given the wrong address, that he was looking for someone else, apologize for disturbing him, and leave.

If she answered the door . . . what choice would he have? The most troubling question would have been answered. He would turn and walk away, never look back, and get on with his life.

All these contingencies had been based on the probability that she was married to the doctor. To Hammond that was the logical explanation for her placing a call to him furtively and then acting guilty when caught redhanded. Because she appeared the picture of health, and had certainly exhibited no visible symptoms of illness, it never had occurred to him that she might be a *patient*.

Not until he reached the house number. In the small square of yard demarcated by an iron picket fence stood a discreet white wooden signpost with black cursive lettering.

Dr. A. E. Ladd was a psychologist.

Was she a patient? If so, it was slightly unsettling that his lover had felt the need to consult her psychologist within moments of leaving his bed. He consoled himself by acknowledging that it was now commonplace to have a therapist. As confidants they had replaced trusted spouses, older relatives, and clergymen. He had friends and colleagues who kept standing weekly appointments, if only to ease the stress of contemporary life. Seeing a psychologist carried no stigma and was certainly nothing to be ashamed of.

Actually, he felt tremendously relieved. Sleeping with Dr. Ladd's patient was acceptable. What was unacceptable was sleeping with his *wife*. But a cloud moved across that small ray of hope. If she was his patient, what then? It would be nearly impossible to learn her identity.

Dr. Ladd wouldn't divulge information about his patients. Even if Hammond stooped to use the solicitor's office as his entrée, the doctor would probably stand on professional privilege and refuse to open his files unless they were subpoenaed, and Hammond would never take it that far. His professional standards wouldn't allow it.

Besides, how could he ask for information about her if he didn't even know her name?

From the opposite side of the street, Hammond mulled over this dilemma while studying the neat brick structure in which Dr. Ladd had his office. It typified a unique architectural style—the single house, so called because from the street it was only one room wide, but was several rooms deep. This one had two stories, with deep side porches, or piazzas, running from front to back on both levels.

Behind an ornate gate, the front walkway extended straight up the right side of the yard to a front door painted Charleston Green—a near-black with only a dollop of green mixed in. The door had a brass knocker in its center, and like the front doors to most single houses, opened not into the house itself, but onto the piazza, from which one entered the house.

Fig vine had a tenacious hold on much of the facade, but it had been neatly trimmed around the four tall windows that offset the front door. Beneath each of these windows was a window box overflowing with ferns and white impatiens. No lights were on.

Just as Hammond was stepping off the curb to cross the street for a closer look, the door of the house behind him opened and an enormous gray and white sheepdog bounded out, dragging his owner behind him.

"Whoa, Winthrop!"

But Winthrop would not be restrained. He was raring to go and straining against his leash as he reached the end of the walkway and came up on his back legs, throwing himself against the gate. Instinctively Hammond took a couple steps back.

Laughing at his reaction, the dog owner pulled the gate open and Winthrop bolted through. "Sorry about that. Hope he didn't scare you. He doesn't bite, but given the chance, he might lick you to death."

Hammond smiled. "No problem." Winthrop, showing no interest in him, had hiked his leg and was peeing against a fence post.

Hammond must have looked harmless but lost, because the man said, "Can I help you?"

"Uh, actually I was trying to locate Dr. Ladd's office."

"You found it." The young man pointed his chin toward the house across the street.

"Right, right."

The man gave him a politely quizzical look.

"Uh, I'm a salesman," he blurted. "Medical forms. Stuff like that. The sign doesn't say what time the office opens."

"About ten, I think. You could call Alex to confirm."

"Alex?"

"Dr. Ladd."

"Oh, sure. Yeah, I should've called, but . . . you know . . . just thought I'd . . . well, okay." Winthrop was sniffing beneath a camellia bush. "Thanks. Take it easy, Winthrop."

Hoping the neighbor would never connect the inarticulate idiot to the assistant D.A. frequently seen addressing reporters on TV, Hammond patted the shaggy dog on the head, then set off down the sidewalk in the direction from which he had come.

"Actually, you just missed her."

Hammond whipped back around. *"Her?"*

Mr. Daniels avoided looking either Smilow or Steffi in the eye when they returned to his hospital room and took up positions on either side of his bed. To Smilow the patient seemed more uncomfortable now than he had fifteen minutes earlier, but it wasn't gastrointestinal discomfort. It looked more like a bad case of guilty conscience.

"The nurse said you remembered something that might help our investigation."

"Maybe." Daniels's eyes nervously sawed back and forth between Smilow and Steffi. "See, it's like this. Ever since I strayed—"

"Strayed?"

Daniels looked at Steffi, who had interrupted. "From my marriage."

"You had an affair?"

Leave it to Steffi to cut to the chase, thought Smilow. "Tact" wasn't in her vocabulary. Mr. Daniels looked completely miserable as he stammered on.

"Yeah. This, uh . . . a woman where I work? We . . . you know." Uneasily he shifted his skinny frame on the hard mattress. "But it didn't last long. I saw the error of my ways. It was just one of those things that happens before you know it. Then you wake up one morning and think to yourself, what the hell am I doing this for? I love my wife."

Smilow was sharing Steffi's obvious impatience with Daniels's longwinded confession. He wished the man would get to the point. Nevertheless, he warned Steffi with a hard look to give Daniels time to tell his story at his own pace.

"The reason I'm telling you this . . . She, my wife, gets all worked up if I so much as give another woman the time of day. Not that I blame her," he rushed to add. "She's got a right to be suspicious. I handed her that right when I committed adultery.

"But the least little thing—even a kind word to another woman—sets her off. Know what I mean? She goes to crying. And saying that she's not woman enough for me. That she can't fulfill my needs." He looked up at Smilow with weary eyes. "You know how they get."

Again, Smilow shot Steffi a look that told her not to jeopardize this by lambasting the man's sexist editorial.

"I didn't describe that lady to y'all in detail because I didn't want my wife to get upset. We've been doing pretty good here lately. She even brought along some, you know, sexual aids on this trip to spice up our time alone. She sorta looked on it as a second honeymoon. Isn't much you can do on a church choir bus, but once we get in our room each night . . . whew."

He grinned up at them, but then his smile deflated as though someone had pulled the plug on a rubber mask. "But if the missus thought I had paid attention to another woman's face and figure, she might have thought I was lusting in my heart after a stranger. I'd have had hell to pay over nothing."

"We understand." Steffi laid her hand on his arm with rare and, Smilow knew, insincere compassion.

"Mr. Daniels, are you now saying that you can describe the woman you saw in the hotel corridor in greater detail?"

He looked across at Smilow. "You got something to write with?"

*Slowly, he pulled the old T-shirt over her head. Before, he had touched her in darkness. He knew what she felt like, but he wanted to see what his hands had touched.*

*He wasn't disappointed. She was lovely. He liked seeing his hands on her breasts, liked watching them respond to his caresses, liked hearing her hum of pleasure when he lowered his lips to them.*

*"You like this."*

*"Yes."*

*He took her nipple into his mouth and sucked it. She clasped his head and moaned softly. "Too hard?" he asked.*

*"No."*

*But he was concerned, especially when he spotted whisker burns on her pale skin. He ran his finger over the spot. "I didn't realize."*

*She looked down at the light abrasion, then raised his finger to her lips and kissed it. "Neither did I."*

*"I'm sorry."*

*"It didn't matter."*

*"But if I hurt you—"*

*"You didn't. You won't." She curled her hand around his neck and tried to draw his head back to her.*

*But he resisted. "Do you mind if . . ." He nodded toward the bed.*

*"No."*

*They lay down, not bothering to straighten the linens. He leaned over her and, holding her face between his hands, kissed her so passionately that her body arched off the bed in order to touch his.*

*His hand skimmed over her breasts, down her rib cage, onto a smooth stomach. "Jesus. Look at you. Beautiful." He fitted his hand into the vee of her thighs, covering her mound with his palm, his fingers tapering downward. Inward. Into her softness. "You're already—"*

*"Yes."*

"*So sweet. So—*"

"*Oh . . .*" *she gasped.*

"*Wet.*"

*He rose above her for another kiss. It was a silky, sexy kiss that ended only when she gave a soft cry and climaxed around his fingers, against his thumb.*

*Moments later she opened her eyes and saw him smiling down at her.* "*I'm sorry, sorry.*"

"*Sorry?*" *he repeated, laughing softly and kissing her damp forehead.*

"*Well, I mean . . . you . . .*"

*His lips barely grazed hers. His whisper was soft and urgent.* "*Don't be sorry.*"

*He coughed a harsh sigh of surprise when she closed her hand around him. He almost protested, almost told her that she didn't have to feel obligated, almost told her that reciprocation wasn't necessary, that he couldn't possibly get any harder than he was. But when she began to explore and massage, the only sounds he made were soft groans of supreme pleasure. Not fully aware of what he was doing, he folded his hand around hers and enhanced her motions.*

*She nuzzled his neck. She buried kisses in his chest hair and took love bites of his skin. Unintentionally—or maybe not—her erect nipple rubbed against his. It was exciting. It was goddamn erotic. And it nearly made him come.*

*When he removed her hand, she angled herself up and frantically kissed his jaw, his cheek, his lips, murmuring,* "*Let me touch you.*"

*But it was too late. He repositioned himself and sank into her. Withdrew. Pressed. Deep. Deeper. Then, resting his forehead on hers, clenching his teeth and squeezing his eyes shut, experiencing more ecstasy than he had in all previous sexual encounters put together . . .*

"*No, let me touch you.*"

*. . . he came.*

The ringing telephone rudely jarred Hammond from his steamy recollection. He was embarrassed to realize that he had an erection and he was bathed in sweat. How much time had he lost to that particular memory? He checked the dashboard clock. Twenty minutes, give or take.

The phone rang a third time. He jerked it to his ear. "What?"

"Where the hell have you been?"

Irritably he said, "You know, Steffi, you need to get some new material. That's the second time today you've asked me that, and in that same tone of voice."

"Sorry, but I've been calling your house for an hour and leaving messages. I finally decided to try your cell. Are you in your car?"

"Yes."

"You went out?"

"Right again."

"Oh. I didn't imagine you'd be going out tonight."

She was hinting that he explain to her where he had gone and why, but he no longer owed her an accounting of his time. It probably stung her pride that on the night he ended their relationship, he wasn't too despondent to go out.

It would really wound her to know that he was staked out on a dark street like a pervert, steeping in a sweat of sexual arousal, and waiting to see if Dr. A. E. Ladd was the woman who, about this time last night, had been stretched out alongside him naked—his sex cozily sandwiched between their bellies, his hands caressing her ass—asking if he was aware that his eyes were the color of storm clouds.

He had a mean impulse to tell Steffi. But of course he didn't.

He wiped his face on his shirtsleeve. "What's going on?"

"For starters, why didn't you tell me that Mason gave you the Pettijohn case?"

"It wasn't my job to."

"That's a bullshit reason, Hammond."

"Thank you, Rory Smilow," he muttered.

"He told me as a friend."

"My ass. He told you because he's no friend of mine. Now, are you going to tell me what's up?"

"Not knowing that I was going to be playing second fiddle," she said sweetly, "I joined Smilow at Roper Hospital, and we lucked out."

"How so?"

"One of those people stricken with food poisoning?"

"Yeah?"

Headlights turned onto the street at the opposite end from where Hammond was parked. He started his car.

"Where are you, Hammond?" Steffi demanded impatiently. "Are you listening? It sounds like you're cutting out."

"I can hear you. Keep talking. One of the people stricken with food poisoning . . ."

"Saw a woman outside Pettijohn's suite. Well, actually, he can't swear that it was outside Pettijohn's suite, but that's a technicality we can iron out if everything else falls into place."

The car stopped in front of Dr. Ladd's office. *She drove off with some guy in a convertible,* Winthrop's owner had told him.

Steffi was saying, "So after a lot of hem-hawing about an affair—"

Driving slowly, Hammond got close enough to see that the car was a convertible.

"On second thought, never mind about the affair," Steffi said. "It's irrelevant. Believe me. Anyway, Mr. Daniels got a much better look at the woman than he had first led us and Mrs. Daniels to believe."

The glare of the convertible's headlights blinded Hammond from seeing anything behind them. But as he pulled even with the car, he turned his head in time to see the occupants. A man behind the steering wheel. A woman in the passenger seat. His woman. No question.

"Mr. Daniels now admits that he remembers her approximate height and weight, hair color, and so forth."

Hammond tuned Steffi out. Once he was past the other car, he cut his eyes to his external side mirror in time to see the man reach across the console and hook his hand around the back of her neck, bringing her face up close to his.

Hammond stamped his accelerator, taking the corner too fast and causing his tires to squeal. Sure, it was an immature, jealousy-inspired reaction, but that's what he felt like doing. He felt like hitting something. He really felt like telling Steffi to shut the fuck up.

"Just do it, Steffi," he said, abruptly stopping her in midsentence.

Taken aback, she took a quick breath. "Do what?"

He didn't know what. He had been only half listening, but he wouldn't admit that to her. She'd been telling him about a potential witness. Someone who had seen someone near Pettijohn's suite and could provide a fairly accurate description.

Steffi might also have suggested a sketch artist. She had mentioned that about the time Hammond had rolled past the convertible, and her prattle had been drowned out by the blood that had rushed to his head. The gist of what Steffi told him had registered, but most of it had been obscured by a wild, primal urge to go back and put his hands around the throat of the bastard in the convertible.

One thing was certain: He had to assert himself or explode. Now. Immediately. He had to establish that there was something over which Hammond Cross still had control.

"I want an artist there first thing in the morning."

"It's late, Hammond."

He knew what time it was. For hours he'd been sitting in a sweltering automobile, entertaining sexual fantasies. For his trouble, all he'd got was *Dr. Ladd* in the company of another man. "I know how late it is."

"My point is, I don't know if I can get—"

"What's the guy's room number?"

"Mr. Daniels's room number? Uh . . ."

"I want to talk to him myself."

"That really isn't necessary. Smilow and I questioned him at length. Besides, I think he's being discharged in the morning."

"Then you'd better set it up early. Seven-thirty. And have the police sketch artist standing by."

# MONDAY

# CHAPTER | 1 3

AT SEVEN-THIRTY THE FOLLOWING MORNING, Hammond entered the hospital carrying a copy of the *Post and Courier* and his briefcase. He stopped at the information desk to ask the room number, which he had failed to get from Steffi. He also stopped at a vending machine for a cup of coffee.

He was wearing a necktie, but in deference to the hot day that was promised, he had left his suit jacket in his car, rolled up his shirtsleeves, and unbuttoned his collar button. His bearing was militant, his face as dark as a thundercloud.

To Steffi's credit, the others were already assembled when he arrived. She was there, along with Rory Smilow, a frumpy woman in an ill-fitting police uniform, and the man in the hospital bed. Steffi's eyes were puffy, as though she hadn't slept well. After a muttered round of greetings, she said, "Hammond, you remember Corporal Mary Endicott. We've worked with her before."

He dropped his briefcase and newspaper in a chair in order to shake hands with the policewoman sketch artist. "Corporal Endicott."

"Mr. Cross."

Steffi then introduced him to Mr. Daniels, a guest of their city from Macon, Georgia, who was presently nibbling at the bland food on his breakfast tray. "I'm sorry your visit to Charleston hasn't been the best, Mr. Daniels. Are you feeling better?"

"Good enough to get out of here. If possible, I'd like to get this over with before my wife comes to pick me up."

"How quickly we finish depends on how precise your descriptions are. Corporal Endicott is excellent, but she can only do as well as you can."

Daniels looked worried. "Would I have to testify in court? I mean, if you catch this lady and she turns out to be the one who killed that man, would I have to point her out at the trial?"

"That's a possibility," Hammond told him.

The man sighed unhappily. "Well, if it comes to that, I'll do my civic duty." He shrugged philosophically. "Let's get on with it."

Hammond said, "First, I'd like to hear your story, Mr. Daniels."

"He's related it to us several times," Smilow said. "It really doesn't amount to much."

Beyond his perfunctory good morning, up to this point Smilow had remained as silent and still as a lizard sunning itself. Often Smilow's posture seemed indolent, but to Hammond he gave off the impression of a reptile lying in wait, constantly watching for an opportunity to strike.

Hammond acknowledged that comparing Smilow to a serpent was based solely on his unmitigated dislike of the man. To say nothing of being unfair to serpents.

Smilow's gray suit was perfectly tailored and well pressed. His white shirt was crisp enough to bounce a quarter, his necktie tightly knotted. Not a hair was out of place. His eyes were clear and alert. After the rough night Hammond had spent tossing and turning, he resented Smilow's bandbox appearance and unflappable composure.

"It's your call, of course," he said politely. "This is your investigation."

"That's right, it is."

"But as a courtesy—"

"You didn't show much courtesy to me when you arranged this meeting without consulting me first. You say it's my investigation, but on surface it appears that it's yours. As usual, your actions belie your words, Hammond."

Leave it to Smilow to pick a fight on a morning when he was feeling truculent himself. "Look, I went out of town the day Pettijohn was killed, so I'm playing catch-up. I've read the newspaper accounts, but I know you don't share all your leads with the media. All I'm asking is that the details be filled in for me."

"When the time is right."

"What's wrong with now?"

"Okay, guys, King's X!" Steffi stepped between them, forming a cross with her index fingers. "It really doesn't matter who arranged this meeting, does it? In fact, Hammond, Smilow had already called Corporal Endicott by the time I reached her last night." The plump, matronly officer confirmed this with a nod. "So technically Smilow had the idea first, as he should since the case is his baby until he turns it over to us. Right?

"And, Smilow, if Hammond also thought of the artist, that only means that great minds think alike, and this case can use all the great minds it can muster. So let's get started and not detain these people any longer than necessary. Mr. Daniels is in somewhat of a hurry, and we've all got other work to do. Speaking for myself, I wouldn't mind hearing his account once more."

Smilow conceded with a curt semi-nod. Daniels recounted his experience of Saturday afternoon. When he concluded, Hammond asked him if he was certain he had seen no one else.

"You mean once I reached the fifth floor? No, sir."

"You're sure?"

"Just that one lady and me were the only ones around. But I couldn't have been in the hall more than . . . hmm . . . say, twenty, thirty seconds from the time I got off the elevator."

"Did anyone share the car with you?"

"No, sir."

"Thank you, Mr. Daniels. I appreciate your repeating your story for my benefit."

Ignoring Smilow's I-told-you-so expression, Hammond turned Daniels over to Mary Endicott. Smilow excused himself to make some telephone calls. Steffi hovered over the artist's shoulder and followed the questions she was asking Daniels. Hammond carried his lukewarm coffee to the window and stared out over a day that was much too sunny to match his mood.

Eventually Steffi sidled up to him. "You're awfully quiet."

"It was a short night. I couldn't fall asleep."

"Any particular reason for your insomnia?"

Catching the underlying meaning to her question, he turned his head and looked down at her. "Just restless."

"You're cruel, Hammond."

"How so?"

"The least you could have done was get stinking drunk last night and second-guess your decision to break up with me."

He smiled, but his tone was serious. "It was the only decision for us, Steffi. You know that as well as I do."

"Particularly in light of Mason's decision."

"It was his decision, not mine."

"But I never stood a fighting chance of getting this case. Mason favors you and makes no bones about it. He always will. And you know *that* as well as I do."

"I was here first, Steffi. It's a matter of seniority."

"Yeah, right." Her droll tone contradicted her words.

Before Hammond could respond to it, Smilow returned. "This is interesting. One of my guys has been nosing around the Pettijohns' neighborhood to see if anyone had overheard Lute quarreling with a tradesman or neighbor. Dead end there."

"I hope there's a *but*," Steffi said.

He nodded. "But Sarah Birch was at the supermarket on Saturday afternoon. She asked the butcher to butterfly some pork chops she wished to stuff for Sunday dinner. He was busy, so it took him a while to get to it. Rather than waiting, she did her other shopping. The store was crowded. She didn't return to the butcher for nearly an hour, he said. Which means she lied about being at home with Mrs. Pettijohn all afternoon."

"If she would lie about something as insignificant as going to the market, it stands to reason that she might also tell a whopper."

"Only the lie isn't so insignificant," Smilow said. "The time frame works. The butcher remembers delivering the chops to Sarah Birch just before his shift ended at six-thirty."

"Meaning that she was in the store anywhere from, say, five until six-thirty," Steffi mused aloud. "About the time Pettijohn was getting whacked. And the supermarket is two blocks from the hotel! Damn! Can it be this easy?"

"No," Smilow said with reluctance. "Mr. Daniels said that the woman he saw in the hotel corridor wasn't ethnic. Sarah Birch definitely is."

"She could be covering for Davee, though."

"Nor was the woman he saw blond," Smilow reminded her. "Davee Pettijohn, by any description, is a blonde."

"Are you kidding? She's the Queen of Clairol."

It didn't surprise Hammond that Davee's faithful housekeeper would lie for her. But he was put off by Steffi's catty comment and uneasy that his childhood friend was seriously being considered a suspect with an alibi that wasn't as ironclad as she had claimed.

"Davee wouldn't have killed Lute." The other two turned to him. "What motive would she have?"

"Jealousy and money."

He shook his head in disagreement. "She has her own lovers, Steffi. Why would she be jealous of Lute's? And she has her own money. Probably more than Lute."

"Well, I'm not ready to mark her off the list just yet."

Leaving the other two to their speculations, Hammond wandered toward the bed. A book of sketches lay open on Daniels's lap, picturing what seemed an endless variety of eye shapes. Hammond glanced down at Endicott's rendering, but so far she was still working to get the shape of the face correct.

"Maybe a little thinner through here," Mr. Daniels said, stroking his own cheek. The artist made the suggested adjustment. "Yeah, more like that."

When they progressed to eyebrows and eyes, Hammond rejoined Steffi and Smilow. "What about former business associates?" he asked the detective.

"Naturally they're being questioned," Smilow answered with cool civility. "That is, those who don't have prison as their alibi."

Unless the cases had fallen under federal jurisdiction, Hammond had helped put some of those white-collar criminals behind bars. Lute Pettijohn had bent the rules often enough, frequently coming a hairbreadth away from criminal wrongdoing. He flirted with it, but never crossed the line.

"One of Pettijohn's most recent ventures involves a sea island," Smilow told them.

Steffi scoffed. "What else is new?"

"This one's different. Speckle Island is about a mile and a half offshore and is one of the few that has escaped development."

"That's enough to give Pettijohn a hard-on," Steffi remarked.

Smilow nodded. "He had set things in motion. His name isn't on any of the partnership documents. At least not the documents we've been able to find. But be assured that we're checking it out." Looking at Hammond, he added, "Thoroughly."

Hammond's heart sank like a lead ball inside his chest. Smilow wasn't telling him anything about Pettijohn's Speckle Island venture that he didn't already know. He knew much more, more than he wanted to know.

About six months ago, he had been asked by South Carolina's attorney general to conduct a covert investigation into Pettijohn's attempt to develop the island. His discoveries had been alarming, but none as much as seeing his own father's name listed among the investors. Until he learned what connection, if any, Speckle Island had to Pettijohn's murder, he was keeping his knowledge of this under wraps. Just as Smilow had rudely said to him, he would give the detective those details only when the time was right.

Steffi said, "One of those former associates might have held a grudge so strong that it drove him to commit murder."

"It's a viable possibility," Smilow said. "The problem is, Lute operated in a circle of movers and shakers that included government officials on every level. His friends were men who wielded power of one kind or another. That complicates my maneuverability, but it doesn't keep me from digging."

If Smilow was digging, then Hammond knew the name of Preston Cross was lying out there like a buried treasure waiting to be disinterred. It was only a matter of time before his father's alliance with Pettijohn was uncovered.

Silently Hammond cursed his father for placing him in this compromising position. Soon he might be forced to choose between duty and family loyalty. At the very least, Preston's dirty dealing could cost Hammond the Pettijohn murder case. If it came to that, Hammond would never forgive him.

He glanced at the hospital bed, where the artist seemed to be making progress.

"Her hair. Was it long or short?"

"About here," Daniels said, indicating the top of his shoulder.

"Bangs?"

"On her forehead, you mean? No."

"Straight or curly?"

"More curly, I guess. Fluffy." Again he used his hands to illustrate.

"She was wearing it down, then?"

"Yeah, I guess. I don't know too much about hairstyles."

"Thumb through this magazine. See if there's a picture in there that resembles her hair."

Daniels frowned and worriedly glanced at the clock, but he did as instructed and began listlessly turning the pages of the hair fashion magazine.

"What color was it?" the artist asked.

"Sorta red."

"She was a redhead?"

Hammond felt himself drawn forward by Daniels's words, as though they were working hand-over-hand on a rope, inexorably pulling him in.

"She wasn't a carrot-top."

"Dark red, then?"

"No. I guess you'd just say brown, but with lots of red in it."

"Auburn?"

"That's it," he said, snapping his fingers. "I knew there was a word for it, I just couldn't think of it. Auburn."

Hammond swallowed a sip of coffee that had suddenly turned bitter inside his mouth. He inched toward the hospital bed with the reluctance of an acrophobic approaching the rim of the Grand Canyon.

Corporal Endicott made rapid pencil strokes against the paper in her tablet. Scratch, scratch, scratch. "How's that?" she said, showing Daniels her work.

"Hey, that's pretty good. Except she had, you know, strands around her face."

Hammond moved a few steps closer.

"Like this?"

Daniels told Endicott that she had nailed the hairstyle. "Good. That just leaves the mouth," she said. Setting aside the magazine, the artist flipped the sketchbook open to another section. "Do you remember anything distinctive about her mouth, Mr. Daniels?"

"She was wearing lipstick," he mumbled as he studied the myriad sketches of lips.

"So you noticed her lips?"

Raising his head, he darted an uneasy glance toward the door, as though fearful that Mrs. Daniels would be standing there eavesdropping. "Her mouth looked kinda like this one." He pointed to one of the standard sketches. "Except her lower lip was fuller." Endicott consulted the drawing in the book, then replicated it on her own sketch.

Watching, Daniels added, "When she glanced at me, she sorta smiled."

"Did her teeth show?"

"No. A polite smile. You know, like people do when they get into an elevator or something."

Like when eyes accidentally connect across a dance floor.

Hammond couldn't work up enough courage to look down at Endicott's handiwork, but in his mind's eye he saw an alluring, closed-mouth smile that had been deeply impressed on his memory.

"Anything resembling this?" Endicott turned her pad toward Daniels to afford him a better look.

"Well, I'll be doggone," he said in awe. "That's her."

And no more than a quick glance confirmed to Hammond that indeed it was. It was her.

Smilow and Steffi had been engrossed in their own conversation. Hearing Daniels's soft exclamation, they rushed to the bedside. Hammond allowed Steffi to elbow him aside because he didn't need to see any more.

"It's not exact," Daniels told them, "but it's pretty damn good."

"Any distinguishing marks or scars?"

*A freckle.*

"I think she had a molelike thing," Daniels said. "It wasn't ugly. More like a freckle. Under her eye."

"Do you remember—" Steffi began.

"Which eye?" Smilow asked, finishing her thought.

*The right.*

"Uh, let's see, I was facing her . . . so that means it would be . . . her left. No, wait, her right. Definitely her right," Daniels said, pleased that he could be so helpful and provide this detail.

"Were you close enough to see the color of her eyes?"

"No. 'Fraid not."

*Green, flecked with brown. Widely spaced. Dark lashes.*

"How tall was she, Mr. Daniels?"

*Five-six.*

"Taller than you," he said, answering Steffi. "But several inches shorter than Mr. Smilow here."

"I'm five-ten," he offered.

"So about five-six or -seven?" Steffi asked, doing the math in her head.

"About that, I'd say."

"Weight?"

*One hundred and fifteen.*

"Not much."

"One thirty?" Smilow ventured.

"Less than that, I think."

"Do you happen to remember what she was wearing?" Steffi wanted to know. "Slacks? Or shorts? A dress?"

*A skirt.*

"Either shorts or a skirt. I'm sure because you could, you know, see her legs." Daniels squirmed. "Some kinda top. I don't remember the color or anything like that."

*White skirt. Brown knit tank top and matching cardigan. Brown leather sandals. No stockings. Beige lace brassiere that closed in front. Matching panties.*

Endicott began gathering up her supplies and stuffing them into the overstuffed black bag. Smilow took the sketch from her and then shook hands with Mr. Daniels. "We have your number in Macon if we need to contact you. Hopefully this will be sufficient. Thank you so much."

"Same for me," Steffi said, smiling at the man before following Smilow toward the door.

Having no voice, Hammond merely nodded a goodbye to Mr. Daniels. Out in the hallway, Smilow and Steffi profusely thanked the artist before she got into the elevator.

They stayed behind to study the sketch and congratulate themselves. "So that's our mystery woman," Smilow remarked. "She doesn't look like a murderess, does she?"

"What does a murderess look like?"

"Good point, Steffi."

She chuckled. "I see now why Mr. Daniels didn't want his wife around when he described our suspect. In spite of the pressure in his bowels, I think he *was* lusting in his heart. He remembered every minute detail, even down to the freckle beneath the chick's right eye."

"You've got to admit, it's a memorable face."

"Which doesn't mean squat when you're talking guilt or innocence.

Pretty women can kill with just as much alacrity as ugly ones. Right, Hammond?" Steffi turned to him. "Jeez, what's with you?"

He must have looked as nauseous as he felt. "Bad cup of coffee," he said, crushing the empty Styrofoam cup he'd been holding clenched in his hand.

"Well, Smilow, go get her." Steffi tapped the drawing with her fingernail. "We've got the face."

"It would help if we knew her name."

*Dr. Alex Ladd.*

# CHAPTER | 14

THE TEMPORARY HEADQUARTERS of the judicial building was located in North Charleston. It was an unattractive two-story structure situated in an industrial district. Its nearest neighbors were a convenience store and a day-old bakery shop. This out-of-the-way location was serving until an extensive renovation of the stately old building downtown was completed. It had been already in need of attention when Hurricane Hugo rendered the building unsafe and unusable, forcing the move.

It was only a ten-minute drive from downtown. Hammond wouldn't remember making the drive that morning. He parked and went inside. He responded by rote to the guard who manned the metal detector at the entrance. Turning left, he went into the county solicitor's office and passed the receptionist's desk without slowing up. He brusquely asked her to hold all calls.

"You already have—"

"I'll take care of everything later."

He soundly closed his private office door behind him. Tossing his suit jacket and briefcase on top of the paperwork waiting for his attention on his desk, he threw himself into the high-backed leather chair and pressed the heels of his hands against his eye sockets.

It simply couldn't be. This had to be a dream. Shortly, he would wake up startled and alarmed and breathing heavily, his sheets damp with sweat. After orienting himself to familiar surroundings, he would realize with relief that he had been in a deep sleep and that this nightmare wasn't a reality.

But it was. He wasn't dreaming it, he was living it. Impossible as it seemed, the sketch artist had drawn Dr. Alex Ladd, who had shared Hammond's bed within hours after she was seen at the site of a murder.

Coincidence? Highly unlikely.

She must have some connection to Lute Pettijohn. Hammond wasn't sure he wanted to know what that connection was. In fact, he was dead certain he didn't want to know.

He dragged his hands down his face, then, propping his elbows on his desk, he stared into near space and tried to arrange his chaotic thoughts into some semblance of order.

First, without a doubt, Corporal Endicott had sketched the face of the woman he had slept with Saturday night. Even if he hadn't seen her as recently as last night, he wasn't likely to forget her face that soon. It had attracted him from the start. He had spent hours late Saturday night and early Sunday morning studying, admiring, caressing, and kissing it.

*"Where did this come from?"* He touched a spot beneath her right eye.

*"My blemish?"*

*"It's a beauty mark."*

*"Thank you."*

*"You're welcome."*

*"When I was younger I hated it. Now I must admit I've grown rather fond of it."*

*"I can see how that could happen. I could grow fond of it myself."* He kissed it once, then a second time, touching it lightly with the tip of his tongue.

*"Hmm. It's a shame."*

*"What?"*

*"That I don't have more spots."*

He had come to know her face intimately. The artist's sketch was a two-dimensional, black and white drawing. Given those limitations, it couldn't possibly capture the essence of the woman behind the face, but it had been such a close representation that there was no doubt Dr. Ladd had been seen near a murder victim's room shortly before placing herself in the path of someone from the county solicitor's office, specifically one Hammond Cross, who had himself been in Pettijohn's company that afternoon.

"Jesus." Plowing his fingers through his hair and holding his head between his hands, he almost surrendered to the disbelief and despair that assailed him. What the hell was he going to do?

Well, he couldn't collapse from within, which is what he felt like doing. What a luxury it would be to slink away from this office, leave Charleston, leave the state, run away and hide, let this mess erupt on its own, and spare himself having to withstand the incendiary lava flow of scandal that would inevitably follow.

But he was made of sterner stuff than that. He had been born with an indomitable sense of responsibility, and his parents had nourished that trait every day of his life. He could no more fathom running away from this than he could imagine sprouting wings.

So he forced himself to confront a second point that seemed unarguable—withholding her name from him hadn't been the flirtation he had mistaken it for. They had been together at the fair for at least an hour before he even thought to ask her name. They'd laughed because it had taken them that long to get around to what was usually the first order of business when two people meet and must make their own introductions.

*"Names aren't really that important, are they? Not when the meeting is this amiable."*

*He agreed. "Yeah, what's in a name?" He proceeded to quote what he could remember of the passage from* Romeo and Juliet.

*"That's good! Have you ever thought of writing it down?"*

*"In fact I have, but it would never sell."*

From there it had become a running joke—his asking her name, her declining to tell him. Like a sap he had thought they were playing out the fantasy of making love to an anonymous stranger. Namelessness had been an enticement, part of the adventure, integral to the allure. He had seen no harm in it.

What was disturbing but likely was that Alex Ladd had known his name all along. Theirs hadn't been a random meeting. It wasn't happenstance that she had arrived at that dance pavilion shortly after him. Their meeting had been planned. The remainder of the evening had been orchestrated in order to either embarrass or totally compromise him and/or the solicitor's office.

To what extent remained to be seen. But even the slightest extent could be calamitous for his burgeoning career. Even a hint of scandal would be a stumbling block. One of this magnitude would certainly damage, if not destroy, his hopes of ever succeeding Monroe Mason and distinguishing himself as the top-ranking law enforcer of Charleston County.

Leaning over his desk, he buried his face in his hands again. *Too good to be true.* A trite but sound adage. During law school he and his friends had hung out in a bar called Tanstaafl, an acronym for "There ain't no such thing as a free lunch." His fantasy evening with the most exciting woman he had ever met not only came with strings attached, those strings were probably going to form a noose that would ultimately hang him.

What an idiot he had been not to recognize the carefully baited trap for what it was. Ironically, he didn't blame the person, or persons—if she was in league with Pettijohn—who had trapped him as much as he blamed himself for being so goddamn callow.

With both eyes wide open, he had walked into the oldest snare known to man. Sex was a trusty method by which to compromise a man. Countless times throughout recorded history, it had proven itself to be timely, reliable, and effective. He wouldn't have thought himself that gullible, but obviously he was.

Gullibility was forgivable. Obstruction of justice wasn't.

Why hadn't he immediately admitted to Smilow and Steffi that he recognized the woman in the sketch?

Because she could be completely blameless. This Daniels could be mistaken. If in truth he had seen Alex Ladd in the hotel, the timing of his seeing her would become critical. Hammond knew almost to the minute when she had appeared in the dance pavilion. Given the distance she would have driven to get there, and taking the traffic congestion into consideration, she couldn't have made it if she had left the hotel . . . He did a quick calculation. Say, after five-thirty. If the coroner pinpointed the time of death anytime after that, she couldn't be the murderer.

*Good argument, Hammond. In hindsight. A terrific rationalization.*

But the fact of the matter was, it had never entered his mind to identify Alex Ladd.

From the heart-stopping instant he looked at the drawing and knew with absolute certainty who the subject was, he knew with equal certainty that he wasn't going to reveal her name.

When he saw the face on the artist's sketch pad and remembered it from the vantage point of his pillow, he didn't weigh his options, didn't deliberate the pros and cons of keeping silent. His secret had been instantly sealed. At least for the time being, he was going to protect her identity. Thereby, he had consciously breached every rule of ethic he advocated. His silence was a deliberate violation of the law he had sworn to uphold, and an intentional attempt to impede a homicide investigation. He couldn't even guess at the severity of the consequences he might pay.

All the same, he wasn't going to turn her over to Smilow and Steffi.

The loud rap on his office door came a millisecond before it opened. He was about to rebuke the secretary for disturbing him after expressly asking not to be bothered, but the harsh words were never spoken.

"Good morning, Hammond."

*Fuck. This is all I need.*

As always when in his father's presence, Hammond put himself through something similar to a pre-flight inspection. How did he look? Were all systems and parts in optimum working condition? Were there any malfunctions that required immediate correction? Did he pass muster? He hoped his father wouldn't be examining him too closely this morning.

"Hello, Dad." He stood and they formally shook hands across his desk. If his father had ever hugged him, Hammond had been too young to recall it.

He gathered up his suit coat and hung it on a wall hook, set his briefcase on the floor, and invited his father to sit down in the only spare chair in the cramped room.

Preston Cross was considerably stockier and shorter than his son. But his lack of stature didn't reduce the impact he made on people, whether in a crowd or one-on-one. His ruddy complexion was kept perpetually sunburned by outdoor activities that included tennis, golf, and sailing. As though on command, his hair had gone prematurely white when he turned fifty. He wore it like an accessory to ensure he was given the respect he demanded.

He had never known a day of illness, and actually disdained poor health as a sign of weakness. He had given up cigarettes a decade ago, but smoked cigars. He drank no less than three tall bourbons a day. He considered it a sacrilege not to have wine with dinner. He always had a snifter of brandy before bedtime. Despite these vices, he thrived.

In his mid-sixties, he was more robust and in better shape than most men half his age. But it wasn't his imposing physicality alone that created a powerful aura. It was also his dynamic personality. He took his good looks as his due. He intimidated men who were usually self-confident. Women adored him.

In both his professional and personal life he was rarely second-guessed and never contradicted. Three decades ago, he had combined several small medical insurance companies into a large one that, under his leadership, had grown huge, now boasting twenty-one branches statewide. Officially, he was semi-retired. Nevertheless, he was still CEO of the company, and it was more than a titular position. He monitored everything down to the price of bulk pencils. Nothing escaped him.

He served on numerous boards and committees. He and Mrs. Cross were on every invitation list that mattered. He knew everyone who was anyone in the southeastern United States. Preston Cross was well connected.

While Hammond wished to love, admire, and respect his father, he knew Preston had taken full advantage of his God-given qualities to do ungodly things.

Preston began his unannounced visit by saying, "I came as soon as I heard."

The words ordinarily prefaced a condolence. Hammond was filled with cold dread. How could his father possibly have found out about his indiscretion with Alex Ladd this soon? "What'd you hear?"

"That you'll be prosecuting Lute Pettijohn's murder case."

Hammond tried to hide his relief. "That's right."

"It would have been nice to hear that kind of good news directly from you, Hammond."

"No slight intended, Dad. I only spoke with Mason last night."

Ignoring Hammond's explanation, his father continued. "Instead, I had to hear it from a friend who attended a prayer breakfast with Mason this morning. When he casually mentioned it to me later at the club, he naturally assumed that I already knew. I was embarrassed that I didn't."

"I went to my cabin on Saturday. I was told about Pettijohn as soon as I returned last evening. Since then, things have been happening so quickly I haven't had a chance to absorb them all myself." An understatement if ever there was one.

Preston brushed an invisible piece of lint off the knife-blade crease of his trousers. "I'm sure you appreciate what an incredible opportunity this is for you."

"Yes, sir."

"The trial will generate a lot of publicity."

"I'm aware—"

"Which you should exploit, Hammond." With the zeal of a fire-and-brimstone evangelist, Preston raised his hand and closed it into a tight fist as though grasping a handful of radio waves. "Use the media. Get your name out there on a routine basis. Let the voters know who you are. Self-promotion. That's the key."

"Winning a conviction is the key," Hammond countered. "I hope my performance in court will speak for itself, and that I won't need to rely on media hype."

Preston Cross waved his hand in a gesture of impatient dismissal. "People don't care how you handle the case, Hammond. Who really gives a damn whether the killer goes to prison for life, or gets the needle, or gets off scot-free?"

"I care," he said heatedly. "And the citizenry should."

"Maybe at one time closer attention was paid to how public officials performed. Now all folks care about is how good they perform on TV." Preston laughed. "If polled, I doubt most people would even have a basic understanding of what a district attorney does."

"Yet those same people are outraged over the crime statistics."

"That's good. Appeal to that," Preston exclaimed. "Talk a good talk and the public will be pacified." He eased back in his chair. "Schmooze the reporters, Hammond, and get on their good side. Always give them a statement when they ask for one. Even if it's bullshit, you'll be amazed to see how a little goes a long way. They'll start giving you free air time." He paused to wink. "Get yourself elected first, then you can crusade to your heart's content."

"What if I can't get elected?"

"What's to stop you?"

"Speckle Island."

Hammond had dropped a bombshell, but Preston didn't even flinch. "What's that?"

Hammond didn't even try to hide his disgust. "You're good, Dad. You're very good. Deny it all you want, but I know you're lying."

"Watch your tongue with me, Hammond."

"Watch my tongue?" Hammond angrily sprang from his chair and thrust his hands into his pockets. "I'm not a child, Father. I'm a county prosecutor. And you're a crook."

Bourbon-flushed blood rushed to the capillaries of Preston's face. "Okay, you're so smart. What do you think you know?"

"I know that if Detective Smilow or anyone else discovers your name in conjunction with the Speckle Island project, it could cost you a hefty fine, maybe even jail time, and spell the end of my career. Unless I prosecute my own father. Either way, your alliance with Pettijohn has placed me in an untenable situation."

"Relax, Hammond. You've got nothing to worry about. I'm out of Speckle Island."

Hammond didn't know whether to believe him or not. His father's face was calm, implacable, giving off no telltale signs of dishonesty. He was talented that way. "Since when?" he asked.

"Weeks ago."

"Pettijohn didn't know that."

"Of course he did. He tried to talk me out of withdrawing. I got out anyway, and took my money with me. Pissed him off something fierce."

Hammond felt his face growing warm with embarrassment. Pettijohn had told him last Saturday afternoon that Preston was up to his neck in Speckle Island. He had shown him signed documents on which his father's signature was readily recognizable. Had Pettijohn been playing with him? "One of you is lying."

"When did you exchange confidences with Lute?" Preston wanted to know.

Hammond ignored the question. "When you pulled out, did you sell your partnership for a profit?"

"It wouldn't have been good business not to. There was a buyer wanting to get in on the deal, and ready to pay my price for my share."

The sour coffee in Hammond's stomach roiled. "It doesn't matter whether you're out now or not. If you were ever connected to that project, you're tainted. And by association, so am I."

"You're making far too much of this, Hammond."

"If it ever becomes public knowledge—"

"It won't."

"It might."

Preston shrugged. "Then I'll tell the truth."

"Which is?"

"That I was unaware of what Lute was doing out there. When I found out, I disapproved and pulled out."

"You've got it figured from all angles."

"That's right, I do. Always have."

Hammond glared at his father. Preston was practically daring him to make a case out of it—literally. But Hammond knew it would be futile to do so. Probably even Lute Pettijohn had known that Preston would have all his ducks in a row. He had used Preston's temporary affiliation with the Speckle Island project to manipulate Hammond.

"My advice to you, Hammond," Preston was saying, "is to learn a valuable lesson from this. You can get by with just about anything, as long as you leave yourself a dependable escape hatch."

"That's your advice to your only son? Fuck integrity?"

"I didn't make the rules," he snapped. "And you might not like them." Leaning forward in his chair, he punctuated his words by stabbing the air with a blunt index finger. "But you've got to abide by them, or those who aren't so high-minded will leave you choking on their heel dust."

This was familiar territory. They'd tramped over it a thousand times. When Hammond became old enough to question his father's infallibility and to dispute some of his principles, it soon became apparent that they differed. A line had been drawn in the sand. These were arguments that neither could win because neither would concede an inch.

Now that Hammond had seen written proof of his father's involvement in one of Pettijohn's more nefarious schemes, he realized how vastly different their viewpoints were. He didn't believe for an instant that Preston was ever unaware of what was taking place on that sea island. Conscience had played no part in his decision to pull out when he did. He had merely waited for an opportunity to make a profit on his own investment.

Hammond saw the gulf between them yawning wider. He saw no way to span it.

"I have a meeting in five minutes," he lied, coming around the corner of his desk. "Tell Mom hi. I'll try and call her later today."

"She and some of her friends are calling on Davee this afternoon."

"I'm sure Davee will appreciate that," Hammond said, remembering how Davee had scorned the whole idea of receiving callers who would flock to her house more out of curiosity than to pay their respects.

At the door, Preston turned. "I made no secret of how I felt when you left the law firm."

"No, sir, you didn't. You made it abundantly clear that you thought it was the wrong choice," Hammond said stiffly. "But I stick by my decision. I like my job here, on this side of the law. Beyond that, I'm good at it."

"Under Monroe Mason's tutelage you've done well. Exceptionally well."

"Thank you."

The compliment didn't warm Hammond because he no longer valued his father's opinion. Furthermore, Preston's praise always came with a qualifier attached.

*"I like the looks of all those A's, Hammond. But that B-plus in chemistry is unacceptable."*

*"The runners you batted in on that triple won the game. Too bad you couldn't have made it a grand slam. That would have really been something!"*

*"Second in your law school class? That's wonderful, son. Of course, it's not as good as placing first."*

That had been the pattern since his childhood. His father didn't break with tradition this morning.

"You now have a chance to validate your decision, Hammond. You abandoned the promise of a full partnership in a prestigious criminal law firm and went into public service. That would make a whole lot more sense if you were the boss." With false affection, his hand landed on Hammond's shoulder like a sack of cement. Already he had forgotten, or had chosen to disregard, their recent argument.

"This is the case that could earn you your spurs, son. Pettijohn's murder case is an open-door invitation to the solicitor's office."

"What if your misdeeds cancel my chances, Father?"

With obvious impatience he said, "That's not going to happen."

"But if it does, considering your ambition for me, wouldn't that be a cruel irony?"

Dr. Alex Ladd didn't see patients on Mondays.

She used that day to catch up on paperwork and personal business. Today was a special Monday. Today she was paying off Bobby Trimble and getting rid of him, she hoped forever. That was the deal they had struck last night. She would give him what he demanded, and he would disappear.

However, she had learned through experience that Bobby's promises were worthless.

As she unlocked the door to her office, she wondered how many times in the future she would be forced to go to her safe to extract cash. For the rest of her life? That was a bleak prospect, but a valid one. Now that Bobby had found her again, it was unlikely he would leave her alone.

Her well-appointed office reminded her of all she stood to lose if Bobby were to expose her. With her patients' comfort uppermost in mind, she had selected understated but expensive furnishings. Like the other rooms of the house, it was a blend of traditional styling with a few antique pieces used for accent.

The Oriental rug muted her footsteps. Sunlight shone in through the windows that overlooked the downstairs piazza and, beyond that, the walled garden, which she kept beautifully maintained through all four seasons. The blooming plants and flowers that thrived in Charleston's semitropical climate were at their peak. Basking in the humidity, they provided patches of vibrant color in the cultivated beds.

She had been fortunate to find the house already restored and renovated with modern conveniences. It had needed only personal touches to make it hers. At one time this front corner room had been the formal parlor of the single house. The matching room adjacent to it, originally a dining room, now functioned as her living room. When she entertained, she took her guests out. Meals at home were eaten in the kitchen, which was the back room on the first floor. Upstairs were two large bedroom suites. Each room in the house opened onto one of the two shady piazzas. The jasmine-covered wall surrounding the garden guaranteed privacy.

Alex swung aside the framed painting that concealed her wall safe. Deftly she spun the dial on the combination lock and when she heard the tumblers line up, she cranked the handle down and pulled open the heavy door.

Inside were several stacks of currency, banded together according to denomination. Perhaps because she had known want, even hunger, in her early years, she was never without cash on hand. The habit was childish and unreasonable, but one she forgave herself, considering the basis of it. It wasn't sound economics to keep the money in a safe where it earned no interest. But it gave her a sense of security to know that it was there, available should an emergency arise. Such as now.

She counted out the agreed-upon amount and placed the money in a zippered bag. Because of what it represented, the sack felt inordinately heavy in her hand.

Her hatred for Bobby Trimble was so intense it frightened her. She didn't begrudge giving him the money. Happily she would give him even more if it meant that she never had to see him again. It wasn't the amount that she resented, it was his intrusion into the life she had built for herself.

Two weeks ago, he had materialized out of nowhere. Unaware of what awaited her, she had blithely answered her ringing doorbell to discover him on her threshold.

For a moment she hadn't recognized him. The changes were startling. His flashy, cheap clothes had been replaced by flashy, expensive fashions. There was a sprinkling of gray at his temples, which would have made any other man appear distinguished. It only made Bobby seem more sinister, as though his youthful meanness had matured into pure evil.

The sardonic grin, however, was all too familiar. It was a triumphant, gloating, suggestive smile that she had spent years trying to eradicate from her recall. When countless therapy sessions and seas of tears hadn't rid her of it, she had begged God to remove it. Now, only on rare occasions, it resurfaced in a bad dream, from which she would awaken bathed in sweat and shivering in terror. Because that smile was representative of the control he had wielded over her.

"Bobby." Her voice had carried the hollow tone of a death knell. His unheralded reappearance in her life could only mean disaster, especially since the subtle changes in him underscored the threat he embodied.

"You don't sound very glad to see me."

"How did you find me?"

"Well, it wasn't easy." His voice was also changed. It was smoother, more refined, absent the twang. "If I didn't know any better, I'd think you've been hiding from me all these years. As it turns out, it was a fluke that brings me to your door. A twist of fate."

She didn't know whether to believe him or not. Fate could have played this cruel trick on her. On the other hand, Bobby was resourceful. He might have been tracking her relentlessly for years. Either way, it didn't matter. He was here, exhuming her worst memories and darkest fears from the deep places of her soul where she had buried them.

"I want nothing to do with you."

Stacking his hands over his heart, he had pretended her words were wounding. "After all we meant to each other?"

"*Because* of what we meant to each other."

He found her far more poised and self-assertive than she had been as a youth, and his face had turned dark with anger. "Do you really want to start comparing our past experiences? You want to match up what happened to who? Remember, I was the one who—"

"What do you want? Besides money. I know you want money."

"Don't jump to conclusions, *Dr. Ladd.* You're not the only one to make good. Since we last saw each other, I've prospered, too."

He had boasted about his career as a nightclub emcee. When she had heard all she could stomach about his glory days at the Cock'n'Bull she said, "I have a patient in fifteen minutes."

She had hoped to bring the reunion to a quick close. Bobby, however, had been building up to a big flash. As though playing a winning ace, he proudly disclosed the scheme that had brought him to Charleston.

Without question, he was stark, staring mad, and she had told him so.

"Be careful, Alex," he said with terrifying softness. "I'm not as nice as I used to be. And I'm much smarter."

Fighting her fear, she said, "Then you don't need me."

But his scheme did involve her. "In fact, you're key to its success."

When he told her what he wanted her to do, she had said, "You're delusional, Bobby. If you think I would give you so much as the time of day, you're sorely mistaken. Go away and don't come back."

But he had come back. The next day. And the day after that. For a week he persisted, showing up at all hours, interrupting her sessions with patients, leaving repeat messages on her voice mail that grew increasingly threatening. He had reattached himself to her life like the parasite he was.

Finally she had agreed to meet with him. Thinking that she had capitulated, his pleasure turned to rage when she declined to participate. "You may have more polish, Bobby. More refinement. But you haven't changed. You're the same as you were when hustling in the streets for pocket change. Scratch the surface of this thin veneer, and you're still scum underneath."

Infuriated by the truth, he removed one of her diplomas from the office wall and hurled it to the floor, splintering the frame and shattering the glass. "You listen to me," he said in a voice more like the one she remembered. "You had better reconsider and do me this little favor. Otherwise, I'll mess up your life real good. Real good."

She realized then that he wasn't just a street hustler any longer. Not only was he capable of damaging her, he could destroy her.

So she had agreed to play her small role in his ridiculous scheme—but only because she had already devised a way to thwart it.

But, as with all Bobby's schemes, it had gone awry.

Terribly awry.

She had been unable to implement her own plan. Now it was imperative that she disassociate herself from Bobby. If that meant paying him what he demanded, it was a small sacrifice to make compared to the enormity of what she could lose if their alliance was exposed.

Feeling that this decision was justified, she closed the wall safe, moved the painting back into place, and left her office, relocking the door behind her. As though on cue, her doorbell chimed. Bobby was right on time. She slipped the zippered bag behind a vase on the foyer table, stepped out onto the piazza, and answered the street door.

But it wasn't Bobby on the threshold. Two uniformed policemen stood on either side of a man with pale eyes and a thin, unsmiling mouth. Alex's heart plummeted, knowing already what had brought them to her home. Once again, her life was about to be pitched into chaos.

To conceal her anxiety, she smiled pleasantly. "Can I help you?"

"Dr. Ladd?"

"Yes."

"I'm Sergeant Rory Smilow, a homicide detective with Charleston P.D. I'd like to talk to you about the murder of Lute Pettijohn."

"Lute Pettijohn? I'm afraid I don't know—"

"You were seen outside his penthouse suite on the afternoon he was murdered, Dr. Ladd. So please don't waste my time by pretending that you don't know what I'm talking about."

She and Detective Smilow stared at one another, taking each other's measure. It was Alex who finally relented. She stood aside. "Come in."

"Actually, I was hoping you would come with us."

She swallowed, although her mouth was dry. "I'd like to call my lawyer."

"That isn't necessary. This isn't an arrest."

She looked pointedly at the stoic policemen flanking him.

Smilow's lips lifted in what could have passed as a wry smile. "Volunteering to be questioned without an attorney present would go a long way toward convincing me that you're innocent of any wrongdoing."

"I don't believe that for an instant, Detective Smilow." She scored a point. Her directness seemed to take him aback. "I'll be happy to accompany you as soon as I notify my lawyer."

# CHAPTER | 1 5

$R$ORY SMILOW SAT ON THE CORNER of his desk. Unlike all other desks in the Criminal Investigation Division, his was uncluttered. The files and paperwork were neatly stacked. Thanks to Smitty's shoeshine early that morning, his lace-up shoes reflected the overhead lights. His suit jacket remained on.

Alex Ladd was seated with her hands calmly clasped in her lap, legs decorously crossed. Smilow thought she was remarkably composed for someone who, appearance-wise at least, seemed out of place in a homicide detective's office.

For half an hour they had been waiting for her solicitor, who had agreed to meet her there. If she was uncomfortable with the prolonged silence and Smilow's close scrutiny, she gave no sign of it. She exhibited no fear or nervousness, merely a grudging tolerance for the inconvenience.

Solicitor Frank Perkins arrived looking flushed, rushed, and apologetic. Except for cleats, he was dressed for the golf course. "I'm sorry, Alex. I was on the tenth hole when I got your page. I came as soon as I could. What's this about, Smilow?"

Perkins had a solid reputation and an excellent track record. Rarer than that, he was known to be a decent human being with unimpeachable integrity. Smilow wondered in what capacity the defense attorney had served Alex Ladd before, so he asked.

"It's a rude question," Perkins replied, "but I don't mind answering if Alex doesn't."

"Please," she said.

"Up till now, we've been social friends. We met a couple of years ago when she and Maggie, my wife, served on a Spoleto committee together," he explained, referring to Charleston's renowned arts festival in May.

"Then, to your knowledge, Dr. Ladd has never been faced with criminal charges before?"

"Come to the point, Smilow." Perkins's tone demonstrated why prosecutors considered him a tough adversary in the courtroom.

"I wish to question Dr. Ladd in connection to the Lute Pettijohn murder."

Perkins's jaw dropped. He gaped at them like he was waiting for the punch line. "You've got to be kidding."

"Unfortunately, no, he's not," Alex said. "Thank you for coming, Frank. I'm terribly sorry I interrupted your golf game. Were you winning?"

"Uh, yeah, yeah," he replied absently, still trying to digest what Smilow had told him.

"Then I'm doubly sorry." Glancing at Smilow, she said, "This is all so ridiculous. It's a waste of time. I just want to get through it and get out of here."

In a manner that looked like she was granting him permission to proceed, she nodded at Smilow. He leaned across his desk, clicked on a tape recorder, then stated their names, the time, and the date.

"Dr. Ladd, the attendant of a public parking lot on East Bay Street identified you by an artist's sketch. Since the lot doesn't have an automated ticketing system, he keeps a record of each car by writing down the license plate number and the time it came in."

Unfortunately for Smilow, no record was kept of the time a car exited the lot. The charge was based on the time of entry. For any stay under two hours, the fee was five dollars. Incremental charges didn't start until after that first one hundred twenty minutes. The charge was noted, but not the exact exit time.

"We traced you through your car tag. On Saturday afternoon you left your car in that lot for up to two hours."

Perkins, who had been listening intently, laughed. "That's your earthshaking discovery? That's your big breakthrough on this case?"

"It's a start."

"One hell of a slow start. How does the parking lot business connect Dr. Ladd to the murder?"

"I tipped—"

Perkins held up his hand in caution, but she waved it down. "It's okay, Frank. I gave that young man at the parking lot a ten-dollar bill, which was the smallest denomination I had. That represented a five-dollar tip. I'm sure that's why he remembered me well enough to describe me to a sketch artist."

"He wasn't the one who provided us with the description," Smilow told them. "That was a Mr. Daniels of Macon, Georgia. His room in the Charles Towne Plaza was located down the hallway from the penthouse suite briefly occupied by Lute Pettijohn on Saturday afternoon. Did you know him?"

"You don't have to answer, Alex," the attorney told her. "In fact, I recommend that you don't say anything else until we've had a chance to speak privately."

"It's all right," she repeated, this time with a small laugh. Looking back to Smilow, she said, "I've never heard of Mr. Daniels of Macon, Georgia."

She was not only cool, but clever, thought Smilow. "I was referring to Mr. Pettijohn. Did you know *him?*"

"Everyone in Charleston has heard of Lute Pettijohn," she said. "His name was constantly in the news."

"You knew he had been murdered."

"Of course."

"You saw it on TV?"

"I was out of town for a portion of the weekend. But when I got back, I heard it on the news."

"You didn't know Pettijohn personally?"

"No."

"Then why were you standing outside his hotel suite near the time he was murdered?"

"I wasn't."

"Alex, please, don't say anything more." Placing his hand beneath her elbow, Perkins indicated the door. "We're leaving."

"It won't look good."

"Detective, you're the one who doesn't look good. You owe Dr. Ladd an apology."

"I don't mind answering the questions, Frank, if it means stopping this nonsense here and now," she said.

Perkins looked at her for a long moment. He obviously disagreed, but he turned toward Smilow. "I insist on consulting with my client before this goes any further."

"Fine. I'll give you a moment alone."

"Be sure and turn off the microphone before you leave."

"Believe me, Frank, I want this to go by the books. I don't want a murderer to be set free on a technicality." Looking pointedly at Alex, he switched off the recorder and left her alone with her solicitor.

"Can you believe it?" Steffi Mundell was outside in the narrow hall, staring through the two-way mirror into Smilow's private office. "The artist was right on. What's she like?"

"Don't you have any other cases, Steffi? I thought all of you A.D.A.s were overworked and underpaid. At least that's what you would have everyone believe."

"With Mason's sanction, I've lightened my caseload so I can concentrate on this one. He wants me to assist Hammond any way I can."

"Where is the boy wonder?" He watched Alex Ladd adamantly shake her head to one of Frank Perkins's inquiries.

"Barricaded inside his office. I haven't seen him since we left the hospital this morning. I left him a message that I was coming over here to take a gander at our suspect. Good work on the capture, by the way."

"Duck soup. Will Hammond be joining us?"

"Would you mind?"

Smilow shrugged. "I'd like to gauge his reaction."

"To Dr. Ladd?"

"It might be interesting to see if Saint Hammond could demand the death penalty for a beautiful woman."

Steffi reacted with a start. "You think she's beautiful?"

Before Smilow could answer, Frank Perkins opened the door and, after giving Steffi a blunt greeting, waved them inside.

Bobby Trimble breathed deeply in an effort to bring his heart rate under control. It had been racing ever since he saw Alex talking to cops on her front door step.

That was bad. Very bad. Were the cops wise to his Pettijohn plot? Had Alex called them with the intention of turning him in to save herself?

He had cruised past her house at a moderate speed with studied indifference. What he saw in his peripheral vision, however, was cause for alarm—two uniforms, a plainclothesman, and a vindictive woman who made no secret of despising him. A foolproof recipe for disaster.

There was one positive sign. Alex hadn't fingered him. She hadn't pointed to him and shouted, "Get him!" But he wasn't sure what that signified, or where it left him. It might mean only that she hadn't seen him driving past.

Deliberating his next move, he aimlessly wove the convertible through downtown Charleston's midday traffic. Last night he had thought he was home free. After a lot of arm-twisting, Alex had agreed to give him the money he demanded.

"If you think you can steal my idea and use it for your own gain, you've got another thing coming, missy!" When agitated, his accent returned. Hating the sound of that hick whine, he had paused to modulate his voice.

"Don't even think about double-crossing me, Alex," he told her in a softer, but no less threatening tone. "That money belongs to me, and I want it."

Alex had cleaned up her act, too. She spoke better. Dressed better. Lived well. But for all her snooty high-and-mighty airs, she hadn't really changed. No more than he had. Just as she knew his true nature, he knew hers. Did she think he was born yesterday? He saw what was happening. She had seized on his brainstorm and was trying to cheat him out of his half.

When he accused her of it, she had said, "For the last time, Bobby: I don't have any money to give you. Leave me alone!"

"That's simply not going to happen, Alex. I'm in your life until I get what I came for. If you want me to disappear, pay up."

Her weary sigh had been as good as a waving white flag. "Be at my house at noon tomorrow."

So he was at her house at noon, and guess what? She had cops for company. There might already be a warrant out for his arrest.

Although maybe not, he thought, forcing himself to calm down. If she and the police had been laying a trap for him, why was the patrol car parked in plain sight? And how could she rat on him without ratting out herself, too?

In any event, until he knew for certain what was going on, it would be wise for Bobby Trimble to lay low. *Bor-ing.*

Stopping for a red light, he folded his hands over the steering wheel and contemplated his immediate future. Out of the corner of his eye, he noticed another convertible pull up alongside his. He turned his head.

The two faces looking back at him were partially concealed by sunglasses with bright yellow lenses. The coeds were young and attractive. Their grins were saucy and challenging. Spoiled, rich daddy's girls looking for mischief on a hot summer afternoon.

In other words, prey.

The light changed, and with a screech of tires, their car shot forward. They made a right turn at the next corner. Bobby switched lanes and made the same turn. The girls, glancing over their bare shoulders, were aware he was following them. He saw them laughing.

The BMW convertible whipped into the parking lot of a trendy luncheon restaurant. Bobby followed. He watched them as they made their way toward the entrance. They were dressed in short shorts that showed an inch of butt cheek and seeming miles of tanned legs. Their halter tops left little to the imagination. They were a walking, giggling, flirting reminder to Bobby of what he did best.

He made his way through the crowded restaurant and spotted them seated at a table on the patio beneath the shade of an umbrella, giving their drink order to a waitress. When she left, Bobby dropped into an empty chair at their table.

Their lips were glossy, framing very white, very straight teeth. Diamond studs glittered in their ears. They smelled of expensive perfume.

"I'm a vice cop," he said in a sexy drawl. "Are you young ladies old enough to drink?"

They giggled.

"Don't worry about us, *officer*."

"We're way past the age of consent."

"Consent to do what?" he asked.

"We're on vacation, so we're open to just about anything."

"And we do mean anything."

He gave them a smile of naughty intent. "Is that right? And here I figured y'all for traveling missionaries."

That brought on another round of giggles. The waitress arrived with two drinks. Bobby leaned back in his chair. "What are we drinking, ladies?"

He had scored.

The intrepid receptionist finally broke the invisible barrier into Hammond's office. "That sketched suspect? She's been identified as Dr. Alex Ladd. As we speak, she's in Detective Smilow's office undergoing questioning."

His palms broke a cold sweat. "Did he arrest her?"

"Came in voluntarily is what Ms. Mundell said. But she has her solicitor with her. Are you on the way over there, or what?"

"Maybe later."

The receptionist withdrew.

The ramifications of this news rebounded as quickly as echoes. Hammond was assailed by them. Smilow's interrogation tactics could have wrung a confession from Mother Teresa. Hammond had no way of knowing how Alex Ladd might respond to them. Would she be hostile or cooperative? Would she have something to confess? When she saw him again, what might she reveal? What might he reveal?

To be on the safe side, he wanted to postpone an inevitable face-to-face meeting for as long as possible. Until he knew more about Alex Ladd, and learned the nature and extent of her involvement with Pettijohn, it was best for him to keep his distance from the case.

Ordinarily, that would have been doable. Except for rare exceptions, his office didn't become directly involved until the detectives felt they had enough evidence to press formal charges, or for Hammond to make a case to the grand jury. Unlike Steffi, who didn't know the meaning of finesse, he let the police department do its job until it was time for him to take over.

But this was one of those rare exceptions. His involvement was required, if for no other reason than politics. City and state officials, some of whom had been Pettijohn's avowed enemies in life, others his cohorts, were using his murder as a political platform. Through the media, they were demanding a quick arrest and prosecution of his murderer.

Fanning public interest, an editorial in this morning's paper had sounded a wake-up call to the sad truth that no one, not even a seemingly invulnerable individual like Lute Pettijohn, was safe from violence.

On the noon edition of the news, a reporter had conducted a man-on-the-street poll, asking people if they were confident that Pettijohn's killer would be captured and justly punished.

The case was creating the media frenzy his father wished for.

What Hammond wished for was to avoid joining the fray for as long as possible. To that end, he spent another half hour creating busywork for himself.

Monroe Mason appeared immediately upon his return from lunch. "I hear Smilow's already got a suspect." His booming voice bounced off the walls of Hammond's office like a racquetball.

"News travels fast."

"So it's true?"

"I just got the message a while ago."

"Give me the condensed version."

He explained about Daniels and the sketch. "A flyer with Endicott's drawing and a written description was circulated around the area of the Charles Towne Plaza. Dr. Ladd was identified by a parking lot attendant."

"I understand she's a prominent psychologist."

"That's the rumor."

"Ever heard of her?"

"No."

"Me either. My wife probably has. She knows everybody. You figure Pettijohn was a patient of hers?"

"At this point, Monroe, you know as much as I do."

"See what you can find out."

"I'll keep you informed as the case progresses."

"No, I mean this afternoon. Now."

"Now? Smilow doesn't like our butting in," Hammond argued. "He especially dislikes *my* butting in. Steffi's already there. If I go, too, he'll resent the hell out of it. It'll look like we're checking up on him."

"If he gets his ire up, Steffi will smooth it over. I've got to have something to tell all the reporters calling my office."

"It can't go on record that Dr. Ladd is a suspect, Monroe. We don't know that she is. She's only being questioned, for chrissake."

"She was worried enough to bring Frank Perkins along with her."

"Frank's her lawyer?" Hammond knew him well, and he respected him. It was always a challenge to argue a case against him in court. She couldn't have a more capable attorney. "Any sensible person would have her lawyer along when invited to the police station for questioning."

Mason wasn't deterred. "Let me know what she's about." With a thundering goodbye, he left, taking any choice Hammond had with him.

Reaching the police station, he went up to the second floor and depressed the buzzer on the locked double doors leading into the Criminal Investigation Division. They were opened for him by a policewoman. Knowing why he was there, she said, "They're in Smilow's office."

"Why not the interrogation room?"

"I think it was occupied. Besides, Solicitor Mundell wanted to watch through the glass."

Hammond was almost glad Alex wasn't being questioned in that windowless cubicle that stank of stale coffee and guilty sweat. He couldn't imagine her in the same room where he'd watched pedophiles and rapists and thieves and pimps and murderers become completely dismantled under the pressure of tough interrogation.

He rounded the corner into the short hallway where the homicide detectives had their offices. He had hoped it would be over and Alex would be gone by the time he arrived. No such luck. Steffi and Smilow were peering through the mirrored glass, looking like vultures waiting for their victim to draw a final breath.

He heard Steffi say, "She's lying."

"Of course she's lying," Smilow said. "I just don't know which part is a lie."

They didn't notice Hammond until he spoke. "What's up?"

Turning around, Steffi looked thoroughly put out. "Well, it's about time. Didn't you get my messages?"

"I couldn't get away. What makes you think she's lying?" He nodded toward the small window, so far too gutless to look through it.

"Normally, an innocent person is nervous and edgy," Smilow said.

"Our lady doctor hardly blinks," Steffi told him. "No hem-hawing. No throat clearing. No fidgeting. She answers each question directly."

Hammond said, "I'm surprised Frank is letting her answer at all."

"He doesn't want her to. She insists. She has a mind of her own."

Following Smilow's thoughtful gaze, Hammond finally turned his head. He could see only a partial profile, but even that had a profound effect on him. His first impulse was to smooth back the strand of hair that had curled against her cheek. The second was to grab her and shake her angrily, demanding to know just what the hell she was up to and why she had dragged him into it.

"What do we know about her?" he asked.

Even Smilow appeared impressed as he rattled off a long list of credentials. "Besides being published twice in *Psychology Today*, she's often asked to lecture, specifically on the study she conducted on panic attacks. She's considered an expert on the subject. A few months ago, she talked a man off a window ledge."

"I remember that," Hammond said.

"It made the newspaper. The man's wife credits Dr. Ladd with saving his life." Referring to his notepad, Smilow added, "Her personal life is personal. All we know is that she's single, no children. Frank is pissed. He says we've got the wrong person."

"What else is he going to say?" Steffi remarked snidely.

Trying to appear impassive, Hammond said, "She seems like a woman who's got it all together."

"Oh, she's together, all right," Steffi said. "You couldn't melt ice on her ass. Once you've talked to her, you'll see what we mean. She's so cool, she's practically bloodless."

*How little you know, Steffi.*

"Ready for the next go 'round?" She and Smilow moved toward the door.

Hammond hung back. "Do you want me to go in?" They turned, surprised.

"I thought you'd be chomping at the bit to get your first crack at the murderess," Steffi said.

"It remains to be seen whether or not she's a murderess," he said testily. "But that's not the point. The point is that since you're here, we outnumber Smilow. I don't want him to think that we're monitoring him."

"You can address me directly," Smilow said.

"Okay," Hammond said, looking at the detective. "Just so we're clear, my coming over here was Mason's idea, not mine."

"I got the same lecture on peaceful coexistence from Chief Crane. I can tolerate you if you can tolerate me."

"Fair enough."

Steffi expelled a deep breath. "So ends round one of the pissing contest. Now can we please get down to business?"

Smilow held the door open for them. Hammond let Steffi precede him. Smilow entered behind him and closed the door, cramming too many people into such a small space. There was hardly enough room for Smilow to squeeze past Hammond on his way to his desk. "Are you sure you won't have something to drink, Dr. Ladd?"

"No, thank you, Detective."

To Hammond, hearing her voice was as stirring as if she had touched him. He could almost feel again her breath against his ear. His heart was a hard, dull thudding against his ribs. He could barely breathe. And, dammit, it was all he could do not to touch her.

Smilow made the superfluous introductions. "Dr. Ladd, this is Special Assistant Solicitor Hammond Cross. Mr. Cross, Dr. Alex Ladd."

She turned her head. Hammond held his breath.

## CHAPTER 16

*S*pecial *Assistant Solicitor Cross can tell you where I was and what I was doing Saturday evening, can't you, Special Assistant Solicitor Cross?"*

*"I didn't kill anybody on Saturday, but if I had, it would have been in self-defense. You see, Detective Smilow, Solicitor Cross lured me to his cabin in the woods and there he raped me repeatedly."*

*"Solicitor Cross, how lovely to see you again. How long has it been? Oh, I remember. It was last Saturday night when we screwed our brains out."*

Alex Ladd said none of that. Nor did she say any of the other horrific things that Hammond had imagined her saying. She didn't scream invectives, or denounce him in front of his colleagues, or wink suggestively, or give any other sign of recognition.

But when she turned toward him and their eyes connected, everything else around him seemed to vanish and all his focus belonged to her. Their eyes were engaged for only a second or two, but if the exchange had lasted an eternity, it couldn't have been more puissant or meaningful.

He wanted to ask, *What have you done to me?* and mean it more ways than one. He had been thunderstruck on Saturday evening. He had thought, even hoped, that seeing her again, under bright fluorescent lighting and in a far less romantic surrounding, would have less of an impact on him. Just the opposite. His desire to reach for her was a physical ache.

All this shot through his mind in less time than it took to blink. Hoping his voice wouldn't betray him, he said, "Dr. Ladd."

"How do you do?"

Then she turned away. That routine acknowledgment dashed Hammond's desperate hope that he actually *had* been a stranger to her on Saturday, and that their meeting at the fair *had* been purely accidental. If so, upon being introduced now, her green eyes would have widened and she would have blurted out something to the effect of, "Why, hello! I didn't expect to see you here." But she had registered no surprise whatsoever. When she turned her head to speak a greeting, she had known exactly whom she would be addressing.

In fact, it appeared that she had been braced for the introduction, just as he had been. She had almost overplayed the aloofness, had turned away almost too quickly to be polite.

There was no longer any question about it—their meeting had been by design, and, for reasons that were still unapparent, the time they had spent together was as compromising to her as it was to him.

Frank Perkins spoke first. "Hammond, this is a complete waste of my client's time."

"Very possibly it is, Frank, but I would like to make that determination for myself. Detective Smilow seems to think that what Dr. Ladd can tell us warrants my hearing it."

The lawyer consulted his client. "Do you mind going through it again, Alex?"

"Not if it means that I can go home sooner rather than later."

"We'll see."

That comment had come from Steffi, and it made Hammond want to slap her. Turning the Q and A over to Smilow, he propped himself against the closed door, where he had an unrestricted view of Alex's profile.

Smilow restarted the tape recorder and added Hammond's name to those present. "Did you know Lute Pettijohn, Dr. Ladd?"

She sighed as though she had already answered that question a thousand times. "No, Detective, I did not."

"What were you doing downtown Saturday afternoon?"

"I could argue that I live downtown, but in answer to your question, I went window-shopping."

"Did you buy anything?"

"No."

"Go into any stores?"

"No."

"You didn't duck into any stores or chat with any shopkeepers who could corroborate that you were there for the purpose of shopping?"

"Unfortunately, no. I didn't see anything that caught my eye."

"You just parked your car and walked around?"

"That's right."

"Wasn't it a little hot outside for a stroll?"

"Not for me. I like the heat."

Her eyes flickered toward Hammond, but he didn't need that glance to stir his memory.

*"Now that the sun has gone down, it's not so hot."*

*She smiled up at him, the lights of the spinning carousel reflected in her eyes. "Actually, I like the heat."*

Hammond blinked Smilow back into focus.

"Did you go into the Charles Towne Plaza?"

"Yes. Around five o'clock. To get something to drink. A soft drink. I'm certain that's where this Mr. Daniels saw me. That's the only time and place he could have seen me because I was never on the fifth floor standing outside Mr. Pettijohn's room."

"He gave us a vivid account of you doing just that at around five o'clock."

"He's wrong."

"You had a drink in the bar."

"Just off the lobby, yes. Unsweetened iced tea."

Steffi leaned toward Hammond and whispered. "The waitress bears that out. But that only confirms that at least two people saw her in the hotel."

He nodded, but he didn't comment because Smilow was asking another question, and he was interested in Alex's answer.

"What did you do after finishing your drink?"

"I walked back to the parking lot where I'd left my car."

"What time was that?"

"Five-fifteen. No later than five-thirty."

Hammond's knees went weak with relief. John Madison's initial guess had placed the time of death later than that. So his silence was justified. Almost. If she were entirely innocent, the victim of a mistake made by a man suffering food poisoning, why hadn't she reacted when he came in? Why had she pretended they'd never met? He had his reasons for keeping their meeting a secret. Obviously she did, too.

"I gave the parking lot attendant ten dollars, which was the smallest bill I had," she was saying.

"That's a very generous tip."

"I thought asking for change would seem cheap. The lot was full and he was busy, but he had been very nice and polite."

"What did you do after retrieving your car?"

"I left Charleston."

"And went where?"

"To Hilton Head Island."

Hammond swallowed audibly. So much for truth-telling. Why was she lying? To protect him? Or herself?

"Hilton Head."

"Yes."

"Did you stop anywhere along the way?"

"I stopped for gasoline." She lowered her eyes, but only momentarily, and probably only Hammond noticed.

His heart was knocking hard against his ribs. That kiss. *The* kiss. The kiss he would remember for the rest of his life. None had ever been that good, or felt so goddamn right, or been so goddamn wrong. That kiss could ultimately change his life, ruin his career, condemn him.

"Do you remember the name of the place?"

"No."

"Texaco? Exxon?"

She shrugged and shook her head.

"Location?"

"Somewhere along the highway," she replied impatiently. "It wasn't in a town. Self-serve. Pay at the window. There are dozens of them along that highway. The cashier was watching a wrestling match on TV. That's all I remember."

"Did you pay by credit card?"

"Cash."

"I see. With one of those large bills."

Hammond saw the trap and hoped that she did. Most self-serve stations and convenience stores didn't take bills larger than a twenty, especially after dark.

"With a twenty, Mr. Smilow," she said, giving him a retiring smile. "I bought twenty dollars' worth. I didn't get change."

"Veddy, veddy cool."

Steffi had spoken beneath her breath, but Alex heard her. She glanced in their direction, looking first at Steffi, then at Hammond, and he vividly remembered holding her face between his hands and bringing her mouth up to his.

*"Don't say no. Don't say no."*

Smilow's next question drew Alex's attention back to him. Hammond exhaled without making it obvious that he'd been holding his breath.

"What time did you arrive at Hilton Head?"

"That was the beauty of the day. I had no plans. I wasn't on a schedule. I wasn't watching the clock, and I didn't take a direct route, so I don't remember what time it was when I actually got there."

"Approximately."

"Approximately . . . nine o'clock."

At approximately nine o'clock, they were eating corn on the cob that had left her lips greasy with melted butter. They had laughed over how messy it was, and elected to forget their manners and shamelessly lick their fingers.

"What did you do on Hilton Head?"

"I drove the length of the island down to Harbour Town. I walked around, enjoyed the music from the various open-air bars. Listened to the young man performing for the children there under the large live oak. Basically I strolled around the marina and out onto the pier."

"Did you talk to anybody?"

"No."

"Eat in a restaurant?"

"No."

"You weren't hungry?"

"Apparently not."

"This is ridiculous!" Frank Perkins protested. "Dr. Ladd admits to being in the hotel on Saturday, but so were hundreds of other people. She's an attractive lady. A man—this Daniels being no exception—is likely to notice her even in a crowd."

Hammond was still watching her, so when her eyes shifted to him, it was a repeat of that first glance across the pavilion. He felt an instantaneous connection, a sudden tug in his gut.

Perkins was still making his argument. "Alex says she wasn't anywhere near Pettijohn's suite. You have nothing that places her there. This is only a lame stab in the dark because you've got nothing else. While I sympathize with your ability to come up with a viable suspect, I'm not going to allow my client to suffer the consequences."

"Just a few more questions, Frank," Smilow said. "Indulge me."

"Make them brief," the lawyer said curtly.

Smilow fixed the psychologist with a hard stare. "I'd like to know where Dr. Ladd spent the night."

"At home."

Her answer seemed to surprise him. "Your home?"

"I berated myself for not making a reservation on Hilton Head. Once I got there, I considered staying over. I would have liked to, but I called several places and everything was booked. So I drove back to Charleston and slept in my own bed."

"Alone?"

"I'm not afraid to drive after dark."

"Did you *sleep* alone, Dr. Ladd?"

She stared at him coldly.

Frank Perkins said, "Tell him to go to hell, Alex. If you don't, I will."

"You heard my solicitor's advice, Detective."

Smilow's mouth slanted upward in what passed for a smile. "While you were at Harbour Town didn't you speak to anyone?"

"I browsed in one of the art galleries, but I didn't talk to anyone. I also bought an ice-cream cone at the base of the lighthouse, but it's a walk-up place and they were very busy. I couldn't pick out the young woman who served me. She had so many customers that night, I seriously doubt she would remember me, either."

"So there's no one who can corroborate that you were there?"

"I suppose not, no."

"From there you drove home. No stops?"

"No."

"What time did you get home?"

"The wee hours. I didn't notice. By then I was very tired and sleepy."

"I've indulged all I'm going to." Frank Perkins assisted her from her chair politely, but in such a way that brooked no argument from either her or Smilow. "Dr. Ladd deserves an apology for this. And if you so much as breathe her name to the media in connection with this case, you'll have not only an unsolved murder to contend with, but a staggering lawsuit as well."

He nudged Alex toward the door, but before everyone could shift positions and make room for their departure, another detective opened the door. He held a folder in his upraised hand. "You asked for this as soon as it was available."

"Thanks," Smilow said, reaching for the folder. "How'd it go?"

"Madison's persnickety. Says he apologizes for the time it took."

"As long as he was thorough."

"It's all in there."

The detective withdrew. For the benefit of the others, Smilow said, "That detective witnessed the autopsy. This is Madison's report."

Steffi crowded up against Smilow as he removed the documents from the envelope. She scanned them along with him.

Without looking up from the report, Smilow asked, "Dr. Ladd, do you own a weapon?"

"Lots of things could be used as a weapon, couldn't they?"

"The reason I'm asking . . ." Smilow said as he raised his head to look at her, "is because it was exactly as we thought. Lute Pettijohn didn't die from the blow to his head. He died of gunshot."

"Pettijohn was *shot*?"

\*     \*     \*

"I think it was genuine."

Steffi squeezed lime into the drink that had just been brought to their table. "Come on, Hammond. Get real."

"It was the first and only time that she showed any emotion or spontaneity," he persisted. "I think her surprise was authentic. Up to that time she didn't even know how Pettijohn had died."

"I was surprised when I read that he had stroked out."

That had been one startling fact to come out of the autopsy. Lute Pettijohn had suffered a stroke. It hadn't killed him, but John Madison deduced that the stroke was massive enough to have caused his fall, which resulted in the head wound. He also determined that, had Pettijohn survived, he might have suffered paralysis and other disabilities. It wasn't until after Frank Perkins had escorted Alex Ladd from Smilow's office that they read the report more thoroughly and added this new information to the increasingly complex mystery.

"Was the stroke caused by an event, do you think?" Steffi wondered. "Or a medical condition he was unaware of?"

"We'll need to find out if he was on medication for an existing condition," Smilow said, sliding a napkin beneath his club soda. "Not that it matters. The stroke wasn't fatal, but the gunshots were. That's how he died."

"Alex Ladd didn't know that," Hammond stated. "Not until she heard it from us."

Thoughtfully Steffi sipped from her gin and tonic, then she shook her head firmly and gave him a smart-aleck smile. "Nope. She faked that astonishment. Women are good at playacting because we're constantly having to fake orgasms."

The remark was meant to insult him. It didn't. But it pissed him off. "Women with penis envy."

"Ah, that was a pretty good comeback, Hammond," she said, raising her glass in a mock salute. "With practice, you might develop into a real jerk."

Smilow, who had been following this repartee with divided attention, said, "Much as it pains me, I tend to agree with Hammond."

"You think I have penis envy?"

He didn't even crack a smile. "I agree with him that Ladd's shock was the real article."

"You're sharing an opinion with Hammond? That's almost as shocking as your sharing a table," she said.

The lobby bar at the Charles Towne Plaza was packed to capacity with the happy hour crowd. Even though the hotel was across town from police headquarters, it had seemed a fitting place for them to meet and discuss Alex's interrogation.

Tourists, whether or not they were registered guests, shopped in the boutiques that rimmed the lobby. They photographed the impressive staircase and the chandelier it embraced. They photographed each other.

Two barefoot women wrapped in hotel bathrobes, their heads swathed in towels, giggled as they avoided being caught in a snapshot. Following Hammond's empty gaze, Steffi said, "Ridiculous to walk around like that for the sake of a beauty treatment. Can you imagine what Pettijohn must have looked like stamping through here like that?"

"Huh?"

"Where are you, Hammond, lost in space?" she asked irritably.

"I'm sorry. I was just thinking."

He hadn't noticed the robed women. He had barely noticed anything since leaving Smilow's office. He was thinking about her. About Alex Ladd and her reaction to how Pettijohn died.

She had seemed genuinely shocked, making him hopeful that she was right about Mr. Daniels when she surmised that he had noticed her in the hotel, but he was mistaken about when and where.

Hopeful of having an ally in Smilow, he leaned across the table, propping his forearms on the edge of it. "You said you agree with me. How so? How do you read it?"

"I think she's clever enough to fake her surprise and make it appear real. For whatever reason, I don't know. Yet. But it's not her surprised reaction that concerns me so much as her story."

"We're listening," Steffi said.

"If she had popped Pettijohn, wouldn't she have left the hotel and immediately sought to establish an alibi?"

Striving for nonchalance, Hammond reached for his glass of bourbon and water. "Interesting notion. Care to expound?"

"They can place time of death with amazing accuracy. Within minutes, in fact."

"Between five-forty-five and six o'clock," Hammond said. Upon seeing that in the autopsy report, he had been overwhelmingly relieved. Alex couldn't possibly be the murderer because she couldn't have been two places at one time. "Dr. Ladd said she left no later than five-thirty."

"Too close for comfort," Smilow said. "A good prosecutor like you would manipulate that time frame, allow for a margin of error. But, given that we don't know exactly what time she got her car from the lot, Frank Perkins could chop that time line like a salami and use it to establish reasonable doubt. But it would only work if—"

"I see where you're going—" Steffi interjected.

"If Dr. Ladd had an excellent—"

"Alibi."

While Steffi and Smilow talked over one another, Hammond took another drink. The whiskey stung his throat. "Makes sense," he said huskily.

Smilow frowned. "The problem I have with her story is that she *didn't* have an alibi. She says she went to Hilton Head and talked to no one who could corroborate that."

"I'm confused," Steffi said. "Are you thinking that by not having an alibi, she appears more innocent than if she did?"

The detective looked across at her. "Not exactly. But it makes me wonder if she's waiting to see how far this goes before springing an alibi on us."

"Like she's holding one in reserve just in case?"

"Something like that."

Hammond, who had listened while they unknowingly played upon his greatest fear, joined in the speculation. "What makes you think she's got this standby alibi?"

"Did you mean to rhyme?" Steffi asked.

"No," he replied, irritated with her because he wanted to hear Smilow's thoughts. "You were saying?"

"I was saying what I've said from the beginning," Smilow explained. "She's not nervous. From the time she answered her door and saw me and those cops on her porch, until Frank escorted her out a half hour ago, she was too unruffled to be completely innocent.

"Innocent people can't wait to convince you of their innocence," he continued. "They chatter nervously. They elaborate and expand their stories with each telling. They tell you more than you ask to know. Accomplished liars stick to the basics and are usually the most composed."

"It's a sound theory," Hammond said. "But it's not foolproof. Being a psychologist, wouldn't Dr. Ladd have a tighter grip on her emotions than the average person? She must hear shocking things when she's treating patients. Wouldn't she know how to screen her reactions?"

"Possibly," Smilow said. Hammond didn't like the detective's smile, and within seconds he learned why he seemed so complacent. "But Dr. Ladd *is* lying. I know that for fact."

Steffi leaned forward so eagerly she almost spilled her drink. "What fact?"

Bending down, Smilow took a newspaper from his briefcase. "She must have missed this item in this morning's news."

He had used a red marker to circle the story. It wasn't that long, but to Hammond it was a devastating four paragraphs.

"Harbour Town evacuated," Steffi read aloud.

Smilow provided a summary. "Last Saturday evening there was a fire aboard one of the yachts moored in the harbor. The wind was up. Sparks were blown onto trees and awnings around the marina. As a safety precaution, the fire department cleared everyone out. Even people aboard other boats and those who were staying in the condos were evacuated.

"The fire was extinguished before it could do too much damage. But that's some of the most expensive real estate in the country. Firemen were taking no chances. They closed Lighthouse Road to incoming traffic and put the whole area through an extensive check. Essentially Harbour Town was shut down for several hours."

"From when to when?"

"From nine o'clock on. Restaurants and bars saw no reason to reopen when they got the go-ahead sometime after midnight. They remained closed until Sunday morning."

Steffi whispered, "She wasn't there."

"Had she been, she would have mentioned this."

"Good work." Steffi raised her glass to Smilow.

"I think raising toasts is a little premature," Hammond said angrily. "Maybe she has a logical explanation."

"And maybe the pope's a Baptist."

He ignored Steffi's wisecrack. "Smilow, why didn't you confront Dr. Ladd with this when you were interrogating her?"

"I wanted to see how far she would carry it."

"You were giving her enough rope to hang herself."

"My job is easier when a suspect does it for me."

Hammond searched his mind for a fresh approach. "Okay, so she wasn't in Harbour Town. What does that prove? Nothing, except that she wants to safeguard her privacy. She doesn't want it known where she was."

"Or with whom."

He shot a cold look at Steffi, then continued speaking to Smilow. "You've still got nothing on her, nothing that places her inside Pettijohn's suite, or even near it. When you asked if she owned a gun, she said no."

"But of course she would," Steffi argued. "And we've got Daniels's testimony."

Hammond wasn't finished with his own arguments. "According to Madison's report, the bullets removed from Pettijohn's body were .38-caliber. Your garden-variety bullets from your garden-variety pistol. There are hundreds of .38s in this city alone. Even in your own evidence warehouse, Smilow."

"Meaning what?" Steffi wanted to know.

"Meaning that unless we find the weapon in the murderer's possession, it will be nigh unto impossible to trace," Smilow said, following Hammond's thought.

"As for Daniels," Hammond continued while he was on a roll, "Frank Perkins would make hash of him on the witness stand."

"You're probably right about that, too," Smilow said.

"So what does that leave you?" Hammond asked. "Nothing."

"I've got SLED running some test on evidence collected from the scene."

"Hand-carried to Columbia?"

"Absolutely."

The South Carolina Law Enforcement Division was located in the state capital. Evidence that was collected, bagged, and labeled by the CSU was usually hand-delivered to SLED by an officer to prevent chain of evidence discrepancies.

"Let's see what turns up," Smilow said in the unflappable manner that only emphasized to Hammond his own unraveling temperament. "We didn't get much from that suite of rooms, but we picked up a few fibers, hairs, particles. Hopefully something—"

"Hopefully?" Hammond scoffed. "You're relying on hope? You'll have to do better than that to catch a killer, Smilow."

"Don't worry about me," he said, his mood growing just as fractious as Hammond's. "You tend to your job and I'll tend to mine."

"I just don't want to face the grand jury with nothing but my dick in my hand."

"I doubt you could find your dick with your hand. But I'll find the link between Alex Ladd and Pettijohn."

"And if you don't," Hammond said, raising his voice, "you can always invent one."

Smilow came out of his chair so fast, it scraped against the floor. Likewise, Hammond was on his feet within a heartbeat.

Steffi popped up, too. "Guys," she said beneath her breath. "Everybody's looking."

Hammond realized that they did indeed have the attention of everyone in the bar. Conversations around them ceased. "I gotta go." He tossed a five-dollar bill down on the table to cover his drink. "See you tomorrow."

He didn't take his eyes off Smilow until he turned and began making his way through the crowd toward the exit. He heard Steffi tell Smilow to order her another drink and that she would be right back, and then she came after him. He didn't want to talk to her, but once they were outside she grasped his arm and brought him around.

"Would you like some company?"

"No," he said, more harshly than he intended. Then, pushing his fingers up through his hair, he took a deep breath and let it out slowly. "I'm sorry, Steffi. It's just been one of those Mondays. My dad came by this morning. This case is going to be a bitch. Smilow's a bastard."

"You're sure that's what's bothering you?"

He lowered his hand and looked at her closely, afraid he had given himself away. But her eyes weren't suspicious or accusatory. They were limpid, soft, and inviting. He relaxed. "Yeah, I'm sure."

"I just thought that maybe . . ." She paused to raise her shoulder in a small shrug. "Maybe you were wishing we had talked things through before you decided to end the relationship." She touched the front of his shirt. "If you're wanting to let off some steam, I remember something that used to work very well."

"I remember, too." He gave her a kind smile which he hoped would appease her ego. But he removed her hand, squeezing it gently before releasing it. "Better get back inside. Smilow's waiting with your drink."

"He can go to hell."

"In that regard, you probably won't be disappointed. I'll see you tomorrow."

He turned and walked away, but she called after him. "Hammond?" When he was facing her again, she asked, "What did you think of her?"

"Who, Dr. Ladd?" He faked a thoughtful frown. "Articulate. Cool under pressure. But unlike Smilow, I'm not ready to—"

"I mean *her*. What did you think of her?"

"What's to think about?" he quipped, forcing a laugh. "She's gorgeous to look at and obviously very intelligent."

Then, with a jovial wave, he turned away.

Since he didn't have Alex Ladd's capacity for lying, he figured it would be safer to stick to the truth.

## CHAPTER 17

THE CITADEL, RESPECTED AS ONE of the outstanding institutions of higher learning in America, was located only a few blocks from the Shady Rest Lounge. Beyond their proximity, the bar and the military academy were worlds apart in every respect.

Unlike the renowned academy with its guarded gate and pristine grounds, the Shady Rest didn't boast an impressive facade. It had no windows, only cinder-block patches where windows had once been. The entrance was a metal door on which a vandal had carved an obscenity. After the infraction, a slapdash attempt had been made to cover the word with a thin, low-grade paint which, unfortunately, didn't quite match the original color or fill in the scratch. As a result, the expletive now drew more attention than if it had been left alone. The only thing that indicated the nature of the establishment was a neon sign above the door that spelled out the name. The sign buzzed noisily and worked only sporadically.

In spite of its lofty neighbor and all its own shortcomings, the Shady Rest Lounge was perfectly at home in its environment, a neighborhood of poverty- and crime-ridden streets where windows were barred and visible signs of prosperity made one a target.

With self-protection in mind, Hammond had replaced his business suit with blue jeans and T-shirt, a baseball cap and sneakers. All had seen better days . . . better decades. But a change of clothing alone wasn't sufficient. In this section of the city, one needed to adopt an attitude in order to survive.

When he pulled open the defaced door to go into the lounge, he didn't politely stand aside for the pair of guys on their way out. Instead he shouldered his way between them, acting tough enough to make a statement but hopefully not being so aggressive as to spark a confrontation he would most certainly lose. He escaped with only a muttered slur directed toward him and his mother.

Once inside the lounge, it took several moments for his eyes to adjust to the darkness. Shady deals were transacted in the Shady Rest. He had never been in this particular bar before, but he knew instantly the kind of place it was. Every city had them, Charleston being no exception. He was also uneasily aware that he wouldn't last long if any of the other patrons discovered that he represented the County Solicitor's Office.

Once his eyes had adjusted and he got his bearings, he spotted whom he sought. She was sitting alone at the end of the bar, morosely staring into a highball glass. Affecting disregard for the wary, hostile stares sizing him up, Hammond made his way over to her.

Loretta Boothe's hair was grayer than the last time he had seen her, and it looked like it had been a while since her last shampoo. She had made an attempt to apply makeup, but either she had done an inept job or this application was several days old. Mascara had flaked onto her cheeks, and her eyebrow pencil had been smudged. Lipstick had bled into the fine lines radiating from her mouth, though none of the color remained on her lips. One cheek was rosy with rouge, the other sallow and colorless. It was a pathetic face.

"Hey, Loretta."

She turned and focused bleary eyes on him. Despite the baseball cap, she recognized him immediately, and her delight to see him was plain. Eyelids that were saggy and webbed beyond their years crinkled as she grinned, revealing a lower front tooth in bad need of a dentist's attention.

"Lord have mercy, Hammond." She looked beyond him, as though expecting an entourage. "You're the last person in the world I'd expect to see in a dive like this. You slumming tonight?"

"I came to see you."

"Same as," she said, snorting a humorless laugh. "I didn't think you were speaking to me."

"I wasn't."

"You had every right to be pissed."

"I still am."

"So what put you in a forgiving mood?"

"An emergency." He glanced down at her nearly empty glass. "Buy you a drink?"

"Ever know me to turn one down?"

Wishing the privacy of a booth, Hammond gallantly helped her off the barstool. If he hadn't lent a supporting hand, her knees might have buckled when she stood up. The drink she left on the bar hadn't been her first, or even her second.

As she teetered along beside him, he acknowledged to himself that there was a very good chance he was going to sorely regret doing this. But as he had told her, it was an emergency.

He ensconced her in a booth, then returned to the bar and ordered two Jack Daniel's black, one straight, one with water over rocks. He passed the former to Loretta as he slid into the booth.

"Cheers." She raised her glass to him before taking a hefty swallow. Fortified by the drink, she turned her attention to Hammond. "You're looking good."

"Thanks."

"I mean it. You always did look good, of course, but you're just now coming into your own. Growing into your bones. Whatever it is that you men do that makes you get better-looking with age while we women rapidly go to pot."

He smiled, wishing he could exchange compliments with her. She was barely fifty, but looked much older.

"You're better-looking than your daddy," she observed. "And I always thought Preston Cross was a right handsome man."

"Thanks again."

"Part of your problem with him—"

"I don't have a problem with him."

She frowned, squelching his denial. "Part of your problem with him is that he's jealous of you."

Hammond scoffed.

"It's true," Loretta pronounced with the superior air of drunks and sages. "Your daddy's afraid that you might surpass him. You might achieve more than he has. You might become more powerful than he is. Earn more respect. He couldn't stand that."

Hammond looked down into his own drink, which he didn't want. The one he'd had a couple hours ago with Smilow and Steffi had left him slightly queasy. Or maybe it had been the subject matter that had turned his stomach. In any case, he wasn't thirsty for Tennessee sipping whiskey. "I didn't come here to talk about my father, Loretta."

"Right, right. An emergency." She took another drink. "How'd you find me?"

"I called the last number I had."

"My daughter lives there now."

"It's your apartment."

"But Bev is paying the rent, and has been for months. She told me if I didn't pull myself together, she was going to kick me out." She raised her shoulders. "Here I am."

Suddenly he realized why she looked so disheveled and unwashed, and the realization increased his queasiness. "Where are you living now, Loretta?"

"Don't worry about me, hotshot. I can take care of myself."

He allowed her a remnant of pride by not coming right out and asking if she was living on the streets or in a homeless shelter. "When I spoke to Bev, she told me this had become one of your favorite hangouts."

"Bev's an ICU nurse," she boasted.

"That's great. She's done well."

"In spite of me."

There was no argument for that, so Hammond said nothing. Feeling self-conscious and awkward for her, he studied the handwritten OUT OF ORDER sign taped to the record selector on their table. The sign had been there a long time. Both the paper and the Scotch tape had yellowed with age. The jukebox in the distant corner stood dark and silent, as though it had succumbed to the pervasive despondency inside the Shady Rest.

"I'm proud of her," Loretta said, still on the subject of her daughter.

"As you should be."

"She can't stand the sight of me, though."

"I doubt that."

"No, she hates me, and I can't say that I blame her. I let her down, Hammond." Her eyes were watery with remorse and hopelessness. "I let everybody down. You especially."

"We finally got the guy, Loretta. Three months after—"

"After I fucked up."

Again, the truth was unarguable. Loretta Boothe had served on the Charleston Police Department until her alcohol abuse got so bad she was fired. Her increasing dependency had been blamed on her husband's death. He had died instantly and bloodily when his Harley crashed into a bridge abutment. His death had been ruled accidental, but in a boozy, confidential conversation with Hammond, Loretta had confessed her misgivings. Had her husband chosen suicide over living with her? The question haunted her.

About that same time, she became increasingly disenchanted with the CPD. Or possibly her disenchantment was a result of her deteriorating personal life. Either way, she created problems for herself at work and eventually found herself unemployed.

She got licensed as a private investigator and for a time worked regularly. Hammond had always liked her; when he joined the prestigious firm fresh out of law school, she was the first person to address him as "solicitor." It was a small thing, but he had never forgotten her thoughtful boost to his self-confidence.

When he moved to the County Solicitor's Office, he frequently retained her to investigate on its behalf even though they had investigators on staff. Even when her reliability became chancy, he continued to use her out of a sense of loyalty and pity. Then she had screwed up royally, and the fallout had been disastrous.

The accused in the case was an angry, incorrigible young man who had almost beaten his mother to death with a tire tool. He was a threat to society, and would continue to be until he was put in prison for a long time.

To win a conviction, Hammond desperately needed the eyewitness testimony of the accused's second cousin, who was not only reluctant to testify against a family member, but was also scared of the guy and feared retaliation. Despite the subpoena, he hightailed it out of town. It was rumored he'd gone to hide with other relatives in Memphis. Because the staff investigators were already committed to other cases, Hammond brought Loretta in. He advanced her money to cover her expenses, and dispatched her to Memphis to track down the cousin.

Not only did his witness drop out of sight, so did Loretta.

He learned later that she had used the expense money to binge. The trial judge, who was unsympathetic with Hammond's plight, refused his request for a postponement and ordered him to proceed with what he had, which was the testimony of the battered mother. Also fearing retribution from her violent son, she changed her story on the witness stand, testifying that she had suffered her injuries when she fell off the back porch.

The jury brought in an acquittal. Three months later, the same guy attacked his neighbor in a similar fashion. The victim didn't die, but he sustained severe and irreparable brain damage. This time the criminal was convicted and sentenced to years behind bars. But Steffi Mundell had prosecuted that case.

All these months later, Hammond still hadn't forgiven Loretta for betraying the trust he had placed in her, especially when no one else would hire her. She had abandoned him when he needed her most and had made him look like a fool in the courtroom. Worst of all, her dereliction had caused a man to suffer a brutal beating that had left him mentally and physically impaired for the rest of his life.

When sober, Loretta Boothe was the best at what she did. She had the instincts of a bloodhound and an uncanny ability to ferret out information. She seemed to possess a sixth sense about where to go and whom to question. Her own human frailties were so obvious, that people found her disarming and confidence-inspiring. They relaxed their guard and they talked candidly to her. She was also savvy enough to distinguish between what information was significant and what wasn't.

Despite her talent, seeing her in the reduced state she was in tonight made Hammond question the advisability of retaining her again. Only a desperate person would seek help from a chronic drunk who had already proved her unreliability.

But then he thought about Alex Ladd, and realized that he was just that desperate.

"I have some work for you, Loretta."

"What is this, April Fool's Day?"

"No, but I'm probably a damn fool for entrusting you with anything."

Her features contorted with emotion. "You'd do well to leave right now, Hammond. I would jump at the chance to make up for what I did last time, but you'd be crazy to depend on me again."

He smiled grimly. "Well, I've been called crazy before."

Tears formed in her eyes, but she cleared her throat and squared her shoulders. "What . . . what did you have in mind?"

"You've heard about Lute Pettijohn."

Her lower jaw went slack. "You want me to work on something as important as that?"

"Indirectly." He shifted uncomfortably on the booth's hard bench. "What I want you to do isn't officially for the D.A.'s office. It's strictly confidential. Between you and me. Nobody else must know. Okay?"

"I'm a fuckup, Hammond. I've demonstrated that. But I always liked you. I admire you. You're one of the good guys, and I flatter myself into thinking of you as a friend. You were good to me when people would do an about-face to avoid speaking. I may let you down, probably will, but they'd have to cut out my tongue before I would betray your confidence."

"I believe that." He peered deeply into her eyes. "How drunk are you?"

"I've got a good buzz going, but I'll remember this tomorrow."

"Okay." He paused to take a deep breath. "I want you to learn what you can about . . . Should I write this down?"

"Would you ever want it to come back to you?"

He thought about it for a moment. "No."

"Then don't write it down. If it ain't tangible, it ain't evidence."

"Evidence? Whoa, Loretta," he said, holding up both hands. "What I want you to do is confidential. It stretches ethics. But it's not illegal. I just want to level the playing field for a suspect."

Tilting her head, she regarded him curiously. "Maybe I'm drunker than I thought. Did you just say—"

"You heard me right."

"You want to give a suspect in the Pettijohn case a break?"

"In a manner of speaking."

"How come?"

"You're not drunk *enough* for me to explain that."

A laugh rattled out of her chest. "Okay," she said, still dubious. "Who's the suspect?"

"Dr. Alex Ladd."

"Is he in Charleston?"

"It's a she."

She blinked several times, then gave him a long, hard look. "A she."

Hammond pretended not to notice the obvious question posed by her raised eyebrows. "She's a psychologist here in Charleston. Find out everything you can about her. Background, family, schooling, anything. Everything. But in particular any possible connection she might have had with Lute Pettijohn."

"Like if she was a girlfriend?"

"Yeah," he mumbled. "Like that."

"I got the impression that Steffi Mundell was prosecuting the Pettijohn case."

"What made you think that?"

She then told him about seeing Steffi and Rory Smilow in the hospital emergency room the night Pettijohn was murdered. "I had gone to see Bev. Actually I was there to bum money off her. Anyway, Stuff-me-Steffi and Unsmiling Smilow came busting in like storm troopers. For all the good it did them. This little pipsqueak of a doctor stood up to them. They got nowhere with him. Did my heart good." She paused to chuckle, then turned somber again and looked across at Hammond. "You still sleeping with her?"

He couldn't conceal his surprise, but he didn't ask how she knew about his secret affair with Steffi. Her knowing evinced that she was very good at what she did. "No."

She studied him a moment as though to convince herself that he was telling her the truth. "Good. Because I'd hate to speak badly of the woman you're boinking."

"You don't like Steffi?"

"The same way I don't like poisonous snakes."

"She's not as bad as that."

"No, she's worse. She's a viper. She's had her eye on you since she first came to Charleston. Not only to get inside your pants, either. She wants to wear them."

"If you mean that we're vying for the same job again, I'm well aware of that."

"But have you thought of this? Steffi might have been using your dick as a lever to hoist her right into the solicitor's office."

"Are you suggesting that she slept with me only to advance her career? Gee, thanks, Loretta. You're doing my ego a world of good."

She rolled her eyes. "I was afraid that possibility might have escaped you. Men rarely think of their dicks as anything except a magic wand with which to cast spells over grateful women. That's why a stiff prick is so goddamn exploitable."

Alex Ladd sprang immediately to Hammond's mind. If Loretta knew about how gullible he had been last Saturday night, she could really lambast him.

She was saying, "Steffi Mundell would screw a rottweiler if she thought it would get her where she wants to be."

"Cut her some slack. True, she's ambitious. But she's had to claw and scrape for every achievement. She had a domineering father who gauged everyone's value on a testosterone meter. Steffi was expected to cook and clean and wait on the menfolk, first her brothers and father, then her husband. Devout Greek Orthodox family. Not only was she not devout, she was—is—a nonbeliever. She had no help or encouragement through university or law school. And when she graduated at the top of her class, her father said something like, 'Now maybe you'll stop this foolishness and get married.' "

"Please, my heart's bleeding," Loretta said sarcastically.

"Look, I know she can be annoying as hell. But she has good qualities that outweigh the bad. I'm a big boy. I know what Steffi's about."

"Yeah, well. . . ," she muttered, unconvinced, "then there's Smilow." She reached for her glass of whiskey, but Hammond reached across the table and gently removed it from her hands. "Can't I even finish that one?" she wheedled. "It's a waste of good whiskey."

"Starting now, you're on the wagon. Two hundred dollars a day and sobriety. Those are the terms of this agreement."

"You drive a hard bargain, Solicitor Cross."

"I'll also cover your expenses, and you'll receive a hefty bonus when the job is finished."

"I wasn't referring to the pay. That's generous. More than I deserve." She wiped the back of her hand across her mouth. "It's the no-drinking clause that's causing me to balk."

"That's the rule, Loretta. If you take a single drink and I find out about it, the deal is off."

"Okay, I got it," she said irritably. "I'll just have to gut it out, that's all. I need the money to pay Bev back. Otherwise I'd tell you to stuff your 'terms' where the sun don't shine."

He smiled, knowing that her gruff act was just that. She was thrilled to be working again. "What were you about to say about Smilow?"

"That son of a bitch," she sneered. "He's the reason I was fired. He gave me an impossible assignment. Dick Tracy couldn't have done it in the amount of time Smilow specified. When I couldn't produce, he blamed my drinking, not his own impossible deadline.

"He went to the chief and said that demoting me from criminal investigation wasn't good enough. He wanted me out, period. Called me a disgrace, a blight on the entire department, a liability. He actually threatened to quit if they didn't fire me. After being issued an ultimatum like that, who do you think the powers that be were going to choose? A woman cop with a slight drinking problem or an ace homicide detective?"

It could be argued that everything Smilow had alleged was true, and that Loretta's drinking problem was more than "slight," and that Smilow had merely forced his superiors to do what they had needed to do but were hesitant to do, fearing a sex discrimination suit or something equally cumbersome.

As unfortunate as it had been to Loretta, Smilow's ultimatum might have prevented a catastrophe. For months leading up to her dismissal, she had been perpetually drunk. She should not have been working as an armed policewoman, investigating assaults and crimes against persons, a dangerous beat under the best of circumstances.

But Hammond understood her need to vent. "Smilow isn't very tolerant of human weaknesses."

"He has some of his own."

"Such as?"

"His love for his sister and his hatred for Lute Pettijohn."

Recalling the condensed story Davee had told him the night before, he asked, "What do you know about that?"

"Same as everybody knows. Margaret Smilow was one sick ticket. Bipolar, I think. Smilow was a protective older brother. When she fell hard for Lute Pettijohn, Rory disliked the idea from the start. Maybe he was jealous of the new protector in his sister's life, or maybe he simply saw Pettijohn's true colors when everybody else was blind to them. For whatever reason, Rory disapproved of the marriage."

"I understand they had some violent quarrels."

Loretta harrumphed. "One night Rory and I were investigating a convenience store holdup and murder. He got paged to call his sister immediately. Margaret was hysterical and begged him to come right then. He was so upset, we turned the crime scene over to our backup team, and I drove him.

"Hammond," she said, shaking her head in disbelief, "by the time we got there, she had totally wrecked that house. Hurricane Hugo didn't do that much damage. There wasn't a piece of glass that wasn't broken. Not a pillow that wasn't ripped open. Not a shelf that hadn't been swept clean. You couldn't walk across the floor for all the debris.

"Apparently she had discovered that Pettijohn had a girlfriend. When we got there, Margaret was in the bathroom holding a straight razor to her wrist and threatening to kill herself. Smilow sweet-talked her out of the razor. He called her doctor, who was kind enough to come over and medicate her. Then Smilow had me drive him to Pettijohn's rendezvous.

"Long story short . . . he barged in and caught this gal sitting on Lute's face. He and Pettijohn each got in a few good punches before I intervened. I had to physically restrain Smilow because nothing I said was getting through. I honestly believe that if I hadn't been there to wrestle him down, he would have killed Pettijohn that night. I've never seen a man—or woman—that enraged."

Her eyes narrowed and she tapped the ugly Formica with a jagged, dirty fingernail. "And till the day I die, I'll believe that's what Rory Smilow holds against me. To the world he reveals this bloodless persona. He comes across as being unfeeling. Cold. Passionless. But I witnessed him being as human as the next man. *More* human than the next man. He lost control. That's why he couldn't tolerate having me around every day as a reminder."

Hammond didn't question her veracity. For all her flaws, he had never known Loretta to lie or even to embroider a story. "Why did you tell me this?"

"Just throwing out some possibilities."

"*Possibilities?* You think Smilow killed Pettijohn?"

"All I'm saying is that he could have. I don't know about opportunity, but he for damn sure had motivation. He never forgave Lute for Margaret's suicide. And these aren't just the delusions of an old drunk, either. Your friend Steffi thought of it, too. I overheard her bring it up that night at the hospital. She remarked on how much Smilow would enjoy seeing Pettijohn die."

"What did Smilow say?"

"He didn't confess, but he didn't deny it." She chuckled. "Not in so many words, anyway. As I recall, he turned the tables and dumped the deed on her."

"On Steffi?"

"He broached the idea that Pettijohn might have been paving her way into Mason's office when he retires."

Hammond laughed. "Smilow must've been having an off night. If Lute was doing someone a favor, why would they kill him?"

"That's what Steffi came back with, and the conversation died there. Besides, he was only being provoking because Steffi was of the opinion that Davee had rid the world of Pettijohn."

"Davee was her first suspect. But now she's got someone else in her crosshairs."

"This Dr. Ladd?"

Nodding, Hammond passed her an envelope containing some advance money. "If you drink that—"

"I won't. I swear."

"Find out what you can on Alex Ladd. I want the skinny as soon as you can get it to me."

"This may sound presumptuous—"

"And I'm sure it is."

Ignoring him, Loretta continued. "Has she been arrested?"

"Not yet."

"But apparently you think Smilow and company are off base."

"I'm not sure." He gave her a summary of the day's events, starting with Daniels's story and ending with Alex's denial that she even knew Pettijohn. "They've found no connection. Speaking as a prosecutor, his case is weak."

"And speaking otherwise?"

"There is no otherwise."

"Huh." Loretta was watching him like she didn't believe him, but she let it drop. "Well, God help this Dr. Ladd if she didn't kill Pettijohn."

"Don't you mean, God help her if she did?"

"No, I meant what I said."

"I don't follow," Hammond said, puzzled.

"If Dr. Ladd was at the scene, but didn't kill him, she could be a witness."

"A witness? Wouldn't she have told us?"

"Not if she was afraid."

"What could she fear more than being accused of murder?"

Loretta replied, "The murderer."

## CHAPTER 18

ALEX DROVE WITH ONE EYE ON HER REARVIEW MIRROR. She recognized her symptoms as paranoia, but she figured she was entitled, having spent most of the day being questioned in connection with a homicide. With Hammond Cross in the room. Knowing she was lying.

Of course, he had been lying, too, by omission. But why? Curiosity? Perhaps he had wanted to see how far she would carry her lies about her whereabouts on Saturday night. But when she concluded her false story about Hilton Head, she had fully expected him to denounce her as a liar.

He hadn't. Which indicated to her that he was protecting his own reputation. He hadn't wanted his colleague Ms. Mundell and the frightening Detective Smilow to know that he had slept with their only lead in the Pettijohn murder case on the very night of the murder. For today, at least, he had been more interested in keeping their meeting a secret than he had been in nailing her as a suspect.

But that could change. Which left her vulnerable. Until she knew how Hammond intended to play this out, she must do everything possible to protect herself from incrimination. It might not come to that, but if it did, she must be prepared.

She arrived at her destination, but eschewed the porte cochere and valets and instead pulled into the public parking lot. Bobby had gone upscale. When she had known him, he'd been no stranger to flophouses. Now he was registered in a chain suite hotel near downtown. She hadn't called first to notify him that she was on her way. Surprising him might give her a slight advantage over what would doubtless be an unpleasant confrontation.

In the elevator, she closed her eyes and rolled her head around her shoulders. She was exhausted. And terribly afraid. She wished she could turn back the clock and rewrite the day Bobby Trimble had reentered her life after twenty years of freedom from him. She wished she could delete that day and all the subsequent ones.

But that would mean also deleting her night with Hammond Cross.

She hadn't known much happiness in her life. Even as a child. Particularly as a child. Christmas had been just another day on the calendar. She'd never had a birthday cake, or an Easter basket, or a Halloween costume. Not until her late teens had she learned that ordinary people, not just people in magazines and on television, were allowed to participate in holiday celebrations.

Her young adulthood had been spent undoing the damage of the past and creating a new individual. She had been greedy to absorb everything she had been denied. At university she had applied herself to her studies with such diligence that little time was left for dating.

By the time her practice was established, her energy had been devoted to it. Through her volunteer and charity work she met eligible men. With some she had forged friendships, but romance had never been an element in these relationships, and that had been her choice.

She had settled on being content with her accomplishments, and with the satisfaction that came from helping troubled people to work through their problems and realize their worth.

Real happiness, the giddy, effervescent kind of joy she had experienced with Hammond that night, had escaped her. It was an elusive stranger to her, so up till now she hadn't realized its addictive powers. Or its potential hazards. She wondered now: Was happiness always this costly?

As soon as the elevator doors opened, she heard music and figured it was probably coming from Bobby's room. She was right. She approached the door and knocked, waited a moment, then knocked again, harder this time. The music was killed.

"Who is it?"

"Bobby, I need to see you."

A few seconds later the door was opened. He was naked except for a towel around his hips. "If you're bringing the heat on me, so help me God, I'll—"

"Don't be absurd. The last thing I want is for the police to know I was ever associated with you."

His eyes scanned the hallway. Finally satisfied that she was alone, he said, "I'm relieved to hear that, Alex. For a while today, I was afraid you had double-crossed me again."

"I—"

Movement behind him drew her gaze beyond his shoulder. First one girl, then a second, appeared. He glanced over his shoulder and, when he saw the girls, smiled and pulled them forward, keeping an arm around the waist of each. If either was eighteen, it wasn't by much. One was wearing a pair of thong underwear, nothing on top. The other was wrapped in a sheet that Alex assumed had been stripped from the bed.

"Alex, this is—"

"I don't care," she interrupted. "I need to talk to you." She leveled an impatient stare on him.

"Okay." He sighed. "But you know what they say about all work and no play."

Shooing both girls back into the room, he swatted their fannies and asked them to give him a few minutes alone with Alex. "We've got business to settle. Then the party will really begin. Okay? Go on, now."

With their whining admonitions not to keep them waiting long, he stepped out into the hallway and closed the door.

Alex said, "You're stoned, aren't you?"

"Don't I have a right to be? Seeing cops at your front door wasn't exactly what I had in mind when I came to see you today."

"Where did you buy the dope?"

"I didn't have to buy it. I know how to pick my friends."

"Your victims."

He grinned, taking no offense. "These girls were well supplied. Quality stuff. Why don't you have some?" He reached out and gave her knotted shoulder a squeeze. "You're all tense, Alex. How about a little pick-me-up?"

She slapped his arm away.

"Suit yourself," he said with an affable shrug. "Where's my money?"

"I don't have it."

His smile slipped a notch. "You're fucking with me, right?"

"You saw the policemen at my house, Bobby. How could I possibly bring you that cash now? I came here to warn you not to come near me again. I don't want to see you. I don't want you to drive past my house. I don't want to know you."

"Hold on just one goddamn minute. We agreed, remember?" He waggled his hand between his chest and hers. "We made a deal."

"The deal is off. Circumstances have changed. They questioned me about Lute Pettijohn's murder."

"That isn't my fault, Alex. You can't blame me for your screwup."

"I told you last night—"

"I know what you *told* me. That doesn't mean I *believe* it."

It was pointless to argue with him. He hadn't believed her yesterday, and he wasn't going to believe her now. Not that she cared what he believed. She just wanted to be rid of him.

"As agreed, I'll give you the hundred thousand."

"Tonight."

She shook her head. "In a few weeks. As soon as this is cleared up. It would be crazy to give it to you now when the police are watching me so closely."

Placing his hands on his lean hips, he leaned forward from the waist, bringing his face down to the level of hers. "I warned you to be careful. Didn't I warn you?"

"Yes, you warned me."

"So how'd they mark you?"

She wasn't going to stand in the hallway of a family hotel with a nearly naked man and discuss her police interrogation. Besides, he didn't really care how the police had linked her to Pettijohn. He cared about only one thing. "You'll get your money," she said. "I'll contact you when I feel it's safe for us to meet. Until then, stay away from me. If you don't, you'll only be shooting yourself in the foot."

Apparently his high was wearing off, because his expression was no longer cool and congenial, but belligerent. "You must think I'm really dense. Do you honestly believe that you can get rid of me just because you want to, Alex?"

He snapped his fingers hard only inches from her nose. "Think again. Until I get my cut of that cash, I'm your shadow. You owe me this."

"Bobby," she said evenly, "if I repaid you what you were owed, I would have to kill you."

"Threats, Alex?" he said silkily. "I don't think so." Then he surprised her by poking her hard in the chest with his index finger, causing her to fall back several steps. "You're in no position to be threatening me. You're the one with the most to lose. Remember that. Now, I'm going to say it for the last time. Get me that money."

"Don't you understand that I can't? Not now."

"Like hell. You've got an alphabet soup of letters strung out behind your name. You've got all the smarts you need to figure this one out." His eyes narrowed into mean slits. "You get that money to me. That's the only way I'll disappear."

Hatred burned red-hot inside her. "Do those girls realize that they'll wake up tomorrow morning without their jewelry and money?"

"They'll get what they want in return." He winked. "And then some."

Disgusted, Alex turned and headed for the elevator. "Stay away from me until I notify you."

Softly he called after her, "Your shadow, Alex. Look around. I'll be there."

Hammond switched on the bedside lamp, bathing the pastel striped walls with a warm glow. Looking around, he had to hand it to Lute Pettijohn— he had hired a good decorator for his Charles Towne Plaza and hadn't skimped on amenities. At least not in the penthouse suite.

The room was spacious and laid out to be user-friendly. Behind the doors of the French armoire was a twenty-seven-inch TV, larger than standard hotel/motel issue and equipped with a VCR. Inside the cabinet were also a CD player and a selection of disks, last week's issue of *TV Guide*, and a remote control for the television. Nothing else.

He moved into the bathroom. The towels appeared not to have been touched since the housekeeper had placed them on the decorative bars. A small silver basket on the marble dressing table still contained bottles of shampoo and other grooming products, a miniature sewing kit, a shoeshine cloth, a shower cap.

He switched out the light and went back into the bedroom, his footsteps muted by the plush carpeting. The bedroom had its own minibar in addition to the one in the parlor. The contents had already been inventoried by the CSU. All the same, he gloved his hand with a handkerchief and opened the refrigerator. A quick inventory checked against the printed menu of stocked items revealed that none were missing. When he closed the door, the motor kicked on and it began to hum.

He welcomed the sound. The suite, its luxurious decor and abundant amenities notwithstanding, was now a crime scene. Its eerie silence pressed in on him from all sides.

He had left the Shady Rest Lounge with the intention of going home and putting an end to this terrible Monday. Instead, he had felt drawn here. He didn't need to guess the reason for this compulsion. Loretta's last comment had found a foothold in his mind and wouldn't let go.

Had Alex Ladd been here last Saturday? Had she witnessed something that she was reluctant to reveal because it might put her life at risk? He would rather believe that than entertain the idea of her being the murderer, although neither was a cheery prospect. Subconsciously he had come here in the hope of finding something that had been previously overlooked, something that would exonerate Alex Ladd and possibly implicate someone else. Irrationally, he felt compelled to protect a woman who had proved to be an elaborate and unconscionable liar.

It hadn't been easy to return to this suite of rooms where last Saturday he had met Lute and exchanged heated words. He hadn't gone beyond the parlor, hadn't really gone far beyond the threshold. He had said what he had come to say from just inside the door.

Lute had been sitting on the sofa, sipping his drink, a picture of complacency as he warned Hammond that if he was bent on building a grand jury investigation around him, he must be prepared to prosecute his own father as well.

"Of course," Lute had added, smiling, "there is a way to avoid all this ugliness. If you agree to my way, everybody gets what he wants and goes home happy."

His proposal amounted to Hammond selling his soul to the devil. He had turned down the offer. Needless to say, Pettijohn hadn't taken kindly to his declination.

Disturbed by the memory, Hammond stepped to the closet, the only area of the bedroom he hadn't inspected. Behind the tall, mirrored sliding doors was an empty safe and empty clothes hangers. Hanging with the belt still tied was a fluffy white terry-cloth robe. Matching slippers were still sealed inside their cellophane packaging. It seemed nothing had been disturbed.

He slid the doors closed, and that's when he saw an image reflected in the mirror.

"Looking for something?"

Hammond spun around. "I didn't know anyone else was here."

"Obviously," Smilow said. "You jumped like you'd been shot." Throwing a glance over his shoulder at the bloodstains on the carpet in the parlor, he added, "Forgive the poor choice of words."

"Come now, Rory," Hammond said, using sarcasm to conceal the chagrin he felt at having been caught snooping. "You've never been one to mince words."

"Right. I haven't. So what the fuck are you doing here?"

"What the fuck do you care?" Hammond fired back, matching the detective's angry tone.

"There's tape across the door to keep people out."

"I'm entitled to visit the scene of the crime I'm going to prosecute."

"But protocol demands that you notify my office and have someone accompany you."

"I know the protocol."

"So?"

"I was out," Hammond said curtly. Smilow was right, but he didn't want to lose face. "It's late. I didn't see the need to drag a cop over here. I didn't touch anything." He waved the handkerchief still in his hand. "I didn't take anything. Besides, I thought you were finished with it."

"We are."

"So what are you doing here? Looking for evidence? Or planting some?"

The two men glared at one another. Smilow was the first to get a grip on his temper. "I came here to think through some of the elements the autopsy turned up."

In spite of himself, Hammond was interested. "Like what?"

Smilow turned back into the parlor and Hammond followed. The detective stood over the bloodstain on the floor. "The wounds. The trajectory of the bullets is hard to determine because of all the tissue damage they caused, but Madison's best guess is that the muzzle of the pistol was aimed at him from above, at a distance probably no more than a foot or two."

"The killer couldn't miss."

"He saw to it that he couldn't."

"But he showed up not knowing that Lute had stroked out."

"He came to kill him, regardless."

"At close range."

"Indicating that Pettijohn knew his killer."

They contemplated the ugly dark stain on the carpet for a moment. "Something's been bothering me," Hammond said after a time. "I just now figured out what it is. Noise. How do you pop someone with a .38 without anyone hearing it?"

"Only a few guests were in their rooms. Turn-down service wasn't scheduled to begin until after six. The housekeepers weren't in the corridor yet. The shooter could have used a sound suppressor of some sort, even a jerry-rigged one. Although Madison didn't find any debris around the area or in the wounds to indicate that. My guess is that Pettijohn's boast of virtually soundproof rooms wasn't bogus like his state-of-the-art video security system."

"Another thought just occurred to me." Smilow looked across at him and motioned for him to continue. "Whoever popped him not only knew Lute well, he also knew a lot about his hotel. It's like the killer had made himself a scholar on everything Pettijohn did. Like he was obsessed with him." He probed Smilow's cold eyes. "Do you see what I'm getting at here?"

Smilow held his stare for a ten count, but, refusing to be provoked, nodded toward the door to the suite. "After you, Solicitor."

# TUESDAY

## CHAPTER 19

LUTE PETTIJOHN'S WILL STIPULATED that he be cremated. As soon as Dr. John Madison released the body on Monday afternoon, it had been transported to the funeral home. The widow already had made the arrangements and taken care of the necessary paperwork. She declined to view the body before relinquishing it to the crematorium.

A memorial service had been scheduled for Tuesday morning, which some regarded as inappropriately soon, especially in light of the circumstances of Pettijohn's demise. However, considering the widow's habitually improper conduct, no one was surprised by her nose-thumbing of time-honored ritual.

The morning dawned hazy and hot. By ten o'clock, St. Philip's Episcopal Church was packed to capacity. The famous and infamous were there, as were those who had come to gawk at the famous and infamous, including South Carolina's venerable United States senator and a movie star who lived in Beaufort.

Some had never met Pettijohn, but deemed themselves important enough to attend an important man's funeral. Almost without exception, most of those in attendance had disparaged the deceased when he was alive. Nevertheless, they filed into the church shaking their heads and mourning his tragic, untimely death. The altar was barely large enough to accommodate the plethora of floral arrangements.

At exactly ten o'clock, the widow was escorted to the front pew. She was wearing black from head to toe, unrelieved by anything except her signature string of pearls. Her hair had been pulled back into an unadorned ponytail, over which she wore a wide-brimmed straw hat that obscured her face. Throughout the service she kept on dark, opaque sunglasses.

"Is she hiding her eyes because they're swollen from crying? Or because they're not?"

Steffi Mundell was seated next to Smilow. Her question caused him to frown. His head was bowed and he appeared actually to be listening to the opening prayer.

"Sorry," she whispered. "I didn't know you had a religious streak."

She remained respectfully silent throughout the remainder of the service, even though she professed no religion. She wasn't as interested in the afterlife as much as she was in the present one. She wished her ambitions to be realized here on earth. Stars in a heavenly crown weren't her idea of achievement.

So, tuning out the scripture readings and eulogies, she used the hour to mull over the pertinent aspects of the case, specifically how she could use them to her advantage.

The case had been assigned to Hammond, but it was she, not him, who had placed a call to Solicitor Mason last evening. She had apologized for interrupting his dinner, but when she told him about Alex Ladd's lie regarding her whereabouts Saturday night, he thanked her for keeping him apprised. She was satisfied that the call had earned her a few brownie points. Taking it one step further, she had assured their boss that Hammond probably would have given him this latest update sometime today . . . when he got around to it . . . intimating that Hammond wouldn't have given it priority.

After what seemed as long as the eternity the minister extolled, the memorial service concluded. As they stood, Steffi said, "Now, isn't that sweet?" From everyone clustered around Davee Pettijohn to pay their respects, she singled out Hammond. The widow embraced him warmly. He kissed her cheek.

"Old family friends," Smilow remarked.

"How good of friends?"

"Why?"

"He seems reluctant to consider her a viable suspect."

They continued to watch as Mr. and Mrs. Preston Cross also embraced Davee. Steffi had met the couple only once at a golf tournament. Hammond had introduced her to his parents not as his girlfriend but as his co-worker. She had admired Preston, seeing in him a strong, daunting personality. Amelia Cross, Hammond's mother, was her husband's direct counterpart, a small, sweet southern lady who probably had never expressed an independent opinion in her life. She probably had never formed an independent opinion in her life.

"See?" Smilow said. "The Crosses are Davee's surrogate family since she has none here."

"I guess."

Because of the crowd, it took them several minutes to get outside. "What have you got against Davee?" Smilow asked as they made their way toward his car. "Now that she's no longer on your list of suspects."

"Who said that?" Steffi opened the passenger door and got in.

Smilow settled behind the steering wheel. "I thought Alex Ladd was your suspect of choice."

"She is. But I'm not ruling out the merry widow, either. Can we have some A.C. please?" she asked, fanning her face. "Have you confronted Davee with her housekeeper's lie?"

"One of my men did. It seems that Sarah Birch's trip to the supermarket that day had completely slipped their minds."

With exaggerated sincerity, Steffi said, "Oh, I'm sure that's true."

They drove several blocks before Smilow surprised her by quietly saying, "We found a human hair."

"In the suite?"

"On the sleeve of Pettijohn's jacket." He glanced at her and actually laughed at her expression. "Don't get too excited. He could have picked it up off the furniture. It could belong to any guest who has previously been in that room, or any housekeeper, room service waiter. Anybody."

"But if it matches Alex Ladd's—"

"You're back to her, I see."

"If it matches her hair—"

"We don't know yet that it does."

"We know she lied!" Steffi exclaimed.

"There could be dozens of reasons for that."

"Now you sound like Hammond."

"The amateur sleuth."

Steffi listened as he told her about finding Hammond in the hotel suite the night before. "What was he doing there?"

"Looking around."

"At what?"

"At everything, I guess. A sly insinuation that I had missed something."

"What were you doing there?"

Somewhat sheepishly he said, "I might have missed something."

"Testosterone!" she scoffed. "What it does to otherwise reasonable *Homo sapiens.*" After a beat, she added, "For instance, look how it colors your opinion of Alex Ladd."

"What's that mean?"

"If Alex Ladd wasn't a noted doctor with a long list of credentials, if she weren't so educated and attractive and articulate, so damn poised, if instead she was a tough girl with teased hair and tattoos on her tits, would you two be this reluctant to apply more pressure?"

"I won't even honor that question with an answer."

"Then why are you soft-pedaling?"

"Because I can't make an arrest based solely on a lie about her going to Hilton Head Island. I've got to have more than that, Steffi, and you know it. Specifically I've got to place her in that room. I need hard evidence."

"Like a weapon."

"Working on it."

Continuing to study his profile, a slow smile broke across her face. "Come on, Smilow, what gives? You've practically got yellow feathers sticking out of your mouth."

"You'll find out the latest development when everybody else does."

"When will that be?"

"This afternoon. I've asked Dr. Ladd to come in for further questioning. Against her solicitor's advice, she has agreed."

"Without realizing she's walking into a carefully laid trap." Feeling buoyant again, Steffi laughed. "When you spring it, I can't wait to see her face."

Her face mirrored complete surprise, just as Hammond's did.

The way it came about was crazy.

Hammond, Steffi, Smilow, and Frank Perkins were congregated outside Smilow's office waiting for Alex to arrive. Steffi complained of leaving a file on the desk sergeant's counter. Feeling claustrophobic, Hammond quickly offered to go downstairs and retrieve it for her.

He left the Criminal Investigation Division on the second floor and went to the elevators. The doors slid open. The only occupant was Alex, obviously on her way to Smilow's office. They looked at each other for one stunned second before Hammond stepped in and punched the button to go down.

The doors closed, sealing them inside the small, confined space. He could smell her fragrance. He noted everything at once—hair, face, form. Her tousled hairstyle, soft makeup, and compact figure lent femininity to the tailored business suit she was wearing. The jacket was sleeveless. Her skin looked smooth and soft. Her skin *was* smooth and soft. On her arms. Breasts. Behind her knees. Everywhere.

Her eyes were as busy as his, touching on every feature of his face, exactly as they had at the gas station seconds before he kissed her. That was part of her sexiness, that seemingly total absorption in whatever her eyes focused on. The intensity with which she looked at him made him feel as though his face were the most captivating visage in the world.

He began. "Saturday night—"

"Please don't ask me—"

"Why did you lie about where you were?"

"Would you rather I had told them the truth?"

"What is the truth? Did that man see you standing outside Lute Pettijohn's hotel suite?"

"I can't discuss this with you."

"The hell you can't!"

The doors opened on the first floor. No one was waiting for the elevator. Hammond stepped out, but kept his hand on the rubber bumper to keep the door from closing behind him. "Sarge, did Ms. Mundell leave a file down here?"

"File? I haven't seen anything, Mr. Cross," he called back. "If I see it, I'll have it run up."

"Thanks."

Stepping back into the elevator, he depressed the button for them to go back up. The doors closed.

"The hell you can't," he repeated in a harsh whisper.

"We've got a few precious seconds. Is this what you want to be talking about?"

"No. Hell, no." He took one step nearer and growled softly, "I want to be all over you."

She raised her hand to the base of her throat. "I can't breathe."

"That's what you said the second time you came. Or was it the third?"

"Stop. Please stop."

"That's one thing you didn't say. Not the whole damn night. So why did you sneak out on me?"

"For the same reason I had to lie about being with you."

"Pettijohn? I know you didn't kill him. The time doesn't fit. But in some way you're culpable."

"I had to leave you that morning. And we can't be caught talking privately now."

"If you weren't somehow implicated," he said, taking another step closer, "why would you need to establish an alibi by spending the night fucking me?"

Anger sparked in her eyes. Her lips parted as though she were about to refute him. The elevator came to a stop. The doors opened. Steffi Mundell was waiting for it.

"Oh," she exclaimed softly when she saw the two of them together. She sliced her eyes over to Alex, then back to Hammond. "Uh, I was just coming to get you. I found it," she said, absently raising her hand to show him the file she had mistakenly sent him to retrieve. "Sorry."

"Doesn't matter."

"Excuse me," Alex said, stepping between them so she could get out.

"Mr. Perkins is already here, Dr. Ladd," Steffi told her as she moved past.

She acknowledged that information with a dignified thank-you, then continued down the hallway toward the secured double doors.

"Where did you two hook up?"

Steffi's question set his teeth on edge, but he tried not to show it. "She was downstairs waiting on the elevator," he lied.

"Oh. Well, I guess everybody's here now, so we can start."

"Stall them a few minutes longer. I gotta use the men's room."

Hammond went into the rest room, glad to see that it wasn't in use. At the sink, he bent from the waist and splashed cold water onto his face, then braced his hands on the cool porcelain and hung his head between his shoulders, letting the water drip from his face into the basin. He took several deep breaths, releasing them on a stream of low curses.

He had requested a few minutes, but it was going to take longer than that to restore himself. Actually he would probably never be free of the tight band of guilt squeezing his chest and restricting his breathing.

What was he going to do? This time last week, he had never even heard of this woman. Now Alex Ladd was the eye of a maelstrom that threatened to suck him under and drown him.

He saw no way out. He hadn't committed just one malfeasance; he had compounded it, and he continued to. If he had come clean when he first saw the sketch of her, he might have redeemed himself.

*"Smilow, Steffi, you are not going to believe this! I spent the night with this woman Saturday night. Now you're telling me that she bumped off Lute Pettijohn before luring me into bed?"*

He might have weathered the storm if he had admitted his culpability early on. After all, when he took her to his cabin he hadn't known she would later be implicated in a crime. He had been the innocent victim of a carefully planned seduction.

He might have been ridiculed for taking a total stranger to bed. He might have been censured for being indiscreet. His father would have accused him of being just plain stupid. Hadn't he taught him better than to have sexual intercourse with a woman he didn't know? Hadn't he warned him about the calamities that could befall a young man at the hands of a devious female?

It would have been embarrassing for him, his family, and the solicitor's office. He would have been the hot topic of gossip and the butt of a thousand lewd jokes, but he would have survived it.

But the point was moot. He hadn't revealed her identity, and he hadn't exposed her when she lied about a nonexistent trip to Hilton Head. He had stood there, juggling duty and desire, and desire had won. He had consciously and deliberately withheld information that could be a key element to a homicide case, just as he had omitted telling Monroe Mason about his Saturday afternoon meeting with Pettijohn. According to any prosecutor's rule book, his conduct over the last few days was unforgivable.

What was even worse, given the opportunity to rethink those decisions, he feared he would make the same wrong choices.

Alex distrusted the polite manner in which Smilow pulled out a chair for her. He wanted to know if she was comfortable, if she would like something to drink.

"Mr. Smilow, please stop treating this like a social visit. The only reason I'm here is because you requested it, and I felt it was my civic responsibility to grant that request."

"Very commendable."

Frank Perkins said, "Let's dispense with the pleasantries and get on with it, shall we?"

"Fine." Smilow resumed his position of the day before on the corner of his desk, a distinct and calculated advantage because it forced Alex to look up at him.

When the door opened behind her, she knew that Hammond had come in. His vitality stirred the air in a particular way. She hadn't fully recovered from being alone with him again. Those moments in the elevator had been brief, but their impact was profound.

Her reaction had been physical and apparently noticeable, because when she joined Frank Perkins, he had commented on her flushed cheeks and asked if she was feeling all right. She had blamed the heat outside. But the weather hadn't caused her blush any more than it had brought on the tingling in the erogenous parts of her body.

Those sexual and emotional stirrings were coupled with the guilt she harbored for unfairly placing Hammond in such a dilemma. She had deliberately compromised him.

*Initially,* she emphasized to her conscience. *Only initially.* Then biology had taken over.

And she could feel the tug of it now that he had entered the room.

She curbed the impulse to turn around and look at him, afraid that Steffi Mundell might detect that something was afoot. The prosecutor had seemed avidly inquisitive when she saw them together in the elevator. Alex had tried to seem unperturbed as she alighted, but she'd felt Steffi's stare like a branding iron between her shoulder blades as she walked down the hallway. If anyone picked up the signals she and Hammond inadvertently gave off, it would be Steffi Mundell. Not only because she came across as being sharp as a razor, but because, generally speaking, women were more attuned to romantic frequencies than men.

Alex was brought back to attention when Smilow turned on the tape recorder and recited the day and time along with the names of those present. He then handed her a laminated newspaper clipping. "I'd like for you to read this, Dr. Ladd."

Curious, her eyes scanned the short headline. She had to read no further than that to realize that she had made a dreadful blunder and that it was going to cost her dearly.

"Why don't you read it out loud?" Smilow suggested. "I'd like for Mr. Perkins to hear it also."

Knowing the detective was trying to humiliate her, she kept her voice even and emotionless as she read the story about the evacuation and shutdown of Harbour Town on Hilton Head, at the precise time she had told them she was there taking in the attractions. When she finished, a long, weighty silence ensued.

Finally, in a very quiet voice, Perkins asked to see the clipping. She passed it to him, but she kept her eyes on Smilow, refusing to submit to his accusatory gaze. "Well?"

"Well, what, Detective?"

"You lied to us, didn't you, Dr. Ladd?"

"You don't have to answer," Frank Perkins told her.

"Where were you late Saturday afternoon and evening?"

"Don't answer, Alex," her attorney instructed again.

"But I would like to, Frank."

"I strongly urge you not to say anything."

"There's no harm in my answering." Heedless of his advice, she said, "I had planned to go to Hilton Head, but at the last minute I changed my mind."

"Why?"

"Caprice. I went instead to a fair outside of Beaufort."

"A fair?"

"A carnival, which can be easily checked out, Mr. Smilow. I'm certain it was advertised. It was a large event. That's where I went after leaving Charleston."

"Can anyone vouch for that?"

"I doubt it. There were hundreds of people there. It's unlikely anyone would remember me."

"Sort of like that ice-cream scooper on Hilton Head."

Smilow didn't seem to appreciate Steffi Mundell's remark any more than Alex did. They both shot her an angry look before Smilow continued. "If you saw advertisements for the fair, you could be making this up, couldn't you?"

"I suppose I could, but I'm not."

"Why should we believe this when we've already caught you in one lie?"

"It doesn't make any difference where I was. I've told you that I didn't even know Lute Pettijohn. I certainly know nothing about his murder."

"She didn't even know the method by which he died," Frank Perkins interjected.

"Yes, we all remember your client's stunned reaction to the fact that Pettijohn was shot."

Alex burned under Smilow's sardonic gaze, but she maintained her composure. "I left Charleston with every intention of going to Hilton Head. When I came upon the fair, I made a spur-of-the-moment decision to stop there instead."

"If it was so innocent, why did you lie about it?"

*First for my own protection. Then to protect Hammond Cross.*

If they wanted the truth, that was it. But Hammond Cross's obligation for truth-telling was more binding than hers, and he had maintained his silence. Upset following her encounter with Bobby last night, she had lain awake thinking about her predicament.

After torturous deliberation, she had concluded that if she could keep Bobby at arm's length, she would be all right. No connection could be made between her and Pettijohn. As long as Hammond believed in her innocence, her whereabouts on Saturday night would remain their secret, because he would think it irrelevant.

But if ever he was convinced of her guilt, it would be his obligation as a prosecutor . . .

She didn't allow herself to think about that. For now, she would continue cooperating with Smilow until, she hoped, he gave up on her having any involvement and redirected his investigation.

"It was silly of me to lie, Mr. Smilow," she said. "I guess I thought that a trip to Hilton Head sounded more convincing than a stop-over at a county fair."

"Why did you feel the need to convince us?"

Frank Perkins held up a hand, but Alex said, "Because I'm unaccustomed to being interrogated by the police. I was nervous."

"Forgive me, Dr. Ladd," Smilow said wryly. "But you're the least nervous person I have ever questioned. We've all commented on it. Ms.

Mundell, Mr. Cross, and I all have agreed that you're remarkably composed for someone under suspicion of murder."

Unsure if he meant that as an insult or a compliment, she didn't respond. It made her uneasy to know that they had discussed her. What had Hammond's "comments" on her been? she wondered. She had certainly provided him a lot to talk about, hadn't she?

*"You're a fraud, you know."*

*"I beg your pardon." Pretending to be affronted, she grabbed two handfuls of his hair and tried to lift his head. But he was unyielding.*

*"You come across as a woman who's all calm, cool, and collected." The stubble on his chin lightly scratched her tummy. "That's what I thought after I rescued you from the marines. This is one cool chick."*

*She laughed. "Between a fraud and a chick, I'm not sure which is the most offensive."*

*"But in bed," he continued, undeterred both in his vein of conversation and his intent, "your participation is anything but contained."*

*"It's hard—"*

*"It certainly is," he groaned. "But it can wait."*

*"—to keep one's composure when . . ."*

*"When?"*

*"When . . ." Then his tongue touched her and her composure was shattered.*

"You went to this fair alone?"

"What?" For one horrifying moment, she feared she had gasped out loud, echoing her orgasm. Even more horrifying, she had unintentionally turned and was looking at Hammond. His eyes were hot, as though he had been following her thoughts. A blood vessel in his temple was distended and ticking.

She whipped her head back around to Smilow, who repeated his question. "You went to this fair alone?"

"Yes. Yes, alone. That's right."

"And you remained alone throughout the evening?"

Looking into Rory Smilow's implacable eyes, it was difficult to lie. "Yes."

"You didn't join a friend there? You didn't meet anyone?"

"As I said, Mr. Smilow, alone."

He paused for a beat. "What time did you leave? Alone."

"When the attractions began closing. I don't remember the exact time."

"Where did you go from there?"

Frank Perkins said, "Irrelevant. This whole interrogation is irrelevant and improper. There's no basis for it, so it doesn't matter where Alex was, or whether or not she was alone. She doesn't have to account for her whereabouts on Saturday evening any more than you do, because you still can't place her inside Pettijohn's hotel suite. She's told you she didn't even know him.

"It's appalling that someone with her impeccable reputation and high standing in the community is being subjected to questioning. Some guy from Macon claims to have seen her at a time when his bowels were about to burst. Do you honestly consider him a reliable witness, Smilow? If you do, then you've lowered your own rigid standards of criminal investigation. In any event, you've inconvenienced my client all you're going to." The lawyer motioned for Alex to stand.

"That was a nice speech, Frank, but we're not done here. My investigators have caught Dr. Ladd in another lie that concerns the murder weapon."

Vexed but wary, Frank Perkins backed down. "It better be good."

"It is." Smilow turned back to her. "Dr. Ladd, you told us yesterday that you don't own a gun."

"I don't."

From a file, he produced a registration form, which Alex recognized. She scanned it, then passed it to Frank for his perusal. "I bought a pistol for protection. As you can see by the date, that was years ago. I no longer have it."

"What happened to it?"

"Alex?" Frank Perkins leaned forward, a question in his eyes.

"It's all right," she assured him. "Beyond a few rudimentary lessons, I never even fired it. I kept it in a holster beneath the driver's seat of my car and rarely thought about it. I even forgot about it when I traded the car in on a newer model.

"It wasn't until weeks after the trade-in that I remembered the revolver was still beneath the seat. I called the dealership and explained to the manager what had happened. He offered to ask around. No one claimed to have any knowledge of it. I figured that someone cleaning the car, possibly even the person who later purchased it, had found the gun, thought 'finders-keepers,' and never returned it."

"It's a pistol that fires the caliber bullet that killed Lute Pettijohn."

"A .38, yes. Hardly a collector's item, Mr. Smilow."

He smiled the cold smile she had come to associate with him. "Granted." He rubbed his brow as though worried. "But here we've got proof of your owning a pistol, and an uncorroborated story of how you came to lose it. You were spotted at the scene about the time Mr. Pettijohn died. We've caught you in one lie about where you were that evening. And you haven't provided an alibi." He raised his shoulders. "Look at it from my perspective. All these circumstantial elements are beginning to add up."

"To what?"

"To you being our killer."

Alex opened her mouth to protest but was dismayed to find that she couldn't speak. Frank Perkins spoke for her. "Are you prepared to book her, Smilow?"

He stared down at her for a long moment. "Not just yet."

"Then we're leaving." This time the lawyer didn't leave room for argument. Not that Alex felt like arguing. She was frightened, although she tried to keep her fear from showing.

An important part of her job was reading the expressions of her patients and interpreting their body language in order to gauge what they were thinking, which often differed from what they were saying. How they stood, or sat, or moved frequently contradicted their verbal assertions. Moreover, when they spoke, their phrasing and inflection sometimes conveyed more than the words themselves.

She applied her expertise to reading Smilow now. His face could have been carved from marble. Without even a nod toward diplomacy, he had looked her straight in the eye and accused her of murder. Only someone with absolute confidence in what he was doing could be that resolute and unemotional.

Steffi Mundell, on the other hand, seemed ready to hop up and down and clap her hands in glee. Based on her experience of reading people, Alex could say accurately that the police felt the situation was definitely in their favor.

But their reactions weren't as important to her as Hammond Cross's. With a mix of anticipation and dread, she turned toward the door and looked at him.

One shoulder was propped against the wall. His ankles were crossed. His arms were folded over his midriff. The straighter of his two eyebrows was drawn down low, almost into a scowl. To an untrained eye, he might appear comfortable, even insouciant.

But readily apparent to Alex were the emotions roiling dangerously close to the surface. He wasn't nearly as relaxed as he wanted to appear. The hooded eyes, the clenched jaw were dead giveaways. His folded arms and crossed ankles weren't components of an indolent pose.

Indeed, they seemed essential to holding him together.

H E WAS A CASTING DIRECTOR'S DREAM for the role of "the nerd." First because of his name—Harvey Knuckle. It was an open invitation to ridicule. Knuckle-head. What have you got for lunch today, Harvey, Knuckle-sandwiches? No-nuts-Knuckle. Let's pop our Knuckle. Classmates and later co-workers had coined a variety of such taunts and they'd been merciless.

In addition to his name, Harvey Knuckle looked the part. Everything about him fit the stereotype. His eyeglasses were thick. He was pale and skinny and had chronic post-nasal drip. He wore a bow tie every day. When Charleston's weather turned cold, he wore argyle V-neck sweaters beneath tweed jackets. In the summer they were substituted for short-sleeved shirts and seersucker suits.

His one saving grace, which ironically was also stereotypical, was that he was a computer genius. The very people around city hall who poked the most fun at him were at his mercy when their computers went on the fritz. A familiar refrain was, "Call Knuckle. Get him over here."

On Tuesday evening, he entered the Shady Rest Lounge, shaking out his wet umbrella and apprehensively squinting into the smog of tobacco smoke.

Loretta Boothe, who had been watching for him, felt a twinge of sympathy. Harvey was a disagreeable little twerp, but he was entirely out of his element in the Shady Rest. He relaxed only marginally when he spotted her coming toward him.

"I thought I'd written down the wrong address. What a horrible place. Even the name sounds like a cemetery."

"Thank you for coming, Harvey. It's good to see you." Before he could bolt, which he appeared to be on the verge of doing, Loretta grabbed his arm and dragged him toward a booth. "Welcome to my office."

Still jittery, he propped his wet umbrella beneath the table, readjusted the lapels of his jacket, and pushed his eyeglasses up his long, narrow nose. Now that his eyes had adjusted to the gloom and he had gotten a better look at the other customers, he shuddered. "You're not afraid to come here alone? The clientele appear to be the dregs of society."

"Harvey, I *am* the clientele."

Abashed, he began stammering an apology.

Loretta laughed. "No offense taken. Relax. What you need is a drink." She signaled the bartender.

Harvey folded his delicate hands on the table. "That would be nice, thank you. A short one. I can't stay long. I'm allergic to secondhand smoke."

She ordered him a whiskey sour and a club soda for herself. Noticing his surprise, she said, "I'm on the wagon."

"Really? I had heard you . . . I had heard otherwise."

"I've had a recent conversion."

"Well, good for you."

"Not so good, Harvey. Cold turkey sucks. I hate it."

Her candor made him laugh. "You always were a straight shooter, Loretta, and you haven't changed. I've missed seeing you around. Do you miss the P.D.?"

"Sometimes. Not the people. The work. I miss that."

"Are you still doing some private investigating?"

"Yes, I'm freelancing." She hesitated. "That's why I called and asked you to meet me."

He moaned. "I knew it. I said to myself, 'Harvey, you're going to regret accepting this invitation.'"

"But your curiosity got the best of you, didn't it?" she teased. "That and recollections of my ready wit."

"Loretta, please don't ask me for a favor."

"Harvey, please don't be such a goddamn hypocrite."

Officially he was a county employ, but his computer access also allowed him to delve into city and state records. He had so much information at his fingertips, he was frequently approached by people willing to pay handsomely to know their co-workers' salaries, or such. But Harvey refused to be part of anything unethical or illegal. To anyone who came to him trying to wheedle a favor, he was irritatingly adamant in his refusal.

That's why Loretta's blunt statement shocked him. He blinked rapidly behind the thick lenses of his glasses.

"You're not the good little boy you would have everyone believe."

"How altogether boorish of you to remind me of my one little indiscretion."

"The only one I know about," she said intuitively. "I still think you pulled the plug, so to speak, on that asshole who hassled you at the Christmas party. Come on, now, Harvey, fess up. Didn't you retaliate by scrambling all his programs?"

He pursed his lips.

"Never mind." She chuckled. "I don't blame you for not confessing, but your secret would be safe with me. In fact, I like you better for showing a weakness. I can identify with human frailty." She wagged her finger at him. "You love the thrill you derive from occasionally breaking the rules. It's how you get your rocks off."

"What horrid terminology! Furthermore, it's untrue." Despite his public avowal to be a teetotaler, he quaffed his drink and didn't object when she ordered another round.

As a policewoman working overtime in county records one night, she had caught Harvey Knuckle in his superior's office, scrolling through his personal finance files and sipping from his secreted bottle of brandy.

The little man had been mortified to be caught red-handed doing the very thing he vowed never to do for someone else. Barely able to contain her laughter, Loretta had assured him that she had no intention of tattling and had wished him good luck on his treasure hunt.

The next time she approached him needing a favor, Harvey didn't hesitate to grant it. From that night on, whenever she needed information, she went to Harvey. He never failed to produce. She had been tapping that valuable resource ever since.

"I know I can count on you, Harvey."

"I'm making no promises," he said prissily. "You're no longer with the police department. That changes things significantly."

"This is very important." She scooted forward on her bench and whispered confidentially, "I'm working on the Pettijohn murder case."

He gaped at her, absently thanked the bartender who delivered his drink to the table, and took a quick sip. "You don't say?"

"It's very hush-hush. You can't breathe a word of this to a single soul."

"You know you have my confidence," he whispered back. "Who're you working for?"

"I'm not at liberty to say."

"They haven't made an arrest yet, have they? Are they close to making one?"

"I'm sorry, Harvey. I can't discuss it. It would violate my client's confidence if I did."

"I understand the necessity for confidentiality, I do."

He wasn't all that disappointed. The intrigue kindled his unappeased sense of adventure. Being let in on a secret, to any extent, gave him a place in an inner circle when he was excluded from most. It twinged Loretta's conscience a little to manipulate him this way, but she was willing to do just about anything to please Hammond and make up for her past mistake.

"What I need is everything you can unearth on a Dr. Alex Ladd. Middle initial E. I also have her Social Security number, driver's license number, and so on. She's a psychologist who practices here in Charleston."

"A shrink? Is that her connection to Pettijohn?"

"I can't tell you."

"Loretta," he whined.

"Because I don't know. I swear. So far all I've got on her is the run-of-the-mill stuff. Income tax returns, banking records, credit cards. Nothing out of joint on any of them. She owns her home, has no major debts. No one's suing her. She hasn't even had a traffic ticket. Her university and postgrad transcripts are impressive. She was an excellent student and had offers to join several existing practices. However, she opted to set up her own."

"Just starting out? She must come from money."

"She inherited a wad from her adoptive parents, one Dr. Marion Ladd, a general practitioner in Nashville. Wife Cynthia, a teacher turned homemaker. They had no other children. They were killed several years ago in a commuter plane crash during a skiing trip in Utah."

"Was foul play suspected?"

Loretta hid her smile behind a sip of her club soda. Harvey was getting into the spirit of the project. "No."

"Hmm. It sounds to me as though you have quite a lot already."

Loretta shook her head. "I know nothing about her early life. She wasn't adopted until she was fifteen."

"That old?"

"Oddly, that's when it seems her life began. The circumstances of her adoption and her life prior to it are a black hole. It's giving up no information, and I've had no luck trying to penetrate it."

"Huh," Harvey said, taking another quick slurp of his drink.

"She attended a private high school. The people I talked to there—and I worked my way up the chain of command—were nice and polite but tight-lipped. They wouldn't even commit to sending me a yearbook of her graduating year. Very into protecting the Ladds' privacy and wouldn't talk about them at all.

"According to everything I read about them, they were highly respected and above reproach. Cynthia Ladd was awarded Teacher of the Year before she left the profession. Dr. Ladd's patients mourned him when he died. He was a church deacon. She . . . Never mind, you get the idea. No scandal or even close to one."

"So what can I do?"

"Get into the juvenile records."

Again he groaned theatrically. "I was afraid you were going to say that."

"There's probably nothing there. I just want you to take a look."

"Just looking could get me fired. You know how CPS is," he whined. "They guard those records like they're holy relics. They're not to be tampered with."

"Not by anyone less than a genius who won't get caught. I need them from Tennessee, too."

"Forget it!"

"I know you can do it," she said, reaching across the table to pat his hand.

"If Child Protection finds out what I was doing, I could get into a lot of trouble."

"I have every confidence in you, Harvey."

He was viciously gnawing his lip, but she could see that he was enticed by the challenge it presented. "I'll agree to try, that's all. I'll try. Also, something this delicate can't be rushed."

"I understand. Take your time. But hurry." She downed her club soda and belched softly. "And Harvey, while you're at it . . ."

He grimaced. "Uh-oh."

"I want you to check on something else for me."

"It's Smilow."

"You'll have to speak up," Steffi told him. "I'm on my cell."

"So am I. A guy at SLED just called."

"Good news?"

"For everybody except Dr. Ladd."

"What? What? Tell me."

"Remember the unidentified particle John Madison took off Pettijohn?"

"You told me about it."

"Clove."

"The spice?"

"When did you last see a spike of clove?"

"Easter. On my mother's ham."

"I saw some yesterday morning when I went to Alex Ladd's house. There was a cut-glass bowl of fresh oranges on her entry table. They were spiked with cloves."

"We've got her!"

"Not yet, but we're getting closer."

"What about the hair?"

"Human, not Pettijohn's. But we don't have one to compare it to."

"Not yet."

He chuckled. "Sleep tight, Steffi."

"Wait, are you going to call Hammond with this update?"

"Are you?"

After a pause, she said, "See you tomorrow."

Hammond seriously considered not answering the telephone. He changed his mind seconds before the machine kicked in. Immediately he regretted it.

"I was beginning to think you weren't going to answer." His father's tone of voice turned the simple statement into a reprimand.

"I was in the shower," Hammond lied. "What's up?"

"I'm in my car on my way back home. I just dropped your mother off at her bridge game. I didn't want her driving in this rain."

His parents had an old-fashioned marriage. The roles were traditional, clearly defined, and the lines never blurred. His father made all the major decisions independently; it would never have occurred to Amelia Cross to challenge that arrangement. Hammond couldn't understand her blind devotion to an archaic system that robbed her of individuality, but she seemed perfectly content with it. He would never enflame his father or hurt his mother by pointing out the inequities of their relationship. Besides, his opinion of it didn't matter. It had worked for them for more than forty years.

"How are things going with the Pettijohn case?"

"Fine," Hammond replied.

Preston chuckled. "Could you elaborate a little?"

"Why?"

"I'm curious. I played nine holes with your boss this afternoon before it started raining. He said Smilow has questioned a female suspect twice, and that you were present both times."

His father was more than idly curious. He wanted to know if his son was performing competently. "I'd rather not discuss it over a cell phone."

"Don't be silly. I want to know what's going on."

Trying to keep from sounding too defensive, Hammond gave him the highlights of Alex's interrogation. "Her lawyer—"

"Frank Perkins. Good man."

Preston was well apprised of the details. Hammond knew he wasn't violating any confidentiality because it had already been violated. Preston's friendship with Monroe Mason dated back to prep school days. If they had played nine holes of golf today, Mason would have already divulged the details, and there would be little left for Hammond to disclose.

"Perkins thinks we've got nothing on her."

"What do you think?"

Hammond chose his words carefully, not knowing when something he said would come back to haunt—or trap—him. Unlike Alex, he wasn't an accomplished liar. It wasn't his habit to lie, and he disdained even the slightest fib. Yet he already had two whoppers of omission to his credit. He discovered he could lie to his father with relative ease.

"She's been caught in a couple of lies, but in Frank's able hands, they would probably be disregarded."

"Why?"

"Because of our side's failure to produce hard evidence linking her to the crime."

"Mason says she lied about where she was that night."

"Mason didn't leave anything out, did he?" Hammond said under his breath.

"What's that?"

"Nothing."

"Why would she lie if she doesn't have something to hide?"

Feeling cavalier and ornery, Hammond said, "Maybe she had a secret rendezvous that night, and she's lying to protect the man she was with."

"Maybe. In any event she's lied, and Smilow is right on top of it. I know you don't like him, but you've got to admit that he's an excellent detective."

"I can't argue that."

"He's got a law degree, you know."

Hammond recognized that as one of those statements that his father threw out like a quick jab to the face. It was intended to distract you from the right uppercut that was coming.

"I hope he never decides to move from the police department over to the solicitor's office. You might find yourself out of a job, son."

Hammond ground his teeth to keep from saying the two words that flashed through his mind.

"I told your mother—"

"You discussed the case with Mom?"

"Why not?"

"Because . . . because it's unfair."

"To whom?"

"To everybody concerned. The police, my office, the suspect. What if this woman is innocent, Dad? Her reputation will have been trampled for nothing."

"Why are you so upset, Hammond?"

"I hope Mom doesn't regale her bridge club with all the juicy details of the case."

"You're overreacting."

Maybe he was, but the longer this telephone conversation got, the more it was pissing him off. Mostly because he didn't want his father monitoring him through every step of this case. A murder trial of this magnitude consumed a lawyer's life. Hours stretched into days, and days into weeks, sometimes months. He could handle it. He would relish handling it. But he wouldn't welcome being critiqued at the end of each day. That could become demoralizing and cause him to start second-guessing every strategy.

"Dad, I know what I'm doing."

"No one ever questioned—"

"Bullshit. You bring my ability into question every time you consult with Mason and ask him for a report. If he weren't pleased with the work I've done, he wouldn't have assigned me to this case. He certainly wouldn't be touting me as his successor."

"Everything you've said is true," Preston said with maddening control. "All the more reason for me to be worried that you'll blow it."

"Why would you think I might blow it?"

"I understand the suspect is a beautiful woman."

Hammond hadn't seen that one coming. If it had been an actual uppercut, it would have been a knockout and he would be on the mat. He reeled from the impact. One hundred percent of the time, his father seemed to know where to strike him where he would feel it the most.

"That's the most insulting thing you've ever said to me."

"Listen, Hammond, I'm—"

"No, you listen. I will do my job. If this case warrants the death penalty, that's what I'll ask for."

"Will you?"

"Absolutely. Just as I'll indict you if my investigation warrants it."

After a slight pause, Preston said softly, "Don't bluff me, Hammond."

"Call it, Dad. See if I'm bluffing."

"Then do it. Just be sure to examine your motives first."

"Meaning?"

"Meaning, be certain you have substantial evidence and not just a petty grudge. Don't cause us both a lot of time, effort, and embarrassment just because you're pissed off at me for being hard on you. I would never be convicted. In your attempt to spite me, you'd only be spiting yourself."

Hammond's fingers had turned white and were aching from gripping the telephone receiver so hard. "Your phone is cutting out. Goodbye."

*   *   *

Ignoring the rain, Alex had decided to go out for a run. Through the downpour, her legs pumped at a steady pace. Adherence to her exercise regimen seemed essential when the rest of her life had been pitched into chaos. Besides, after seeing rescheduled patients late into the evening, it gave her a physical outlet for cerebral overload. It cleared her head and allowed her mind to wander freely.

She worried about her patients. If and when it became public that she was a suspect in a murder case, what would happen to them? What would they think of her? Would it change their opinion of her? Naturally it would. It wouldn't be realistic to hope that they would disregard her involvement with a murder investigation.

Maybe she should begin as early as tomorrow trying to place them with interim therapists so there would be no suspension of their treatment if she were to be incarcerated.

On the other hand, finding replacements for them might not become her problem. When they learned that their psychologist had been accused of murder, they would probably leave her practice in flocks.

As she ran past a car parked at the curb only a half block from her house, she noticed that the windows were fogged, indicating that someone was inside the vehicle. The motor was idling, although the headlights were out and the windshield wipers were still.

She ran another twenty yards or so before glancing back. The car lights were now on. It was turning onto a side street.

Probably nothing, she told herself. She was just being paranoid. But her apprehension lingered. *Was* someone watching her?

The police, for instance. Smilow might have ordered surveillance. Wouldn't that be standard operating procedure? Or Bobby could be watching her to make certain she wouldn't abscond with "his money." It hadn't been his convertible she'd just seen, but he was resourceful.

There was another possibility. One much more threatening. One that she didn't want to entertain, but knew it would be foolish and naive not to. It hadn't escaped her that she might be of interest to Lute Pettijohn's murderer. If it got out that she had been identified at the scene, the killer might fear she had witnessed the killing.

The thought made her shiver, and not strictly because she feared a murderer. Her life was presently out of her control. That's what she feared most—that loss of control. In its way, that was a death more real than death itself. Living, but having no choices or free will, could be even worse than being dead.

Twenty years ago, she had determined that her life would never again be given over to someone else to manage. It had taken her almost that long to convince herself that she was finally free of the bonds that had fettered her, that she alone would chart her destiny.

Then Bobby had reappeared and everything had changed. Now it seemed that everyone around her had a say-so in her life, and she was powerless to do anything about it.

After a half-hour run, she let herself into the house through a door off the piazza. In the laundry room she stripped off her drenched running clothes, then wrapped herself in a towel for the walk through her house.

She had lived alone all her adult life, so when by herself at home, she was never afraid. Loneliness was more frightening to her than the threat of an intruder. She didn't feel the need to protect herself from burglars, but she steeled herself against the emptiness felt on holidays when even the company of good friends didn't compensate for the lack of a family. Solitude didn't make for coziness even when sitting in front of the fireplace on a cold night. When she was startled awake in the middle of the night, it wasn't because of imagined noises, but because of the all-too-real silence of living alone. The only fear she had of being by herself was of being by herself for the rest of her life.

Tonight, however, she felt slightly ill at ease as she switched out the lights on the lower floor and made her way upstairs. The treads creaked beneath her weight. She was accustomed to the protests of the old wood. Usually a friendly sound, tonight it seemed ominous. On the second-floor landing, she paused to look down the shadowed staircase. The hallway and rooms below were empty and still, exactly as she had left them when she went out to run.

As she continued on into her bedroom, she blamed her nervousness on the rain. After days of oppressive heat, it was a relief, but it was almost too much of a good thing. It was coming down in torrents that pelted windowpanes and hammered against the roof. It spilled over gutters and gushed from the downspouts.

Opening a door onto the second-story piazza, she stepped out to drag a potted gardenia bush beneath the sheltering overhang. Below, in the center of the walled garden, the concrete fountain was overflowing. Flower petals had been beaten off their stalks, leaving the vegetation looking bare and forlorn. Returning inside, she secured the door, then moved from window to window to close the shutters.

The rainfall was enough to make anyone nervous. The Battery had been deserted tonight. Without the usual joggers, bicyclers, and people walking their dogs, she had felt isolated and vulnerable. The large trees in White Point Gardens had seemed looming and menacing, where usually she thought of their low, thick branches as being protective.

In the bathroom, she draped her towel over the brass bar and leaned into the tub to turn on the faucets. It took a while for the hot water to travel through the pipes, so she used that time to brush her teeth. When she straightened up out of the sink, she caught a reflection in the medicine cabinet mirror and whirled around.

It was her robe hanging on a hook on the back of the door.

Knees weak, she leaned against the pedestal sink and ordered herself to stop this silliness. It was so unlike her to jump at shadows. What was wrong with her?

Bobby, for one thing. Damn him. *Damn him!*

Silly or not, she allowed herself the same weaknesses she would have advised a patient to allow himself. When one's carefully constructed world begins to fall apart, one is entitled to a few natural reactions, including bitter anger, even rage, certainly childlike fear.

She remembered being a child afraid. The bogeyman had nothing on Bobby Trimble. Very capably he could destroy lives. He had nearly destroyed hers once, and he was threatening to destroy it again. That's why she feared him, now even more than before.

That's why she could be startled at bathrobes, and lie, and do irresponsible things such as involve a decent man like Hammond Cross in something ugly.

*But only at first, Hammond. Only at the start.*

She stepped into the tub and pulled the curtain. For a long while, she stood beneath the spray, head bowed, letting the hot water drum against her skull while the rising steam swirled around her.

A Saturday night in Harbour Town had seemed like such a safe lie. It placed her a credible distance from Charleston, in a crowded place where it was plausible that no one would remember seeing her. Damn the luck!

What she had told them about the pistol was the truth, but there was little chance of them believing that story now. Having been trapped in one lie, everything she said thereafter would sound untrue.

Steffi Mundell wanted her to be guilty. The prosecutor hated other women. Alex had determined that the instant they met. Her studies had covered personalities like Mundell's. She was ambitious and shrewd and competitive to a fault. Individuals like Steffi were rarely happy because they were never satisfied, not with others, but especially not with themselves. Expectations were never met because the bar was continually being raised. Satisfaction was unattainable. Steffi Mundell was an overachiever to the extreme and to her detriment.

Rory Smilow was harder to read. He was cold, and Alex had no doubt he could be cruel. But she also detected in him an inner demon with which he constantly struggled. The man never knew a moment of inner peace. His outlet was to torment others in an effort to make them as miserable as he. That kernel of discontent left him vulnerable, but he battled it with a vengeance that made him dangerous to his enemies—such as murder suspects.

Between the two of them, it would be hard to choose whom she feared most.

Then there was Hammond. The others thought of her as a murderer. His opinion of her must be even lower than that. But she couldn't dwell on him or she would become immobilized by despondency and remorse. She had no surplus time or energy to devote to regretting what might have been had they met at another time and place.

If ever a man had a chance of touching her—her mind and heart, the spot in her spirit where Alex Ladd really lodged—it might have been him. He might have been the one allowed to relieve the self-imposed loneliness and solitude, fill the emptiness, relieve the silence, share her life.

But romantic notions were a luxury she couldn't afford. Her priority must be to get out of this predicament with her practice, her reputation, and her life intact.

She squeezed fragrant gel into a scrubbing sponge and used the lather liberally. She shaved her legs. She shampooed her hair. She rinsed for a long time, letting the hot water ease her muscles even if it couldn't ease her anxiety.

Eventually she turned off the faucets and sluiced off excess water with her hands, then she whisked back the curtain.

Never one to scream, she did.

## CHAPTER 21

Bobby was in the chips again.

He considered it only a temporary setback that he hadn't yet collected his money from Alex. She would produce. She had too much at stake not to.

In the meantime, however, he wasn't without funds. Thanks to the two coeds with whom he had spent the night, he was several hundred dollars richer. While they lay snoring in his bed, he had packed his belongings and sneaked out. The experience should teach them a valuable lesson. He had felt almost altruistic.

Finding other accommodations was a minor inconvenience when weighed against the reward. As soon as he was settled in another hotel across town, in a room with a river view, he ordered an enormous room-service breakfast of eggs, ham, grits and tasso gravy, a short stack, and an extra portion of hash browns, which he hadn't particularly wanted, but ordered just because he was feeling so flush.

Next on his agenda was a shopping expedition. A new suit of clothes wasn't an extravagance. It was a business expense. If he paid income taxes, he could have counted his wardrobe as an allowable deduction. In his line of work, one had to look sharp.

He had spent the remainder of the afternoon lounging around the hotel pool, working on his tan.

Now, decked out in his new suit of cream-colored linen with a royal blue silk shirt underneath, he entered a bar that had come highly recommended by a cabbie. "Where can I find some action?"

"Action?" Then, sizing Bobby up in the rearview mirror, the taxi driver had drawled, "You're hustling pussy, aren't you, sport?"

Flattered, Bobby smiled in reply.

"I know just the place."

The moment Bobby entered the bar, he realized the driver knew his stuff. This was a place for prime pickings. The music was blaring. Lights flashing. Dancers sweating. Waitresses scrambling to fill the drink orders being placed by people on a desperate quest for fun. Lots of single women. Fair game.

It took him two watered-down drinks before he homed in on his target. She sat at a table alone. No one had asked her to dance. She smiled a lot, to whomever happened to be passing, evidence that she was feeling self-conscious, conspicuous, and in need of someone to talk to. Best of all, she had glanced his way several times while he pretended not to notice.

And then he charitably graced her with a return smile.

Nervously she looked away. Her hand flew to her throat, where she played with the silver beading on the collar of her shirt.

"Bingo," Bobby said to himself as he settled his tab with the bartender.

He came up from behind her, so she didn't see him until he said, "Excuse me. Is someone sitting here?"

Her head came around with a quick snap. She gave away her delight with the widening of her eyes, which she then tried to cover by being flirtatious. "Now there is."

He smiled and joined her at the small table, intentionally bumping her knees with his, then offering a quick apology. He asked if he could buy her a drink, and she said that would be awfully nice of him.

Her name was Ellen Rogers. She was from Indiana and this was her first time in the Deep South. She loved it except for the heat, but even that had a certain charm. The food was divine. She complained of gaining five pounds since she'd been in Charleston.

Although she could have stood to lose fifteen, Bobby said gallantly, "You certainly don't need to watch your weight. I mean, you have a terrific figure."

Slapping his hand, she demurred. "I get plenty of exercise at work."

"Are you an aerobics instructor? Personal trainer?"

"Me? Goodness gracious, no. I'm a middle school teacher. English grammar and remedial reading. I probably walk ten miles a day, going up and down those halls."

He was from the South, she observed correctly. She could tell by his soft drawl and the melodic pattern of his speech. And southern people were *so* friendly.

Smiling, he leaned toward her. "We try, ma'am."

He proved it by inviting her to dance. After they had gyrated through several songs, the DJ played a slow dance. Bobby pulled her against him, apologizing for being so sweaty. She said that she didn't mind at all. Sweat was manly. By the end of the dance, his hand was riding her ass and no way was Miss Ellen Rogers in doubt that he was aroused.

When he released her, her cheeks were red and she was flustered.

"I'm sorry about . . ." he stammered. "It's . . . Lordy, this is embarrassing. I haven't held a woman . . . If you want me to leave you alone, I'll—"

"You don't have to apologize," said Miss Rogers gently. "It's only natural. It's not like you could control it."

"No, ma'am, I couldn't. Not with holding you close against me."

She took his hand and led him back to the table. It was she who ordered another round of drinks. Midway through them, Bobby told her about his wife. "She died of cancer. Two years ago in October."

Her eyes misted. "Oh, how awful for you."

Only recently had he been able to go out and start enjoying life again, he told her. "At first I thought it was good we didn't have kids. Now I sorta wish we had. It's lonesome, you know, being all by yourself in the world. People aren't supposed to be alone. It goes against nature."

Her hand crept beneath the table to give his thigh a sympathetic pat and then stayed there.

*Jesus, I'm good!* Bobby thought.

Hammond was standing on the other side of the shower curtain.

"You scared me half to death!" Alex gasped. "What are you doing here? How'd you get in? How long have you been here?"

"You scared me, too."

"Me? How?"

"I figured out why you've been lying. You're afraid of Pettijohn's killer."

"It occurred to me that I might be in jeopardy, yes."

"I wanted to warn you and didn't trust the telephone."

She glanced toward the bedroom. "Tapped?"

"I wouldn't put it past Smilow. Even without a court order."

"I think he might have me under surveillance."

"If he does, I don't know about it. Anyway, I scaled your back wall. Wouldn't suit to be seen at your house, would it? I've been knocking on the kitchen door for five minutes. I could see your upstairs lights on, but when you didn't answer, my imagination went wild. I thought maybe I was too late, that something terrible . . ." He stopped. "You're shivering."

"I'm cold."

He reached for a towel and placed it around her, folding it closed in front but not letting it go. "What makes you think you're under surveillance?"

"I saw a suspicious-looking car while I was running. Engine on. Lights out."

"You went running tonight? In this weather? Alone?"

"I'm usually alone. But I'm always careful."

He smiled weakly. "I'm sorry I scared you."

"I already had the jitters."

"I couldn't very well come up to your front door and ring the bell, could I?"

"I guess not."

"Would you have let me in?"

"I don't know." Then, more quietly, "Yes."

He stared at the hollow of her throat, where a droplet of water shimmered in the shallow depression. Releasing his grip on the towel, he stepped away from her, a move that deserved a goddamn merit badge for valor. "We've got to talk," he said thickly.

"I'll be right out."

Woodenly, he moved into the bedroom, actually seeing nothing, but noticing her stamp on everything. Every item in the room was a reflection of her. When she joined him, she was wearing a robe, the old-fashioned, no-nonsense kind that folded over her front and had a tie belt at the waist, as opaque as a lead apron, yet sexy as hell because she was naked and wet underneath.

"Your hand is bleeding."

He looked at the cut on his thumb, which had gone unnoticed until now. "I guess I did that when I busted your lock."

"Do you need a bandage?"

"It's fine."

The last thing he wanted to do was talk. He longed to touch her. He wanted to open the robe and press his face against her softness, taste her skin, inhale her essence. His whole body pulsed with physical desire, but he resisted yielding to it. He couldn't be held accountable for last Saturday night. But he was accountable for everything that followed.

"You knew my name all along, didn't you? Knew who I was."

"Yes."

He nodded slowly, assimilating what he had known but hadn't wanted to accept. "I don't want to have this conversation."

"Because. . . ?"

"Because I know you'll lie to me. That will make me angry. I don't want to be angry with you."

"I don't want you to be angry with me, either. So maybe we shouldn't talk."

"There is something I'd like to hear you say. Even if it is a lie."

"What?"

"I'd like to hear you say that Saturday night . . . that it had never been like that for you before."

She tilted her head slightly.

"Not just the passion," he added. "The . . . All of it."

He saw her swallow, dislodging the drop of water he had noticed earlier. It trickled beneath the collar of her robe. Her voice was husky with emotion. "It had never been like that for me before."

It was what he had hoped to hear, but if anything his expression became more bleak. "Whether we want to or not, we must talk."

"We don't have to."

"Yes, we do. When you and I showed up at the dance pavilion at approximately the same time, it wasn't by accident, was it?"

She hesitated for a few seconds, then shook her head no.

"How in God's name did you know I was going to be there? I didn't even know myself."

"Please don't ask me any more questions."

"Were you with Lute Pettijohn earlier that afternoon?"

"I can't talk to you about this."

"Dammit, answer me."

"I can't."

"It's a simple question."

On a humorless laugh, she shook her head. "It's not simple at all."

"Then answer it with an explanation."

"If I did, I would leave myself too vulnerable."

" 'Vulnerable' is a strange word for you to use, when it would appear that I am the one who's hanging out in the wind."

"You're not the one suspected of murder."

"No, but wouldn't you agree that I'm in an awkward situation? I'm prosecuting the murder case of our city's best-known citizen, who also happened to be married to my best friend."

"Your best friend?"

"Davee Burton, now Lute Pettijohn's widow. We've been friends all our lives. She campaigned for me to be assigned this case. A lot of people are depending on me, people I would rather not disappoint. Can you even fathom what would happen to my reputation, career, my future, if anyone found out I was here with you tonight?"

"That's why I left you Sunday morning." Restlessly she began to prowl the bedroom. "I wanted to remain anonymous. I didn't want you to feel conflicted, the way you're feeling now."

"By Sunday morning it was a little too late for concern and circumspection. If you were so worried about preserving my reputation, you shouldn't have picked me up in the first place."

She turned to stare at him with patent disbelief. "Pardon me, but your memory is slightly skewed. You picked me up."

"Yeah, right," he snorted.

"Who tried to leave? Twice. Twice I tried to leave, and both times you came after me, begging me to stay with you longer. Who followed who from the fair? Who stopped and—"

"Okay," he said, slicing the air with his hands. "But that hard-to-get act is the strongest turn-on there is, and women have known it since creation. You knew exactly what you were doing."

"Yes, I did," she exclaimed in a raised voice. Then she clasped her hands at her waist and searched his face with tearful eyes. "Yes, I knew what I was doing. And you're exactly right. At first I just wanted to . . . make contact with you."

"Why?"

"Insurance."

"In other words, to establish an alibi."

She cast her eyes downward. "I didn't know I was going to like you," she said softly. "I hadn't counted on the chemistry between us. I started feeling badly about using you. So I tried to get away from you. I didn't want you to be compromised because of an association—even a brief one—with me.

"But you came after me. You kissed me. After that . . ." She lifted her eyes to his again. "After that kiss, my initial reasons for meeting you ceased to matter. At that point I just wanted to be with you." She brushed tears off her cheeks. "That is the truth. You can believe it or not."

"Why did you need an alibi?"

"You know I didn't kill Pettijohn. You said so in the elevator."

"Right. So I repeat, why did you need an alibi?"

"Don't ask me, please."

"Just tell me."

"I can't."

"Why not?"

"Because I don't want you to think . . ." She paused and drew a deep breath. "I just can't, that's all."

"Has it got something to do with the man?"

The question took her aback. She blinked rapidly. "What man?"

"I traced you here Sunday night. I saw you with a man in a Mercedes convertible, approximately twelve hours after you left my bed."

"Oh. Sunday night? That was . . . an old friend. From college. He was in Charleston on business. He called and invited me out for a drink."

"You're lying."

"Why don't you believe me?"

"Because part of my job is to detect lies and liars, and you're goddamn lying!"

She pulled herself up straight and crossed her arms at her waist. "We should just as well let this be the end of it. Now. Tonight. This is an impossible situation. Your career is at stake. I don't want the responsibility of wrecking it. And I certainly don't want to be with someone who thinks I'm a liar."

"Who . . . was . . . he?"

"What does it matter who my friends are, when *your* friends, Steffi and Smilow, are itching to charge me with murder?"

"Is it any wonder that I don't believe you when you continue to avoid answering the simplest question?"

"They're not simple questions," she shouted. "You have no idea how difficult they are. They dredge up things I would rather forget, that I've tried to forget, that have haunted—" She stopped, realizing she was about to reveal too much. "You can't trust me. All the more reason for you to leave now and not come back. Ever."

"Fine."

"As long as we were in bed—"

"It was bloody great."

"But if you distrust me—"

"I do."

"Then—"

"Did you fuck Pettijohn?"

Her features went slack. *"What?"*

"Were you lovers?"

Hammond advanced on her, backing her into the wall. This was what was really bugging him. This was what had driven him to act like he had taken complete leave of his senses, to rant and rave and behave with reckless disregard for his career and everything else he had previously thought important. The desire to know the answer to this question was so imperative, the cautious, careful, and controlled Hammond Cross was ranting like a lunatic. "Were you ever Lute Pettijohn's lover?"

"No!" Then her voice dropped from a shout to a hoarse whisper. "I swear it."

"Did you kill him?" He pressed her shoulders between his hands and lowered his face to within inches of hers. "Tell me the truth about this, and I'll forgive all the other lies. Did you kill Lute Pettijohn?"

She shook her head. "No. I did not."

He struck the wall behind her with his fists, then left them planted there. Dropping his head forward, he aligned his cheek with hers. His breathing was harsh and loud even above the rain that continued to lash at the windows.

"I want to believe you."

"You can believe that." Turning her head, she spoke to his profile. "Don't ask me anything more, because I can't tell you anything more."

"Why? Tell me why."

"Because the answers are too painful for me."

"Painful, how?"

"Don't put me through this, please. If you do it will break my heart."

"You're breaking mine with your lies."

"I beg you, if you have any regard for me at all, spare me having to disillusion you. I would rather never see you again than for you to know . . ."

"What? Tell me."

She shook her head hard, and he realized it was useless to press her further. As long as her private torment had nothing to do with the Pettijohn case, he must respect her wish for privacy.

"That's not all," she continued. "We're going to be on opposite sides of a brewing crisis."

"So all this does relate to the case," he said dejectedly.

"I knew our being together was going to result in a mess, but I still made it happen. I wanted it to happen. Even at the gas station, I could have said no to you. I didn't."

He raised his head and tilted it back to better see her face. "Knowing what you know now, if you had it to do over again . . ."

"That's unfair."

"Would you do it again?"

Her answer was to steadily hold his gaze for a very long time as a tear slid down her cheek.

Hammond groaned. "God help me, so would I."

A heartbeat later his arms were around her and his mouth was grinding against hers. Water dripped from her hair onto his shirt. Her lips were warm, her tongue soft, her mouth sweet.

When they finally pulled apart, they spoke each other's name for the first time, laughed at themselves, then kissed again, if possible with more passion than before. He untied the belt at her waist, slipped his hands inside the robe, and touched her, stroking the smooth skin of her belly, eliciting soft moans from her when his fingertips feathered across her mound.

Hammond's blood pounded against his eardrums as hard as the rain pounded the roof. It drowned out everything else. The cautious murmurings of his common sense and conscience didn't stand a chance against such a racket.

He lifted her against him and carried her to the bed. Then, in a frenzy of impatience, he removed his clothes. When he stretched out on top of her he sighed with a mix of desire and despair. Her thighs parted and in the next breath he was enveloped in her warmth.

Sinking deeper, he swore softly, his voice cracking with emotion.

"I didn't sleep with you because I needed an alibi, Hammond."

Planting his hands on either side of her head, he looked down into her face and began to move. "Then why?"

She arched her back up to meet his thrusts. "For this."

He buried his face in her neck. The sensations were incredible. They shimmied up through his penis into his belly, spread through his chest and outward to his extremities, making them tingle. He allowed everything else to drift out of his consciousness so he could savor being inside her. But a climax was rushing upon him too quickly, so he stopped moving and whispered urgently, "I don't want to come yet. Not without you."

"Touch me."

She guided his hand between their bodies and placed it where they were joined. He moved his fingers lightly, stroking her simultaneously inside and out. She cupped her breast and pressed it up against his lips. He flicked the nipple with his tongue. The sound she made was almost a sob. They climaxed together.

They got beneath the covers. He drew her up against him, nestling her bottom against his lap. That's when he realized that he hadn't worn any protection. But, somehow, he didn't care overly much. What good would it do to fret? There was no help for it now. He just wanted to hold her. Smell her. Be near her and share her body heat.

He was content to gaze at her face where it lay in the crook of his elbow. He thought she was asleep because her eyes were closed, but he noticed her lips curving into a smile. He kissed her eyelid. "Penny for them."

She laughed softly and looked up at him. Lightly she traced the shape of his mouth with her fingernail. "I was thinking what it would be like to dress up and go out on a date with you. To dinner. A movie. Out in public and for all the world to see."

"Maybe. Someday."

"Maybe," she whispered, sounding no more optimistic than he.

"I'd love escorting you around Charleston, showing you off to all my friends."

"Truly?"

"You sound surprised."

"I am, a little. For a back-alley affair—"

"That's not what this is, Alex."

"Isn't it?"

"No."

"I'm a relative newcomer, but I've learned how things work here."

"What things?"

"Social circles."

"I don't care about that crap."

"But most Charlestonians do. I have no pedigree. Your family practically invented the concept."

"In the words of a famous Charlestonian, albeit a fictitious one, 'Frankly, my dear, I don't give a damn.' But even if I did, I would still choose you over any other woman in this city. I *have* chosen you over any other."

"Over Steffi Mundell." His expression caused her to laugh. "You should see your face."

"How did you know?"

"Women's intuition. I disliked her on sight. The feeling was mutual, and it had nothing to do with my being a suspect and her being a prosecutor. It was more elemental than that. Today, when she caught us in the elevator together, I knew. You were lovers, weren't you?"

" 'Were' being the operative and important word here. It lasted almost a year."

"How long since you broke up?"

"Two days."

Then it was her turn to register dismay. "Sunday?" He nodded. "Because of Saturday?"

"No. For me it had been over a long time. But after being with you, I knew with absolute certainty that, as a couple, Steffi and I were a lost cause." He threaded his fingers through her hair. "In spite of your bent for lying, you are the most desirable woman I've ever met. In every way. It goes beyond the physical."

Pleased, she smiled. "For instance?"

"You're smart."

"Kind to animals and the elderly."

"You're funny."

"Even-tempered. Most of the time."

"You're thrifty, brave, clean, and reverent."

"Somehow I knew you were a Boy Scout."

"An Eagle Scout. Where was I? Oh, your tits are perfect."

"What happened to going beyond the physical?"

Dispensing with the frivolity, he kissed her meaningfully. When at last he pulled away, her troubled expression alarmed him. "What?"

"Be careful, Hammond."

"No one will know I was here."

She shook her head. "Not that."

"Then what?"

"You may have to put me on trial for my life. Please be careful that you don't make me fall in love with you first."

# WEDNESDAY

"THANK YOU FOR SEEING ME."

Solicitor Monroe Mason offered Steffi a chair in his office. "I only have a minute. What's on your mind?"

"The Pettijohn case."

"I guessed as much. Anything specific?"

Steffi's hesitation had been planned and rehearsed. As though uneasy, she said, "I hate to bother you with what will seem like petty office politics."

"Is it Hammond and Detective Smilow? Are they behaving like rival bullies instead of professionals?"

"There have been a few verbal skirmishes, with some snide volleys being fired from both sides. I can handle that. It's something else."

He glanced at his desk clock. "You'll have to forgive me, Steffi. I have a meeting in ten minutes."

"It's Hammond's general attitude," she blurted out.

Mason frowned. "His attitude? Toward what?"

"He seems . . . I don't know . . ." She hem-hawed as though searching for the right word and finally coming up with, "Indifferent."

Mason leaned back in his chair and studied her over his steepled fingers. "I find that hard to believe. This case is right up Hammond's alley."

"That's what I thought, too," she exclaimed. "Ordinarily he would be chomping at the bit. He would be hounding Smilow to gather enough evidence to take to the grand jury. He would be anxious to start preparing for trial. This case has got all the ingredients that usually make him salivate.

"That's why I'm at a total loss," she continued. "He seems not to care if the mystery is solved. I've been briefing him on everything I get from Smilow. I've kept him apprised of what leads are hot and which have turned cold. Hammond reacts to every scrap of information with the same degree of disinterest."

Mason thoughtfully scratched his cheek. "What do you make of it?"

"I don't know what to make of it," she said with just the right mix of exasperation and puzzlement. "That's why I came to you. For guidance. I'm in the second seat on this case and don't want to overstep my bounds. Please tell me how to handle this."

Monroe Mason was approaching his seventieth birthday. He had grown tired of the grind of holding public office. For the last couple of years, he had delegated a lot of responsibility to the young and eager assistant solicitors, advising them when necessary, but for the most part giving them their heads to operate as they saw fit. He looked forward to retirement so he could golf and fish to his heart's content and not have to deal even with the political aspects of the job.

But it wasn't by accident that he had served as county solicitor for the past twenty-four years. He had been a shrewd operator when he assumed the office, and he had lost none of that edge. His instincts were as keen as ever. He could still sense when someone was being less than entirely upfront with him.

Steffi had counted on her boss's intuitiveness when she planned this meeting.

"Are you sure you don't know what's bothering him?" he asked her, lowering his booming voice to a dull roar.

With feigned anxiety, Steffi pulled her lower lip through her teeth. "I've painted myself into a corner, haven't I?"

"You don't want to speak badly of a colleague."

"Something like that."

"I appreciate the awkwardness of your situation. I admire your loyalty to Hammond. But this case is too important for sensitivities. If he is shirking his duties—"

"Oh, I didn't mean to imply that," she said hastily. "He would never drop the ball. It's just that I don't think he's running full out with it. His heart isn't in it."

"Do you know why?"

"Every time I've broached the subject, he reacts as though I've smashed a sore toe. He's touchy and cranky." She paused as though mulling it over. "But if you asked me to speculate on what's bothering him . . ."

"I have."

She pretended to think it over carefully before finally saying, "At this point, our suspect is a woman. Alex Ladd is an intelligent, successful woman. She's refined and articulate, and some might think attractive."

Mason actually laughed. "You think Hammond's got a crush on her?"

Steffi laughed with him. "Of course not."

"But you're saying that her gender is influencing his approach to the case."

"I'm saying it's a possibility. But it makes a weird sort of sense. You know Hammond better than I do. You've known him all his life. You know how he was brought up."

"In a home with very traditional values."

"And clearly defined roles," she added. "He's a native Charlestonian, southern to the marrow. He was weaned on mint juleps and chivalry."

Mason contemplated that for a moment. "You're afraid he might go soft if it came down to asking for the death penalty for a woman such as Dr. Ladd."

"It's only a guess." She lowered her eyes as though relieved that a terrible task was now behind her.

Covertly she watched her boss tug thoughtfully on his lower lip. Several moments passed. Her theory, and the reluctant manner in which she had vocalized it, had been perfect. She failed to tell him that Hammond had gone to the crime scene last night. Mason might regard that as a favorable sign. Steffi wasn't certain how she regarded it. Ordinarily Hammond let the detectives do their job without his interference, so this turnabout struck her as odd. It was something to think about, but later.

Right now, she was anxious to hear Mason's response to what she had told him. Saying anything more would be overkill, so she sat quietly and gave him plenty of time to cogitate.

"I disagree."

"What?" Her head came up with an almost audible snap. So confident had she been that she'd successfully made her point, his disagreement was totally unexpected.

"Everything you've said about Hammond's upbringing is correct. The Crosses drilled manners into that boy. I'm sure those lessons included a code of behavior toward women—all women—that harkens back to the days of knights in armor. But his parents, Preston in particular, also instilled in him an unshakable sense of responsibility. I believe that would override the other."

"Then how do you explain this ennui?"

Mason shrugged. "Other cases. A full court calendar. A toothache. Something in his private life. There could be any number of reasons for his distraction. But we're only a few days distant from the murder. The investigation is still in the preliminary stage. Smilow admits that he doesn't have enough evidence to make an arrest." He smiled and his boom returned. "I'm confident that when Smilow does charge Dr. Ladd—or whomever—with this crime, Hammond will step to the plate, bat in hand, and if I know the boy, he'll knock a home run."

Although Steffi felt like gnashing her teeth, she expelled a sigh of relief. "I'm so glad you see it that way. I was reluctant to bring this to your attention."

"That's what I'm here for." Clearly dismissing her, he stood up and retrieved his jacket from a coat tree.

Following him to the door of his office, Steffi pressed on. There was more he needed to hear. "I was afraid you would become dissatisfied with Hammond's performance and assign the case to someone else. Then I would no longer be working on it, either, and I would hate that because I'm finding the case absolutely fascinating. I'm anxious for the police to give us a suspect. I can't wait to sink my teeth into the trial preparation."

Amused by her enthusiasm, Mason chuckled. "Then you'll be happy to hear what Smilow's been up to this morning."

"My time is almost up—"

A groan of protest went up from the medical students who had filled the hall to standing-room-only capacity to hear Alex's lecture.

"Thank you," she said, smiling. "I appreciate your attention. Before we're forced to dismiss, I want to comment on how vital it is that the patient suffering panic attacks not be dismissed as a hypochondriac. Sadly, that's too often the case. Family members can—understandably—become intolerant of the patient's chronic complaints.

"The symptoms are sometimes so bizarre, they seem ridiculous and are frequently believed to be imaginary. So, even as the patient is receiving treatment and learning ways in which to cope with acute anxiety disorder, his family should also be instructed on how to deal with this phenomenon.

"Now I really must let you go, or your other instructors will have my head. Thank you for your attention."

They applauded enthusiastically before they began filing out. Several came up to speak with her, shake her hand, and tell her how interesting and informative her talk had been. One even presented her a copy of an article she had authored and asked her to autograph it.

Her host didn't come forward until the last student departed. Dr. Douglas Mann was on the faculty at Medical University of South Carolina. He and Alex had met in med school and had been friends ever since. He was tall and lanky, as bald as a billiard ball, an excellent basketball player, and a confirmed bachelor for reasons he had never shared with Alex.

"Maybe I should charter a fan club," he remarked as he joined her.

"I'm just relieved I held their attention."

"Are you kidding? They were hanging on to every word. You've made me the hero of the hour," he told her with a broad smile. "I love having famous friends."

She laughed at what she considered to be a misplaced compliment. "They were easy. A good audience. Were we that bright when we were their age?"

"Who knew? We were stoned."

"*You* were stoned."

"Oh, yeah." He shrugged bony shoulders. "That's right, you were no fun. All work, no play."

"Excuse me. Dr. Ladd?"

Alex turned to find herself face-to-face with Bobby Trimble. Her heart lurched.

Reaching for her hand, he pumped it enthusiastically. "Dr. Robert Trimble. Montgomery, Alabama. I'm on vacation here in Charleston, but I saw a notice about your lecture this morning and just had to come and meet you."

Doug, unaware of her discomfiture, introduced himself and shook Bobby's hand. "Colleagues are always welcome at our lectures."

"Thanks." Back to Alex, Bobby said, "Your studies on anxiety have been of particular interest to me. I'm curious as to what made you focus on that particular syndrome. Something in your own experience, perhaps?" He winked. "Afraid past sins will catch up with you?"

"You'll have to excuse me, Dr. Trimble," she said frostily. "I have patients scheduled."

"I apologize for detaining you. It's been a pleasure."

Turning abruptly, she headed for the exit. Doug mumbled a hasty goodbye to Bobby, then rushed to catch up with her. "One ardent fan too many, huh? Are you all right?"

"Of course," she replied brightly. But she wasn't all right. She was anything but all right. Bobby's unexpected appearance was his way of letting her know that he could intrude at any time. Easily. There wasn't an area of her life that he couldn't penetrate if he wanted to.

"Alex?" Doug asked if she would join him for a late breakfast. "By way of thanks, the least I can do is buy you a plate of shrimp and grits."

"That sounds delicious, Doug, but I have to pass." She couldn't have swallowed a bite of food if her life depended on it. Seeing Bobby in what she had considered a safe realm had left her terribly shaken and upset, as was most certainly his intention. "I've got a patient scheduled in fifteen minutes. I'll barely get there in time as it is."

"We're on our way."

Doug had insisted on picking her up that morning and driving her to the MUSC Medical Center because parking spaces near the sprawling complex were scarce. On the way downtown, he thanked her again.

"No need. I enjoyed it." *Until Bobby ruined it,* she thought.

"Anytime I can return a favor, I owe you one," he said earnestly.

"I'll remember that."

Trying to hide her agitation, she kept the conversation light. They exchanged gossip about friends and colleagues they had in common. She inquired about the AIDS research paper he was working on. He asked if anything new and exciting was going on in her life.

If she told him, he wouldn't believe her. *Or maybe he would,* she amended when they turned onto her street.

"What the hell?" Doug exclaimed. "You must've had a burglary."

She knew instantly, with a sinking sense of dread, that the police car parked in front of her house had nothing to do with a burglary. Two uniformed policemen were flanking her front door like sentinels. A plain-clothesman was peering into the front windows. Smilow was talking with her patient, who apparently had arrived early for her appointment.

Doug pulled his car to a stop and was about to get out when Alex forestalled him. "Don't get involved in this, Doug."

"Involved in what? What the hell's going on?"

"I'll fill you in later."

"But—"

"Please. I'll call you."

She squeezed his arm, then got out and hastily went through her gate and up her walkway, noting as she went that the scene being played out at her front door had attracted the attention of several passersby. A tourist was taking photographs of her house, which was nothing out of the ordinary. The street was featured on all the walking tours. While similar in design, each house on her block boasted at least one distinctive feature of historical significance. This morning, her house was set apart from the others by the police car parked in front.

"Dr. Ladd!" Her patient rushed forward. "What's going on? I got here just as these policemen arrived."

Alex glared at Smilow over the shoulder of the woman in distress. "I'm terribly sorry, Evelyn, but I'll have to reschedule your appointment."

Placing her arm around the woman's shoulders, she turned her about and walked her to her car. It took several minutes for Alex to reassure her that everything was all right and that her appointment would be rescheduled for the earliest possible time.

"Are you okay?" Alex asked kindly.

"Are you, Dr. Ladd?"

"I'm fine. I promise. I'll call you later today. Don't worry."

Not until she drove away did Alex turn back. This time, as she strode up her walkway, she had Smilow in her sights.

"What the hell are you doing here? I had a patient and—"

"And I have a search warrant."

He produced the document from the breast pocket of his suit jacket.

Alex looked toward the three other officers loitering on her porch before her eyes swung back to Smilow. "I see my last patient at three o'clock. Can this wait until after that session?"

"I'm afraid not."

"I'm calling Frank Perkins."

"Be my guest. But we don't need his permission to come inside. We don't even need yours."

Without further ado, he motioned his men forward.

Perhaps the thing Alex found most offensive was the plastic gloves they pulled on before entering her home, as though it and she were contaminants that needed to be guarded against.

First she cried.

Waking up and finding herself in the worst nightmare a single woman can fathom—at least a single middle school teacher from suburban Indianapolis—Ellen Rogers sat up in bed, clutched the sheet to her throat, and sobbed her heart out.

Hungover. Naked. Violated. Abandoned.

Reliving the events of last night, it first had seemed that she had dropped into one of her own fantasies, in which a good-looking stranger had chosen her over the younger, prettier, thinner girls in the nightclub. He had made the initial move. He had chosen her to dance with and buy drinks for. The attraction had been instantaneous and mutual, just as she had always imagined it would be when "it" finally happened to her.

Furthermore, he wasn't vapid and shallow. He had a *story*. His was a tale of love and loss that had wrenched her heart. He had loved his wife to distraction. When she became ill, he had dedicated himself to her care until she finally succumbed. Despite the hardship it had imposed on him and his business, he had done all the cooking and cleaning and laundry. He had performed personal tasks for his wife, even the most unpleasant ones. On the rare occasions that she was able to go out, he had applied her makeup.

Such sacrifice! That was what love was all about. This was a man worth knowing. This was a man worthy of all the love Ellen had been storing up for years and wished desperately to share.

He had also been a fantastic lover.

Even with her experience being limited to an older male cousin who had once forced a French kiss on her, a sweetheart who had talked of love through two awkward couplings in his car before jilting her, and a married teacher with whom she had carried on an exciting but unconsummated flirtation until he was transferred to another school, she had recognized that Eddie—that was his name—was exceptional in bed. He had done things to her that she had only read about in the novels she collected in labeled boxes in her basement. He had exhausted her with his passion.

But now, the rosy glow of romance was dimmed by the dark terrors accompanying one-night stands with total strangers. Pregnancy. (Hey, it could happen to women in their forties.) STDs. AIDS.

Any one of those consequences would dash her dream of marrying one day. Her shot at matrimony had been growing slimmer with each passing year, but last night's indiscretion had made it a truly impossible dream. What man would want her now? Not a decent man. Not now that she had a *past*.

Her situation couldn't get much worse.

But it did.

She'd been robbed, too.

She discovered that when she finally left the bed to go into the bathroom to assess the damage. She realized that her handbag wasn't in the chair where she had dropped it the night before. She remembered distinctly. It wasn't something she was likely to forget because that had been the first time a man had ever come up behind her and started grinding his . . . you know . . . against her. He had reached around her and put his hand inside her dress to caress her breasts. Bones virtually melting, she had dropped her purse on the chair. She was certain of that.

Nevertheless, she searched the room frantically, berating herself for not heeding the television commercials that strongly urged never to leave home without traveler's checks.

Whether it was that blistering self-incrimination or recollections of the ease with which glib Eddie had convinced her of all his lies, Ellen Rogers suddenly stopped her futile searching for the handbag and stood stock-still in the center of the hotel room. Still mother-naked, she placed her hands on her hips, stepped out of her decorous self, and swore like a sailor.

She no longer felt sorry for herself. She was pissed.

# CHAPTER | 23

I<small>T WAS ALMOST NOON</small> by the time Hammond reached the judicial building. On his way past the receptionist's desk, he asked her to bring him a cup of coffee. He wasn't happy to see Steffi lying in wait for him inside his office.

To his further annoyance, she took one look at him and said, "Rough night?"

He hadn't returned home until nearly dawn. Once he fell asleep, he had slept hard for several hours. When he finally woke up, he cursed the time he read on his bedside clock. He didn't need Steffi to point out how late a start he was getting on the day.

"What happened to your thumb?"

It had taken two Band-Aids to cover the gash. "I cut myself shaving."

"Hairy thumbs?"

"What's up, Steffi?"

"Smilow's got some more evidence on its way up to SLED. He's hoping for a hair match."

He hid his inward knee-jerk reaction by calmly going about his business—setting his briefcase on his desk, shrugging off his suit jacket and hanging it up, flipping through a stack of mail and phone messages. Studying one, he asked absently, "Which case?"

Extremely perturbed, Steffi folded her arms across her waist. "The Lute Pettijohn murder case, Hammond."

He sat down behind his desk and thanked the receptionist when she brought in a cup of coffee. "Want one, Steffi?"

"No, thanks." None too gently she closed the door behind the departing receptionist. "Now that you're settled and have your coffee, may we please discuss this latest development?"

"Smilow found a hair in Pettijohn's hotel suite?"

"Correct."

"And he's having it matched to . . . ?"

"To one he took from Alex Ladd's hairbrush this morning during the search."

That jolted him. "Search?"

"He obtained a warrant first thing this morning. They've already conducted the search."

"I didn't even know he was going for a warrant. Did you?"

"Not until a while ago."

"Why didn't you call me?"

"I saw no reason to until we had something."

"It's my case, Steffi."

"Well, you're sure as hell not acting like it is," she said, raising her voice.

"How am I acting?"

"You figure it out. For starters you might ask yourself why you're dragging in here so late. Don't get mad at me because you weren't here when things started rolling."

They glared at each other across his desk. He was angry over being excluded from the tight loop that she had formed with Smilow. They were practically joined at the hip over this case. But, as much as he hated to admit it, her arguments were valid. He was angry at himself and at the situation, and he was taking it out on her.

"Anything else?" he asked in a more civil tone.

"He got the cloves, too."

"Cloves? What the hell are you talking about?"

"Remember the fleck of something removed from Pettijohn's sleeve?"

"Vaguely."

She explained that the speck had been identified as clove, and that Alex Ladd had clove-spiked oranges in a bowl in her entryway. "They scent the rooms like a natural potpourri. Plus, they found a wad of money in her home safe. Thousands of dollars."

"Which is supposed to prove what?"

"I don't know what it *proves* yet, Hammond. But you must admit it's unorthodox and suspicious for someone to keep that much cash in a home safe."

Throat tight, he asked. "What about the weapon?"

"Unfortunately, that didn't turn up."

His telephone beeped, and the receptionist informed him that Detective Smilow was on the line.

"He's probably calling me," Steffi said, reaching for the receiver. "I told him I would be in your office."

She listened for a moment, consulted her wristwatch, then said cheerfully, "On our way."

"On our way where?" Hammond asked when she hung up.

"I guess Dr. Ladd realizes she's up you-know-what creek. She's coming in for further questioning."

Although his desk was covered with untouched paperwork, briefs, memos, and unanswered messages, he didn't even think of sending Steffi on his behalf. He needed to be there to hear what Alex had to say, even if it was something he didn't want to hear.

His living nightmare continued. The horror of it escalated. Smilow was irrepressible, although the man couldn't be faulted for doing his job and doing it well. Alex . . . hell, he didn't know what to think about Alex. She had admitted to deliberately compromising him by sleeping with him, but she refused to explain why. What other reason could there be except for a link with Pettijohn and/or his murder?

Dreading the unknown, Hammond moved as though slogging through quicksand as they left the building. The sun felt like a broiler. The air was heavy and still. Even the air-conditioning in Steffi's car was insufficient. He was sweating as they climbed the steps to the entrance of police headquarters. Today, he rode the elevator with Steffi up to Smilow's territory.

Steffi knocked once on his office door before barging in. "Did we miss anything?"

Smilow, who had started without them, continued speaking into the tape recorder's microphone. "Assistant D.A.s Mundell and Cross have joined us." He stated the time and date.

Alex turned toward Hammond where he was crowded in behind Steffi. When he had bent down from the side of the bed to kiss her goodbye early this morning, she had curved her hands around the back of his neck and lifted her mouth to his for a sustained, deep kiss. When it finally ended and he groaned his regret, she had smiled up at him from her pillow sleepily, sexily, her eyes slumberous and heavy-lidded.

Now he read in them an apprehension that matched his own.

Once the formalities were out of the way, Frank Perkins said, "Before you start, Smilow, my client would like to amend some of her previous statements."

Steffi smirked. Smilow, showing no reaction, signaled for Alex to proceed.

Her steady voice filled the expectant silence. "I lied to you before about being in Mr. Pettijohn's penthouse suite. I was there last Saturday afternoon. As I was waiting for him to answer his door, I saw the man from Macon going into his room, just as he told you."

"Why did you lie about it?"

"To protect one of my patients."

Steffi snorted with disbelief, but Smilow cut her off with a hard look. "Please continue, Dr. Ladd."

"I went to see Mr. Pettijohn on a patient's behalf."

"What for?"

"To deliver a verbal message. I can't divulge any more than that."

"Professional privilege is a very convenient shield."

She conceded the point with a small nod. "Nevertheless, that's what I was doing there."

"Why didn't you tell us this before?"

"I was afraid you would browbeat me into disclosing the patient's name. That individual's best interests came before mine."

"Until now."

"The situation has become precarious. More so than I anticipated. I've been forced to tell what I had hoped to keep confidential for my patient's sake."

"Do you usually go to such lengths for your patients? Delivering messages and so forth?"

"Customarily, no. But it would have been terribly upsetting for this patient to have a face-to-face meeting with Mr. Pettijohn. It was a small favor to grant."

"So you saw Mr. Pettijohn?" She nodded. "How long were you inside the suite with him?"

"A few minutes."

"Less than five? More than ten?"

"Less than five."

"Isn't a hotel suite an odd setting for that kind of meeting?"

"I thought so, too, but it was at Mr. Pettijohn's request that we meet there. He said the hotel would be more convenient for him since someone else was joining him there later."

"Who?"

"I wouldn't know. In any case, I didn't mind going there because, as I told you, the remainder of my day was free. I had no other commitments. I did some window-shopping in the area of the Charles Towne, then left the city."

"And went to the fair."

"That's right. Everything else I told you stands."

"Which version?"

Frank Perkins frowned at Steffi's wisecrack. "There's no need for sarcasm, Ms. Mundell. It's clear now why Dr. Ladd was reluctant to tell you about her brief meeting with Pettijohn. She was protecting a patient's privacy."

"How noble of her."

Before the solicitor could admonish Steffi again, Smilow continued, "How did Mr. Pettijohn seem to you, Dr. Ladd?"

"How did he seem?"

"What was his mood?"

"I didn't know him so I have nothing with which to compare his mood that afternoon."

"Well, was he jovial or cranky? Happy or sad? Complacent or upset?"

"None of those extremes."

"What was the gist of the message you delivered?"

"I can't tell you."

"Was it provoking?"

"Do you mean did it make him angry?"

"Did it?"

"If it did, he didn't show it."

"It didn't make him upset to the point of causing a stroke?"

"No. Not in the slightest."

"Did he seem nervous?"

She smiled at that. "Mr. Pettijohn didn't strike me as a person who would get nervous easily. Nothing I've read about him suggests that he was timid."

"Was he basically friendly toward you?"

"Polite. I wouldn't go so far as to say friendly. We were strangers."

"Polite." Smilow pondered that. "Did he play host? For instance, did he offer you a seat?"

"Yes, but I remained standing."

"Why?"

"Because I knew I wouldn't be there long, and I preferred standing to sitting."

"Did he offer you a drink?"

"No."

"Sex?"

Everyone in the room reacted to the unheralded question, but none more violently than Hammond. He jumped as though the wall he had been leaning against had bit him. "What the hell?" he exclaimed. "Where'd that come from?"

Smilow switched off the microphone, then turned toward Hammond. "Butt out. This is my interrogation."

"The question was inappropriate, and you damn well know it."

"I couldn't agree more," Frank Perkins said, his anger almost matching Hammond's. "Your investigation has turned up nothing to indicate that Pettijohn had a sexual encounter that afternoon."

"Not in the bed in the hotel suite. That doesn't preclude all sexual activity. Oral sex, for instance."

"Smilow—"

"Did you perform oral sex on Mr. Pettijohn, Dr. Ladd? Or he on you?"

Hammond lunged across the crowded room and shoved him hard. "You son of a bitch."

"Get your goddamn hands off me," Smilow said, shoving him back.

"Hammond! Smilow!" Steffi tried to step between them and got knocked aside for her efforts.

Frank Perkins was beside himself. "This is outrageous."

"That was a cheap shot, Smilow!" Hammond shouted. "Even you've never stooped that low. If you're going to take potshots like that, at least have the guts to keep the tape recorder on."

"I don't need lessons from you on how to conduct an interrogation."

"This isn't an interrogation. It's a character assassination. For no good reason."

"She's a suspect, Hammond," Steffi countered.

"Not in a sex scam, she's not," he fired back.

"What about the hair, Smilow?" Steffi asked.

"I was getting to that." He and Hammond continued facing off like leashed pit bulls. Smilow was the first to collect himself. He smoothed back his hair and shot his cuffs. Returning to his desk, he switched the recorder back on. "Dr. Ladd, we found a hair in the hotel suite. I've just heard from the state lab in Columbia that it matches strands taken from your hairbrush."

"So what, Detective?" She no longer appeared passive to what was going on. There were spots of color in her cheeks, and her green eyes were flashing angrily. "I've admitted to being in the suite, and I've explained why I didn't tell you the truth before. I shed a hair, which is a natural biological occurrence. I'm sure mine wasn't the only human hair you collected from that room."

"No, it wasn't."

"But I'm the only one you singled out to insult."

Hammond wanted to shout, *Bravo, Alex.* She had every right to be indignant. Smilow's question had been calculated to shake her, to throw her off, to break her concentration so he could trap her in a lie. It was an old trick used by pros, and it usually worked. Not this time. Smilow had failed to rattle her, and had only succeeded in making her mad as hell.

"Can you explain how a speck of clove got on Mr. Pettijohn's sleeve?"

Her angry expression relaxed somewhat, then she actually laughed. "Mr. Smilow, clove can be found in most kitchens in the world. Why did you isolate *my* clove? I'm sure there's a supply in the kitchen at the Charles Towne Plaza. Maybe Mr. Pettijohn picked it up from his home kitchen and brought it into the hotel room with him."

Frank Perkins smiled, and Hammond knew what the defense attorney was thinking. On cross-examination, he would follow this same track until the jurors were also laughing at the prosecution's allegation that *the* clove was Dr. Ladd's clove.

"I think you'd better cut your losses here, Smilow," Perkins said. "Against my advice, Dr. Ladd has cooperated fully. She's been terribly inconvenienced and so have the patients whom she had to reschedule. Her house has been turned upside down, and she's been unforgivably insulted. You owe her several apologies."

If Smilow heard the solicitor, he gave no sign of it. His crystal stare didn't waver from Alex's face. "I'd like to know about the money we found in your safe."

"What about it?"

"Where did you get it?"

"You don't have to answer, Alex."

She ignored her solicitor's advice. "Check my tax returns, Mr. Smilow."

"We have."

She raised her eyebrows as though to say, *So what's your question?*

"Wouldn't it be more financially sound to keep your money in an interest-bearing bank account instead of a wall safe?"

"Her finances and how she manages them are totally irrelevant," Perkins said.

"That remains to be seen." Before the lawyer could further object, Smilow held up his index finger. "One more thing, Frank, and then I'll be done."

"This is getting you nowhere."

"When did you have the break-in, Dr. Ladd?"

Hammond sure as hell didn't see that question coming. Apparently neither did Alex. For once her reaction was visible and telling.

"At the kitchen door?"

Watching her closely, Smilow said, "Off the piazza, yes."

"I don't remember exactly. A few months ago, I think."

"Were you robbed?"

"No, I think it was just some neighborhood kids up to mischief."

"Hmm. Okay, thanks." He turned off the recorder.

Perkins held her chair for her as she stood up. "This is getting very old, very fast, Smilow."

"No apologies, Frank. I've got a murder to solve."

"You're barking up the wrong tree. You're harassing Dr. Ladd while the culprit's trail grows colder."

He nudged his client toward the door. Hammond tried to keep his eyes off her but couldn't. She must have felt his stare because she looked over at him as she moved past. Consequently they were looking at each other when Smilow said, "Who's your boyfriend?"

She turned quickly toward the detective. "Boyfriend?"

"Your lover."

This time the barb worked. Alex's self-control slipped. She didn't exercise her customary caution, or hear her lawyer's admonishment for her not to speak. She reacted on reflex. "I don't have a lover."

"Then how do you account for the sheets we found in your dirty clothes hamper that are stained with blood and semen?"

"That story about covering for a patient was pure fiction," Steffi chortled. "I recommend that you charge her without further delay."

She, Smilow, and Hammond had remained behind after Frank Perkins had furiously hustled his client out. The two men weren't listening to anything Steffi had to say, however. They were squared off like gladiators about to engage in a fight to the finish. Last one to die wins.

Hammond got in the first thrust. "Where the hell do you get off—"

"I don't give a damn what you think about my tactics. I'll do this my way."

"You want her to walk?" Hammond fired back. "You keep up that bullshit about her personal life, Frank Perkins will be all over that. A sheet in her clothes hamper? Jesus," he said, sneering in disgust.

"Don't forget the robe," Steffi interjected. That was the part she found most amusing. "Miss Goody-two-shoes fucks with her robe on."

Hammond looked at her with fire in his eyes, but Smilow demanded his attention. "Why did she lie about having a boyfriend?"

"How the hell do I know?" Hammond yelled. "How the hell do *you* know? She explained that she wasn't presently involved with anyone. Enough said."

"Hardly," Steffi threw in. "The semen stains—"

"Have nothing to do with her seeing Pettijohn last weekend!"

"Maybe not," she said curtly. "It's plausible that she nicked her leg shaving, as she explained. Okay, that accounts for the blood, although I think it should be typed. But sperm is sperm. Why would she deny having a personal relationship with a man if it doesn't somehow relate to Petti-john?"

"There could be a thousand reasons."

"Name one."

Hammond pushed his face close to hers. "Okay, here's one. It's none of your goddamn business who she sleeps with."

The cords in his neck were strained. His face was red, and a vein in his forehead was ticking. She had seen him furious with cops, judges, juries, her, himself. But she had never seen him this angry before. It raised questions in her mind, questions that she would mull over when she was alone and had time to think about them carefully. Now she said, "I don't understand why you're so upset."

"Because I know what he's capable of." He pointed at Smilow. "He finesses evidence to make his case."

"We gathered this evidence during a legal search," Smilow said, straining the words through his teeth.

Hammond snickered. "I wouldn't put it past you to jack off on those sheets yourself."

Smilow looked like he might strike Hammond. With an effort, he pulled air into his nostrils, which were pinched almost shut by rage.

Steffi thought it prudent to step in. "How often would you guess that a Miss Priss like Alex Ladd does her laundry?"

"At least every three or four days," Smilow said stiffly, his hard eyes still fixed on Hammond.

"I'm not believing this." Hammond backed against the wall as though trying to distance himself from the discussion.

Steffi said, "That means that in the last few days, Alex Ladd has had sex and then lied about it. When you mentioned a lover, she didn't simply decline to identify him, or ask what bearing her love life had on our murder investigation, or tell us all to take a flying leap. She blanched, she lied, and then when trapped in her lie, she tried qualifying it: 'What I meant to say is that I'm not presently involved with someone.' "

Both men were listening, or appeared to be. But since neither commented, she continued. "It could be semantics. Maybe she's taking the politician's way out. Not exactly lying, but not exactly telling the truth, either. Maybe she doesn't have a steady lover, but she enjoys occasional, recreational sex."

Smilow's brows drew together. "I don't think so. We didn't find any oral contraceptives in the medicine cabinet. No diaphragm, or even condoms. Nothing to suggest sexual activity on a more or less routine basis. Consequently, that's why I was frankly surprised when we found those stained items in the hamper."

"But you must have thought of her in a sexual connotation, Smilow. Otherwise, where were you going with that question about her having sex with Pettijohn?"

"Nowhere in particular," he admitted. "It was saying more about Lute than her."

"It was a mean attempt to trip her up."

Steffi ignored Hammond's sulky remark. "So you don't really believe that she went down on her knees in that hotel suite and gave Pettijohn head?"

Smilow grinned. "Maybe that's what caused his stroke."

Hammond practically launched himself away from the wall. "Is discussing Dr. Ladd's sex life going to be the extent of this meeting? Because if it is, I've got real work to do."

Smilow nodded him toward the door. "Feel free to leave."

"What else is there to talk about?"

"The break-in on her back door."

"She explained that."

Steffi was becoming increasingly impatient with Hammond's obtuseness. "You didn't believe that explanation, did you? She was obviously lying about that, too. Just as she's been lying all along, about everything. What's the matter with you? Usually you can smell a lie a mile away."

"She claims the break-in occurred months ago," Smilow said. "But the splintered wood hadn't weathered. It was raw. The scratches on the metal lock were fresh, too. Besides these signs of a recent break-in, as meticulously as she's groomed, and as immaculate as the house is, I can't see her waiting months to have repair work done."

"It's still conjecture," Hammond said. "All of it. Everything."

"But to dismiss it would be preposterous," Steffi argued.

"No more preposterous than tying up a bunch of unrelated, unsubstantiated guesses and considering them facts."

"Some of them *are* facts."

"Why do you want so badly for her to be guilty?"

"Why do you want so badly for her not to be?"

The ensuing silence was so sudden and tension-laden that the knock at the door sounded like a cannon blast.

Monroe Mason opened the door and poked his head around. "I heard that Dr. Ladd was being questioned again, and thought I'd come over and see how it was going. Not too well, I gather. I could hear the shouting as soon as I came through the security doors."

Everyone mumbled greetings, then for half a minute no one said anything.

Eventually Mason addressed Steffi. "You're usually so outspoken. What's wrong? Cat got your tongue? What did I interrupt?"

She glanced at Hammond and Smilow before going back to Mason. "The search of Dr. Ladd's house yielded some items of interest. Hammond and I were evaluating their relevance to the case. It's Smilow's opinion, and I tend to agree, that they constitute valid evidence against her."

He turned to Hammond. "You obviously don't share their opinion."

"In my opinion we've got zilch. They're getting off on it, but then they don't have to present the case to the grand jury."

Steffi realized that the next few moments could be key to her future. Hammond was Monroe Mason's protégé. As recently as this morning, when she had aired her concerns over Hammond's seeming indifference toward the case, Mason had jumped to his defense. Contradicting his anointed successor might not be the wisest thing to do.

On the other hand, she couldn't let a perfect suspect get away just because Hammond had turned squeamish. If she played this right, Mason might see a weakness in his heir apparent that he hadn't before seen. He might spot a character flaw that would hinder a hard-hitting prosecutor's effectiveness.

"I think what we've got on Dr. Ladd is compelling enough to make an arrest," she declared. "I don't understand what we're waiting for."

"Evidence," Hammond said crisply. "How's that for a concept?"

"We've got evidence."

"Flimsy, circumstantial evidence, to say the least. The worst defense lawyer in the state of South Carolina could easily maneuver around everything we've compiled. Far from being the worst, Frank Perkins is one of the best. I doubt the grand jury would even indict her if all I went in with was a strand of hair and a condiment."

"Condiment?" Mason asked.

"Clove is a spice," Steffi countered irritably.

"Whatever," Hammond shouted.

"He's right." Smilow's soft-spoken interjection silenced them instantly. Steffi couldn't believe that Smilow had agreed with Hammond, and Hammond appeared as astonished as she.

Mason was interested in what Smilow had to say. "You agree with Hammond?"

"Not entirely. I think Dr. Ladd is involved. In what way and to what extent, I don't know yet. She was there with Pettijohn on Saturday. My hunch is that she was there for no good purpose. Otherwise, why has she been heaping lie upon lie to cover this up? However, from a legal standpoint, Hammond is right. We've got no weapon. And no—"

"Motive," Hammond supplied.

"Exactly." Smilow smiled sourly. "If she wasn't intimate with Petti-john, it really doesn't matter if she sleeps with every other man in Charleston. What do we care if someone did break into her house for no apparent reason? It's odd, but not illegal to hoard thousands of dollars in a home safe when there are several banks within walking distance of her home.

"From what I've discerned of her character, I believe she would let her-self be sentenced to death row before betraying a patient's confidence, even if that patient were her only defense. Not that I believe that story about delivering a message for a patient. Which I don't. No more than I believe that nonsense about going to the fair and all the rest.

"But," he said emphatically, "the bottom line is that I've established no motive for her to kill Lute Pettijohn. I haven't even made a connection be-tween them in either their personal lives or professional ones. If he was a patient, he never wrote a check to her. If she invested in one of his devel-opment deals, there are no records of it. I can't even place them at a din-ner party together.

"I've got a guy digging around in Tennessee where she comes from, but so far he hasn't turned up much except her school records. If Pettijohn was ever in the state of Tennessee, he left no trace of himself there."

"So," Mason said, "either she's telling the truth or she's covered her tracks well."

"I tend to think the latter," the detective said. "She's hiding something. I just don't know what it is."

Steffi said, "But if you did—"

"He doesn't."

"If you did have a motive—"

"But he *doesn't.*"

"Shut up, Hammond, and let me talk," she snapped. "Please." He waved his hand, giving her the floor. She addressed Smilow. "If you could make a connection, find a motive, could you move forward with the evidence we've got?"

Smilow looked across at Hammond. "That's up to him."

Hammond looked hard at Smilow, then glanced at her. He then looked at Mason, who seemed anxious to hear his answer. Finally he said, "Yeah. I could go with what we've got. But it would have to be damn strong mo-tivation."

Y OU KNOW, DAVEE, that this is in very poor taste."

"Very." Davee Pettijohn was practically purring with self-satisfaction as she traded her empty highball glass for the full one the roving waiter brought her. "As I told you before, Hammond, I refuse to be a hypocrite."

"Your late husband's funeral was only yesterday."

"God, don't remind me. What a freaking dismal event that was. Weren't you just bored out of your gourd?"

In spite of himself Hammond smiled and thanked the waiter for his own made-to-order drink. "They'll be talking about this for years."

"That's the general idea, sweetheart," Davee said. "This little soiree was meant to offend all the bitches who'll be gossiping about me no matter what I do. Why not go all out?"

The gathering could hardly be called a little soiree. The lower level rooms of the Pettijohn mansion were teeming with friends, acquaintances, and hangers-on who were too flamboyantly rebellious in their own right to give a fig if the widow threw a party the day following her husband's funeral or not. There was no way it could be misconstrued as a wake. It was a highly improper, ill-timed bacchanal, which, of course, was the general idea.

"Wouldn't this make Lute furious? He'd have a stroke."

"He did," Hammond remarked.

"Oh, yeah. I almost forgot that."

"Did he have warning of a pending stroke?"

"Blood pressure readings off the charts."

"Didn't he take medication for it?"

"He was supposed to. But it made his dick limp, so he stopped taking it."

"And you knew that?"

She laughed "What do you think, Hammond? That I caused him to have a stroke? Look, it was his own damn, stubborn fault. He said if it came to a choice between screwing or blowing a gasket, he'd choose blowing a gasket."

"The stroke didn't kill him, Davee."

"No. The bastard was shot. In the back. Here's to the one who did it." She raised her glass.

Hammond couldn't drink to that, and it made him uneasy that she could. He turned his attention back to the party. They were standing on the second-floor gallery, an excellent vantage point from which to watch the merrymaking. "I don't see any of the Old Guard here."

"They weren't invited." She sipped from her drink, smiling wickedly. "Why spoil their pleasure of speculating on all the sin and iniquity taking place?"

The party would supply the gossips with plenty of material. The rock band's amps were maxed out. The catered food was ample. Liquor was in even more abundant supply. Drugs were available, too. Earlier Hammond had recognized a well-known dealer who had eluded conviction numerous times.

He spotted a bestselling novelist who'd recently come out of the closet. In celebration of this liberating decision, he was overtly making out with his date for the evening. Their unabashed public display might have drawn attention, except for a stunning young woman nearby who was showing off her newly augmented breasts to a group of avid admirers who were invited to touch and test.

"She paid too much for those," Davee remarked cattily.

"Do you know a discount boob doctor?"

"No, but I know one who would have done a better job." Hammond looked at her askance, and she laughed in her throaty, sexy way. "No, darling. Mine are all me. But I've slept with him. He's a lousy lover, but when it comes to his work he's an absolute perfectionist."

Hammond gave her a once-over. "Ever since I got here, I've been meaning to ask."

"What?"

"Have you taken up belly dancing?"

"Isn't it divine?"

Davee spread her arms and executed a pirouette to show off her outfit. Made of red raw silk, it consisted of tight hip-hugger pants and a top cropped just below her breasts. The pants rode dangerously low on her abdomen. Her waist was encircled by a thin gold chain. On each arm she wore at least a dozen gold bangles.

She ended the turn with a nasty bump and grind. Hammond laughed. "Divine."

Lowering her arms, she frowned at him. "Fat lot of good it does me for you to think so. Hammond, why aren't we lovers?"

"I'd have to take a number."

"Fuck you." He laughed, but her frown only deepened. "How can you say something so mean when I don't even have a date for my own party?"

"Where's the masseur?"

"Sandro. I had to let him go."

"Since Sunday? That was quick."

"You know how I am once I make up my mind about something."

"He was rubbing you the wrong way?"

In response to his bad joke, she gave him a sarcastic, "Ha-ha."

"Sore subject?"

"God, no. He wasn't a heartthrob, just a crotch throb. His penis is a whole lot bigger than his brain."

"Every woman's fantasy man."

"For a while, maybe. I got bored."

"And boredom is anathema to you."

"Positively." Looking down at the crowd, she sighed. "And I'm there now." She reached for his hand. "Come with me. I want to show you something."

She drew him down the hallway and into her bedroom. By closing the door, they were granted a blessed reprieve from the music. She leaned against the door and closed her eyes. "Enough of that. I was developing a bitching headache."

"You can't abandon your own party, Davee."

"Only a handful of those people know me. They were just looking for a party and they found one. It doesn't matter whether or not I mingle. Besides, they're all on their way to becoming blind drunk." As she moved across the room, she stepped out of her high-heeled sandals and set her drink on the small table near the chaise. "Want another?"

"No, thanks."

She took his sweating glass from him and set it down beside hers. What happened next caught him completely by surprise. She reached for his hands and positioned them on her bare waist, then came up on her tiptoes and kissed him, doing another bump and grind against his middle that wasn't as exaggerated as the first, but even more suggestive.

He reacted with a start, jerking his head up and back. "What are you doing?"

"You have to ask?"

She looped her arms around his neck and tried to kiss him again, but when he didn't respond, she lowered her heels and gazed up at him with evident disappointment. "No?"

"No, Davee."

"Just for the hell of it? If you can't fuck an old friend, who can you fuck?"

"*Whom* can you fuck."

She grinned and tried to lock lips again, but he angled his head back.

"We're not kids any longer, Davee. We're past the experimental age."

"It would be good," she promised seductively. "Much better than the first time."

"No doubt about that." He smiled and gave her waist an affectionate squeeze before lowering his hands to his sides. "But I can't."

"You mean you won't."

"I mean I won't."

"Oh, Jesus," she groaned. As she lowered her arms, she dragged her hands down his chest all the way to his belt before letting them fall away from him. "Tell me it isn't so."

"What?"

"You've fallen for her."

His heart all but stopped. "How did you find out?"

"Oh, please, Hammond. For months it's been in the grapevine that you two take your work home with you."

"Steffi!" he exclaimed on an expulsion of relief. "You're talking about Steffi."

Davee cocked her head with perplexity. "Who else could I be talking about?"

Admitting to his affair with Steffi was less harmful than answering her question. "I had a relationship with Steffi, but it's over."

"Swear?" She narrowed her eyes suspiciously.

"Scout's honor."

"Well, I can't tell you how glad I am to hear that. Sunday night when you were here, I gave you ample opportunity to talk trash on Ms. Mundell. When you didn't, I figured the rumors were true. I was floored. I mean, Hammond, where was the appeal? She has no style, no sense of humor, no class, and I'd be willing to bet she doesn't know any better than to wear white shoes after Labor Day."

Hammond laughed. "You big phony. You're not nearly as unconventional as you want everyone to believe."

She assumed a haughty air. "Some things simply aren't done."

"And that white shoes bit is strictly taboo."

"But you are interested in someone, aren't you?" she asked suddenly. "And don't try that 'who, me?' face on me, because I know I'm right."

He neither admitted nor denied it.

Exasperated, she propped her fists on her hips. "I threw this at you," she said of her shapely body. "I offered you no-strings-attached, mindless boffing, and you turned me down. So either you've gone gay, you're hung up on another woman, or I've lost all my sex appeal and might just as well kill myself tonight. Now which is it?"

"Well, I haven't gone gay, and you haven't lost all your sex appeal."

She didn't make any of the triumphant exclamations she was entitled to. No "I knew it!" No "You can't fool me, Hammond Cross!" None of that.

Instead she responded to his solemnity, saying quietly, "I thought so. When did you meet her?"

"Recently."

"A new armpiece? Or is she special?"

Hammond stared at her a moment, debating whether or not to try lying. Before his affair with Steffi, he had dated many women but never stayed with one for long. Around Charleston, he was known as an eligible bachelor with family money and plenty of promise. Scores of single women boldly sought his company. Potential mothers-in-law considered him an excellent catch.

His own mother was constantly arranging introductions to her friends' daughters and nieces. "She's a lovely young woman from a wonderful family." "Her people are from Georgia. They're into timber. Or maybe it's tires. Something like that." "She's simply a precious girl. I think you two would have a lot in common." A flip answer would probably convince Davee that this amounted to nothing more than that.

But Davee was his oldest friend, and he was sick of lies and lying. He lowered himself to the edge of the chaise and clasped his hands between his spread knees. His shoulders slumped forward slightly.

"Jesus," she said as she picked up her drink. "Is it as bad as all that?"

"She's not an armpiece. About the other, whether or not she could be special, I don't know."

"Too soon to tell?"

"Too complicated."

"She's married?"

"No."

"Then why is it complicated?"

"More than complicated. Impossible."

"I don't understand."

"I can't talk about it, Davee." He spoke more sharply than he had intended, but his tone must have alerted her to how sensitive the subject was.

In any case, she backed down. "Okay. But if you need a friend . . ."

"Thanks." He reached for her hand, pushed back the bangles, and kissed the inside of her wrist. Then, as his finger absently traced the pattern etched into one of the bracelets, he asked, "What gave me away?"

"The way you're acting."

He dropped her hand. "How am I acting?"

"Like there's a line for mandatory castration and you're next." She moved to the cart across the room and mixed a fresh drink. "The minute I saw you at the funeral yesterday I knew something was wrong. Career-wise—thanks in part to me—things are going great for you. So I figured you were suffering from a heart problem."

"It bothers me that I'm so transparent."

"Relax. Probably no one else has noticed. Besides knowing you so well, I recognize the symptoms. That particular brand of misery can only spell l-o-v-e."

He raised his eyebrows. "I don't believe it."

"Hmm."

"You never told me."

"It ended badly. I was just coming off of it that summer we were in the wedding together. A wedding," she snorted. "Just the environment I needed to make me thoroughly miserable. That's why I acted like such a royal bitch at all the prenuptial parties. That's also why I needed a friend that night. A very intimate friend," she said with a soft smile, which he returned. "Our little escapade in the swimming pool restored my self-confidence."

"Glad to have been of service."

"You're damn right you were."

Gradually Hammond's smile receded. "I never would have guessed, Davee. You covered it well. What happened?"

"We met at the university. He was a preacher's kid. Can you believe it? Me with a preacher's kid. He was a real gentleman. Smart. Sensitive. Didn't treat me like a tramp, and, hard as you may find this to believe, I didn't act like one with him."

She finished her drink and poured another. "But I had, of course. By the time I met him, I had whored my way across campus, through one dormitory, up one side of fraternity row and down the other. I'd even had a fling with one of my instructors.

"Miraculously he was blissfully unaware of my reputation. Some of my former partners thought it would be a great joke to tell him." She moved to the window and stared through the louvers of the shutters.

"He was an excellent student. Dean's list. Very straight. He didn't party much. For all those reasons, he wasn't well liked. The guys enjoyed humiliating him, figured it was his comeuppance for being so superior. They didn't spare a single detail. They even had some pictures from a party where I was one of the favors.

"When he confronted me with all they'd told him, I was devastated that he knew the truth about me. I pleaded with him to forgive me. To try and understand. To believe that I had changed when I met him. But he refused even to listen." She leaned forward, resting her forehead on the shutter. "That same night, to spite me, he slept with another girl. And she got pregnant."

She remained so still that even her bracelets didn't jangle. "From a moral and religious standpoint, abortion was out of the question. Nor would it ever have occurred to him to do other than what was right. So he married the girl. As strange as it may seem, Hammond, that's when I loved him most. I had so wanted to have his children."

He waited until he was certain that she was finished, until she moved again, and that was to raise her glass to her lips. "Have you kept track of him?"

"Yes."

"Is he still married?"

"No."

"Do you ever see him?"

She turned away from the window and looked at him. "Yesterday. At Lute's funeral. He was seated near the back with Steffi Mundell. He's still not very well liked."

When Hammond pulled all the clues together, his jaw dropped open. Soundlessly his lips formed the name. "Rory Smilow?"

She gave a wry laugh. "There's no accounting for taste, is there?"

Hammond pushed his hand up through his hair. "No wonder he hated Lute so much. First for his sister. Then you."

"Well, actually it was the other way around. Lute's marriage to Margaret didn't come until years later. I remember when Rory moved to Charleston to accept the job with the police department. I read about it in the newspaper. I wanted to contact him then, but my pride wouldn't let me.

"The woman he married had died giving birth to their stillborn baby." She paused to reflect on the irony of that. "His parents were dead, so responsibility for Margaret had fallen on him. He moved her here with him. She got a clerical job in the courthouse. County records, plats, things like that. That's where she met Lute. It wouldn't surprise me if the romance developed after she did him a favor, like fudging a property line or something."

"It wouldn't surprise me, either," Hammond remarked. "I've heard the marriage was a nightmare."

"Margaret was emotionally fragile. She was certainly no match for a bastard like Lute." She finished her drink. "On occasion I had got good and tanked, swallowed my pride, and accidentally-on-purpose put myself in Rory's path. He always looked right through me, as though we'd never known one another. That hurt, Hammond. It also pissed me off.

"So after Margaret's suicide, I went after Lute and didn't stop chasing him until he married me. Rory had broken my heart. So I tried to break his by marrying the man he most despised." She added ruefully, "Revenge has a way of kicking the avenger in the ass, doesn't it?"

"I'm sorry, Davee."

"Ah, well, don't be," she said with a breeziness that Hammond knew was false. "I've still got my looks. This," she said, holding up her highball glass, "didn't destroy Mama's beauty. She's as gorgeous as ever, so I'm counting on good genes to ward off the ill effects of demon alcohol. I've got lots of money. As soon as Lute's will is probated, I'll have lots more. Speaking of which . . ."

She walked to an antique desk and opened the slender lap drawer. "This fucking stroll down memory lane almost made me forget. I found this while going through some papers in Lute's desk. It's in his handwriting." She handed him a pale green Post-It note. "That's last Saturday's date, isn't it?"

Hammond's vision blurred around the notation.

"Lute wrote down your name and a five o'clock time. Looks to me like an appointment. Which I'm sure you would rather no one knew about."

He looked across at her. "It's not what you think."

She laughed. "Hammond, honey, I'd sooner believe in cellulite-reducing creams than I would believe you capable of committing murder. I don't know what it signifies and don't want to know. I just thought you should have it."

He stared at the second notation on the small square of paper. "He wrote down another time. Six o'clock. No name. Any ideas?"

"None. There's nothing on his official day planner about any appointments on Saturday, with you or anyone else."

Obviously Lute had intended to meet with someone else that afternoon, following his appointment with him. Who? he wondered. Thoughtfully, he folded the small piece of paper and put it in his pocket. "Rightfully, you should have given this to Smilow."

"When have you ever known me to do the right thing?" Her mischievous smile turned wistful. "I learned the hard way that it's a waste of time to try and hurt Rory. I don't believe he can be hurt." Then her smile disappeared altogether. "But I don't feel compelled to do him any favors, either."

## CHAPTER 25

HE WAS HERE WITH ME LAST NIGHT." Ellen Rogers had to shout to make herself heard above the music. "We sat at that table for hours and ordered several rounds of drinks. You must remember."

The bartender, a hunky young man with a sleek ponytail and a silver hoop in his eyebrow, looked her over in a way that said she was remarkably forgettable. "I see lots of people. Night after night. I don't remember all their faces. They sorta run together in my head, you know?"

A leggy blonde in a tight black dress undulated onto the neighboring barstool. The bartender reached across Ellen to light the blonde's cigarette. "What are you having?"

"What's good?"

He propped his elbows on the bar and leaned closer to her. "That all depends on what you're after."

"Excuse me," Ellen interrupted. She wound up having to tap the bartender on the shoulder to regain his attention. "If he comes back—the guy I was with last night—call me. Okay?"

With little hope it would do any good, she pushed a slip of paper toward him. "Here's the number of my hotel."

"Okay."

She watched him pocket the telephone number, knowing that his dry cleaner would probably find it in a couple of days. She had entered the club with the proud, purposeful stride of a crusader. She was a woman on a mission.

This morning, after the initial shock had worn off and she'd had time to pull herself together, she had determined to track down the lying son of a bitch and turn him over to the police.

When darkness fell, she had set out with the intention of canvassing every nightclub in Charleston if that's what it took to find and expose him. This character had hustling down to an art. Looking back, she realized that he had been too smooth for her to have been his first victim. Nor would she be his last. Feeling heady and confident after last night's success, her seducer would be on the prowl again tonight.

But now as she left the club, her zeal was already on the wane. She acknowledged how foolhardy it was to be traipsing around Charleston looking for a liar and thief she knew only as Eddie, which in all likelihood was an assumed name.

The new patent leather pumps she had bought especially for this vacation trip were pinching her toes, reducing her march to a hobble. She was hungry, but each time she had tried to eat today, her stomach had grown queasy from last night's liquor consumption and this morning's self-loathing.

Not that she could afford to eat at any decent restaurants, she reminded herself sourly. She had notified the credit card companies of the theft, but it would be days before she received replacement cards. Luckily she had remembered tucking some cash into the pocket of a blazer. It was a fraction of the amount Eddie had stolen, but if she was frugal it would see her home.

So why not just cut her losses and go?

Charleston had been spoiled for her. The sultry heat that had enhanced the city's romantic appeal now made her irritable and headachy. If she stayed as long as planned, she wouldn't be able to afford any tours or attractions. Fewer nights here would mean a smaller hotel bill.

Common sense told her to return to Indianapolis tomorrow. The airline would charge her for changing her ticket, but the fee would be worth it. In her safe little house, with her two cats and familiar belongings, she could retreat to lick her wounds until the fall semester began. Eventually work and routine would crowd the nasty incident from her mind.

In any case, slogging through Charleston searching for Eddie was a waste of time and effort.

On the other hand, even now, while she was limping along in her uncomfortable, blister-rubbing patent leather shoes, he was probably working his con on another lonely lady who would wake up tomorrow morning relieved of her pocketbook and her self-respect. The crime would go unreported because the victim was too ashamed to report it to the authorities. That's why Eddie could do it with such arrogance—he could get away with it.

Well, he wasn't going to get away with it this time. "Not if I can help it," Ellen Rogers said out loud.

With renewed determination, she entered the next club.

Hammond slid into the booth across from Loretta. "What have you got for me?"

"No hello or how are you?"

"I'm fresh out of pleasantries today."

"You look like shit."

"You must be out of pleasantries, too." Hammond smiled grimly. "Actually, that's the second time today that it's been noted how ragged I look. That's how my day started out, in fact."

"What's wrong?"

"You haven't got that much time. I'm running out of time myself, so do you have something for me, or not?"

"I called you, didn't I?" she retorted.

He didn't blame her for taking umbrage. He was acting like a jerk. His visit with Davee had left him more disconcerted than before. When he got in his car and used his cell phone to check for messages, he was only half glad to hear Loretta's voice urging him to meet her as soon as possible at the Shady Rest Lounge. Seeing her meant extending a day he was ready to put to a close. Conversely, he was anxious to know what her probe had turned up.

Shaking his head and sighing heavily, he apologized. "I'm in a pisser of a mood, Loretta, but I shouldn't be taking it out on you."

"You need a drink."

"Your solution for everything."

"Not for everything. Not by a long shot. But it can be a Band-Aid cure for a bad mood." She ordered him a bourbon and water.

In less than a minute, he had the drink in his hand and was taking a sip. "You look good."

She laughed around a swallow of club soda. "Maybe when viewed through the bottom of a highball glass."

She had undergone noticeable improvements since Monday night. She was far better groomed, her clothes were clean and pressed. Correctly applied makeup had softened the lines in her face. Her eyes were bright and clear. Although she had tried to laugh off his compliment, he could tell she was flattered.

"I've cleaned up a little, is all."

"Put some color in your hair?"

"Bev's idea."

"Good one."

"Thanks." Self-consciously she raised her hand and patted her rejuvenated hairdo. "She was happy to hear I had a job. I told her it was just temporary, but, well, she was still glad. She let me move back into the apartment, under the condition—she's big on conditions, just like you—that I keep perfect attendance at the AA meetings."

"How're you doing?"

"I get the morning shakes, but I'm dealing with it."

"That's good, Loretta. That's real good," he said, meaning it. He paused, signaling the conclusion of that topic before moving on to the reason for the meeting. "What have you got for me?"

She winked. "The motherlode. You'll probably recommend that I get a staff position with the solicitor's office. You might even ask me to have your children."

"That good?"

He set his drink aside. It wasn't mixing well with the one he'd drunk at Davee's party. Besides, he got the feeling that the information he was about to receive would be upsetting, and it would be better dealt with if his head were clear.

"I have a mole who shall remain nameless, a real computer geek—"

"Knuckle."

"You know him?"

"Harvey's my mole, too. He's everybody's mole."

"Are you shitting me?" she asked, astonished and more than a little abashed and angry.

"You weaseled him, right?"

"Damn!" she said, slapping the tabletop. "I can't believe that pompous little fucker made me feel guilty for twisting his arm and trying to get him to compromise his integrity."

"He's thoroughly corruptible. That's why I didn't go to him directly. He's untrustworthy."

Hammond wasn't worried that Harvey's delving into Alex's records would be traced back to him. He believed Loretta when she vowed they would have to cut out her tongue before she would betray his confidence. But he wondered if anyone else had tried to coerce Knuckle for the same purpose. "When you approached him, did Harvey know anything about the case?"

"He didn't appear to. But now I'm doubting him, as well as my own instincts. Why?"

Hammond raised a shoulder. "I'm just curious if anyone else asked him to run a trace on Dr. Ladd."

"Like Steffi Mundell?"

"Or Smilow."

"If Harvey is everyone's mole, I guess that's a possibility. But, honestly, Hammond, he acted surprised and pleased that I was including him on my investigation."

Nodding, he indicated the letter-size envelope beneath her right hand. "Let's have the scoop."

She opened the envelope and removed several folded sheets of paper. From what Hammond could tell, they were typewritten notes. By now Loretta had reviewed the information so many times, she had practically memorized it. She referred to the typewritten data only to verify specific dates.

"Impressive," he murmured as she enumerated Alex Ladd's scholastic accomplishments, most of which he already knew. Any relief he felt, however, was short-lived.

"Hold on. I haven't got to the good stuff yet."

"By good, do you really mean bad?"

"She doesn't have as impressive a record in Tennessee."

"What happened there?"

"What didn't?"

She then told him what Harvey Knuckle had mined from unmineable juvenile records. It didn't make for easy listening. By the time Loretta finished, half an hour had passed and Hammond was wishing he hadn't drunk any whiskey that evening. He was fairly certain he was going to see it recycled. Now he understood what Alex had meant last night about his being disillusioned, about explanations being painful. She hadn't wanted to share, and now he knew why.

Loretta replaced the sheets of paper in the envelope and triumphantly handed it to him. "I didn't find the link between her and Pettijohn. That remains a mystery."

"I think—thought," he amended, "that she was too classy to have any link to Lute. Apparently I was wrong."

He slid the envelope and its incriminating contents into the inside breast pocket of his jacket. His dejection wasn't lost on her. "You don't seem very excited."

"I couldn't have asked for more thorough coverage. You should feel very good about the way you pulled yourself together and came through for me. You more than made up for past mistakes. Thanks."

He scooted to the end of the booth, but Loretta reached across the table and seized his hand. "What is with you, Hammond?"

"I don't know what you mean."

"I thought you'd be over the moon."

"It's good stuff, no question."

"And it only took me two days."

"Can't complain about the short turnaround, either."

"It definitely gives you something to work with, doesn't it?"

"Definitely."

"So why do you look so goddamn glum?"

"I guess I'm embarrassed."

"By what?"

"This," he said, tapping his jacket outside the breast pocket. "It indicates that I'm a lousy judge of character. I honestly didn't think she was capable of . . ." His voice trailed off, leaving his complete thought unspoken.

"Alex Ladd, you mean?" He nodded. "You think she's innocent? That Smilow is barking up the wrong tree? Has she come up with an alibi?"

"It's weak. She says she went to a county fair in Beaufort. No corroboration." It seemed lying came easily now. Even to trusted friends. "Anyway, in light of this information, an unsubstantiated alibi seems academic."

"I could—"

"Excuse me, Loretta. As I said earlier, it's been a rough day, and I'm exhausted."

He tried to smile, but knew he failed. The gloomy interior of the bar was suffocating him. The smoke seemed thicker. The odor of despair more pervasive. His head was throbbing and his gut was churning. Loretta's eyes were as sharp as boning knives. Afraid they would see too much, he avoided looking straight into them.

"I'll get your fee to you tomorrow."

"I turned over every stone I could, Hammond."

"You did a terrific job."

"But you were hoping for more."

Actually he had been hoping for nothing, but certainly less than what he had got. "No, no. With this, I'll be able to move the case forward."

Pathetically eager to please him, Loretta gripped his hand tighter. "I could try digging even deeper."

"Give me time to assimilate this first. I'm sure it'll be sufficient. If not, I'll be in touch."

Without fresh air, he was going to die. He worked his hand out of Loretta's damp grip, told her to stay sober, thanked her again for a job well done, and tossed a hasty goodbye over his shoulder.

Outside the Shady Rest, the air was neither fresh nor bracing. It was stagnant and thick and seemed to take on the properties of cotton as he sucked it into his lungs.

Even hours after sundown the sidewalk was emanating heat that burned his feet through the soles of his shoes. His skin was clammy. Like when he was a kid, sick. After a fever broke, his mother would remove his damp pajamas and change his bed sheets, assuring him that the sweat was a good sign. It meant he was getting better. But it didn't feel better. He preferred the dryness of fever to the cloying moisture on his skin.

The sidewalk was congested with people milling from doorway to doorway but having no real place to go. They were looking for something interesting to do, which might include, but wasn't limited to, getting drunk in one of the taverns, stealing something they needed, destroying or defacing property just for the hell of it, or satisfying a vendetta with bloodshed.

Ordinarily Hammond would have been attuned to the potential danger the neighborhood posed to one who obviously didn't belong there. Both blacks and whites sneered at him with palpable prejudice and cultivated hatred. He was definitely a "have" in an area of "have nots," and resentment ran high. At any other time, he would have been looking over one shoulder as he made his way back to his car, half expecting to find it stripped when he reached it. Tonight, preoccupation made him careless and indifferent to the hostile glances cast at him.

Loretta's report on Alex had plunged him into a moral morass. The incriminating information was stultifying. The emotional impact of it severe. The whole of it was so devastating, he couldn't separate individual aspects of it.

When Smilow learned her history—and it was only a matter of time before one of his detectives uncovered it—he would have wet dreams. Steffi would break out a bottle of champagne. But for him and Alex, professionally and personally, the discovery would be disastrous.

Disclosure was like a lead weight hanging by an unraveling filament just above his head. When would it drop? Tonight? Tomorrow? The next day? How long could he stand the suspense? How long could he wrestle with his own conscience? Even if the time of death eliminated her as the actual murderer, she must have been involved to some extent.

These thoughts were so dreary, so absorbing, they were almost immobilizing. He had lost all sense of where he was. He was thinking about disbarment, not dismemberment. When he reached the alley where he had left his car, he used the keyless door lock and opened the driver's door without even glancing around to see if it was safe.

Startled by sudden movement behind him, he reacted quickly. He came around in a blur of motion, his arm raised, ready to protect and defend himself.

He came close to striking Alex before arresting the momentum of his arm.

"What the hell!" Reflexively he scanned the immediate area, only now becoming aware of the dark, menacing surroundings. "What the hell are you doing in this neighborhood?"

"I followed her here."

"Who?"

Green eyes snapped angrily. "Who do you think, Hammond? The woman you hired to follow *me*."

"Shit!"

"My sentiment exactly," she said heatedly. "I thought it was strange that the same tourist came down my street twice in one day taking pictures of my house. First this morning, then again shortly after Smilow's raiders left. On my way home from that humiliating interrogation this afternoon, I stopped at the supermarket. She was there, too, trying to look interested in watermelons. It finally dawned on me that I was under surveillance."

"Not surveillance."

"True. That would imply professionalism. While this is classless, gutless, ordinary spying."

"Alex—"

"So I dodged her, doubled back, turned the tables, and started following her. I thought Detective Smilow must be behind it. Imagine my surprise when you showed up to meet her here."

"Don't put me on a level with Smilow."

"Oh, you're much lower than Mr. Smilow," she said, her voice cracking with mounting emotion. "You're sneakier. More underhanded. You sleep with me first."

"It's not like that."

"Really? Then what is it like? Which part is inaccurate? Is she a policewoman?"

"Private investigator."

"Even worse. You paid her to snoop on me."

"Okay, you caught me," he said, his anger rising to match hers. "You're a very clever lady, Dr. Ladd."

"Did you two have a nice chat about me?"

"There wasn't anything nice about it, but what she dug up on you was damned interesting. Especially the records from Tennessee."

She closed her eyes and reeled slightly. But she recovered quickly, reopened her eyes, and told him to go to hell.

She turned on her heel, but Hammond caught her arm and brought her back around. "What she dredged up about you isn't my fault, Alex. When I hired her, I thought I was doing us both a favor."

"In God's name, how?"

"I had hoped, stupidly, that she would find something exculpatory. But that was before you started lying to the police with every breath, and painting yourself into inescapable corners."

"Would you rather I had told them the truth?"

She had asked him the same question when they accidently met in the elevator. He'd had no answer for her. But since then he had given it a lot of thought. "It doesn't matter that we spent Saturday night together."

"Then why haven't you told them? When I was being put through that humiliating interrogation about my dirty laundry, literally, why did you just stand there? Why didn't you tell them everything, including who broke into my house last night and stained my sheets?"

"Because it's irrelevant."

She laughed without mirth. "You're delusional, Solicitor Cross. Even given your brilliance, I think you would have a hard time persuading anyone of its irrelevance. And while we're on the subject, I explained away the blood. But there's only one explanation for semen. Which wouldn't have been there if you'd worn some protection."

"I didn't think about it." Lowering his face close to hers, he added on an angry whisper, "And neither did you." He knew he had scored on that round when she averted her face. "Besides, one has nothing to do with the other."

She looked back at him. "I have trouble following that logic."

"Our sleeping together has no bearing on the case." If he could convince her, he might be able to convince someone else. He might even come to believe it himself. "I've been thinking about it. Last Saturday, you could have murdered Pettijohn before leaving Charleston."

She sucked in a quick breath, and folded her arms across her middle as though a pain had just shot through her. "That's what you've been thinking? You said the time of death didn't fit."

"Because I didn't want it to."

"And now you do?"

"You killed him, then finagled our meeting to establish an alibi."

"I told you last night, I did not kill Pettijohn."

"Right, right. Like you didn't fuck him, either."

Once again, she spun around to leave. Hammond's arm shot out. This time, she put up more of a struggle. "Damn you! Let me go!"

He turned her around and trapped her in the wedge formed by the open car door. In order for her to escape she would either have to go around or through him. He was determined that she would hear him out first. "I don't want to think that, Alex."

"Well, gee, thanks. I'm so glad you don't want to think of me as a slut and a murderer."

"What else am I supposed to believe?"

"Believe anything you like, just leave me alone."

"All along, even when it stretched credibility, I've been giving you the benefit of the doubt. Until tonight." He opened his jacket far enough for her to see the envelope inside his breast pocket.

Suddenly she ceased to struggle. She stared at the envelope for a moment, and he saw her lips twitch with what looked like remorse. But to her credit, when she raised her eyes to his, they were defiant and proud. "Juicy reading?"

"Damaging. Very damaging. This is the ammunition they need to nail you."

"Then why are you standing here talking to me?"

"Smilow will take this and run with it."

"So call him up. Give him the lowdown. You got what you wanted, what you paid for."

"I'm giving you a chance to explain it."

"I rather imagine it's self-explanatory."

"So I'm supposed to take it at face value?"

"I don't give a damn how you take it."

"Okay. I'll interpret it the only way I can." He pressed his lower body against her. "It means you've come a long way, baby."

Her composure and hauteur deserted her. With both hands, she pushed hard against his chest. "Get away from me."

He didn't yield. "What this indicates to me is that last Saturday night was more than a simple seduction."

"I didn't seduce you."

"Like hell, but we've been through that before. You're implicated in a felony crime, and you deliberately drew me in. Why, Alex? You intentionally created a conflict of interest for me as a prosecutor. You made me part of it—whatever the hell *it* is."

"There is no 'it.' There never was. Not until Lute Pettijohn turned up dead."

"Was he in on it?"

"Aren't you listening?" she cried.

"Was I the target of his last scheme? Was he plotting my downfall when he was murdered?"

"I don't know. His being murdered had nothing to do with me."

"I wish I could believe that. Our meeting was not accidental, Alex. You've admitted that much."

She tried to sidestep him, but he blocked her and placed his hands on her shoulders.

"You're not leaving until I get to the truth. How did you know I would be at that fair?"

She shook her head.

"How did you know?"

She remained stubbornly mute.

"Tell me, Alex. How did you know I was going there? You couldn't have. The only way you could have known is if—" Suddenly he broke off. He gave her a hard, piercing look and gripped her shoulders tighter.

Her eyes spoke eloquently to his.

"You followed me there," he said quietly.

She hesitated for what seemed an interminable time before slowly nodding her head. "Yes. I followed you from the Charles Towne Plaza."

Y OU'VE KNOWN ALL THIS TIME THAT I WAS THERE?"

"Yes!"

"With Pettijohn?"

"Right again."

"And you didn't say anything? Why?"

"If I told you now, you wouldn't believe me."

Looking straight at his jacket, she stared at it as though she could see through the fabric to the envelope inside the breast pocket. She was angry. But she also appeared profoundly sad.

"That's an ugly report, but it can't come close to capturing how ugly it was in reality. You can't begin to imagine." Her eyes moved back up to his. "I'll be judged on a damn report, not on what I am now."

"I won't—"

"You already have," she said hotly. "I see it in the way you're looking at me and I hear it in your nasty insinuations. It's easy to judge from your lofty position, isn't it? You of the wealthy family with the pedigree. Have you ever gone hungry for days on end, Hammond? Been cold because the utility bill hadn't been paid? Gone dirty because there was no soap to wash with?"

He tried to reach for her, but she flung off his arm. "No, don't pity me. Sometimes I'm glad for it because it made me strong. It made me who I am, made me better at helping people. Because nothing they tell me shocks me. I'm wholly accepting of people and their aberrations, because until you've been where someone else has been, you've no right to judge their behavior.

"Until you've gone hungry, and suffered humiliation, and come to hate yourself for what you're doing . . . until you come to believe you're filth, unworthy of anyone's love, of a man's love—"

She stopped and sucked in a quick breath that caused her chest to shudder. Then she sniffed her nose and tossed her head in defiance of the tears streaming down her cheeks. "Happy reading, Hammond."

She pushed him aside and stalked off, turning the corner and out of the alley. Hammond watched her go, knowing that nothing he said now would reach beyond her anger. He cursed, braced his elbow on the roof of the car, and rested his head on his forearm. But the respite lasted only a few seconds.

A muffled cry brought his head up and around.

Alex was running back into the alley. A man was chasing her.

"He's got a knife!" she shouted.

The attacker grabbed her by the hair, jerking her to a sudden halt. He raised his arm and Hammond saw the glint of steel. Without even thinking about it, he launched himself against the attacker, his shoulder catching him beneath his rib cage and knocking him off-balance.

In order to keep from falling, the man released Alex. She scrambled out of the way. Hammond barely had time to register that she was momentarily out of harm's way when he saw a flash of silver arcing horizontally toward his middle. Acting on reflex, he protected his belly with his arm. The switchblade sliced it open from elbow to wristbone.

Unarmed, in a knife fight, he would lose. The only self-defense he knew, he'd learned playing football. To please his father, he had played with a bloodthirsty competitiveness.

Instinctually, he relied now on a blocking tactic that was effective if you could get away with it and not draw a flag from the official. He thrust his head forward as though he were going to ram his attacker in the throat but stopped just short of making contact. The mugger reacted as hoped by jerking his head backward, leaving his Adam's apple vulnerable to Hammond's ramming forearm. He knew it hurt like hell and would incapacitate the mugger for a precious few seconds.

"Get in the car!" he yelled to Alex.

Hammond thrust his foot toward the man's groin but missed and caught him in the thigh. The kick didn't do any real damage, but it bought him another half second in which to run backward toward the car while dodging slashing motions of the switchblade. Alex had gotten in through the open door on the driver's side and climbed over the console. He practically fell into the driver's seat, then leaned backward across the console and drove his heel into the guy's gut. The mugger stumbled backward but managed another swipe with the blade. Hammond heard the fabric of his trousers rip.

Lunging for the door handle, he pulled the door closed and locked it. His attacker, having rapidly regained his balance, pounded on the window and door, shouting obscenities and death threats.

Hammond's right hand was slippery with blood, but he managed to cram the key into the ignition and start the motor. He dropped the gear stick into drive and stamped on the accelerator. The tires laid down rubber as his car shot down the alley and fishtailed out into the street.

"Hammond, you're hurt!"

"What about you?" He took his eyes off the road long enough to glance at Alex. She was sitting on her knees in the passenger seat, reaching across the console to examine his arm.

"I'm okay. But you're not."

What was left of his right sleeve was soaked with blood. It dripped from his hand, making the steering wheel almost too slippery to hold on to, and forcing him to drive left-handed. But that didn't slow him down. He ran a red light. "He's probably got friends. They'll rob us and then steal the car. I've got to get us out of this neighborhood."

"He wasn't trying to steal anything," she said with remarkable composure. "He was after me. He called me by name."

Hammond gaped at her; the car veered off the road, nearly striking a telephone pole.

"Hammond!" she shouted. Once he had regained control of the car, she said, "Head for the emergency room. You're going to need stitches."

He released the steering wheel long enough to drag his left sleeve across his forehead. He was sweating profusely. He could feel it on his face, in his hair, trickling down his ribs, gathering in his groin. Now that the adrenaline surge was over, he was feeling the impact of what had happened, and what might have happened. He and Alex were lucky still to be alive. *Jesus, she could have been killed.* The thought of how close she had come to dying made him very weak and shaky.

At the first major intersection they came to, he was forced to stop for a traffic light. He took deep breaths in an effort to clear his head of a buzzing noise that sounded like a thousand swarming bees.

"Your leg is bleeding, too, but it's your arm that concerns me," Alex said. "Do you think he cut into the muscle?"

Green light. Hammond pressed the accelerator hard and the car bucked forward like a bronco charging out of the chute. Within seconds it was exceeding the posted speed limit. He could see the hospital complex a few blocks ahead.

"Hammond, are you okay?"

Alex's voice seemed to drift toward him from far away. "I'm fine."

"Can you drive the rest of the way?"

"Hmm."

"I don't think so. Stop here. Let me drive."

He tried to tell her that he was all right, but he couldn't separate his words, so they came out garbled and unintelligible.

"Hammond? Hammond? You need to turn here. The emergency room—"

"No."

"You're losing a lot of blood."

"You're a doctor." God, his tongue had grown thick.

"Not the kind you need," she exclaimed. "You need a hospital. A tetanus shot. Maybe even blood."

Shaking his head, he mumbled, "My place."

"Please be reasonable."

"Two 'f us . . ." He looked across at her and shook his head. "We' b'screwed."

She grappled with indecision for several seconds, but apparently came to the same conclusion. Reaching across the console, she took control of the steering wheel, which was slick with his blood.

"All right, but I'm driving."

She managed to steer the car to the curb and put it in park. It took some effort, and some gentle but forceful urging, to get Hammond to switch places with her. She got out and went around, opened his door, and assisted him out. He was wobbly on his feet. She tucked him into the passenger seat and secured the seat belt. As soon as he was settled, he laid his head back and closed his eyes.

She couldn't have him pass out on her. "Hammond, what's your address?" She reached for his cell phone and began to dial. "Hammond!"

He mumbled a street address. "'Cross from marina. Just . . ."

He angled his chin in the right direction. Thankfully Alex knew the street. It was only blocks away. She could have him there within minutes.

Convincing Dr. Douglas Mann to make a house call was another matter.

Miraculously, she had memorized his home phone number. He answered on the second ring. "Doug, Alex. Thank God I reached you." She explained the situation as she drove, but omitted telling him that it hadn't been a random attack.

"Sounds to me like he needs a hospital."

"Doug. Please. I'm calling in that favor."

Reluctantly, he asked for the address. She was giving it to him as she pulled onto the street. "We're here now. Come as soon as you can." The remote opener for Hammond's garage was clipped to the sun visor. She opened the garage door, then closed it behind them as soon as she killed the engine.

Getting out, she ran around the hood of the car to the passenger side. Hammond's eyes were still closed. He was pale. When she tried to rouse him, he groaned. "It's not going to be easy, but I've got to get you inside. Can you swing your legs out?"

He moved as though he weighed a thousand pounds, but he managed. She slipped her hands into his armpits. "Stand up, darling, and lean against me."

He did so. But the movement hurt his right arm and he yelped in pain. "I'm sorry," she said earnestly.

It was like handling a hundred-eighty-five–pound rag doll. His coordination was shot. But he followed her instructions, and she managed to get him out of the car and on his feet. She supported him as they shuffled toward the back door. "Is the door locked? Will we set off an alarm?"

He shook his head.

She got him into the kitchen. "Where's the nearest bathroom?"

He pointed with his left hand. The half bath was located in a short hallway between the kitchen and what she could see was the living room. She eased him down onto the commode lid and flipped on the wall switch. For the first time, she got a well-lit look at his wounds.

"Oh, my God."

"I'm okay."

"No, no you're not."

The skin of his arm had been laid open. It was hard to tell how deep the gash was because it was leaking blood all along the cut. She went straight to work. First she removed his jacket, then ripped the sleeve of his shirt up to the shoulder seam. Yanking towels and washcloths off the decorative bars, she wrapped them around his forearm, pulling them tight to form compresses which would hopefully stanch the bleeding.

Kneeling in front of him, she tried to rip his pants leg, but the fabric was too strong, so she impatiently shoved it over his knee. The cut along his shin wasn't as deep as the one on his arm, but it was just as bloody. His sock had absorbed a lot of it. She upturned the empty wastebasket and propped his foot on it, then wrapped his shin in towels as she had his arm.

She stood up, pushed back her hair with a bloody hand, and consulted her wristwatch. "Where is he? He should be here by now."

Hammond reached for her hand. "Alex?"

She stopped fretting and looked down at him.

"He could've killed you," he rasped.

"But he didn't. I'm here." She squeezed his hand.

"Why didn't you tell them?"

"That you were with Pettijohn?"

He nodded.

"Because when they first questioned me, I thought you had killed him."

His face went a shade more pale. "You thought—"

"I can't explain it all now, Hammond. It's too involved. In the state you're in, it's doubtful you would even remember it later. Suffice it to say that at first I lied in order to protect myself. But when I learned that Pettijohn had died of gunshot, I continued lying to protect . . ."

He blinked, looked at her quizzically.

"You."

The doorbell rang. She pulled her hand free. "The doctor's here."

He woke up, startled, her name on his lips. There was something he must tell her, something urgent they must talk about. "Alex." His voice was a croak, alarming him. He moved to get up. The stiffness in his arm caused him to remember.

He opened his eyes. He was lying in his own bed. The room was dark except for a small night-light that had been moved from the hallway and plugged into a wall socket in the bedroom.

"I'm here."

She materialized at his bedside, bent over him, and laid her hand on his shoulder. While he'd been sleeping she had showered and washed her hair. She was no longer covered in his blood, and her clothes had been replaced with one of his oldest and softest T-shirts. Just like at the cabin.

"It's time for another pain pill if you want one."

"I'm okay."

"Would you like some water?"

He told her no.

"Then go back to sleep."

She adjusted the sheet over his bare chest, but when she tried to move away, he covered her hand with his, keeping it trapped against his chest. "What time is it?"

"A little after two. You've been asleep for a couple of hours."

"Who was the doctor?"

"A friend of mine. A good friend. We can trust him."

"You're sure?"

"Let's just say we've swapped professional favors. He strongly advised me to take you to an emergency room, but I prevailed upon him."

"Saying what?"

"That you didn't want to go through the rigmarole of filing a crime report."

"He was okay with that?"

"No, because he saw Smilow and gang at my house this morning. He knows something's amiss. But I left him no room to argue. If your wounds had warranted it, I would have insisted on the hospital myself, no matter what. But once they were cleaned, I was convinced he could treat them here. Actually, you probably got better treatment here than you might have received at the hospital. Much more quickly, too."

"My memory of him is foggy."

"He gave you a shot that more or less knocked you out, so I'm not surprised you don't remember much. You suffered quite a trauma. It exhausted you, and the blood loss made you weak." Smiling, she stroked his forehead. "We had a heck of a time getting you up the stairs. Wish we had it on video. We could send it to *America's Funniest*."

"Will I keep my arm?"

Playing upon his joke, she replied solemnly. "He wanted to take it, but I wouldn't let him. I threw my body across it to protect it."

"Thanks."

"You're welcome. Truthfully, the wound was only skin deep. Several layers of skin, but no muscle or nerve damage was done, thank God. Your leg didn't need to be stitched. He said it would close on its own within a few days. He gave you a tetanus shot and a huge injection of antibiotics. Your butt's going to be sore. He left some oral antibiotics and Darvocet tablets for pain, which you can take every four hours."

His bandaged right arm was propped on a pillow. "It feels like lead, but it doesn't hurt."

"It's full of local anesthetic. As that wears off, the soreness will set in. Tomorrow you'll be glad you have the pain pills. Next week you can have the stitches removed. Until then, you're to keep it in a sling, elevate it when you can, and avoid getting it wet."

"I was covered with blood."

"I gave you a bed bath."

"Sorry I missed that." He grinned, but it was a struggle to keep his eyelids open.

"I also cleaned up your car and the bathroom. They're spotless."

"You're an angel of mercy."

"Only to a point. I should be downstairs now laundering the towels."

"Just throw them away."

"I guessed that's what you would say, so that's what I did. Besides, I would rather be up here watching over you." Tenderly, she combed her fingers through his hair.

He shifted slightly, looking for a more comfortable position. But even that much movement caused him to wince.

"I'm giving you another pill."

This time he didn't argue. He was almost asleep again when she pressed a tablet into his mouth, then cradled his head in the crook of her elbow and eased him up. She tilted a glass of water to his lips. He swallowed the pill.

As she was lowering his head back onto the pillow, he resisted, and nuzzled her breasts instead. They felt full and inviting beneath the soft cloth of his T-shirt. His lips closed around a nipple.

"You need to sleep," she whispered, gently easing him away and back onto the pillow.

He sighed a protest, but his eyes automatically closed. He felt her light kiss on his brow. And something else, too. Opening his eyes again, he saw her tears. Even as he watched, another splashed onto his face.

Remorsefully he said, "Are you crying because of that goddamn report? And because of the way I acted about it? Jesus, Alex, I'm sorry." And he was. For everything. For the horror of her childhood and adolescence and his sanctimonious reaction to it. "I acted like a bastard."

She shook her head. "You saved my life. You were hurt because of me. If I hadn't been there—"

"Shh." Reaching across his body with his left hand, he touched her cheek. She clasped his hand and clutched it to her chest, bending over it and repeatedly kissing the ridge of knuckles.

"I was so afraid, Hammond." Her lips moved against his hand. She pressed the back of it to her cheek, which was moist with tears. "You have been so hurt because of me. And you will continue to be hurt."

He struggled to stay awake because this was important. "Alex . . . I love you."

She let go of his hand as though it had burned her. "What?"

"I love—"

"No, you don't, Hammond," she exclaimed, softly but adamantly. "Don't say that. You don't even know me."

"I know you." He closed his eyes for a few precious seconds of rest and tried to work up the energy to say what he wanted to say. "I've loved you from . . ." . . . *from the night I met you. When I saw you across the dance floor, I knew you immediately.*

He thought the words, but wasn't sure whether or not he actually spoke them out loud. Opening his eyes and focusing on her face, he smiled sadly. "Why did it have to be such a fucking mess?"

She licked a tear from the corner of her lips. She opened her mouth to speak but couldn't find the words. It must have been as puzzling to her as it was to him that the first time in his life he was truly in love, it couldn't be more wrong.

He patted the bed on his left side.

She shook her head no. "I could hurt you."

"Lie down."

Hesitating only a moment longer, she came around to the far side of the bed and slipped in beside him. She didn't touch him except for laying her hand on his chest. "I can't get any closer or I might bump your leg."

There was more he wanted to say, and much they needed to talk about, but the drug was taking effect. Having her close was some consolation. He wanted to enjoy it. But against his will, he slipped into oblivion.

Some time later he awakened. Partially. Not completely. He didn't want to awaken completely. He wasn't in pain. In fact, he was in a sublime state. Good stuff, those painkillers.

Beside him, Alex stirred. He felt her sit up. "Hammond, are you awake?"

"Hmm."

"Can I get you anything?"

He mumbled something that she must have taken as a no because she lay back down. However, a few moments later he muttered something that even he couldn't distinguish.

"Pardon?" Her head came back up. At least he thought so. He still hadn't opened his eyes. "Hammond?" Concerned, she placed her hand on his chest. "Are you in pain? Do you want some water?"

Covering her hand with his, he guided it down beneath the sheet.

Then he floated backward into a semiconscious state that was better than the best of dirty dreams. As in an erotic fantasy, his participation was unnecessary. All he had to do was give over control and submit to the sensations. Let it happen. Go with the flow. Rock adrift on the gentle swells of feeling.

The buildup was deliciously slow. They were on no timetable, under no deadline. There was no pressure or recrimination. Dreams were blissfully void of consequences.

He was aware of her repositioning herself, but a few preliminary, delicate kisses didn't quite prepare him for the wet heat that sheathed him. The sensuous stroking was unlike any other. He held his breath and let the sensations saturate him. His entire body settled heavily into the mattress, as into a warm bath, and soaked in sexual lassitude.

Instinctively he moved his hand. Stretched. Sought. Found. Softness. Silkiness. Mystery deep. Center of the universe. Heartbeat of Man. Pathway to Life.

He had to move his fingers but slightly to elicit little jumps of excitement. The ball of his thumb was possessed of an ancient knowledge. Gifted with a special touch that drew from her soft moans. Not sounds exactly. Vibrations inside her mouth that were transmitted back to him.

This living dream, this oblivion, was so sweet, he didn't leave it, not even after a slow, undulating climax that left him feeling as though he had dissolved.

On the fringes of his consciousness lurked something threatening and ugly, but he refused to acknowledge it. Not now. Not tonight. Tomorrow.

Hammond's tomorrow started three hours later with an explosive "Jesus Christ!"

# THURSDAY

## CHAPTER 27

STEFFI CONTINUED SHOUTING as she bounded up the stairs. Reaching Hammond's bedroom, she barged in to find him sitting bolt upright in bed, holding his head between his hands, and looking like he was only one heartbeat away from cardiac arrest.

"I thought you'd been murdered. I saw the bloody towels—"

"Goddammit, Steffi. You nearly gave me a heart attack."

"You? Myself! Are you all right?"

He glanced anxiously around the room as though looking for something. "What time is it? What are you doing here? How'd you get in?"

"I still have a key. Never mind that. What happened to you?"

"Uh . . ." He glanced at his bandaged arm as though seeing it for the first time. "I, uh, got mugged last night." He motioned toward the bureau. "Get me a pair of underwear, will you?"

"Mugged? Where?" His boxers were kept in the second drawer from the top. She brought him a pair. He swung his legs over the side of the bed.

"Your leg is hurt, too?"

"Yeah. Not as bad as the arm." He bent from the waist and stepped into the shorts, then worked them up his legs to his thighs. Before standing up, he gave her a pointed look.

"Oh, for heaven's sake, Hammond. I've seen it."

Whisking back the sheet, he stood up and pulled on the shorts, then reached for a bottle of water on the nightstand and drained it.

"Are you going to tell me what happened or not?"

"I told you I got—"

"Mugged. I got that part. What about your arm?"

"Slashed. My leg, too."

"My God, you could've been killed. Where were you?" When he told her, she said, "Well no bloody wonder. What were you doing in that part of town?"

"Remember Loretta Boothe?"

"The lush?"

He frowned, but nodded. "She's sober, wanting to do some P.I. work again. She asked me to meet her at one of her hangouts. On the way back to my car, this guy jumped me. I resisted. He got slaphappy with his switchblade. I fought him off long enough to get away in my car. I drove home and called a doctor. He stitched my arm."

"Did you notify the police?"

"I didn't want the third degree. Which I'm getting anyway. From you."

"Why didn't you go to the hospital?"

"Same reason." He hobbled toward the bathroom, favoring his left leg. "It wasn't that bad."

"Not that bad! Hammond, there's a trash bag of blood-soaked towels downstairs."

"It looks a whole lot worse than it is. I only needed two pain pills all night. Do you mind?" She had followed him into the bathroom.

She went out and he closed the door. Through it, she hollered, "I've seen you peeing before, too."

Returning to the bed, she sat down where he had been sitting moments earlier. Along with the now-empty bottle of springwater and a drinking glass on the nightstand were a standard-issue cloth sling and a plastic bottle of pills. It was a pharmaceutical sample; the doctor's name wasn't on it.

Hammond came out of the bathroom, limped over to her and nudged her off his bed, then pulled the duvet up over the sheets.

"When did you get to be so prissy?" she asked.

"When did you get to be so nosy?"

"Don't you think I'm entitled to a little nosiness? Hammond, the first thing I saw when I came in was a bagful of bloody towels. Call me sentimental, but it caused me to wonder if my colleague—not to mention my former boyfriend, for whom I still have an affectionate regard—had fallen victim to an ax murderer."

He raised an eyebrow skeptically. "Who cleans up after himself?"

"Some of these guys are compulsive. But you're missing the point."

"No, I'm not, Steffi. You were concerned for my well-being. If the situation had been reversed, I would have reacted in a similar fashion. But as you can see, I am still breathing. Sore, bruised, and battered, but breathing. I'll feel a lot better after a hot shower and a few cups of even hotter coffee."

"My cue to leave?"

"Now you're catching on."

She looked at the bandage on his right forearm. "Who was the doctor?"

"You don't know him. Old college friend. Owed me a favor."

"What's his name?"

"What difference does it make? You don't know him."

"Hmm."

"*What?*"

"Nothing."

"Ask."

"Why didn't you want to file a crime report?"

"It wouldn't have been worth the hassle. The mugger didn't get anything."

"He assaulted you with a deadly weapon."

Looking supremely perturbed and addressing her as though she were a dimwit, he said, "It wouldn't have done any good to report it. I couldn't ID the guy. Honestly I don't even know if he was white or black or Hispanic, tall or short, thin or fat, hairy or bald. It was dark. The incident was over in a flash, and all I really saw was that switchblade coming at me. That's what made an impression on me, and that's why I got the hell out of there.

"It would be a waste of time to recount the episode to the police because all they would do is file the report, and that would be that. They've got better things to do, and so do I." With a grimace, he cradled his right arm in his left. "Now would you please leave so I can shower and dress?"

"Need any help?"

"Thanks, but I'll manage."

"Why don't you take the day off? I could come by around noon, fix you some lunch, and tell you what we learn from this guy."

Hammond opened his drawer of T-shirts. She had often teased him about his collection of nearly threadbare T-shirts, which he loved to wear around the house. He picked the top one from off the stack. It must have been a real favorite, she thought, because he smiled and lifted it to his face, breathing it in. "What guy?"

"I haven't told you!" She slapped her forehead. "Seeing you like this made me forget what brought me over. As I was driving to work, Smilow called me on my cell. There's a guy in our city jail."

His fascination with the T-shirt was lost on her, but he was still fiddling with it. He remarked absently, "There are lots of guys in our city jail."

"But only one claims to be Alex Ladd's brother."

Hammond whipped around. His face went chalk-white. Steffi supposed the sudden blanching was from pain. Turning so abruptly, he had banged the elbow of his injured right arm on the corner of the open drawer. He put his left arm out to stabilize himself.

"I think you're crazy to even consider going into the office today, Hammond. Look at you. You can hardly stand up and you're as white as a sheet. Your arm—"

"Forget my goddamn arm."

"Don't yell at me."

"Then stop mothering me."

"You're hurt."

"I'm fine. What about this guy?"

"His name is Bobby Turnbull. No, that's not it. Something like that."

"What's he in jail for?"

"Smilow didn't get that far before I cut him off and came straight here."

"What did he—"

"Hammond, honestly! Talk about third degree. All I know is that this Trimble—that's it. Bobby Trimble. He was arrested last night and used his one telephone call to call Alex Ladd. She wasn't at home. One of the cops over there at detention was sharp enough to pick up on the name, knew that she'd been connected to the Pettijohn murder, and notified Smilow."

Hammond replaced the T-shirt in the drawer, then slammed it shut. "On second thought, don't leave. It'll be hard to drive with my arm in a sling, so I'll hitch a ride with you. Give me five minutes."

While he was getting ready, Steffi went downstairs to call Smilow and tell him why she was running late.

"Mugged?"

"That's what he says."

After a short pause, Smilow asked, "Do you have reason to doubt him?"

"Not really. It's just . . ." She stared thoughtfully at the doorway of the powder room, now blocked by a Hefty bag stuffed with blood-soaked towels. "It just seems uncharacteristic for our Mr. Crime and Punishment to dismiss an assault with a switchblade. He tried to minimize his injuries, but he looks like he went fifteen rounds with a grizzly."

"Maybe he's just embarrassed for being so careless."

"Maybe. Anyway, we'll be there in fifteen minutes."

She didn't tell him about Hammond's lame excuse for not going to a hospital for treatment. The "old college friend" doctor was a transparent lie. Hammond had never been good at lying. He should take lying lessons from Alex Ladd. He seemed to admire that lady's penchant for—

Steffi's mind slammed on the brakes.

Staring into near space, her eyes unfocused, her head was assailed by unthinkable thoughts that whizzed through her consciousness with the speed of light. Holding those thoughts was like trying to catch comets.

Hammond came clumping down the stairs.

She joined him at the front door, but not before snatching one of the bloody hand towels from the trash bag and stuffing it into her satchel.

Bobby Trimble was scared spitless. But he would be damned before he let them see his fear. Fucking cops.

He owed his present situation to a dowdy, overweight, old-maid schoolteacher. It was an insult to his pride that such a pushover could bring about his downfall. She'd been no challenge at all. Her seduction had been boring and routine. He had struggled to stay awake through it. It had been all he could do to keep from dozing off.

Who would have guessed that the frump would turn out to be a femme fatale in the strictest sense?

Last night he had been well on his way to scoring big time with a widow lady from Denver who had diamonds as big as headlights in her ears and on both hands. They would have financed a luxurious lifestyle for a long time. Immediately she had revealed a raunchy sense of humor and spirit of adventure, so that's what he had appealed to. With his hand up her skirt, he had been describing to her the hard-on she'd given him, sparing no anatomical details, when two cops grabbed him under the arms and hauled him out of the nightclub.

Outside, they had spread-eagled him against the hood of the squad car, frisked him and cuffed him like he was a common criminal, and read him his rights. Out the corner of his eye, he had spotted the Indiana schoolmarm standing nearby clutching a pair of patent leather shoes in one hand.

"Damn bitch," he muttered now, just as the door swung open.

"What's that, Bobby? Did you say something?"

The guy looked vaguely familiar, although Bobby couldn't place him. He wasn't tall, but he gave off that impression as he strode into the room. He was wearing a three-piece suit, which Bobby recognized as quality goods. His cologne smelled pricey, too.

He shook hands with Bobby's pro bono lawyer, a guy named "Heinz, like the ketchup," who looked like a loser, and whose advice to Bobby so far had been to keep his trap shut until they knew what was going on. He then had sat down at the end of the small table and politely covered his yawns behind his hand. However, the man who'd just come in had made him sit up and look sharp.

Taking the chair across from Bobby, he introduced himself as Detective Rory Smilow. Bobby didn't trust his smile any further than he could have thrown the suave son of a bitch. He said, "I'm here to make your life a whole lot easier, Bobby."

Bobby didn't trust the promise, either. "Is that a fact? If so, you can start by hearing my side of this story. That bitch is lying."

"You didn't rape her?"

Bobby's facial features went slack. In contrast, his sphincter tightened. "Rape?"

"Mr. Smilow, my client and I were under the impression that this was a purse-snatching offense. Miss Rogers's complaint doesn't mention rape," Heinz nervously pointed out.

"She's talking it over with a policewoman," Smilow explained. "She was too embarrassed to discuss the details of the offense with the arresting male officers."

"If she's alleging rape, then I need to consult further with my client."

Bobby, having recovered from the initial shock, looked at his attorney with scorn. "There's nothing to consult about. I didn't rape her. Everything we did was consensual."

Smilow opened a folder and skimmed the written report. "You picked her up in a nightclub. According to Miss Rogers, you plied her with liquor and intentionally got her intoxicated."

"We had a few drinks. And, yes, she was tipsy. But I never forced alcohol on her."

"You accompanied her back to her hotel room and had sex with her." He glanced up at Bobby. "Is that true?"

Bobby couldn't resist meeting the silent challenge of the other man's eyes. "Yes, it's true. And she loved every minute of it."

Heinz cleared his throat uneasily. "Mr. Trimble, I'm advising you not to say anything more. Anything you say can be used against you. Remember that."

"Do you think I'm going to let some dumpy broad accuse me of rape and not defend myself?"

"That's what a trial is for."

"Fuck a trial. And fuck you." Bobby turned back to Smilow. "She's lying through those buck teeth of hers."

"You didn't have sex with her while she was under the influence?"

"Of course I did. With encouragement from her."

Looking pained, Smilow sighed and rubbed his eyebrow. "I believe you, Mr. Trimble. I do. But from a legal standpoint you're walking a high wire. The laws have changed. Definitions have been sharpened to a fine point. Because of increased public awareness on the mistreatment of rape victims, prosecutors and judges take a hard line. They don't want to be held responsible for releasing a rapist—"

"I've never had to rape a woman," Bobby exclaimed. "Just the opposite, in fact."

"I understand," Smilow returned calmly. "But if Miss Rogers alleges that she was mentally incapacitated by the alcohol which you urged her to drink, then technically and legally, in the hands of a good D.A., a case could be made for rape."

Bobby folded his arms across his chest, partially because it was a non-chalant pose, but mostly because he was on the brink of panic. When he was eighteen, he'd been sentenced to goddamn prison. He hadn't liked it. Not one freaking bit. He had vowed that he would never go again. Afraid that his voice would give away his fear, he said nothing.

Smilow continued. "You were in possession of drugs when you were arrested."

"A few joints. I didn't give what's-her-name any."

Smilow looked hard at him. "No?"

"I wouldn't have wasted good smoke on her. She was too easy."

"Nevertheless, you still have a problem. Who do you think a jury would believe? A simple, sweet-looking lady like her? Or a worldly stud like you?"

While Bobby was composing a suitable answer, the door opened and a woman came in. She was petite, with short dark hair and bright, black eyes. Good legs. Small pointed tits. But a ball-breaker if Bobby had ever seen one.

She said, "I hope the slime-bucket hasn't confessed."

Smilow introduced her as Stefanie Mundell from the County Solicitor's Office. Heinz had gone a little green around the gills and was swallowing convulsively. It wasn't a good sign that his own lawyer was quaking at the sight of this bitch and looked ready to heave.

Smilow offered her a chair, but she said she preferred to stand. "I won't be here that long. I just wanted to make Mr. Trimble aware that rape cases are my specialty, and that I advocate castration for first-time offenders. And not the chemical kind, either." Placing her palms down on the table, she leaned over it until she was nose to nose with him. "For what you did to poor Ellen Rogers, I can't wait to get your balls on the chopping block."

"I didn't rape her."

His sincere denial didn't faze Ms. Mundell, who smirked at him and said, "See you in court, Bobby." Turning on her high heels, she went out, slamming the door behind her.

Smilow was massaging his jaw and shaking his head sorrowfully. "I feel for you, Bobby. If Steffi Mundell is prosecuting, I'm afraid you're in for a world of hurt."

"Maybe Mr. Trimble would consider pleading guilty to a lesser charge."

Bobby glared at Heinz, who had tentatively offered the suggestion. "Who asked you? I'm not pleading guilty to anything, understand?"

"But stealing—"

"Gentlemen," Smilow said, interrupting. "It has just occurred to me that since Ms. Mundell is involved, there might be a way around this."

With affected calmness, Bobby asked, "What's on your mind?"

"She's prosecuting the Pettijohn murder case."

*Red alert!*

Suddenly he remembered where he had seen Smilow before. On TV the night following Pettijohn's murder. He was the homicide detective in charge of the investigation. Bobby leaned back in his chair and tried to pretend that he wasn't suddenly sweating like a cracker in a cornfield. "Pettijohn murder case?"

Smilow gave him a long, hard, withering stare. Then he sighed and closed the folder. "I thought we might be able to help each other, Bobby. But if you're going to play dumb, you leave me no choice but to let Ms. Mundell have at you."

He scraped back his chair and left the room without another word, closing the door firmly behind him.

Bobby looked over at Heinz-like-the-ketchup and raised his shoulders. "What did I do?"

"You tried to mind-fuck Rory Smilow. Bad idea."

## CHAPTER 28

$F$OR HALF AN HOUR SMILOW AND STEFFI had been patting one another on the back for the excellent job they'd done of manipulating Bobby Trimble. Their self-congratulations were almost more than Hammond could stomach.

"I gave him over an hour to think about it," Smilow told him for what must have been at least the tenth time.

"So you've said."

"As soon as we walked back into the room," Steffi chimed in, "he started talking."

"You must've played the bad cop very well."

"If I do say so myself," she boasted. "Bobby was convinced that he was facing a rape charge."

Ellen Rogers had never alleged rape. On the contrary, she had acknowledged her own culpability for the theft of her credit cards and money. She had wanted only to see Bobby Trimble captured and put out of commission, sparing other women a similar humiliating experience.

She had made arrangements to return to Indianapolis immediately, although she made it clear she was willing to testify against Trimble in court if the case came to trial. She left the city, never knowing the gift she had handed the Charleston Police Department.

"I can't wait to see the expression on Alex Ladd's face when she hears this tape recording. Hammond, you won't believe it," Steffi enthused. "You asked for motive and, brother, did you get it. In spades."

He breathed through his mouth to stave off nausea. It had been threatening since he was informed that Alex's half-brother was in police custody. Steffi and Smilow were so proud of their goddamn tape recording. They were salivating in anticipation of his hearing it, when he already knew the substance of it. He'd heard the incriminating story from Loretta Boothe last night.

The raw facts alone painted an unflattering picture of Alex. By the time Bobby Trimble had embellished the story to suit his own purposes, it would be a character assassination. As Steffi had noted, it provided the motivation the case had lacked. In spades.

Hammond had hoped that Smilow's investigators wouldn't be as resourceful or as diligent as Loretta, and that he could continue stalling the case indefinitely until he determined the nature of Alex's connection to Pettijohn and explained to her about his own meeting with Lute.

He was going to suggest that they both come clean with Smilow. He should have told the detective about his meeting with Pettijohn immediately. But it had been a delicate issue, one he had hoped to avoid anyone knowing about. He was also going to advise Alex to inform Smilow of her past, before he had a chance to uncover it himself and jump to his own conclusions about how it pertained to the Pettijohn investigation.

Unfortunately, he'd been robbed of the opportunity. By the time Steffi had barged in, Alex was gone. He had blessed her for leaving early, and had considered them damn lucky for not being discovered in bed together, which would have damaged their credibility when making their independent confessions to Smilow.

Now this.

Bobby Trimble had appeared out of nowhere, at the worst possible time. Alex had no idea of the trap that had been laid for her. Hammond was powerless to warn her.

A pager beeped. All three of them checked. "Mine," Hammond said.

Smilow pushed the telephone across his desk, nearer to Hammond.

Hammond checked the number on the LED. "I'll use my cell, thanks."

Excusing himself, he stepped out of the office and moved into the hall, which offered a modicum of privacy. "Loretta, what's up?"

"We ended on a sour note last night."

"What do you mean?"

"You were so disappointed when you left."

"Don't worry about it."

"But I did. I wanted to do something for you, so I went over to county records this morning and caught Harvey buying a honey bun out of a vending machine."

"I've only got a minute, Loretta."

"I'm getting there. I asked him if anyone else had leaned on him for information related to the Pettijohn case."

"Specifically Alex Ladd?"

"No, I just laid it out there to see if he would bite."

"And?"

"He broke a cold sweat. I could practically hear his knees knocking."

"Who approached him for information?"

"The little nerd wouldn't say."

"Loretta—"

"I tried everything, Hammond. Believe me. Threats of exposure, torture, physical harm. I wheedled, dealed, cajoled. I offered him unlimited booze, drugs, sex with the professional of his choice. Nothing worked. Whoever approached him, scared him. Speechless. He's not talking."

"Okay, thanks." Hearing motion behind him, he glanced over his shoulder. Frank Perkins was ushering Alex around the corner.

"Anything else you want me to do?" Loretta asked.

"Not for now. Thanks. Got to go."

He clicked off and turned just as Perkins and Alex reached the door to Smilow's office. When the solicitor saw Hammond, his eyes widened. "What happened to you?"

"I got mugged."

"Jeez. Looks like more than the average mugging."

"I'll be all right." He dropped his gaze to Alex. "I was well taken care of."

They had no longer than a millisecond of eye engagement. Hammond tried to telegraph a warning, but her lawyer nudged her forward into the office. "Well, what now, Detective?"

"We've got a recording we want your client to hear."

"A recording of what?"

"Of an interrogation we conducted early this morning with a man in our own jail. Believe me, his statements are relevant to the Pettijohn case."

Perkins held out the only chair for Alex. The others took up standing positions around the small room. Smilow offered to have a chair brought in for Hammond, but he declined. As Alex sat down, she managed a covert inquisitive glance at him, but he had no way of preparing her for what was in store.

Smilow summarized Ellen Rogers's experience for Alex and her lawyer. "Fortunately for us, Ms. Rogers turned out to be no shrinking violet. She tracked the man down herself and reported him to police."

"I fail to see—"

"His name is Bobby Trimble."

Hammond had been closely watching Alex's face. As soon as Smilow began, she had realized what was coming. Her eyes closed briefly, and she took a deep, fortifying breath. But when he said Trimble's name, she revealed no reaction at all.

Smilow said, "You're acquainted with Mr. Trimble, aren't you, Dr. Ladd?"

Frank Perkins said, "I would like a word with my client."

"It's all right, Frank," she said softly. "Unfortunately, I can't deny knowing Bobby Trimble."

Before Perkins could say anything more, Smilow said, "The tape is self-explanatory, Frank." He depressed the play button on the machine.

In Smilow's voice, the people present during the interrogation were identified. The time, place, and date were noted, along with the conditions under which Trimble was giving the statement. He had confessed to seducing Miss Ellen Rogers for the purpose of robbing her, and, although he wasn't guaranteed clemency, he was assured by Stefanie Mundell that the County Solicitor's Office would deal favorably with anyone who voluntarily provided information pertinent to Lute Pettijohn's murder case.

That said, Smilow asked his first question. *"Bobby—may I call you Bobby?"*

*"I'm not ashamed of my name."*

*"Bobby, do you know Dr. Ladd?"*

*"Alex is my half-sister. Same mother. Different fathers. Never knew either one of them, though."*

*"Trimble was your mother's name?"*

*"Right."*

*"You and your half-sister were reared together, in the same home?"*

*"If you want to call it that. It was hardly a home. Our mother wasn't a Martha Stewart, although she did a lot of entertaining."*

*"What kind of entertaining?"*

*"Men, Detective Smilow. She had men in the house all the time. When she did, Alex and I were sent out. If it was hot outside, tough. Cold weather, tough. If we were hungry, too bad. Sometimes we could talk a hamburger out of the old black lady who worked at the Dairy Queen. She didn't like me much, but she had a soft spot for Alex. But if her boss was around, forget it. We went hungry."*

*"Is your mother still alive?"*

*"Who knows? Who cares? She left when I was about . . . hmm, fourteen. Making Alex twelve, I guess. She had fallen hard for a guy, and when he left for Reno, she followed him out there. I don't know if she ever caught him or not. That's the last we ever saw or heard of her."*

*"Didn't Child Protection Services see to your needs after that?"*

*"I'd just as soon be in jail as to have a bunch of busybody bureaucrats*

*breathing down my neck. So I told Alex not to tell anybody that our mother had left. We faked it. We went to school, pretending everything was normal. And"*—he chuckled—*"everything was. I don't think our mother ever darkened the door of the schoolhouse. As far as she was concerned, PTA stood for pussy, tits, and ass."*

"There's no call for that," Smilow said sharply.

"Sorry, ma'am. I didn't mean any disrespect."

Hammond assumed Bobby had apologized to Steffi. His apology sounded insincere. Alex must have thought so, too. She was staring at the recorder with repugnance.

*Smilow asked, "Didn't neighbors notice that your mother was no longer around?"*

*"Alex and I had been fending for ourselves for so long, it wasn't unusual for them to see her toting clothes to the Laundromat or me asking for odd jobs."*

*"You did odd jobs to support yourself and your sister?"*

*He cleared his throat. "For a while." A pause. "Before I continue . . . just so we understand one another . . . I already paid my debt to society for what happened. This isn't going to come back on me, is it? This all happened way back when. In Tennessee. This is South Carolina. I'm free and clear in this state."*

*"Tell us what you know about Lute Pettijohn's murder, Bobby, and you walk out of here."*

*"Sounds good."*

Up to this point Alex hadn't moved. Now she turned to Perkins. "Is it necessary for us to listen to this?"

The lawyer asked Smilow to stop the tape so he could confer with Alex. Smilow courteously complied. Perkins whispered a question to her. She answered quietly. They consulted in undertones for about sixty seconds.

Then Perkins said, "You can't seriously validate this man's statements. He's bargaining for a dismissal of charges against him. Obviously he told you what you wanted to hear."

Smilow said, "If he's lying, then it doesn't matter to Dr. Ladd what he said, does it?"

"It matters in that it could prove embarrassing for her."

"I'm sorry for any embarrassment. But I would think Dr. Ladd would want to hear what's being alleged about her. She's free to jump in and refute anything he says at any time."

Perkins turned to her. "It's up to you."

She gave the attorney a curt nod.

"All right, Smilow," he said. "But this is cheap theatrics and you know it."

The rebuke bounced off Smilow, who restarted the tape at the point where he repeated his question about how Trimble had supported himself and his sister.

*"We got by for a time, with me doing this and that," he replied. "But I was busting my ass trying to keep food on the table and Alex in clothes. She was growing, you know, like teenage girls do. Blossoming."*

*Trimble's tone dropped to a confidential pitch. "It was seeing how she was filling out that first gave me the idea."*

*"What idea?"*

*"I'm getting to it," he said, nettled by Smilow's impatience. "I started noticing how my buddies looked at my baby sister. In a whole new light, you might say. I overheard a few remarks. And that's when the idea first occurred to me."*

Hammond propped his left elbow on the fist of the arm in the sling and covered his mouth with his hand. He wanted to stop up his ears. He wanted to throw the tape recorder against the wall. He wanted to slap the shit out of Steffi, who was smiling smugly at Alex. He was helpless to do anything except to listen, just as she was being forced to do.

The difference in Trimble's diction and syntax was noticeable. Talking about his past had caused him to lapse into the speech patterns of his youth. He sounded more crass. More uncouth. More lewd.

*"The first time it happened by accident. I mean, I didn't plan it. Alex and I were with this friend of mine. He had stolen a six-pack of beer and we met in this abandoned garage to drink it. He started teasing Alex and . . ."* A squeak of a chair as he shifted his weight. *"Eventually he dared her to raise her shirt and give him a look at her top.*

*"Alex told him no way, José. But she didn't mean it. She was giggling, playing along, you know. And damned if she didn't finally do it. I told him that in exchange for seeing my little sister's tits—sorry, breasts—he had to give me the extra beer. He said no way in hell because all he had really seen was her brassiere. But the next time—"*

Hammond's left hand shot out and stopped the recorder. "We all get the drift, Smilow. Dr. Ladd's half-brother exploited her. It's disputable whether or not she went along willingly. But in any case, it's ancient history."

"Not that ancient."

"Twenty, twenty-five years! What in God's name does this have to do with Lute Pettijohn?"

"We're coming to that," Steffi said. "It all ties in together."

"The rest of you can sit in here and listen to this tripe," Frank Perkins said, also coming to his feet. "But I will not allow my client to be subjected to listening to it."

"I'm afraid I can't allow Dr. Ladd to leave," Smilow said.

"Do you plan to formally charge her with a crime?" Sarcastically Perkins added, "One allegedly committed this decade?"

Smilow evaded giving him a direct answer. "If you don't want to hear the remainder of the tape, I must ask you to wait in the other room until Mr. Cross has heard all of it."

"Fine."

"No." Alex spoke quietly but with resolve. All eyes moved to her. "Bobby Trimble is trash. Over the last twenty years, he's acquired some polish, but he's still a lowlife. I want to hear everything he says. I have a right to know what he's saying about me. As horrible as it is for me even to hear his voice, I need to listen to this, Frank."

Steffi said, "Do you deny anything he's said so far?"

"You don't have to answer that, Alex."

Ignoring her solicitor's advice, she met Steffi's eager eyes head-on. "It all happened a long time ago, Ms. Mundell. I was a child."

"You were beyond the age of accountability."

"I made some bad choices when my only option was to make worse ones. The memories are ugly. Years ago, I expunged them from my mind and got on with my life. I made a new life."

"Very good answer, Dr. Ladd," Steffi said. "But in other words, no. You don't deny anything he's said so far."

If Frank Perkins hadn't intervened at that moment and warned Alex to say nothing more, Hammond would have warned her himself. She heeded her lawyer's advice. Looking thoroughly disgusted with the whole proceeding, Perkins said, "Let's get this over with."

Smilow restarted the tape. Hammond shifted his weight from one leg to the other, ostensibly to work some of the soreness out of his left leg. In reality he was trying to keep himself from doing something very stupid, like grabbing Alex by the hand and dragging her out of there. Last night had proved she needed protection. He would guard her himself. He was almost ready to tell everything, get it out in the open, damn the torpedoes.

*Almost.* In this instance the adverb was a monumental qualifier.

The worst of the tale was yet to come, and it was that which bore an unsettling similarity to the present. According to Loretta's report, upon leaving Florida with a theft rap and a loan shark hot on his trail, Bobby Trimble had dropped from sight. That he had resurfaced here in Charleston within days of a murder in which his half-sister was implicated was a damned uncomfortable coincidence.

It was certainly more than enough to increase Steffi's and Smilow's suspicions. Even though Hammond knew that it was virtually impossible for Alex to have killed Pettijohn and still arrive at the fair when she had, there were still inconsistencies, unanswered questions, that plagued him. Especially in light of her troublesome past.

Unarguably someone saw her as a threat that must be silenced. But what threat did she pose? As a witness? Or as a conspirator who had got cold feet? Until he knew with certainty that Alex was entirely guilty—or entirely innocent—of any wrongdoing, he was trapped between prosecutor and protector.

On the tape, Smilow was asking Trimble about the con game he had devised to bilk money out of his friends.

*"It worked like this. I'd target somebody and start telling him about Alex, how she was maturing. I'd say she was itching to try out the new equipment, that she was in heat, things like that. I'd feed him little tidbits, get him to thinking about her and speculating on the possibilities. Sometimes it took a few days, other times only a matter of hours before he'd get really worked up.*

*"I had this knack, this sixth sense, about when the time was right to close the deal. I'd name our price. Know what? I never had one of those suckers try to haggle down the fee,"* he said, laughing. *"I'd set the time and place. They'd pay me, then it was up to Alex to do her thing."*

*"What thing?"*

*"Whatever she had to do to get them . . . you know, vulnerable."*

*"Aroused?"*

*"That's a nice way of putting it. When they were good and aroused, I would rush in and demand all their money, or else."*

*"Or else what?"*

*"I gave them some legal-sounding bullshit about molestation of a minor. If they balked or threatened us with the law, I'd say that it was our word against theirs, and who wouldn't believe a twelve-year-old virgin? They kept quiet, all right. That's how we stayed in business so long. None wanted to look like a jackass in front of his friends, so none ever admitted to being taken."*

*"Your half-sister willingly participated?"*

*"What do you think? That I forced her? A woman loves showing off. Meaning no disrespect, Ms. Mundell. But I'll bet Mr. Smilow here agrees with me, even if he doesn't own up to it. All women are exhibitionists at heart. They know what they've got. They know men are panting after it. They love baiting us with it."*

*"Thank you for that psychological insight."*

Steffi Mundell's sarcasm wasn't lost on him. *"I didn't write the rules, Ms. Mundell. I'm only telling it like it is, and you know it."*

Smilow resumed the questioning. *"You didn't run out of suckers?"*

*"We spread into other neighborhoods. Alex looked so fresh and innocent*

*that every mark thought he was the first one. That's why I knew it would work with the older men, too."*

"Tell me about that."

*"Alex was the perfect lure. She knew how to reel them in, too. That's her specialty. She would act innocent and nervous. As a rule, we men can't resist a woman who's being coy. Alex can play hard to get better than any woman I've ever met before or since."*

Hammond ran his shirtsleeve across his sweating forehead, then rested his head against the wall and closed his eyes.

He heard the click when the button was depressed to stop the recorder. "Are you all right?"

Realizing that Smilow's question was aimed at him, he opened his eyes. Everyone except Alex was looking at him. Her eyes were downcast, focused on her hands, which lay folded in her lap. "Sure. Why?"

"You're awfully pale, Hammond. Why don't you let us bring in an extra chair?"

"I'll give you mine, Mr. Cross." Alex stood up and took a step toward him.

"No," he said brusquely. "I'm fine."

"Would you like something to drink?"

"Thanks, Steffi. I'm okay."

Alex was still standing, still looking at him, and he knew that she knew that he was far from okay. In fact, he'd never been more miserable in his entire life.

"How much more?" he asked.

"Not much," Smilow replied. "Dr. Ladd?"

She resumed her seat and he restarted the recorder. The room was silent except for the soft whir of the machine and Bobby's ingratiating voice as he described how they expanded to older, more affluent men, which he enticed from hotel lobbies and bars. Basically Bobby pimped for Alex. Business was good.

*"Once I got them there with her, I'd relieve them of their wallets, which were fatter than the ones we'd taken off the neighborhood boys. Much fatter."*

"Sounds like you two made quite a team."

*"We did. The best." Bobby's voice turned nostalgic. "Then that one guy ruined it for us."*

"You tried to kill him, Bobby."

*"It was self-defense! That son of a bitch came after me with a knife."*

"You were stealing from him. He was protecting his property."

*"And I was protecting myself. It wasn't my fault that the knife got turned around in the scuffle and wound up in his belly."*

*"The judge thought it was your fault."*

*"That bastard judge sent me to that hellhole."*

*"You were lucky the man survived. If he had died, it could have gone a lot worse for you."*

Hammond had heard the rest of the story from Loretta. Trimble went to prison. Alex received a probated sentence which included mandatory counseling and foster care.

She was placed with the Ladds. The couple loved her. For the first time in her life she was treated well, shown affection, and taught by example how healthy relationships worked. She thrived under their care and positive influence. They officially adopted her, and she took their name. Whether the credit belonged to the late Dr. and Mrs. Ladd or to Alex herself, her life underwent a one-hundred-eighty-degree turnaround.

By Bobby Trimble's own admission, he resented her good fortune.

*"I went to prison, but Alex got off scot-free. It wasn't fair. I wasn't the one flashing those guys, you know."*

*"Is that all she did? Flash them?"*

*"Now, what do you think?" Trimble scoffed. "At first, yeah. But later? Hell, she was whoring, plain and simple. She liked doing it. Some women are just made for it, and Alex is one of them. That's why, even with this psychology thing she's got going for her, she misses doing it."*

*"What do you mean, Bobby?"*

*"Pettijohn. If she didn't miss whoring, why did she take it up again with Pettijohn?"*

Alex shot to her feet and cried, "He's lying!"

## CHAPTER 29

FRANK PERKINS SAID, "I'VE NEVER HEARD ANYTHING SO preposterous." The lawyer motioned for Alex to stand. "Bobby Trimble is a lying, immoral thief who shamelessly exploited his half-sister in her youth, and is using her now to worm out of a rape charge. Make that a *bogus* rape charge, devised by you to encourage this fabrication. Such manipulation is beneath even you, Smilow. I'm taking my client home."

Smilow said, "Please don't leave the building."

Perkins bristled. "Are you prepared to charge Dr. Ladd now?"

Smilow looked inquiringly at Steffi and Hammond. But when neither of them voiced an opinion, he said, "There are a few matters left for us to discuss. Please wait outside."

Hammond took the coward's way out and didn't even glance at Alex before the solicitor escorted her from the room. His expression would have underscored the precariousness of her situation. The chips were definitely stacking up against her. It didn't bode well that she and Trimble were former partners in crime, and they hadn't been petty crimes. Except for a medical miracle, the stabbing victim would have died.

After years of separation, she and Trimble had reunited mere weeks before Lute Pettijohn was killed. Young Alex had been the lure that enabled Trimble to fleece their victims. Alex had a home safe full of cash. The implications were brutal.

Hammond's pain medication had worn off hours ago. To keep a clearer head he had refrained from taking more. His discomfort must have been obvious, because as soon as Perkins showed Alex out, Steffi turned to him. "You look like you're on the verge of collapse. Are you in pain?"

"It's tolerable."

"I'll be happy to get you something."

"I'm fine."

He wasn't fine. He dreaded hearing Smilow's take on Bobby Trimble's statement and what it meant to their case against Alex, but he had no choice except to give the homicide detective the floor and hear him out as he summarized the information.

"Here's the way it went down. Last spring, Bobby Trimble got in a barroom fight in some hick town. He came out on top of the fracas. One of Pettijohn's talent scouts, so to speak, witnessed the brawl and recommended Trimble for the job on Speckle Island where they needed a heavy."

"To put the squeeze on landowners who didn't wish to sell."

"Right, Steffi. Pettijohn was trying to buy up the entire island, but he met with a resistance he didn't expect. The landowners had inherited the real estate from slave ancestors who were deeded the property by their previous owners. Generations have worked that land. It's all they know. It's their legacy and heritage. It's more important to them than money, which is a concept that Lute couldn't grasp. Anyway, they didn't want their island 'developed.'"

"Pettijohn might not have developed it," Steffi surmised. "He probably wanted only to acquire it, let it appreciate for a few years, then turn around and sell it for a nifty profit." She turned to Hammond. "Do you have anything to contribute?"

"You two are doing fine. I haven't heard anything yet that I disagree with. A cockroach like Trimble isn't above strong-arming hardworking people who wish only to be left alone to live their lives. His tactics were probably much worse than he made them out to be."

"They were," Smilow said. "My investigator reported cross burnings, beatings, and other Klan-type activities. Trimble organized the thugs who did the deeds."

"Jesus," Hammond said with disgust.

Was it even conceivable that his own father had been involved in such atrocities? Preston had claimed to be unaware of Pettijohn's terrorism. He had said that when he learned of it, he had sold his partnership. Hammond hoped to God that was true.

Referring back to Bobby Trimble, he sneered, "And this is our reliable character witness?"

Ignoring that editorial comment, Steffi said, "Trimble claims he realized the error of his ways and refused to do any more of Pettijohn's dirty work.

More likely he simply got tired of it. That island doesn't offer many amenities. It couldn't have been nearly as exciting as his emcee job at the strip club."

"Lute was a stingy bastard," Smilow said. "He wouldn't have paid Trimble that much. Not too many places on Speckle for Bobby to wear his fancy clothes, either."

Steffi referred to the handwritten notes she'd taken. "And didn't he refer to the island people as being stubborn? Maybe he wasn't very successful at arm-twisting. Pettijohn might have become dissatisfied with his performance and threatened to fire him."

"In any case, Trimble was a disgruntled employee whose boss was bending the law and who coincidentally had a lot of money."

"In other words, extortion waiting to happen."

"Exactly. The blackmailing scheme made good economic sense," Smilow observed with a wry smile. "Trimble figured he was working way too hard when he could get a lot more money out of Pettijohn by threatening to reveal what was happening over on Speckle."

"Do you believe Pettijohn ordered Bobby to hurt those people? Beat them up? Set fires? Or was Bobby elaborating?"

"I'm sure some of it was exaggerated," Smilow said. "But if you're asking me if I think Lute was capable of nefarious tactics like that, the answer is yes. He would go to any lengths to get what he wanted."

"Whatever he was doing, it must have been bad, because he agreed to pay Bobby one hundred thousand dollars cash to keep quiet about it."

Smilow picked up the story again. "But in Bobby's own words, he 'wasn't born yesterday.' Lute capitulated almost too quickly to his demands. Bobby was mistrustful of the haste with which Lute had agreed. Collecting the cash was risky business. Even Bobby is smart enough to figure out that he could have been walking into a trap."

"Enter his sister."

"Half-sister," Hammond corrected. "And she didn't 'enter.' "

"Okay, he looked her up and recruited her."

"He found her on a fluke. He spotted her picture in the *Post and Courier.*"

No doubt Alex rued the day she had signed on as a volunteer to help organize Worldfest, a ten-day film festival scheduled in Charleston each November. A seemingly innocuous newspaper write-up and an accompanying group photo had exposed her to her nemesis.

On the recording Trimble had said, "*I couldn't believe my eyes when I saw Alex's picture in the newspaper. I read the names twice before I realized she must've changed hers. I looked up her address in the phone book, staked out her place, and sure enough, Dr. Ladd was my long-lost half-sister.*"

Hammond said, "Until he saw that write-up, he didn't even know she lived in Charleston. After years of hiding from him behind her new identity, she was not pleased to see him."

"Or so she claims," Steffi said.

"If he were your brother, would you be happy to have him reappear in your life?"

"Maybe. If we'd been successful partners before."

"Partners my ass. He used her sexuality in the worst imaginable way, Steffi."

"You believe she was an innocent?"

"Yes, I do."

"Hammond, she was a whore."

"She was *twelve!*"

"Okay, she was a young whore."

"She was not."

"She granted sexual favors for money. Isn't that the definition of a whore?"

"Children." Smilow's quiet rebuke put an end to their shouting match. He gathered a stack of written materials into his case file and passed it to Hammond. "That's everything you need to take to the grand jury. They meet next Thursday."

"I know when they meet," Hammond snapped. "I've got some other cases pending. Can't this wait a month, until they meet again? What's the rush?"

"You have to ask?" Smilow said sardonically. "I have to tell you the importance of this case?"

"All the more reason to make sure we've got it sewed up before the grand jury hears it." He grappled for another argument. "You made Trimble a sweet deal. A measly purse snatching. One night in jail, max. He's probably laughing his ass off."

"Your point being?"

"Trimble might have killed Pettijohn, and is using his sister as a scapegoat."

Smilow thought about it for a second, then shook his head. "There's no evidence placing him at the crime scene, whereas physical evidence puts Alex Ladd in the room with Pettijohn. Daniels's statement puts her there at the estimated time of his death."

"Frank Perkins could easily fudge that time frame. And you've got no weapon."

"If we had the weapon, I would charge her today," Smilow said. "As it is, remind the grand jury that Charleston is surrounded by water. She could have dumped the gun at any time Saturday evening."

"I agree," Steffi said. "We could search till doomsday and not find that pistol. You really don't need it, Hammond," she said confidently.

He dragged his hand down his face, realizing for the first time that he hadn't taken time to shave that morning. "I'll have a hard time selling them on her motive."

"That'll be a breeze," Steffi argued. "You'll have Trimble's testimony about her past."

"You're dreaming, Steffi," he said. "It happened more than twenty years ago. But even if it had happened yesterday, Frank will never permit it to come out during trial. He'll argue her juvenile record's irrelevance, and any fair judge will rule it inadmissible. The jury will never hear that shit. *If* by some legal maneuvering on my part it is ruled admissible, I'm not sure I would use it. It could have the opposite effect and work against us."

Smilow's eyes narrowed on Hammond. "Well, Mr. Prosecutor, maybe you're representing the wrong side. You're ready to throw up any and all obstacles to this case, aren't you?"

"I know what can happen in court, Smilow. I'm only being realistic."

"Or cowardly. Maybe Steffi should alert Mason that you've developed cold feet."

Hammond withheld an obscene comeback. Smilow was deliberately provoking him, and an angry outburst would give him exactly what he was hoping for. Instead he spoke very quietly. "I have an idea. Why don't you dispense with all the legal ways to win a conviction? Let's see, what underhanded methods could you use? I know." He snapped his fingers. "You could withhold exculpatory evidence. Yeah, you could do that. It wouldn't be the first time, either, would it?"

Smilow's very clean-shaven jaw knotted with rage.

"What are you talking about?" Steffi asked.

"Ask him," he said, never taking his eyes off Smilow. "Ask him about the Barlow case."

"If you weren't already banged up—"

"Don't let that stop you, Smilow."

"Guys, cut the crap," Steffi said impatiently. "Don't we have enough to worry about without you two slapping each other with gloves?" She turned to Hammond. "What were you saying about Ladd's juvenile record working against us?"

Several seconds passed before Hammond pulled his eyes away from Smilow and focused on Steffi. "As Dr. Ladd was listening to the Trimble recording, you only had to watch her face to see how much she detests him. The jury will be watching her, too."

"Though maybe not as closely as you."

If she had jabbed him with a hot poker, he couldn't have reacted more fiercely. "What the fuck?"

"Nothing."

"Something," he insisted angrily.

"Just an observation, Hammond," she replied with maddening calmness. "You couldn't take your eyes off our suspect today."

"Jealous, Steffi?"

"Of her? Hardly."

"Then keep your snide remarks to yourself." He cautioned himself not to go too far down that track or he might not be able to get safely back. He picked up the topic where they'd left off. "Trimble is slime. He even offended you, and you're not easily offended. His testimony will repulse women jurors."

"We'll coach him on what to say and how to say it."

"Have you ever seen Frank Perkins on cross-examination? He'll flatter Trimble into expounding on some of his chauvinistic theories. Trimble will be too vain to see the trap. He'll orate himself right into it, and we'll be sunk. It would be tough for me to sell a jury on the notion that Dr. Ladd— and you can bet Frank will line up a legion of character witnesses—was in cahoots with a guy like him."

Steffi thought on it for a moment. "Okay, for the sake of argument, let's say she's as pure as the driven snow. When her criminal half-brother showed up with his blackmail scheme, why didn't she immediately report him to the authorities?"

"Association," Hammond replied. "She wanted to protect her practice and her reputation. She didn't want all that garbage from the past dredged up."

"Maybe, but she could have called his bluff and threatened to sic the cops on him. Or she could have ignored him until he gave up and went away."

"Somehow I don't think he would be that easy to ignore. He would have kept hacking away at her, threatening to expose her to her patients, and friends, and the community. They weren't empty threats. People are always willing to believe the worst about someone. Patients entrust her with their problems. Would they continue that trust if they heard what Bobby had to tell them? No, Steffi. He could have inflicted some serious damage, and she knew it.

"She's made a name for herself professionally. Established herself as an expert on acute anxiety disorder. She's admired and respected. After the years it took her to work through God knows how many hang-ups from her childhood and construct her life, she would do just about anything to protect it."

"That's our case!" Steffi cried excitedly. "You've just nailed it, Hammond. Bobby threatened her with exposure if she didn't go along with his scheme. In order to get rid of him, she agreed to collect the blackmail money. Something went awry inside that hotel suite, and she had no choice but to kill Pettijohn."

Too late, Hammond realized how ill-chosen his words had been. Steffi was right. He had just made his case. "It might work," he mumbled.

"What other explanation is there for her being in that hotel suite with Lute Pettijohn? She certainly hasn't offered one."

That was the rub. Hammond could waltz around it all he wanted, but his fancy footwork always brought him back to that. If Alex was totally and completely innocent of any wrongdoing, why had she gone to see Pettijohn that afternoon?

Smilow headed for the door. "I'll tell Perkins that the grand jury is hearing our case next Thursday."

"Why don't you just arrest her?" Steffi asked.

The thought of Alex spending any time in jail sickened Hammond, but he thought it wise not to voice any more protests.

Thank God Smilow did it for him. "Because Perkins would cry foul and force us to charge her before incarcerating her. He'd have her out on bail within hours anyway."

"He's right, Steffi," Hammond said, feeling as though he had been granted a reprieve. "When she's charged, I'd rather have a grand jury indictment behind it."

Smilow left, giving his office over to them.

Steffi looked at Hammond sympathetically. "Are you sure you're up to preparing the case? Whether you admit it or not, this mugging took a toll. You'll probably feel even worse over the next several days when the real soreness sets in. I'll be glad to take over this responsibility for you."

On the surface it sounded as though a concerned colleague was offering to do another a favor, but Hammond wondered if the gesture was entirely unselfish. She had wanted the case and probably resented his getting it.

Beyond that, her offer could also be a carefully laid trap. After her innuendo about his being unable to take his eyes off Alex, he was wary. If Steffi was entertaining even the hint of a notion that he was attracted to Alex, she would be watching him like a hawk. Everything he said and did would be filtered through her suspicion. If she discovered that his attraction went much further than even she suspected, it would be disastrous for both him and Alex. He couldn't be obvious about favoring their suspect.

On the other hand, Steffi's offer could be wholly unselfish, her concern genuine. She had every right to be angry and upset with him because of the breakup, but she hadn't let that compromise their professional interaction. He was the one with the hidden motives.

Chagrined, he thanked her for the courteous offer. "I appreciate it, but I've got a week to recuperate. I'm sure by next Thursday, I'll be back to normal and raring to go."

"If you change your mind . . ."

## CHAPTER 30

THERE'S PRESS OUTSIDE?" Frank Perkins asked with angry incredulity.

"That's what I was told," Smilow replied blandly. "I thought you ought to be warned."

"Who leaked it?"

"I don't know."

The solicitor snorted. "Sure you don't." He turned away and, taking Alex Ladd's arm, escorted her toward the elevator.

Steffi sidled up to Smilow, remarking, "I can't wait for Thursday."

"It won't be easy."

She looked at the detective, surprised by his discouraged tone. "Don't tell me Hammond's pessimism is catching? I thought you'd be treating your detectives to cigars."

"Hammond's points have merit," he said thoughtfully. "First, he's got to convince the grand jury that Alex Ladd is indictable. If they do hand down an indictment, he's got to prove to a jury that she's guilty beyond a reasonable doubt. Our evidence is circumstantial, Steffi. Trimble's testimony is tainted by Trimble himself. Not much for a prosecutor to work with."

"More evidence will turn up before the trial begins."

"If there is more."

"There's bound to be more."

"Not if she didn't do it." Her eyes sharpened on him, but he pretended not to notice and turned away. "I've got a slew of work waiting on me."

Crestfallen by his remarks, she dawdled in the hallway until Hammond emerged from the men's room. They got into the elevator together. "There's press outside."

"I heard."

"Are you up for it?" she asked, giving the shoulder of his injured arm a concerned pat.

On the ground floor, they could see through the glass doors the throng of reporters lying in wait on the front steps. "Doesn't matter whether I am or not. I've got to do it."

Afterward, Steffi had to admit that he did it well. Although he downplayed his injuries, they made him seem dashing and courageous, a wounded soldier gearing up for battle.

They said little on the drive back to the judicial building in North Charleston. As soon as they went inside, Hammond excused himself and closed his private office door behind him. Steffi, lost in thought, literally bumped into Monroe Mason as he came bustling around a blind corner. He had a tuxedo draped over his arm.

"The boss is clearing out early," she teased.

Mason frowned. "My wife has committed us to one of those boring charity functions tonight. A banquet where everyone in attendance receives a reward. But who needs me around here, anyway? You're all doing a fine job without any help from me. Dr. Ladd's stepbrother provided Hammond with the missing link, huh? Now he's got her motivation. Sounds solid."

"Trimble's statement made all the difference."

"I'd put my money on our team."

"Thank you."

"Now, enough rhetoric," he said, smiling good-naturedly. "What's your gut feeling, Steffi? What kind of case have you got?"

Recalling Smilow's concerns, she said, "We'd like more hard evidence."

"Name a prosecutor who wouldn't. Rarely do we catch the accused holding a smoking gun. Sometimes—more often than not—we have to make something of little or nothing at all. Hammond will get his indictment, and when the case gets to trial, he'll bring in a guilty verdict. I have no misgivings about his abilities."

Although it pained the muscles of her face to do so, Steffi smiled. "Nor do I. If he doesn't fall head over heels."

Mason was looking at this wristwatch, saying, "I must be on my way. I'm meeting my trainer for a quick workout and massage before I climb into this monkey suit. Cocktails are at five. Mrs. Mason made me swear I wouldn't be late."

"Have a good time."

He frowned. "That's a jibe, right?"

"Yes, sir, that's a jibe." Laughing, she wished him a pleasant evening.

He had almost reached the end of the hall when he stopped and turned back. "Steffi?"

Her back was to him, so he didn't see the triumphant smile that spread across her face. She collapsed it before turning around. "Yes?"

"What were you implying with that remark?"

"Remark?"

"About Hammond falling head over heels."

"Oh." She laughed. "I was joking. It's nothing."

He retraced his steps back to her. "That's the second time you've alluded to Hammond being infatuated with Dr. Ladd. I don't consider that nothing. I certainly don't think it's a joking matter."

Steffi gnawed the inside of her cheek. "If I didn't know him better . . ." she said, faltering. Then she shook her head firmly. "But I do. We all do. Hammond would never lose his objectivity."

"Not a chance."

"Of course not."

"Well then . . . good night."

The county solicitor turned and made his way back down the hallway. Once he was out of sight, Steffi practically skipped into her office. She had planted the seed earlier in the week. Today she had nourished it. "Let's see how fertile his mind is," she said to herself as she sat down behind her desk and rifled through the stack of phone messages. The one she hoped for wasn't among them. Irritably, she placed a call.

"Lab. Anderson speaking."

"This is Steffi Mundell."

"Yeah?"

Jim Anderson worked in the hospital lab and had a chip on his shoulder the size of Everest. Steffi knew this because she had had run-ins with him and his attitude before. She demanded accuracy combined with speed, which he seemed incapable of delivering. "Have you run that test yet?"

"I told you I would call you as soon as I got to it."

"You haven't done it yet?"

"Have I called?"

He didn't even have the courtesy to apologize or offer an explanation. She said, "I need the result of that test for a very important case. It's critical. Perhaps I didn't make that clear to you this morning."

"You made it clear, all right. Just like *I* made it clear that I work for the hospital, not the police department, and not the D.A.'s office. I have other work piled up ahead of you that's just as important."

"Nothing is as urgent as this."

"Get in line, Ms. Mundell. That's how it works."

"Look, I don't need DNA testing. Or HIV. Nothing fancy for now. Just a blood typing."

"I understand."

"All I need to know is if the blood on that washcloth matches the blood on the sheet Smilow took to you a few days ago."

"I got it the first time you told me."

"Well, how hard can it be?" she said, raising her voice. "Don't you just have to look through a microscope or something?"

"You'll get it when I get to it."

Anderson hung up on her. "Son of a bitch," she hissed as she slammed down her own telephone receiver. Nothing aggravated her more than incompetence, unless it was incompetence combined with unwarranted arrogance.

Dammit, she needed that blood test! She was nursing a strong hunch, and her hunches were rarely wrong. Ever since this morning when the idea first took hold, it had consumed her thoughts until she was now obsessed by it.

As impossible as it seemed, it made a weird kind of sense to her that there was something going on between Alex Ladd and Hammond, and that this "something" was sexual. Or at least romantic.

She hadn't dared to discuss her suspicion with Smilow. Probably he would dismiss it as absurd, in which case she would look like a fool at best, and a jealous ex-lover at worst.

He would share her theory with his team of detectives, who would make her a laughingstock. Detective Mike Collins, and others who had a hard time accepting women in authority, never would take her seriously again. Everything she said or did would be undermined by their ridicule. That would be intolerable. Her reputation as a tough, savvy prosecutor had been too hard-won to jeopardize it by something so laughably feminine as envisioning romance where none existed.

But it would be almost as bad if Smilow did give her hunch credence. He would take it and run with it. Unlike her, he had the resources and the muscle to do some serious sleuthing. He would tell assholes like Jim Anderson to hop, and the hospital lab tech would ask how high. Smilow would have the result of that blood test in no time flat. If the samples matched, Smilow would be credited with making the connection between Hammond and their suspect.

If she *was* right, she didn't want to share the credit with Smilow or anyone else. She wanted it all to herself. If Hammond were to be disgraced—dare she even wish for disbarment?—for impeding a murder investigation, she wanted to be the one to expose him. Singlehandedly. No more playing second fiddle, no more group projects for Steffi Mundell, thank you very much.

It would be delicious fun to watch Hammond topple from his pedestal. It would be gratifying to be the one to topple him.

His behavior today as he listened to Trimble's recording had strengthened her suspicion. He had reacted like a jealous lover. It was clear that he saw Alex Ladd as a victim of her half-brother's exploitation. Whenever possible, he had rushed to her defense, finding angles that suggested innocence. Not a good mind frame for a prosecutor to be in when trying to convince others of the accused's guilt.

Maybe he felt nothing more than pity for a girl's lost innocence. Or sympathy for the professional about to be stripped of all credibility and respect. But whatever it was, there was *something* there. Definitely.

"I know it," Steffi whispered fiercely.

She had been gifted with a keen perception. She could sniff out lies and spot motivations that hadn't occurred to anyone else in the solicitor's office. Those skills had served her well today. Her instincts had come alive and buzzed noisily whenever Hammond and Alex Ladd were near one another.

But her surety went beyond her instincts as a prosecutor. She also sensed it with a woman's intuition. As she watched them watch each other, the signs had become glaringly obvious. They avoided making direct eye contact, but whenever they did, there was an almost audible click.

Alex Ladd had looked shattered when Trimble related the more prurient details of her past. Most of her verbal denials had been directed toward Hammond. While he, known for his amazing ability to focus and concentrate on the business at hand, had been unable to keep still. He fidgeted. His hands moved restlessly. He had acted like he had an itch he couldn't scratch.

Steffi recognized the signs. He had behaved like that when their affair first began. Sleeping with a colleague had made him uneasy. He had worried about the impropriety of it. She had teased him, telling him that if he didn't relax when they were together in public, his jitters were going to give them away.

*But I'm not jealous,* Steffi told herself now. *I'm not jealous of him, and I'm certainly not jealous of her. I'm not.*

On the surface, she might look like the classic woman scorned. But it wasn't jealousy that compelled her to get to the bottom of this. It was bigger than jealousy. Grander. Her future hinged on it.

She would keep digging until she had an answer, even if her hunch proved to be wrong. One day, while Dr. Ladd was languishing in prison, she might tell Hammond about this crazy notion she had once entertained. They would have a good laugh over it.

Or she might discover a scandalous secret that would damage Hammond Cross's reputation beyond repair and destroy any chance of his becoming county solicitor.

And if that happened, guess who was groomed and ready to seize the office?

The top-ranking homicide detective in the CPD was ready to submit that Alex Ladd had killed Lute Pettijohn. It was Hammond's job to argue and prove the state's case in a court of law. But the state's case was against the woman with whom he had fallen in love. Moreover, he was a material witness in that case. Those were two powerfully motivating reasons for him to want to *dis*prove the state's allegation.

But there was another reason even more powerful, compelling, and urgent. Alex's life was at risk. The media had picked up the story of her house being searched yesterday. There had been an attempt on her life last night. That couldn't have been a coincidence. The guy in the alley had probably been hired to silence Alex. Since that attempt had failed, there was sure to be another.

Smilow and company had focused all their attention on Alex, leaving it up to him to find another viable suspect or suspects.

To that end, he sealed himself inside his office with the case file Smilow had given him. Mentally he disconnected himself from the case. Discounting his personal investment in it, he focused only on the legal aspects and approached it exclusively from that standpoint.

Who would want Lute Pettijohn dead?

Business rivals? Certainly. But according to Smilow's files, all those questioned had concrete alibis. Even his own father. Hammond had personally verified Preston's alibi.

Davee? Most certainly. But he believed that if she had killed him, she would have made no secret of it. It would have been a production. That was more her style.

Relying on his powers of concentration and cognitive skills, he arranged and absorbed all the data the case file contained. To that information, he added facts that he knew but of which Smilow was unaware:

1. Hammond himself had been with Lute Pettijohn shortly prior to his murder.
2. The handwritten note Davee had given him indicated that Hammond wasn't the only visitor Lute had scheduled last Saturday afternoon.
3. Lute Pettijohn was under covert investigation by the Attorney General's Office.

Alone, none of these facts seemed relevant. Together, however, they piqued his curiosity as a prosecutor and prompted him to ask questions . . . and for reasons beyond his wanting Alex to be innocent. Even had he not been emotionally involved with her, he never wanted to wrongfully convict an innocent person. No matter who the prime suspect was, these questions warranted further investigation.

In his mind, applying these undisclosed facts, he replayed each conversation he had had about the case. With Smilow, Steffi, his father, Monroe Mason, Loretta. He removed Alex from the equation and pretended that she didn't exist, that the suspect remained a mystery. That allowed him to listen to every question, declaration, and offhand remark with a new ear.

Oddly enough, it was one of his own statements that snagged him, yanking him from this lazy stream of consciousness. *"Your garden-variety bullets from your garden-variety pistol. There are hundreds of .38s in this city alone. Even in your own evidence warehouse, Smilow."*

Suddenly he was imbued with renewed energy and a fierce determination to justify his own irrational behavior over the last few days. Everything—his career, his life, his own peace of mind—hinged on exonerating Alex and proving himself right.

He glanced at his desk clock. If he hurried, he might have time to begin his own investigation this afternoon. Hastily gathering up the case file and stuffing it into his briefcase, he left his office. He had just cleared the main entrance of the building and stepped into the blast-furnace heat when he heard his name.

"Hammond."

Only one voice was that imperative. Inwardly Hammond groaned as he turned. "Hello, Dad."

"Can we go back into your office and talk?"

"As you see, I'm on my way out, and I'm in somewhat of a hurry to get downtown before the end of the business day. The Pettijohn case goes to the grand jury on Thursday."

"That's what I want to talk to you about."

Preston Cross never took no for an answer. He steered Hammond toward a sliver of shade against the building's flat facade. "What happened to your arm?"

"Too much to explain now," he replied impatiently. "What's so urgent it can't wait?"

"Monroe Mason called me from his cell phone on his way to the gym this afternoon. He's deeply troubled."

"What's the problem?"

"I dread even to think about the consequences if Monroe's speculation is correct."

"Speculation?"

"That you have developed an improper regard for that Dr. Ladd."

*That* Dr. Ladd. Whenever his father spoke disparagingly of someone, he always placed the generic pronoun in front of their name. The depersonalization was his subtle way of expressing his low opinion of the individual.

Stalling, Hammond said, "You know, it's really beginning to piss me off that every time Mason has a beef with me, he calls you. Why doesn't he come to me directly?"

"Because he's an old friend. If he sees my son about to piss away his future, he respects me enough to warn me of it. I'm sure he hoped that I would intervene."

"Which you're all too glad to do."

"You're goddamn right I am!"

His father's face had turned red up to the roots of his white hair. There was spittle in the corner of his lips. He rarely lost his temper and considered emotional outbursts of any sort a weakness reserved for women and children. Removing a handkerchief from his back pants pocket, he blotted his perspiring forehead with the neat white square of Irish linen. More calmly he said, "Assure me that Monroe's notion is totally groundless."

"Where did he get the idea?"

"Firstly, from your lackadaisical approach to this case."

"I'd hardly call it that. I've been working my butt off. Granted, I've exercised caution—"

"To a fault."

"In your opinion."

"And Mason's, too, apparently."

"Then it's up to *him* to chew my ass, not *you*."

"From the outset you've been dragging your heels. Your mentor and I would like to know why. Is it the suspect that's made you gun-shy? Have you developed a fondness for this woman?"

Hammond's eyes stayed fixed on his father's, but he remained stubbornly silent.

Preston Cross's features turned rigid with fury. "Jesus Christ, Hammond. I can't believe it. Are you insane?"

"No."

"A *woman*? You would sacrifice all your ambitions—"

"Don't you mean all *your* ambitions?"

"—on a woman? After getting this far, how could you behave in such a—"

"Behave?" Hammond barked a scornful laugh. "You've got your nerve, confronting me about a behavior issue. What about your behavior, Father? What kind of moral measuring stick did you set as my example? Maybe I've readjusted mine to match yours. Although I would definitely draw the line at cross-burnings."

His father blinked rapidly, and Hammond knew he had struck a chord.

"Are you Klan?"

"No! Hell, no."

"But you knew about all that, didn't you? You knew damn well what was happening on Speckle Island. Furthermore, you sanctioned it."

"I got out."

"Not entirely. Lute did. He got himself murdered, so he's off the hook. But you're still vulnerable. You're getting careless, Dad. Your name is on those documents."

"I've already made reparation for what happened on Speckle Island."

Ah, his famous quick jab/uppercut. As usual, Hammond hadn't seen it coming.

"I went to Speckle Island yesterday," Preston told him calmly. "I met with the victims of Lute's appalling terrorism, explained to them that I was mortified when I learned what he was doing, and that I separated myself from the partnership immediately. I gave each family a thousand dollars to cover any damage done to their property and, along with my heartfelt apology, made a substantial contribution to their community church. I also established a scholarship fund for their school." He paused and gave Hammond a sympathetic smile. "Now, in light of this philanthropic gesture, do you really think a criminal case could be made against me? Try it, son, and see how abysmally you fail."

Hammond felt dizzy and nauseated, and it wasn't attributable to the heat or to his injuries. "You bought them off."

Again that beatific smile. "With money taken out of petty cash."

Hammond couldn't remember a time when he wanted to hit someone more. He wanted to grind his fist against his father's lips until they were bruised and bleeding, until they could no longer form that condescending smirk. Curbing the impulse, he lowered his voice and moved his face close to his father's.

"Don't be smug, Father. It's going to cost you more than some petty cash to make this go away. You're not off the hook yet. You are one corrupt son of a bitch. You *define* corruption. So do not come to me with lectures about behavior. Ever again." Having said that, he turned and headed for the parking lot.

Preston grabbed his left arm and roughly pulled him around. "You know, I actually hope it comes to light. You and this gal. I hope somebody has got pictures of you between her legs. I hope they publish them in the newspaper and show them on TV. I'm glad you're in this fix. It would serve you right, you goddamn little hypocrite. You and your self-righteous, do-gooding, Boy-Scouting attitude have sickened me for years," he said, sneering the words.

He poked Hammond hard in the chest with his blunt index finger.

"You're as corruptible as the next man. Up till now you just hadn't been tested yet. And was it greed that caused you to stumble off the straight and narrow path? No. The promise of power? No." He snickered.

"It was a piece of tail. As far as I'm concerned, that's where the real shame lies. You could have at least been corrupted by something a little harder to come by."

The two men glared at each other, their animosity bubbling to the surface after simmering for years beneath thick layers of resentment. Hammond knew that nothing he said would make a dent in his father's iron will, and suddenly he realized how little he cared. Why defend himself and Alex to a man he didn't respect? He recognized Preston for what he was, and he didn't like him. His father's opinion of him, of anything, no longer mattered because there was no integrity or honor supporting it.

Hammond turned and walked away.

Smilow had to wait half an hour in the Charles Towne Plaza lobby before one of the shoeshine chairs became vacant. "Shine's holding up just fine, Mr. Smilow."

"Just buff them, then, Smitty."

The older man launched into a discussion of the Atlanta Braves' current slump.

Smilow cut him off. "Smitty, did you see this woman in the hotel the afternoon Mr. Pettijohn was killed?" He showed him the photograph of Alex Ladd that had appeared in the afternoon edition of the newspaper. He'd enlarged it to better define her features.

"Yes, sir, I did, Mr. Smilow. I saw her on the TV this afternoon, too. She's the one y'all think murdered him."

"Whether or not the grand jury indicts her next week will depend on the strength of our evidence. When you saw her, was she with anyone?"

"No, sir."

"Have you ever seen him?"

He showed him Bobby Trimble's mug shot.

"Only on the TV, same story, same picture as this one."

"Never here in the hotel?"

"No, sir."

"You're sure?"

"You know me and faces, Mr. Smilow. I rarely forget one."

The detective nodded absently as he replaced the photos in his breast pocket. "Did Dr. Ladd look angry or upset when you saw her?"

"Not in particular, but I didn't study on her that long. I noticed her when she came in 'cause she's got right nice hair, you know. Old as I am, I still like looking at pretty girls."

"You see a lot of them coming through here."

"Lots o' ugly ones, too," he said, chuckling. "Anyhow, this one was by herself and minding her own business. She went straight on through the lobby to the elevators. Then in a little while she came back down. Went into the bar over yonder. Little later, I saw her crossing back to the elevators."

"Wait." Smilow leaned down closer to the man buffing his shoes. "Are you saying she went upstairs twice?"

"I reckon."

"How long did she stay the first time?"

"Five minutes, maybe."

"And the second time?"

"I wouldn't know. I didn't see her when she came back down."

He gave Smilow's shoes one last whisk. Smilow stepped down and spread his arms to let Smitty go over his coat with a lint brush. "Smitty, have you mentioned to anyone that I got a shoeshine that day?"

"It's never come up, Mr. Smilow."

"I'd rather you keep that between us, okay?" As he turned, he slipped Smitty a sizable tip.

"Sure enough, Mr. Smilow. Sure enough. Sorry about the other."

"What other?"

"The lady. I'm sorry I didn't see her come back down."

"You were busy, I'm sure."

The shoeshiner smiled. "Yes, sir. It was like Grand Central Station through here last Saturday. People coming and going at all times." He scratched his head. "Funny, isn't it? All of you being here that same day."

"All of us?"

"You, that doctor lady, and the lawyer."

Smilow's mind acted like a steel trap that had just been tripped. "Lawyer?"

"From the D.A.'s office. The one on the TV."

Hᴀᴍᴍᴏɴᴅ ᴡᴀɪᴛᴇᴅ ɪɴ ᴛʜᴇ ᴄᴏʀʀɪᴅᴏʀ until he saw Harvey Knuckle leave his office at precisely five o'clock. The computer whiz conscientiously locked the door behind him, and when he turned around, Hammond was crowding him. "Hey, Harvey."

"Mr. Cross!" he exclaimed, backing up against the office door. "What are you doing here?"

"I think you know."

Knuckle's prominent Adam's apple slid up, then down the skinny column of his neck. His hard swallow was audible. "I'm sorry, but I haven't the vaguest."

"You lied to Loretta Boothe," Hammond said, playing his hunch. "Didn't you?"

Harvey tried to disguise his guilty nervousness with petulance. "I don't know what you're talking about."

"What I'm talking about is five-to-ten for computer theft."

"Huh?"

"I could get you on several counts without breaking a sweat, Harvey. That is unless you cooperate with me now. Who asked you to check out Dr. Alex Ladd?"

"Pardon?"

Hammond's eyes practically nailed him to the office door behind him. "Okay. Fine. Get yourself a good defense lawyer." He turned.

Harvey blurted, "Loretta did."

Hammond came back around. "Who else?"

"Nobody."

"Har-veee?"

*"Nobody!"*

"Okay."

Harvey relaxed and wet his lips with a quick tongue, but his sickly smile folded when Hammond asked, "What about Pettijohn?"

"I don't know—"

"Tell me what I want to know, Harvey."

"I'm always willing to help you, Mr. Cross, you know that. But this time I don't know what you're talking about."

"Records, Harvey," he said with diminishing patience. "Who asked you to dig up Pettijohn's records? Deeds. Plats. Partnership documents, things like that."

"You did," Harvey squeaked.

"I went through legal channels. I want to know who else was interested in his business dealings. Who asked you on the sly to go into his records?"

"What makes you think—"

Hammond took a step nearer and lowered his voice. "Whoever it was had to come to you for information, so don't stall, and don't try and bullshit me with that phony innocent, quizzical expression, or I'm liable to get angry. Prison can be tough on a guy like you, you know." He paused to let the implied threat sink in. "Now, who was it?"

"T-two different people. At different times, though."

"Recently?"

Harvey nodded his head so rapidly his teeth clicked together. "Within the last couple of months or thereabout."

"Who were the two?"

"D-detective Smilow."

Hammond kept his expression unreadable. "And who else?"

"You ought to know, Mr. Cross. She said she was asking on your behalf."

A news junkie by habit, Loretta Boothe watched the early evening newscasts, flipping back and forth between channels and comparing their coverage of the Alex Ladd story.

She was dismayed to see Hammond facing TV cameras looking the worse for wear, his arm in a sling. When had he got hurt? And how? She had seen him just last night.

About the time the news ended and *Wheel of Fortune* began, her daughter Bev came through the living room dressed for work. "I made a macaroni casserole for my lunch, Mom. There's plenty left in the fridge for your supper. Salad makings, too."

"Thanks, honey. I'm not hungry just yet, but maybe later."

Bev hesitated at the front door. "Are you okay?"

Loretta saw the worry in her daughter's eyes, the wariness. The harmony between them was still tentative. Both wanted desperately for things to go well this time. Both feared that they wouldn't. Promises had been made and broken too many times for either of them to trust Loretta's most recent pledges. Everything depended on her staying sober. That was all she had to do. But that was a lot.

"I'm fine." She gave Bev a reassuring smile. "You know that case I was working on? They're taking it to the grand jury next week."

"Based on information you provided?"

"Partially."

"Wow. That's great, Mom. You still have the knack."

Bev's compliment warmed her. "Thanks. But I guess this means I'm out of work again."

"After this success, I'm sure you'll get more." Bev pulled open the door. "Have a good evening. See you in the morning."

After Bev left, Loretta continued watching the game show, but only for lack of something better to do. The apartment felt claustrophobic this evening, although the rooms were no smaller today than they had been yesterday or the day before. The restlessness wasn't environmental; it came from within.

She considered going out, but that would be risky. Her friends were other drunks. The hangout places she knew were rife with temptation to have just one drink. Even one would spell the end of her sobriety, and she would be right back where she had been before Hammond had retained her to work on the Pettijohn case.

She wished that job weren't over. Not just because of the money. Although Bev made an adequate salary to support them, Loretta wished to contribute to the household account. It would be good for her self-esteem, and she needed the independence that came with earning her own income.

Also, as long as she was working, she wouldn't notice her thirst. Idle time was a peril she needed to avoid. Having nothing constructive to do made her crave what she couldn't have. With time on her hands, she began thinking about how trivial her life really was, how it really wouldn't matter if she drank herself to death, how she might just as well make things easy on herself and everyone associated with her. A dangerous train of thought.

Now that she thought about it, Hammond hadn't specifically told her he no longer needed her services. After she gave him the scoop on Dr. Alex

Ladd, he had fled that bar like his britches were on fire. Although he had seemed somewhat downcast, he couldn't wait to act upon the information she had provided, and his action must have paid off because now he was taking his murder case to the grand jury.

Contacting Harvey Knuckle today had probably been superfluous. Hammond had seemed rushed and not all that interested when she passed along her hunch that Harvey had lied to her this morning. But what the hell? It hadn't hurt her to make that additional effort.

Despite Hammond's injuries, whatever they were, his voice had been strong and full of his conviction when he addressed the reporters on the steps of police headquarters. He explained that Bobby Trimble's appearance had been the turning point of the case.

"Based on the strength of his testimony, I feel confident that Dr. Ladd will be indicted."

Conversely, Dr. Ladd's solicitor, whom Loretta knew by reputation only, had told the media that this was the most egregious mistake ever made by the Charleston P.D. and Special Assistant County Solicitor Cross. He was confident that when all the facts were known, Dr. Ladd would be vindicated and that the powers-that-be would owe her a public apology. Already he was considering filing a defamation suit.

Loretta recognized lawyerese when she heard it, although Frank Perkins's statements had been particularly impassioned. Either he was an excellent orator or he was genuinely convinced of his client's innocence. Maybe Hammond did have the wrong suspect.

If so, he would be made to look like a fool in the most important case of his career thus far.

He had alluded to Alex Ladd's unsubstantiated alibi, but he hadn't been specific. Something about . . . what was it?

"Little Bo Peep Show," Loretta said mechanically, solving the Before and After puzzle on *Wheel of Fortune* with the *t*'s, the *p*'s, and the *w* still missing.

A fair on the outskirts of Beaufort. That was it.

Suddenly on her feet, she went into the kitchen where Bev stacked newspapers before conscientiously bundling them for recycling. Luckily tomorrow was pickup day, so a week's worth was there. Loretta plowed through them until she located last Saturday's edition.

She pulled out the entertainment section and quickly leafed through it until she found what she had hoped to. The quarter-page advertisement for the fair provided the time, place, directions, admission fees, attractions to be enjoyed, and—wait!

"Every Thursday, Friday, and Saturday evening through the month of August," she read out loud.

Within minutes she was in her car and on her way out of the city, driving toward Beaufort. She didn't know what she would do when she got there. Follow her nose, she supposed. But if she could—by a stroke of luck or an outright miracle—shoot a hole in Alex Ladd's alibi, Hammond would forever be in her debt. Or, if the psychologist's alibi held up, at least he would be forewarned. He wouldn't be unpleasantly surprised in the courtroom. Either way, he would owe her. Big time.

Until he officially dismissed her, she was technically still on retainer. If she came through for him on this, he would be undyingly grateful and wonder what he had ever done without her. He might even recommend her for a permanent position in the D.A.'s office.

If nothing else, he would appreciate her for seizing the initiative and acting on her own razor-sharp instincts, which not even oceans of booze had dulled. He would be so proud!

"Sergeant Basset?"

The uniformed officer tipped down the corner of the newspaper he was reading. When he saw Hammond standing on the opposite side of his desk, he shot to his feet. "Hey, Solicitor. I have that printout you requested right here."

The CPD's evidence warehouse was Sergeant Glenn Basset's domain. He was short, plump, and self-effacing. A bushy mustache compensated for his bald head. Lacking aggressiveness, he had been a poor patrolman, but was perfectly suited for the desk job he now held. He was a nice guy, not one to complain, satisfied with his rank, an affable fellow, friendly toward everyone, enemy to none.

Hammond had called ahead with his request, which the sergeant was flattered to grant. "You didn't give me much notice, but it was only a matter of pulling up the past month's records and printing them out. I could go back further—"

"Not yet." Hammond scanned the sheet, hoping a name would jump out at him. It didn't. "Do you have a minute, Sergeant?"

Sensing that Hammond wished to speak to him privately, he addressed a clerk working at a desk nearby. "Diane, can you keep an eye on things for a minute?"

Without removing her eyes from her computer terminal, she said, "Take your time."

The portly officer motioned Hammond toward a small room where personnel took their breaks. He offered Hammond a cup of the viscous coffee standing in the cloudy Mr. Coffee carafe.

Hammond declined, then said, "This is a very delicate subject, Sergeant Basset. I regret having to ask."

He regarded Hammond inquisitively. "Ask what?"

"Is it within the realm of possibility—not even probable, just possible—that an officer could . . . borrow . . . a weapon from the warehouse without your knowledge?"

"No, sir."

"It's not *possible*?"

"I keep strict records, Mr. Cross."

"Yes, I see," he said, giving the computer printout another quick scan. Basset was getting nervous. "What's this about?"

"Just a notion I had," Hammond said with chagrin. "I've turned up empty on the weapon that killed Lute Pettijohn."

"Two .38s in the back."

"Right."

"We've got hundreds of weapons in here that fire .38s."

"You see my problem."

"Mr. Cross, I pride myself on running a tight ship. My record with the force—"

"Is impeccable. I know that, Sergeant. I'm not suggesting any complicity on your part. As I said, it's a delicate subject and I hated even to ask. I simply wondered if an officer could have fabricated a reason to take a weapon out."

Basset thoughtfully tugged on his earlobe. "I suppose he could, but he would've still had to sign it out."

Nowhere. "Sorry to have bothered you. Thanks."

Hammond took the records with him, although he didn't think they would yield the valuable clue he had hoped they might. He had left Harvey Knuckle on a high, having got the computer whiz to admit that both Smilow and Steffi had coerced him into getting them information on Pettijohn.

But now that he reflected on it, what did that prove? That they were as interested as he in seeing Lute get his comeuppance? Hardly a breakthrough. Not even a surprise.

He wanted so desperately for Alex to be innocent, he was willing to cast doubt on anyone and everyone, even colleagues who, these days, were doing more to uphold law and order than he was.

Despondently, he let himself into his apartment, moved straight into the living room, and turned on the TV. The anchorwoman with the emerald green contact lenses was just introducing the lead story. Masochistically, he watched.

Except for the arm sling, his bandages were covered by his clothing, but his complexion looked waxy and wan in the glare of the leeching TV lights, making his day-old beard appear even darker. When asked about his injury, he had dismissed the mugging as inconsequential and cut to the chase.

Being politically correct, he had complimented the CPD for an excellent job of detective work. He had dodged specific questions about Alex Ladd and said only that Trimble's statement had been a turning point in the investigation, that their case was solid, and that an indictment was practically ensured.

Standing just behind his left shoulder, lending support, Steffi had nodded and smiled in agreement. She photographed well, he noted. The lights shone in her dark eyes. The camera captured her vivacity.

Smilow also had been swarmed by media, and he received equal time on the telecasts. Unlike Steffi, he had been uncharacteristically restrained. His remarks were diluted by diplomacy and more or less echoed Hammond's. He referred to Alex's connection to Bobby Trimble only in the most general terms, saying that the jailed man had been integral to making a case against her. He declined to reveal the nature of her relationship to Lute Pettijohn.

He never referenced her juvenile record, but Hammond suspected that this omission was calculated. Smilow didn't want to contaminate the jury pool and give Frank Perkins grounds for a change of venue or mistrial, assuming the case made it to trial.

Video cameras captured a granite-jawed Frank Perkins ushering Alex out. That segment was the most difficult for Hammond to watch, knowing how humiliating it must have been for her to be in the spotlight as the prime suspect in the most celebrated homicide in Charleston's recent history.

She was described as thirty-five years old, a respected doctor of psychology with impressive credentials. Beyond her professional achievements, she was lauded for her participation in civic affairs and for being a generous benefactor to several charities. Neighbors and colleagues who had been sought for comment expressed shock, some outrage, calling the speculation on her involvement "ludicrous," "ridiculous," and other synonymous adjectives.

When the anchorwoman with the artificially green eyes segued into another story, Hammond turned off the set, went upstairs, and drew himself a hot bath. He soaked in it with his right arm hanging over the rim of the tub. The bath eased some of the soreness out of him, but it also left him feeling light-headed and weak.

In need of food, he went downstairs and began preparing scrambled eggs.

Working with his left hand made him clumsy. He was further incapacitated by a dismal foreboding. When remembered in posterity, he didn't want to be a dirty joke. He didn't want it to be said, "Oh, you remember Hammond Cross. Promising young prosecutor. Caught a whiff of pussy, and it all went to hell."

And that's what they would say. Or words to that effect.

Over their damp towels and sweaty socks in the locker room, or between glasses of bourbon in a popular watering hole, colleagues and acquaintances would shake their heads in barely concealed amusement over his susceptibility. He would be considered a fool, and Alex would be regarded as the piece of tail that had brought about his downfall.

He wanted to lash out at those imagined gossips for their unfairness. He wanted to lambast them for making lewd remarks about her and their relationship. It wasn't what they thought it was. He had fallen in love.

He hadn't been so doped up on Darvocet last night that he didn't remember telling her that this was the real thing for him, and had been from the first. He had met her less than a week ago—*less than a week*—but he had never been more sure of anything in his life. Never before had he been so physically attracted to a woman. He had never felt such a cerebral, spiritual, and emotional connection to anyone.

For hours at that silly fair, and later in his bed at the cabin, they had talked. About music. Food. Books. Travel and the places they wanted to visit when time allowed. Movies. Exercise and fitness regimens. The old South. The new South. The Three Stooges, and why men loved them and women hated them. Meaningful things. Meaningless things. Endless conversations about everything. Except themselves.

He had told her nothing substantive about himself. She certainly hadn't divulged anything about her life, present or past.

Had she been a whore? Was she still? If she was, could he stop loving her as quickly as he had started? He was afraid he couldn't.

Maybe he was a fool after all.

But being a fool was no excuse for wrongdoing. He and his guilty conscience were becoming incompatible roommates. He was finding it increasingly difficult to live with himself. Although he hated to give his father credit for anything, Preston had opened his eyes today and forced him to confront something he had avoided confronting: Hammond Cross was as corruptible as the next man. He was no more honest than his father.

Unable to stomach the thought, or the scrambled eggs, he fed them to the garbage disposal.

He wanted a drink, but alcohol would only have increased the lingering muzziness in his head and left him feeling worse.

He wanted his arm to stop throbbing like a son of a bitch.

He wanted a solution to this goddamn mess that threatened the bright future he had planned for himself.

Mostly, he wanted Alex to be safe.

*Safe.*

A safe full of cash at Alex's house.

An empty safe in Pettijohn's hotel suite.

A safe inside the closet.

The closet. The safe. Hangers. Robe. Slippers. Still in their wrapper.

Hammond jumped as though a jolt of electricity had shot through him, then fell impossibly still as he forced himself to calm down, think it through, reason it out.

*Go slow. Take your time.*

But after taking several minutes to look at it from every conceivable angle, he couldn't find a hole in it. All the elements fit.

The conclusion didn't make him happy, but he couldn't allow himself to dwell on that now. He had to act.

Scrambling from his chair, he grabbed the nearest cordless phone. After securing the number from directory assistance, he punched in the digits.

"Charles Towne Plaza. How may I direct your call?"

"The spa, please."

"I'm sorry, sir, the spa is closed for the evening. If you wish to make an appointment—"

He interrupted the switchboard operator to identify himself and told her with whom he needed to speak. "And I need to talk to him immediately. While you're tracking him down, put me through to the manager of housekeeping."

It didn't take long for Loretta to decide that coming to this fair was a bad idea.

Fifteen minutes after parking her car in a dusty pasture and going the rest of the way on foot, she was sweating like a pig. Children were everywhere—noisy, rowdy, sticky children who seemed to have singled her out to annoy. The carnies were surly. Not that she blamed them for their querulous dispositions. Who could work in this heat?

She would have sold her soul to be inside a nice, dark, cool bar. The stench of stale tobacco smoke and beer would have been a welcome relief from the mix of cotton candy and cow manure that clung to the fairgrounds.

The only thing that kept her there was the constant reminder that she might be doing Hammond some good. She owed him this. Not just in recompense for the case she'd blown, but for giving her another chance when no one else would give her the time of day.

It might not last, this season of sobriety. But for right now she was dry, she was working, and her daughter was looking at her with something other than contempt. For these blessings, she had Hammond Cross to thank.

Doggedly she trudged from one attraction to another.

"I just thought you might remember—"

"You nuts, lady? We've had thousands o' people through here. How'm I s'posed to remember one broad?" The carny spat a stringy glob of tobacco juice that barely missed her shoulder.

"Thank you for your time, and fuck you."

"Yeah, yeah. Now move it. You're holding up the line."

Each time she showed Alex Ladd's photograph to the exhibitors, ride operators, and food vendors, the response was a variation on a theme. Either they were outright rude like the last one, or they were too frazzled to give her their full attention. The shake of a head and a curt "Sorry" was the usual answer to her inquiries.

She canvassed long after the sun went down and the mosquitoes came out in force. After several hours, all she had to show for her trouble was a pair of feet that the humidity had swollen to the size of throw pillows. Analyzing the tight, puffy flesh pressing through the straps of her sandals, she thought it was a shame that this carnival didn't have a freak show. "These babies would have qualified me," she muttered.

She finally acknowledged that this was a fool's mission, that Dr. Ladd had probably lied about being at the fair in the first place, and that the likelihood of bumping into someone who had been there last Saturday and who also remembered seeing her was next to nil.

She swatted at a mosquito on her arm. It burst like a balloon, leaving a spatter of blood. "I gotta be at least a quart low." It was then she decided to cut her losses and return to Charleston.

She was fantasizing about soaking her feet in a tub of ice water when she walked past the dance pavilion with a conical ceiling strung with clear Christmas lights. A scruffy band was tuning up. The fiddler had a braided beard, for crying out loud. Dancers fanned themselves with pamphlets, laughing and chatting as they waited for the band to resume playing.

Singles lurked on the perimeter of the floor, checking out their prospects, assessing their competition, trying to appear neither too obvious nor too desperate to link up with someone.

Loretta noticed that there were a lot of military personnel in the crowd. Young servicemen, with their fresh shaves and buzz haircuts, were sweating off their cologne, ogling the girls, and swilling beer.

A beer sure would taste good. One beer? What could it hurt? Not for the alcohol buzz. Just to quench a raging thirst that a sugary soft drink couldn't touch. As long as she was here, she could show Dr. Ladd's photo around, too. Maybe someone in this crowd would remember her from the weekend before. Servicemen always had an eye out for attractive women. Maybe one had taken a shine to Alex Ladd.

Telling herself she wasn't rationalizing just to get near the beer-drinking crowd, and wincing from the sandal straps cutting into her swollen feet, Loretta limped up the steps of the pavilion.

W HEN FRANK PERKINS OPENED THE FRONT DOOR to his home, his welcoming smile slipped, as though the punch line to a promising joke had turned out to be a dud. "Hammond."

"May I come in?"

Choosing his words carefully, Frank said, "I would be very uncomfortable with that."

"We need to talk."

"I keep normal business hours."

"This can't wait, Frank. Not even until tomorrow. You need to see it now." Hammond removed an envelope from his breast pocket and handed it to the attorney. Frank took it, peeped inside. The envelope contained a dollar bill. "Aw, Jes—"

"I'm retaining you as my lawyer, Frank. That's a down payment on your fee."

"What the hell are you trying to pull?"

"I was with Alex the night Lute Pettijohn was killed. We spent the night in bed together. Now may I come in?" As expected, the declaration rendered Frank Perkins speechless. Hammond took advantage of his momentary dumbfoundedness to edge past him.

Frank closed the front door to his comfortable suburban house. Quickly recovering, he came at Hammond full throttle. "Do you realize how many rules of ethics you've just violated? How many you tricked *me* into violating?"

"You're right." Hammond took back the dollar bill. "You can't be my lawyer. Conflict of interest. But for the brief time that you were on retainer, I confided something to you which you're bound by professional privilege to keep confidential."

"You son of a bitch," Frank said angrily. "I don't know what you're up to. I don't even want to know, but I do want you out of my house. Now!"

"Didn't you hear what I said? I said that I spent—"

He broke off when the open archway behind Frank filled with people who were curious to see what the commotion was. Alex's face was the only one that registered with Hammond.

Frank, following the direction of Hammond's stare, mumbled, "Maggie, you remember Hammond Cross."

"Of course," said Frank's wife. "Hello, Hammond."

"Maggie. I'm sorry to barge in on you like this. I hope I didn't interrupt anything."

"Actually, we were having dinner," Frank said.

One of his nine-year-old twin sons had a smear of what looked like spaghetti sauce near his mouth. Maggie was a gracious southern lady who had descended from valiant Confederate wives and widows. The awkward situation unfolding in her foyer didn't ruffle her. "We've just now sat down, Hammond. Please join us."

He glanced first at Frank, then at Alex. "No, thanks, but I appreciate the offer. I just need a few minutes of Frank's time."

"It was good to see you again. Boys."

Taking each twin by a shoulder, Maggie Perkins turned them around and herded them back to where they had come from, presumably an informal eating area in the kitchen.

Hammond said to Alex, "I didn't know you were here."

"Frank was kind enough to invite me to dinner with his family."

"Nice of him. After today, you probably didn't feel like being alone."

"No, I didn't."

"Besides, it's good you're here. You need to hear this, too."

Finally Frank butted in. "Since I'm probably going to be disbarred over this anyway, I think I'll go ahead and have the drink I desperately need. Either of you interested?"

He indicated for them to follow him toward the rear of the house where he had a home study. The plaques and framed citations arranged in attractive groupings on the paneled walls attested to the honorable man that Frank Perkins was, personally and professionally.

Hammond and Alex declined his offer of a drink, but Frank poured himself a straight scotch and sat down behind a substantial desk. Alex took a leather love seat, Hammond an armchair. The lawyer divided a look between them that ultimately settled on his client. "Is it true? Have you slept with our esteemed assistant county solicitor?"

"There's no call for—"

"Hammond," Frank brusquely interrupted, "you are in no position to correct me. Or even to cross me, for that matter. I should kick your ass out of here, then share your confession with Monroe Mason. Unless he already knows."

"He doesn't."

"The only reason you're still under my roof is because I respect my client's privacy. Until I know all the facts, I don't want to do anything rash which might embarrass her any more than she's already been embarrassed by this travesty."

"Don't be angry with Hammond, Frank," Alex said. There was an honest weariness in her voice that Hammond hadn't heard before. Or perhaps it was resignation. Maybe even relief that their secret was finally out. "This is as much my fault as his. I should have told you immediately that I knew him."

"Intimately?"

"Yes."

"How far were you willing to let it go? Were you going to let him indict you, jail you, subject you to a trial, get you convicted, put you on death row?"

"I don't know!" Alex stood up suddenly and turned her back to them, hugging her elbows close to her body. After taking a moment to compose herself, she faced them again. "Actually I'm more to blame than Hammond. He didn't know me, but I knew him, and I pursued him. Deliberately. I made our meeting look accidental, but it wasn't. Nothing that happened between us was by chance."

"When did this meeting-by-design occur?"

"Last Saturday evening. Around dusk. After the initial contact, I exercised every feminine wile I knew to entice Hammond to spend the night with me. Whatever I did," she said, her voice growing husky, "worked." She looked across at him. "Because he did."

Frank finished his drink in one swallow. The liquor brought tears to his eyes and caused him to cough behind his fist. After clearing his throat, he asked where all this had taken place. Alex talked him through the chain of events, beginning with their meeting in the dance pavilion and ending in his cabin. "I sneaked out the following morning before dawn, prepared never to see him again."

Frank shook his head, which seemed to have become muddled either by a sudden infusion of alcohol or by conflicting facts he was finding difficult to sort out. "I don't get it. You slept with him, but it wasn't . . . you didn't . . ."

"I was her insurance," Hammond said. It was still hard for him to hear her admit that she had set him up, that their meeting wasn't kismet or the romantic happenstance he wished it had been. But he had to get past that. Circumstances demanded that he focus on matters that were much more important. "If Alex found herself in need of an alibi, I was to be it. I was the perfect alibi, in fact. Because I couldn't expose her without implicating myself."

Frank gazed at him with unmitigated puzzlement. "Care to explain that?"

"Alex followed me to the fair from the Charles Towne Plaza, where I'd met with Lute Pettijohn."

Frank stared at him for several beats before looking to Alex for confirmation. She gave a small nod. Frank got up to pour himself another drink.

While he was at it, Hammond took the opportunity to look at Alex. Her eyes were moist, but she wasn't crying. He wanted to hold her. He also wanted to shake her until all the truths came tumbling out.

Or maybe not. Maybe he didn't want to know that he had been as gullible as the horny young boys and dirty old men who had paid half-brother Bobby for her favors.

If he loved her, as he professed, he would have to get past that, too.

Frank returned to his chair. Twirling his refilled glass on the leather desk pad, he asked, "Who's going to go first?"

"I had an appointment with Pettijohn on Saturday afternoon," Hammond stated. "At his invitation. I didn't want to go, but he had insisted that we meet, guaranteeing that it would be in my best interest."

"For what purpose?"

"The A.G. had appointed me to investigate him. Pettijohn had got wind of it."

"How?"

"More on that later. For now, suffice it to say that I was close to turning my findings over to a grand jury."

"I assume Pettijohn wanted to make a deal."

"Right."

"What was he offering in exchange?"

"If I reported back to the A.G. that there was no case to be made, and let Lute carry on his business as usual, he promised to support me as Monroe Mason's successor, including sizable contributions to my campaign. He also suggested that once I achieved the office, we would continue to have a mutually beneficial arrangement. A very cozy alliance which would have enabled him to continue breaking laws and me to look the other way."

"I gather you turned him down."

"Flat. That's when he brought out the heavy artillery. My own father was one of his partners on the Speckle Island project. Lute produced documents proving it."

"Where are those documents now?"

"I took them with me when I left."

"They're valid?"

"I'm afraid so."

Frank was no dummy. He figured it out. "If you proceeded with your investigation of Lute, you'd be forced to bring criminal charges against your father, too."

"That was the essence of Lute's warning, yes."

Alex's face was soft with compassion. Frank said quietly, "I'm sorry, Hammond."

He knew the commiseration was genuine, but he waved it aside. "I told Lute to go to hell, that I intended to uphold my duty. When I turned my back on him, he was screaming invectives and issuing threats. The temper tantrum might have brought on the stroke. I don't know. I never turned around. I wasn't in there for more than five minutes, Max."

"What time was this?"

"We had a five o'clock appointment."

"Did you see Alex?"

They shook their heads simultaneously. "Not until I got to the fair. I was so pissed off at Pettijohn, I was in quite a temper when I left the hotel. I didn't notice anything."

He paused to take a deep breath. "I had planned to go to my cabin for the night. On the spur of the moment I decided to stop at the fair for a while. I saw Alex in the dance pavilion and . . ." He looked from Frank to her, where she was seated on the love seat, listening intently. "It went from there."

The room grew so silent that the ticking clock on Frank's desk sounded ponderous. After a time, the lawyer spoke. "What did you hope to accomplish by coming here and telling me this?"

"It's been weighing heavily on my conscience."

"Well, I'm not a priest," Frank said testily.

"No, you're not."

"And we're on opposite sides of a murder trial."

"I'm aware of that, too."

"Then back to my original question: Why did you come here?"

Hammond said, "Because I know who killed Lute."

## CHAPTER 33

Davee LANGUIDLY ANSWERED HER TELEPHONE.

"Davee, you know who this is." It wasn't a question.

For lack of anything better to do, she had been stretched out on the chaise lounge in her bedroom, drinking vodka on the rocks and watching a black and white Joan Crawford film on a classic movie channel. The urgency behind the caller's voice brought her up into a sitting position, which caused a wave of dizziness. She muted the television set.

"What—"

"Don't say anything. Can you meet me?"

She checked the clock on the antique tea table beside the chaise. "Now?"

In her wild teenage years a call late at night would have spelled adventure. She would have sneaked out of the house to meet a boyfriend or a group of girls for some forbidden cruising until dawn, skinny-dipping at the beach, beer drinking, or pot smoking. Those escapades never failed to get her parents in an uproar. Getting caught and defying punishment had been part of the fun.

Even following her marriage to Lute, it wasn't all that uncommon for her to carry on one-sided telephone conversations that led to late-night excursions. However, those had never caused a disturbance in the household. Either Lute was indifferent to her comings and goings or he was out on a lark of his own. They hadn't been nearly as much fun.

Although this one didn't promise to be fun, her curiosity was piqued. "What's going on?"

"I can't talk about it over the telephone, but it's important. Do you know where the McDonald's on Rivers Avenue is?"

"I can find it."

"Near the intersection with Dorchester. As soon as you can get there."

"But—"

Davee stared at the dead cordless phone in her hand for a few moments, then dropped it onto the chaise and stood up. She swayed slightly and put her hand on the table in order to regain her balance. Her equilibrium gradually returned and brought her reason with it.

This was nuts. She'd had a lot to drink. She shouldn't drive. And, anyway, who the hell did he think he was to summon her to a McDonald's in the middle of the freaking night? No explanation. No please or thank you. No worry that she wouldn't acquiesce. Why couldn't he come to her with whatever was so damned important? Whatever it was must surely relate to Lute's murder investigation. Hadn't she made it clear that she didn't want to become involved in that any more than was absolutely necessary?

Nevertheless, she went into the bathroom, splashed cold water on her face, and gargled a mouthful of Scope. She slipped off her nightgown, then, without bothering with underwear, pulled on a pair of white pants and a matching T-shirt made of some clingy, synthetic microfiber knit that left little to the imagination—which served him right. She didn't bother with shoes. Her hair was a mess of unbrushed curls. If anyone spied them together, her dishabille alone would raise eyebrows. She didn't give a damn, of course, but this recklessness was uncharacteristic of him.

Sarah Birch was watching TV in her apartment off the kitchen. "I'm going out." Davee informed her.

"This time o' night?"

"I want some ice cream."

"There's a freezer full."

"But none of the flavor I'm craving."

The faithful housekeeper always knew when she was lying, but she never challenged her. That was just one of the reasons that Davee adored her. "I'll be careful. Back in a while."

"And if anybody asks me later . . . ?"

"I was in bed fast asleep by nine."

Knowing that all her secrets were safe with Sarah, she went into the garage and climbed into her BMW. The residential streets were dark and sleepy. There was little traffic on the freeway and commercial boulevards as well. Although it went against her natural inclination as well as the automobile's, she kept the BMW within the speed limit. Two DUIs had been dismissed by a judge who owed Lute a favor. A third would be pushing her luck.

The McDonald's was lit up like a Las Vegas casino. Even at this late hour there were a dozen cars in the parking lot, belonging to the teenagers who were clustered around the tables inside.

Davee pulled into a shadowed parking space on the far side of the lot, lowered the driver's-side window, then turned off the engine. In front of her was a row of scruffy bushes serving as a hedge between the McDonald's parking lot and that of another fast food restaurant that had failed. The building was boarded up. Behind her was the empty drive-through lane. On either side of her, nothing but darkness.

He wasn't there yet and that miffed her. Responding to his urgency, she had dropped everything—including a perfectly good highball—and had come running. She flipped down the sun visor, slid the cover off the lighted mirror, and checked her reflection.

He opened the passenger door and got in. "You look good, Davee. You always do."

Rory Smilow closed the car door quickly to extinguish the dome light. Reaching above the steering wheel, he slid the closure back across the vanity mirror, eliminating that light, too.

His compliment spread through Davee like a sip of warm, very expensive liqueur, although she tried not to show the intoxicating effect it had on her. Instead, she spoke crossly. "What's up with the cloak and dagger stuff, Rory? Running low on clues these days?"

"Just the opposite. I have too many. None of them add up."

Her comment had been intended as a joke, but of course he had taken her seriously. Disappointingly, he was getting right down to business, just as he had the night he came to inform her that her husband was dead. He had behaved exactly as protocol demanded. Professionally. Courteously. Detached.

Never in a thousand years would Steffi Mundell ever have guessed that they had been lovers who had once knocked out the glass door of his shower while making love. That a picnic in a public park had ended with him sitting against a tree while she rode him. That one weekend they had subsisted on peanut butter and sex from after classes on Friday afternoon until classes began on Monday morning.

His behavior the day Lute died had betrayed none of the romantic craziness in which they had once engaged. It had broken Davee's heart that he could maintain such goddamn detachment when with every glance she had wanted to gobble him up. His control was admirable. Or pitiable. So little passion must make for a very lonely and sterile life.

Trying to harden her heart against him, she said, "Mark it up to a lapse in good judgment, but here I am. Now, what do you want?"

"To ask you some questions about Lute's murder."

"I thought you had the case sewed up. I saw on the news—"

"Right, right. Hammond's taking it to the grand jury next week."

"So what's the problem?"

"Before today, when you saw the news story, had you ever heard of Dr. Alex Ladd?"

"No, but Lute had a lot of girlfriends. Many of them I knew, but not all, I'm sure."

"I don't think she was a girlfriend."

"Really?"

Turning toward him, she pulled her foot up into the car seat, settling her heel against her bottom and resting her chin on her knee. It was a provocative, unladylike pose that drew his gaze downward, where it remained for several seconds before returning to her face.

"If you're coming to me for answers, Rory, you must truly be desperate."

"You are my last resort."

"Then too bad for you, because I've told you everything I know."

"I seriously doubt that, Davee."

"I'm not lying to you about this Ladd woman. I never—"

"It's not that," he said, shaking his head impatiently. "It's something . . . something else."

"Do you think you're after the wrong person?"

He didn't respond, but his features tensed.

"Ah, that's it, isn't it? And for you, uncertainty is a fate worse than death, isn't it? You of the cold heart and iron resolve." She smiled. "Well, I hate to disappoint you, darlin', but this little tête-à-tête has been a waste of time for both of us. I don't know who killed Lute. I promise."

"Did you speak to him that day?"

"When he left the house that morning, he told me he was going to play golf. The next time I even thought about him was when you and that Mundell bitch showed up to inform me that he was dead. His last words to me were apparently a lie, which more or less summarizes our marriage. He was a terrible husband, a so-so lover, and a despicable human being. Frankly, I don't give a rat's ass who did the deed."

"We caught your housekeeper in a lie."

"To protect me."

"If you're innocent, why did you need protecting?"

"Good point. But if I had said that I spent that Saturday afternoon riding horseback nekkid down Broad Street, Sarah would have agreed. You know that."

"You weren't confined to your bedroom all day with a headache?"

She laughed and ran her fingers through her hair, combing out some of the tangled curls. "In a manner of speaking. I was in bed all day with my masseur, who turned out to be not only a headache, but a boring pain in the butt. Sarah didn't want to sully my good reputation by telling you the truth."

Her sarcasm wasn't lost on him. Turning his head away from her, he stared through the windshield toward the row of straggling shrubbery. His jaw was knotted with tension. Davee didn't know if that was a good sign or bad.

"Am I a suspect again, Rory?"

"No. You wouldn't have killed Lute."

"Why don't you think so?"

His eyes came back to hers. "Because you enjoyed tormenting me by being married to him."

So he knew why she had married Lute. He had noticed, and, furthermore, he had cared. For all his seeming indifference, there was blood in his veins after all, and at least a portion of it had been heated by jealousy.

Her heart fluttered with excitement, but she kept her features schooled and her inflection at a minimum. "And what's more . . . ?"

"And what's more, you wouldn't have put yourself out. Knowing that you could have gotten away with murder, why bother?"

"In other words," she said, "I'm too rich to be convicted."

"Exactly."

"And a divorce is only marginally less trouble than a murder trial."

"In your instance, a divorce is probably more trouble."

Enjoying herself, she said, "Besides, as I told Hammond, the prison uniforms—"

"When did you talk to Hammond?" he asked, cutting her off.

"I talk to him often. We're old friends."

"I'm well aware of that. Did you know he was with Lute the day he was killed? At about the time he was killed?"

No longer relaxed, Davee was instantly on guard and wondering how far Rory would go to pay her back for the torment she had caused him. Would he charge her with obstruction of justice for withholding evidence? She had turned over to Hammond the handwritten notation from Lute, indicating his appointments on Saturday. The information could be totally insignificant. Or it could be key to the solution of Rory's murder mystery.

Whichever, it was the investigator's job, not the widow's, to determine what bearing it had on the case. Even if Hammond's meeting with Lute didn't factor into the murder itself, it could compromise him as the prosecuting attorney. The second appointment had never taken place, if indeed that second notation had indicated a later appointment. There'd been no name with it, and by the time specified, Lute was already dead.

Davee was trapped between being caught for wrongdoing and fierce loyalty to an old friend. "Did Hammond tell you that?"

"He was seen in the hotel."

She laughed, but not very convincingly. "That's it? That's the basis of your assumption that he was with Lute, that he was seen in the same building? Maybe you need to take a vacation, Rory. You've lost your edge."

"Insults, Davee?"

"The conclusion you've reached is an insult to my intelligence as well as yours. Two men were in the same large public place at approximately the same time. What makes you think there's a connection?"

"Because for all the times we've talked about the hotel last Saturday afternoon, never once has Hammond mentioned that he was there."

"Why should he? Why make a big deal out of a coincidence?"

"If it was a coincidence, there would be no reason for him not to mention it."

"Maybe he was having a Saturday afternoon rendezvous. Maybe he likes the dining room's crab cakes. Maybe he took a shortcut through the lobby just to get out of the heat. There could be a hundred reasons why he was there."

He leaned across the console, coming closer to her than he had been in years. "If Hammond met with Lute, I need to know it."

"I don't know if they met or not," she snapped. That much was true. All she had done was give Hammond Lute's note. She hadn't asked, and he hadn't said, whether or not the appointment had been kept.

"What would be the nature of such a meeting?"

"How should I know?"

"Had Lute caught you and Hammond together?"

"What?" she exclaimed on a short laugh. "Heavenly days, Rory, your imagination is truly running amok tonight. Where did you get that idea?" He gave her a hard look, the meaning of which couldn't be misinterpreted. It pierced the tiny, fragile bubble of happiness spawned by seeing him again.

"Oh," she said, her smile turning sad. "Well, you're right, of course. I'm certainly not above committing adultery. But do you honestly think that Hammond Cross would sleep with another man's wife?"

After a brief, tense silence, he asked, "What other reason could they have for meeting?"

"We don't know that they did."

"Has Hammond mentioned seeing anyone else in the hotel?"

"If he was there, I'm sure he saw the sweating hordes of people who are in and out of there every day."

"Anyone in particular?"

"No, Rory!" she said with exasperation. "I've told you, he didn't say anything."

"Something is wrong with him."

"With Hammond? Like what?"

"I don't know, but it bothers me. He's not his fire-breathing self these days."

"He's in love."

His chin went back like it had sustained a quick, unexpected jab. "In love? With Steffi?"

"God forbid," she replied, shuddering slightly. "I was almost afraid to ask about the depth of that relationship, but when I did, he said it was over, which I believe. His lady love is not the charmless Ms. Mundell."

"Then who?"

"He wouldn't say. He didn't look too happy about it, either. Said it wasn't just complicated, but impossible. And no, the lady isn't married. I asked him that, too."

Rory bowed his head slightly. He seemed to grow fixated on her bare toes while he ruminated on what she had told him. She had a coveted few moments to look at him—the smooth forehead, stern brow, rigid jaw, the uncompromising mouth which she knew could be compromised. She had felt it on her lips, on her body, hungry and tender.

"It's a powerful motivator," she said softly.

He raised his head. "What?"

"Love." For ponderous, timeless moments they stared deeply into each other's eyes. "It makes you do things you wouldn't consider doing otherwise. Like marrying a man you hate."

"Or killing him."

A quick breath caused her breasts to tremble beneath the filmy fabric clinging to them. "I wish you had loved me enough to kill him." She placed her hands on his cheeks and ran her thumbs alternately across his lips. "Do you, Rory?" she whispered urgently. "Do you love me that much? Please tell me you do."

As though stretching across the years spent in heartache and yearning, she leaned over the console and kissed him. The first touch of her lips was as cataclysmic as a match striking flint. His reaction was explosive. His mouth devoured hers in a hard and greedy kiss that was almost savage in intensity.

But it ended just as abruptly. Reaching up, he forcibly removed her hands from his face and pushed her away.

"Rory?" she cried, reaching for him as he pushed open the car door.

"Goodbye, Davee."

"Rory?"

But he slipped through the hedge of bushes and disappeared into the darkness. McDonald's had closed. Everyone had left. The lights had been turned out. It was dark, and Davee was alone. No one heard her bitter sobs.

I KNOW WHO KILLED LUTE."

Hammond's statement shocked Alex and Frank Perkins into silence, but it lasted no more than a few seconds before each began firing questions at him. Primarily, Frank wanted to know why Hammond was here in his home study instead of at the police station.

"Later," Hammond said. "Before we go any further, I must hear Alex's account of what happened." Turning toward her, he leaned forward. "The truth, Alex. All of it. Everything. Tonight. Now."

"I—"

Before she could speak, Frank held up his hand. "Hammond, you must think I'm an idiot. I will not allow my client to tell you a damn thing. I want no part of this clandestine meeting you have forced me into. You have behaved in the most reprehensible, irresponsible, unprofessional—"

"Okay, Frank, you're not a priest, remember?" Hammond said. "You're not my Sunday school teacher, or my daddy, either. Both Alex and I have acknowledged how inappropriately we've handled this."

"A peach of an understatement," Frank remarked drolly. "The consequences of your intimacy are potentially disastrous. For all of us."

"How are they disastrous for you?" Alex asked.

"Alex, less than five minutes ago, you admitted to doing everything within your power to get Hammond into bed with you. If you have any defense at all, your being with Hammond that night is it. But how effective will that testimony be in light of your background according to Bobby Trimble?"

"How can that be held against me? It's behind me. I'm not that girl anymore. I'm me." She looked from him to Hammond. "Yes, every ugly detail of Bobby's statement is true. With one exception. I never went beyond letting them look at me."

She shook her head emphatically. "Never. I safeguarded a small, private part of myself, in case my hope for a better way of life was ever realized. There was a line I would not cross. Thank God I had that kernel of self-preservation.

"Bobby exploited me in the most despicable way. But it took years for me to stop blaming myself for my participation. I believed that I was intrinsically bad. Through counseling and my own studies, I realized that I was a classic case, an abused child who felt that I was responsible for the mistreatment."

She smiled at the irony. "I was one of my first cases. I had to heal myself. I had to learn to love myself and consider myself worthy of others' love. The Ladds were instrumental. They had left me a legacy of unconditional love. I came to understand that if they could love me, being as basically good and decent as they were, I could bury the past and at least accept myself.

"But it's an ongoing therapy. Sometimes I have lapses. To this day, I ask myself if there was something I could have done. Was there ever a time when I could have stood up to Bobby and resisted? I was so afraid that he would abandon me as my mother had, and I would be entirely alone. He was my provider. I depended on him for everything."

"You were a child," Frank reminded her gently.

She nodded. "Then, yes, Frank. But not the night I placed myself in Hammond's path and hoped that he would respond to me." Turning to him, she said with entreaty, "Please forgive me for the damage I've done. I was afraid of just this, of what has happened. I did not kill Lute Pettijohn, but I was afraid of being accused of it. Afraid of being considered guilty because of my juvenile record. I went to Pettijohn's hotel suite—"

"Alex, again I must caution you not to say anything more."

"No, Frank. Hammond is right. You need to hear my account. He needs to hear it." The lawyer was still frowning his concern, but she didn't heed the silent warning.

"Let me go back a few weeks." She told them about Bobby's sudden and unwelcome reappearance in her life, how he had shared with her his scheme to blackmail Lute Pettijohn. "I cautioned Bobby that he was way out of his league, that he would do well to leave Charleston and forget this ridiculous plan.

"But he was determined to see it through, and equally determined that I help him. He threatened to expose my past if I didn't. I'm ashamed to admit this, but I was afraid of him. If he had been the same loudmouthed, arrogant, unsophisticated Bobby that he'd been twenty-five years ago, I would have laughed at his threats and called the police immediately.

"But he had acquired some etiquette, or at least he affected good manners and social decorum. This new Bobby could more easily insinuate himself into my life and decay it from the inside. He did in fact appear at a lecture, passing himself off as a visiting psychologist, and my colleague never questioned his authenticity.

"Nevertheless, I called his bluff and told him to leave me alone. I suppose he got desperate. In any event, he contacted Pettijohn. Whatever Bobby said to him must have made an impression, because he agreed to pay one hundred thousand dollars in exchange for Bobby's silence."

"No one who knew Lute Pettijohn will believe that, Alex," Hammond said quietly.

"On that I agree," Frank added.

"I didn't believe it myself," Alex said. "And apparently Bobby wasn't entirely convinced, either, because he approached me again, this time insisting that I be the one to meet Pettijohn and collect the cash. I agreed to."

"In God's name, why?" Frank asked.

"Because I saw it as an opportunity to rid myself of Bobby. My idea was to meet Pettijohn, but instead of collecting the cash, I was going to explain the situation and urge him to report Bobby's extortion to the police."

"Why not go to the police yourself?"

"In hindsight, I see that would have been the better choice." She sighed. "But I feared the association with Bobby. He had boasted about his escape from a loan shark in Florida. There were numerous reasons I wanted to stay one step removed from him."

"So you went to the Charles Towne Plaza at the appointed time."

"Yes."

"You couldn't call Pettijohn on the telephone?"

"I wish I had, Frank. But I thought that meeting him in person would make a stronger impression."

"What happened when you got there?"

"He was courteous. He politely listened as I explained the situation." She sat down on the edge of the love seat and stroked her forehead.

"And?"

"And then he laughed at me," she said shakily. "I should have known the instant he opened the door that something was out of kilter. He wasn't surprised to see me, although he should have been expecting Bobby. But I didn't realize that until later."

"He knew you were coming, not Bobby, and he laughed at your story."

"Yes," she said forlornly. "Bobby had called ahead and told Pettijohn I was coming, told him that I was his double-crossing partner, warned him that I would probably concoct a sob story, one guaranteed to make him feel sorry for me, before luring him into bed and creating my own chance to blackmail him for more of a prize than Bobby was asking."

"I didn't give that son of a bitch enough credit," Hammond muttered angrily. "Trimble doesn't look that smart."

"He's not smart," Alex said. "Just crafty. Bobby's got more gall than sense, and that makes him dangerous. When he sees an opportunity, he takes risks that no intelligent person would consider taking. He also knows the advantage of striking first.

"Nothing I said convinced Pettijohn that I wasn't part of some devious grand scheme involving sex and blackmail. He suggested that I not squander the opportunity. As long as we were there, and I had my heart set on taking him to bed . . . You get my drift."

"He came on to you?" Frank guessed.

"I resisted, of course. Knocked his arm aside. I'm sure that's when the clove got on his sleeve. I'd spiked the oranges with them that morning. A speck must have still been on my hand. Anyway, I spurned him, and he got angry and began issuing his own threats, specifically that he had an appointment with a prosecutor from the County Solicitor's Office. Hammond Cross." She glanced at him. "He said no doubt you would be interested in Bobby's and my scam."

After a moment, she continued, "I panicked. I saw my carefully reconstructed life falling apart. The Ladds, who had placed such confidence in me, would be disgraced. Doubt would be cast on my credibility, rendering my studies worthless. Patients whose trust I had won would feel betrayed.

"So I ran. In the elevator I started shaking uncontrollably. When I reached the lobby level, I went into the bar looking for a place to sit down, because my knees felt ready to buckle.

"But when my panic subsided, I realized what an irrational reaction it was. In seconds, I had regressed to where I'd been when Bobby had controlled my life. There in the bar, I came to my senses. My juvenile record was decades behind me. I am a respected member of my community. I'm acclaimed in my field. What was I afraid of? I had done nothing wrong. If I could convince the right person that once again my half-brother was trying to exploit me, I possibly could get rid of him forever. Who better to make a believer than—"

"Hammond Cross, assistant county solicitor."

"Correct." She nodded up at Frank. "So I returned to the room on the fifth floor. When I got there, the door to the suite was ajar. I put my ear to it, but couldn't hear any conversation. I pushed it open and looked in. Pettijohn was lying face down near the coffee table."

"Did you realize he was dead?"

"He wasn't," she said, drawing a shocked reaction from both men. "I didn't want to touch him, but I did. He had a pulse, but he was unconscious. I didn't want to be caught with him in that condition when my former partner in crime was blackmailing him. So once again I virtually ran from the suite. This time I took the stairs down. We must have just missed each other," she said to Hammond. "When I reached the lobby, I spotted you leaving the hotel by the main doors."

"How did you know me?"

"I recognized you from your media exposure. You looked very upset. I thought—"

"That I had attacked Pettijohn."

"Not attacked. I thought you had punched out his lights, and that, if your meeting had gone anything like mine, he probably deserved it. That's why I followed you. Later, if Pettijohn filed a complaint against Bobby and me, if I was implicated in a crime, who better to have as my alibi than the D.A., who himself had had an altercation with Pettijohn?" She looked down at her hands. "Several times Saturday evening, I began to feel guilty about what I was doing, and tried to leave you."

She glanced at Hammond, who guiltily looked up at Frank, who was scowling at him like the gatekeeper of hell.

"By Sunday morning I was very ashamed and left before Hammond woke up," she told her lawyer. "That evening Bobby came for his money—there was none, of course. But to my astonishment he congratulated me for killing our only 'witness.'"

"You didn't know until then that Pettijohn was dead?"

"No. I had listened to CDs on the drive home, not to the car radio. I didn't turn on the TV. I was . . . was preoccupied." After a brief, tense silence, she said, "Anyway, when I heard that Pettijohn had been murdered, I believed the worst."

"You thought I had killed him," Hammond said. "That he eventually had died from my assault."

"Right. And I continued believing that until—"

"Until you heard that he had died of gunshot," he said. "That's why you were so shocked to learn the cause of death."

She nodded. "The two of you didn't struggle?"

"No, I just stormed out."

"Then his stroke must have caused him to fall."

"That would be my guess," Hammond said. "The cerebral thrombosis caused him to black out. He fell against the table, causing the wound on his forehead."

"Which I couldn't see. I didn't realize how bad his condition was. For the rest of my life, I'll regret that I didn't do something," she said with genuine remorse. "If I had called for help, it probably would have saved his life."

"Instead someone came in after you, saw him lying there, and shot him."

"Unfortunately, Frank, that's right," she said. "Which is partially why I haven't used my alibi."

"And why I came here tonight," Hammond said.

The attorney divided a puzzled glance between them. "What have I missed?"

Alex was the one to explain. "Thanks to Smilow's thoroughness, and now the media, everyone knows that I was in Pettijohn's suite last Saturday afternoon. But the one person who knows with absolute certainty that I did not shoot him is the person who actually did."

"And that person made an attempt on Alex's life last night."

Frank's jaw went slack with disbelief as he listened to Hammond's account of their encounter in the alley.

"Alex was his target. He was no ordinary mugger."

"But how do you know it was Pettijohn's killer?"

Hammond shook his head. "He was only a hireling, and not a very accomplished one. But Lute's murderer is accomplished."

"You actually think you've solved the mystery?" Frank asked.

Hammond said, "Brace yourselves."

He talked uninterrupted for another quarter hour. Frank registered shock, but Alex didn't seem all that surprised.

When he finished, Frank expelled a long breath. "You've already spoken to hotel personnel?"

"Before coming here. Their statements bear out my hypothesis."

"It sounds plausible, Hammond. But, my God. It couldn't be more difficult, could it?"

"No, it couldn't," Hammond admitted.

"You're going out on a limb with a chain saw in your hand."

"I know."

"Where do you go from here?"

"Well, first of all, I want to make damn sure I'm right." Hammond turned to Alex. "Other than me, did Pettijohn mention any other appointments? I know that he had another scheduled for six o'clock. I just don't know with whom."

"No. He only told me about his meeting with you."

"On your way to the suite, did you see anyone in the elevator or in the hallway?"

"No one except the Macon man who later identified me."

"And when you took the stairs, you didn't see anyone in the stairwell?"

"No." He looked at her hard, and she added, "Hammond, you're placing your career on the line for me. I wouldn't lie to you now."

"I believe you, but our culprit might not. If it's *believed* that you saw something, it really doesn't matter if you did or not."

"To the killer, she's still a threat."

"Which would be unacceptable. Remember the crime scene was nearly immaculate. This isn't a person who leaves loose ends untied."

"So what do you suggest?" Frank asked. "Around-the-clock bodyguards for Alex?"

"No," she said adamantly.

"That's what I would prefer," Hammond said. "But reluctantly I agree with Alex. First of all, I know her well enough to know that she wouldn't stand for it, and that arguing about it would be futile. Second, guards, or anything out of the ordinary, would be like a red flag."

"How long do you need, Hammond?"

"I wish I knew."

"Well, that open-ended time frame makes me very nervous," Frank said. "While you're gathering evidence, Alex is at risk. You should take this up with . . ."

"Yeah," Hammond said, reading Frank's unspoken thought. "Who do I take it up with? At this point, who do I trust? And who would believe me? These allegations would sound like sour grapes, especially if anyone learned that Alex and I are lovers."

"'Are'? You mean you've been together since Saturday night?" Their expressions must have given them away. "Never mind," Frank groaned. "I don't want to know."

"As I was saying," Hammond continued, "I've got to do this myself, and I've got to work quickly." He laid out his plan to them.

When he finished, he addressed Frank first. "Do I have your sanction?"

The lawyer pondered his answer for a long moment. "I'd like to believe that people associate my name with integrity. That's what I've worked toward, anyway. This is the first time I've ever deviated from the rule of ethics. If this ends in disaster, if you're wrong, I would probably come through it with no more than a reprimand and a blemish on an otherwise impeccable record. But, Hammond, it's your throat. I'm sure you realize that."

"I do."

"Furthermore, I don't give it a snowball's chance in hell of working."

"Why not?"

"Because in order for it to work, you must confide in Steffi Mundell."

"I'm afraid that's a necessary evil."

"The very word I would have used."

Just then Hammond's pager beeped. He checked the number. "Don't recognize it." Ignoring the page, he asked Frank if he had any questions.

"Are you serious?" the lawyer asked facetiously.

Hammond grinned. "Cheer up. Wouldn't you just as well be hanged a sinner as a saint?"

"I'd rather not be hanged at all."

Hammond smiled, but then he turned away from Frank and addressed Alex. "What are your thoughts?"

"What can I do?"

"Do?"

"I want to help."

"Absolutely not," he countered adamantly.

"I caused this mess."

"Pettijohn would have been murdered last Saturday whether or not you had ever met him. As I've explained, it had nothing to do with you."

"Even so, I can't just stand by and do nothing."

"That's exactly what you'll do. It can't appear that we're in league together."

"He's right, Alex," Frank said. "He's got to work it from the inside."

Eyes filled with anxiety, she said, "Hammond, isn't there another way? You could lose your career."

"And you could lose your life. Which is more important to me than my career."

He reached for her hand. She took his and squeezed it. They stared into one another's eyes until the silence became heavy and uncomfortable.

Frank delicately cleared his throat. "Alex, you'll stay here tonight. No argument."

"I agree," Hammond said.

"And you'll go home." The stern order was directed toward Hammond.

"Reluctantly I agree to that, too."

"The guest room stays ready, Alex. Second bedroom to the left of the landing."

"Thank you, Frank."

"It's late, and I've got a lot to think about." Frank headed for the study door, where he paused and looked back at them. He was about to speak, arrested himself, then finally said, "I was about to ask you both if last Saturday night had been worth it. But your answer is evident. Good night."

Once they were alone, the silence became more uncomfortable, the ticking clock on Frank's desk more ponderous. There was a tension between them, and it wasn't entirely because of what might happen tomorrow.

Hammond was the first to speak. "It doesn't matter, Alex."

She didn't even have to ask what he was referring to. "Of course it matters, Hammond." He reached for her, but she evaded him, stood up, and moved across the room to stand before a bookcase filled with legal tomes. "We're deluding ourselves."

"How so?"

"This won't have a happy ending. It can't."

"Why not?"

"Don't be naive."

"Trimble is garbage. It's ancient history. I knew about all that last night when I told you that I love you." He smiled. "I haven't changed my mind."

"Our love affair started with me playing a dirty trick on you."

"A dirty trick? That's not how I remember last Saturday night."

"I lied to you from the start. That will always be in the back of your mind, Hammond. You'll never completely trust me. I don't want to be with someone who is constantly second-guessing everything I do, and gauging the truthfulness of everything I say."

"I wouldn't."

She smiled, but it was a sad expression. "Then you wouldn't be human. I'm a scholar of human emotion and behavior. I know the lasting impact that events in our lives have on us, the injuries that other people inflict, sometimes deliberately, sometimes without meaning to. I see the result of those injuries every day in my sessions with patients. I've suffered them myself. It took me years to get myself emotionally healthy, Hammond. I worked hard to get free from Bobby's influence. And I did. With God's help I did. That's why I'm able to love you the way—"

"So you do? Love me?"

In an unconscious gesture, she raised her hand and touched her heart. "So much it hurts."

His pager beeped again. Cursing softly, he turned it off. The distance between them seemed wide, and he knew that it would be inappropriate to cross it tonight. "I want to kiss you."

She nodded.

"And if I kissed you, I'd want to make love to you."

Again she nodded, and they exchanged a long, meaningful stare.

"I love making love to you," he said.

Her chest rose and fell gently. "You should go."

"Yeah," he said huskily. "As you know, I've got to get up very early tomorrow." His brows came together in a steep frown. "I don't know how it will play out, Alex. I'll be in constant touch. You'll be all right?"

"I'll be all right." She gave him a reassuring smile.

He started backing out of the room. "Sleep well."

"Good night, Hammond."

"Dammit!" Loretta Boothe glared at the coin-operated telephone as though willing it to ring. Twice she had paged Hammond after getting no answer on either his home or cell phones. The telephone remained stubbornly silent. She checked her wristwatch. Nearly two. Where the devil could he be?

She waited sixty seconds longer, then plunked another coin into the phone and dialed his house again.

"Listen, asshole, I don't know why I'm chasing around in the middle of the night covering your ass, but for the umpteenth time, I left that fucking fair with a material witness in tow. Please advise ASAP. He's antsy and I'm running low on charm."

"Ms. Boothe?"

She hung up and called, "Coming!" to the man riding shotgun in her car.

At first he had been eager to talk about the case and news of Alex Ladd's arrest. Then, when she told him that he could very well be called as a material witness, he had begun to backpedal in double time. He had said he didn't want to get involved. He wanted to be a good citizen, but . . .

It had taken hours of cajoling and all her powers of persuasion to get him to commit to cooperating. But she didn't trust his commitment. At any moment he might have a change of heart and bolt, or conveniently develop a mental block and forget everything he remembered about last Saturday.

"Ms. Boothe?"

Flipping her middle finger at the pay phone, she returned to her car. "Didn't I tell you to call me Loretta? Want another beer?"

"Now that I've had time to think about it . . ." Indecision rearranged his features. "I just don't know if I want to get involved. I could be wrong, you know. I didn't get that good a look at her."

Loretta reassured him again, thinking all the while, *Where the hell is Hammond?*

# FRIDAY

## CHAPTER 35

Steffi drew up short when she opened her office door and found Hammond on the other side of it, fist raised, about to knock.

"Got a minute?"

"Actually, no. I was just—"

"Whatever it is, it can wait. This is important." He backed her into the office and closed the door.

"What's up?"

"Sit down."

Quizzical, she nevertheless did as he asked. In the time it took her to get seated, he had begun pacing the width of her office. He didn't look much better than he had yesterday. His arm was still in the sling. His hair looked like it had been dried with a leaf blower. He had nicked his chin shaving, and the scabbing spot of blood reminded her of the lab report she had received only minutes ago.

"You look frazzled. How much coffee have you had this morning?" she asked.

"None."

"Really? You look like you've been taking caffeine by IV."

Suddenly he stopped pacing and faced her across the desk. "Steffi, we have a special relationship, don't we?"

"Pardon?"

"It transcends our being colleagues. While we were together, I entrusted you with my secrets. That past intimacy elevates our relationship to another plane, right?" He looked closely at her for a moment, then cursed and tried in vain to smooth down his hair. "God, this is awkward."

"Hammond, what is going on?"

"Before I tell you, I've got to clear the air on another matter."

"I'm over it, Hammond. Okay? I don't want a man who—"

"Not that. Not us. Harvey Knuckle."

The name landed like a rock on her desk. She tried to contain her surprise, but knew her shattered expression must be a dead giveaway. Under Hammond's piercing gaze, a denial would be futile.

"Okay, so you know. I had him sneak me some private information on Pettijohn."

"Why?"

She tinkered with a paper clip for a moment, weighing the advisability of dissecting this with Hammond. Finally she said, "Pettijohn approached me several months ago. It seemed innocent enough at first. Then he made his pitch. He said it had occurred to him how comfortable it could be for both of us if I held the county solicitor's job. He promised to make it happen."

"If?"

"If I would keep my eyes and ears open and report to him anything that might be of interest. Such as a covert investigation into his business dealings."

"To which you said?"

"Something not too ladylike, I'm afraid. I turned down the offer, but it made me curious to know what he could be hiding, what he was into. Wouldn't it be a feather in Steffi Mundell's cap if she nailed the biggest crook in Charleston County? So I approached Harvey." She bent the paper clip into an S shape. "I got the information I was after and—"

"Saw my father's name on the partnership papers."

"Yes, Hammond," she replied solemnly.

"And you kept quiet about it."

"It was his crime, not yours. Preston couldn't be punished without you getting hurt. I didn't want that to happen. You know I would love to have the top job. I've made no secret of it."

"But not if it meant getting into bed with Pettijohn."

She shuddered. "I hope you meant that figuratively."

"I did. Thanks for coming clean."

"Actually, I'm glad it's out in the open. It's been like a fester." She dropped the paper clip. "Now what's up?"

He sat down across from her, balancing on the edge of the seat and leaning forward as he spoke. "What I'm about to tell you must remain strictly between us," he said in a low, urgent voice. "Do I have your confidence?"

"Implicitly."

"Good." He took a deep breath. "Alex Ladd did not kill Lute Pettijohn."

That was the big proclamation? After that grand buildup, she'd been expecting a heart-rending confession of their affair, maybe an earnest plea for forgiveness. Instead his verbal drumroll had heralded only another pathetic petition for his secret lover's innocence.

Her temper surged, but she forced herself to lean back in her chair in a deceptively relaxed posture. "Yesterday you were gung-ho to take the case to the grand jury. Why this sudden reversal of opinion?"

"It's not sudden, and I was never gung-ho. All along I've felt we had the wrong person. There are too many factors that don't add up."

"Trimble—"

"Trimble's a pimp."

"And she was his whore," she fired back. "It appears she still is."

"Let's not go there again, okay?"

"Agreed. It's a tired argument. I hope you've got a better one."

"Smilow killed him."

Her jaw involuntarily went slack. This time, she truly couldn't believe that she had heard him correctly. "Is this a joke?"

"No."

"Hammond, what in God's name—"

"Listen for a minute," he said, patting the air between them. "Just listen, and then if you disagree, I'll welcome your viewpoint."

"Save your breath. I can almost assure you that my viewpoint is going to differ."

"Please."

Last Saturday evening when she had teasingly asked Smilow if he had murdered his former brother-in-law, she had intended it as a joke, albeit a bad one. She had asked him out of pure orneriness, trying to provoke him. But Hammond was deadly serious. Obviously he considered Smilow a viable suspect. "Okay," she said with an exaggerated shrug of surrender. "Lay it on me."

"Think about it. The crime scene was practically sterile. Smilow himself has made several references to how pristine it was. Who would know better how to leave no trace of himself than a homicide detective who makes his living picking up after murderers?"

"It's a good point, Hammond, but you're reaching."

He was reaching in order to protect his new lover. It was deeply insulting that he would go to such lengths for Alex Ladd's sake. All that schoolboy stammering about intimacy and entrusting her with his secrets, and clearing the air, and their special, elevated relationship had been just so much bullshit. He was trying to use her to get his lady love off the hook.

She wanted to tell him that she knew about their inappropriate affair, but that would be an impetuous and foolish move. While it would be gratifying to see him humbled, she would sacrifice a long-term advantage. Her knowledge of their secret affair was a trump card. Playing it too soon would reduce its effectiveness.

Meanwhile, the more he talked, the more ammunition he was giving her to use against him. Unwittingly, he was handing her the job of county solicitor gift-wrapped. It took a lot of self-control to maintain her poker face.

"I hope you're basing your suspicion on more than the lack of physical evidence," she said.

"Smilow hated Pettijohn."

"It's been established that many people did."

"But not to the degree that Smilow did. On several occasions, he all but pledged to kill Lute for the unhappiness he had caused Margaret. I have it on good authority that he once attacked Lute and would have killed him on the spot if he hadn't been restrained."

"Who told you that, Deep Throat?"

Unappreciative of her amusement, he said stiffly, "In a manner of speaking, yes. For the time being I'm keeping this as confidential as possible."

"Hammond, are you sure you're not letting your personality conflict with Smilow color your reason?"

"True, I don't like him. But I've never threatened to kill him. Not like he threatened to kill Lute Pettijohn."

"In the heat of the moment? In a fit of rage? Come on, Hammond. Nobody takes death threats like that seriously."

"Smilow often goes for drinks in the lobby bar of the Charles Towne Plaza."

"So do hundreds of other people. For that matter, so do we."

"He gets his shoes shined there."

"Oh, he gets his shoes shined there," she exclaimed, slapping the edge of her desk. "Hell, that's practically a smoking gun!"

"I refuse to take umbrage, Steffi. Because the gun was my next point."

"The murder weapon?"

"Smilow has access to handguns. Probably at least half of them are unregistered and untraceable."

This was the first issue to which Steffi gave serious consideration. Her teasing smile slowly faded. She sat up straighter. "You mean handguns—"

"In the evidence warehouse. They're confiscated in drug raids. Seized in arrests. Being held there until a trial date, or simply awaiting disposal or sale."

"They keep change-of-custody records over there."

"Smilow would know how to get around that. He could have used one, then replaced it. Maybe he threw it away after using it. It would never be missed. He may have used one that hadn't been consigned to the warehouse yet. There are dozens of ways."

"I see what you mean," she said thoughtfully, then shook her head. "But it's still a stretch, Hammond. Just as we don't have a weapon to prove that Alex Ladd shot Pettijohn, we don't have one that proves Smilow did."

He sighed, glanced down at the floor, then looked across the desk at her again. "There's something else. Another motive, perhaps even more compelling than revenge for his sister's suicide."

"Well?"

"I can't discuss it."

"What? Why not?"

"Because someone else's privacy would be violated."

"Wasn't it you who, not five minutes ago, made that flowery speech about our transcendent relationship and mutual trust?"

"It's not that I mistrust you, Steffi. Someone else trusts *me*. I can't betray that individual's confidence. I won't, not until and unless this information becomes a material element in the case."

"The case?" she repeated with ridicule. "There is no case."

"I think there is."

"Do you actually intend to pursue this?"

"I know it won't be easy. Smilow isn't a favorite among CPD personnel, but he's feared and respected. No doubt I'll encounter some resistance."

" 'Resistance' is putting it mildly, Hammond. If you investigate one of their own, you'll never have the cooperation of another city cop."

"I'm aware of the obstacles. I realize what it's going to cost me. But I'm determined to go through with it. Which should give you some indication of how firmly I believe that I'm right."

*Or how besotted you are with your new lover,* she thought. "What about Alex Ladd and the case we've made against her? You can't just throw it out, make it disappear."

"No. If I did, Smilow would smell a rat. I plan to proceed. But even if the grand jury indicts her, we can't win the case we have against her. We can't," he said stubbornly when he saw that she was about to object. "Trimble is a smarmy hustler. A jury will see right through his cheesy veneer. They'll think his testimony is self-serving, and they'll be right. They won't believe him even if he occasionally tells the truth. Besides, how many times has Dr. Ladd earnestly denied that she did it?"

"Naturally she's going to deny she did it. They all deny it."

"But she's different," he muttered.

Even knowing about his affair with the psychologist, Steffi was dismayed by his unshakable determination to protect and defend her. She studied him for a moment, not even trying to hide her frustration. "That's it? You've told me everything?"

"Honestly, no. I checked some things out last night, but the evidence isn't concrete."

"What kind of things?"

"I don't want to discuss them now, Steffi. Not until I'm certain that I'm right. This is a precarious situation."

"You're damn right it is," she said angrily. "If you won't tell me everything, why tell me anything? What do you want from me?"


The last person Davee Pettijohn expected to come calling that morning was the woman suspected of making her a widow.

"Thank you for seeing me."

Sarah Birch had led Dr. Alex Ladd into the casual living room where Davee was having coffee. Even if the housekeeper hadn't announced her by name, Davee would have recognized her. Her picture was on the front page of the morning newspaper, and Davee had seen last evening's newscasts before her troubling, clandestine meeting with Smilow.

"I'm receiving you more out of curiosity than courtesy, Dr. Ladd," she said candidly. "Have a seat. Would you like coffee?"

"Please."

While waiting for Sarah Birch to return with an extra cup and saucer, the two women sat in silence and assessed one another. The TV cameras and newspaper photographs hadn't done Alex Ladd justice, Davee decided.

After thanking the housekeeper for the coffee and taking a sip, Alex said, "I saw your husband last Saturday afternoon in his hotel suite." She indicated the sections of the morning edition scattered about. "The newspaper write-ups subtly suggest that Mr. Pettijohn and I had a personal relationship."

Davee smiled wryly. "Well, he had a reputation to uphold."

"But I don't. There's absolutely no basis for that implication. Although you'll probably think I'm lying if my half-brother ever testifies against me."

"I read about him, too. In print Bobby Trimble comes across as a real asshole."

"You flatter him."

Davee laughed, but as she watched the other woman's face, she realized that the topic wasn't pleasant for her. "You had it rough as a kid?"

"I got past it."

Davee nodded. "We all bear scars from childhood, I guess."

"Some scars are just more visible than others," Alex said by way of agreeing. "In my work, I've learned how clever people can be at hiding them. Even from themselves."

Davee studied her for a moment longer. "You're not what I expected. From the way you were portrayed in the news stories, I would have thought you were . . . coarser. Harder. Devious. Even wicked." She laughed again. "I would have thought you were more like me."

"I have my flaws. Plenty of them. But I swear that I met your husband only once. That was last Saturday. As it turns out, not long before he was killed. But I didn't kill him, and I didn't go to that hotel suite to sleep with him. It's important to me that you know that."

"I'm inclined to believe you," Davee said. "First of all, you have nothing to gain by coming here and telling me that. Moreover, and I mean no offense by this, you're not my dearly departed's type."

Alex smiled at that, but her curiosity was genuine when she asked, "Why wouldn't I have been his type?"

"Physically you would have passed muster. Don't be offended by this, either—Lute would screw any woman whose body was warm. Who knows? Sometimes that might not even have been a qualification.

"But he liked his women to be in awe of him. Submissive and stupid. Silent for the most part, except maybe during orgasm. You wouldn't have appealed to him because you're far too self-confident and bright."

She refilled her coffee cup from a silver carafe, then dropped two sugar cubes into the cup so that they made soft splashes. "FYI, Dr. Ladd, some of the people accusing you of killing Lute don't truly believe you did."

Registering surprise, Alex blurted out, "You've spoken with Hammond?"

"No. It wasn't . . ." A jolt of enlightenment halted Davee in midsentence. "'Hammond'? You're on a first-name basis with the man prosecuting your murder case?"

Clearly flustered, Alex set her cup and saucer on the coffee table. "I hope my coming here wasn't too much of an imposition, Mrs. Pettijohn. I wasn't sure you would even consent to see me. Thank you for the—"

Davee stopped the chatter by reaching across the space separating them and laying her hand on Alex's arm. After a pause, Alex raised her head and stared back at Davee with quiet dignity. They communicated on a different level. Defenses were down. Two women seeing, understanding, accepting.

Peering deeply into the other woman's eyes, Davee said softly, "You're the one who is not just complicated but impossible."

Alex opened her mouth to speak, but Davee forestalled her. "No, don't tell me. It would be like reading the last page of a juicy novel. But I can't wait to find out how the two of you managed to get yourselves into this mess. I hope the circumstances were absolutely decadent and delicious. Hammond deserves that." Then she smiled ruefully. "Poor Hammond. This must be one hell of a dilemma for him."

"Very much so."

"Is there anything I can do?"

"He may soon find himself in need of friends. Be his friend."

"I am."

"So he says." Alex slid the strap of her handbag onto her shoulder. "I should go."

Davee didn't summon her housekeeper but walked Alex to the front door herself. "You haven't commented on my house," she observed as they crossed the front foyer. "Most people do the first time they come. What do you think?"

Alex gave a quick look around. "Honestly?"

"I asked."

"You have some lovely things. But to my taste it's a little overdone."

"Are you kidding?" Davee chortled. "It's gaudy as all get-out. Now that Lute is dead, I plan on detackying it."

The two women smiled at each other. This was a rare thing for Davee— feeling a kinship with another woman. With characteristic straightforwardness, she said, "I don't care whether you slept with Lute or not, I like you, Alex."

"I like you, too."

Alex was halfway down the front walk when Davee called out to her. "You were with Lute shortly before he was killed?"

"That's right."

"Hmm. The killer might think that you're holding something back. Something you saw or heard. Are you?" she asked bluntly.

"Shouldn't we leave the questions to the police?"

She continued down the walk and let herself out through the front gate. Davee closed the door and turned. Sarah Birch had come up behind her.

"What is it, baby?" She reached out and smoothed away the worry lines creasing Davee's forehead.

"Nothing, Sarah," she murmured absently. "Nothing."

## CHAPTER 36

VERY EARLY THAT MORNING, before leaving for the office and his conversation with Steffi, Hammond had checked his voice mail. He returned only one message.

*"Loretta, this is Hammond. I didn't get your messages until this morning. Sorry I put you in a huff last night. I mistook your pages for a wrong number. Uh, listen, I appreciate what you did. But the fact is, I don't want you to bring in this guy you talked to at the fair. Not now anyway. I have my reasons, believe me, and I'll explain everything later. For now, keep him on ice. If it turns out I need him, I'll let you know. Otherwise, just . . . I guess you can . . . what I'm saying is, you're free to take on other work. If I need you further, I'll be in touch. Thanks again. You're the best. Goodbye. Oh, I'll send you a check to cover yesterday and last night. You went above and beyond. 'Bye."*

Bev Boothe listened to the message twice, then stared at the telephone, her fingers tapping lightly on the number pad as she reflected on what to do with the message—save or delete?

What she would like to tell Mr. Cross to do with his message was anatomically impossible.

She was tired and cranky. Overnight someone had dented her car while it was parked in the hospital personnel parking lot. A dull lower backache took hold every morning following her twelve-hour shift.

Mostly, she was worried about her mother, whose bedroom was empty and undisturbed. Where had she been all night, and where was she now? Bev remembered that when she left for the hospital last evening, Loretta had seemed preoccupied and depressed.

This message indicated that she was out doing the county solicitor's dirty work for him, at least for a portion of the night. The bastard didn't sound very appreciative of her mother's efforts.

Spitefully, Bev depressed the numeral three to delete the message.

Five minutes later, as she was stepping from the shower, she heard her mother call into her room. "Bev, just wanted to let you know that I'm home."

Bev grabbed a towel and wrapped it around herself. She tracked wet footprints down the hallway into her mother's bedroom. Loretta was sitting on the side of her bed, easing off a pair of sandals that had cut vivid red stripes into her swollen feet.

"Mom, I was worried," Bev exclaimed, trying not to sound surprised and relieved that her mother was sober, although she looked haggard and unkempt. "Where've you been?"

"It's a long story that can wait until we've both put in a few hours of rack time. I'm exhausted. Did you check the voice mail when you came in? Were there any messages?"

Bev hesitated only a heartbeat. "No, Mom. None."

"I can't believe it," Loretta muttered as she peeled off her dress. "I busted my ass, and Hammond pulls a disappearing act."

Having stripped to her underwear, she pulled back the covers and lay down. She was almost asleep by the time her head hit the pillow.

Bev returned to her own room, slipped on a nightgown, set her alarm, readjusted the thermostat to a cooler temperature, and got into bed.

Loretta had come home sober this time. But what about the next? She was trying so hard to keep her tenuous hold on sobriety. She needed constant reinforcement and encouragement. She needed to feel useful and productive.

Bev's last thought before drifting off to sleep was that if Mr. Hammond Cross was going to relieve her mother of the job she desperately needed for her present and future well-being, then he could damn well relieve her of it in person and not via the lousy voice mail.

"What's that?"

Rory Smilow glanced up from the manila envelope that Steffi had just plunked down on top of a littered desk. As soon as Hammond left her office, she wasted no time driving to police headquarters. She found the detective in the large, open Criminal Investigation office.

She felt no compunction about informing Smilow of this latest development. Loyalty to her former lover never entered her mind. Nor did she let her pledge of confidentiality deter her. From here on, she was playing for keeps.

"It's a lab report." She retrieved the envelope, holding it flat against her chest as though cherishing it. "Can we talk in your office?"

Smilow came to his feet and nodded her in that direction. As they weaved their way through the maze of desks, Detective Mike Collins greeted Steffi in a singsong voice. "Good morning, Miss Mundell."

"Up yours, Collins."

Ignoring the laughter and catcalls, she preceded Smilow down the short hallway and into his private office. When the door closed behind them, he asked her what was up.

"Remember the bloodstains on Alex Ladd's sheets?"

"She nicked her leg shaving."

"No, she didn't. Or maybe she did, but it wasn't her who bled on the sheet. I had the blood typed and compared to another specimen. They match."

"And this other specimen would be . . . ?"

"Hammond's."

For the first time since she had met him, Smilow seemed completely unprepared for what he'd just heard. It left him speechless.

"The night he was mugged," she explained, "he bled. Quite a lot, I think. I got to his place early the following morning to tell him that Trimble was in our jail. He was acting weird. I attributed his weirdness to the rough night he'd had and the medication he was taking.

"But it was more than that. I got this *feeling* that he was lying to cover up a shameful secret. Anyway, before we left, I impulsively sneaked a bloody washcloth out of his bathroom."

"What prompted you to do that? And to test it against the stains on Ladd's sheets?"

"The way he acts around her!" she cried softly, flinging her arms out to her sides. "Like it's all he can do to keep from devouring her. You've sensed it, too, Smilow. I know you have."

He ran his hand around the back of his neck and said the last thing Steffi would have expected. "Jesus, I'm embarrassed."

"Embarrassed?"

"I should have reached this conclusion myself. Long before now. You're right, I did sense something between them. I just couldn't lay my finger on what it was. It's so unthinkable, I never even thought of sexual attraction."

"Don't beat yourself up over it, Smilow. Women are more intuitive about these things."

"And you had another advantage over me."

"What?"

"I've never slept with Hammond."

He grinned wryly, but Steffi didn't find the statement humorous. "Well, it really doesn't matter who sensed what when, or who first defined what is going on between them. The bottom line is that Hammond has been in bed with Alex Ladd since he was appointed prosecutor of the criminal case in which she's a prime suspect." She raised the envelope as though it were a scalp or some other battle trophy. "And we can prove it."

"With evidence illegally obtained."

"A technicality," she said with a shrug. "For now, let's look at the big picture. Hammond is in deep doo-doo. Remember that weak lie about who had busted the lock on her back door? I'm guessing it was Hammond. He broke into her house—"

"For what purpose? To lift the silver?"

She frowned at his making light of this. "They had met before. Before she became a suspect. Each pretended not to know the other. They had to get together to compare notes, so Hammond went to see her. . . . Let's see, that would have been Tuesday night, after we'd caught her in several lies.

"He couldn't go up to her front door and ring the bell, so he sneaked in. When he busted the lock, he cut his thumb. That's what bled on her sheet. I remember he was wearing a bandage the next day.

"And I think she was with him the night he was mugged, too. He was evasive when I asked him about the doctor who had treated his wounds, and why he hadn't gone to the emergency room. He fabricated some farfetched explanations."

The detective was still looking at her with skepticism.

"I know him, Smilow," she said insistently. "I practically lived with him. I know his habits. He's relatively neat, but he's a *guy*. He lets things go until he's forced to straighten up, or he waits on his weekly maid to clean up after him. The morning after the mugging, when he was feeling like shit, do you know what he was worried about? Making up his bed. Now I understand why. He didn't want me to notice that someone had slept beside him."

"I don't know, Steffi," he said, his frown dubious. "As much as I'd like to see this Boy Scout brought down several pegs, I can't believe Hammond Cross would do something this compromising. Have you confronted him about it?"

"No, but I've baited him. Gently. Teasingly. Until this morning when I received the lab report, it was only a hunch."

"Blood type isn't conclusive."

"If it comes to proving malfeasance, we could get a DNA test."

"If you're right—and I'll concede that it has weight—that explains his reaction to Bobby Trimble's statement yesterday."

"Hammond didn't want to hear that Alex Ladd is a whore."

"Was."

"The tense is still up for debate. In any event, that's why he balked at our using Trimble's testimony." When Smilow pulled another steep frown, Steffi said, "What?"

"I tend to agree with him on that. Hammond's arguments make a certain amount of sense. Trimble is so offensive, he could create sympathy for Dr. Ladd. Here she is, a respected psychologist. There he is, a drug-using male prostitute who thinks he's God's special gift to women. He could hurt our case more than help it, especially if you wind up with a largely female jury. It would almost be better if he weren't in the picture."

"If Hammond has his way, there'll be no case against Alex Ladd. At least it will never go to trial."

"That decision isn't entirely his. Does he plan—"

"What he plans is to pin Pettijohn's murder on someone else."

"*What?*"

"You haven't been listening, Smilow. I'm telling you that he'll go to any lengths to protect this woman. In one breath he declined to share the leads he's following, and in the next breath he's asking for my cooperation and help in building a case against someone else. Someone who had motive and opportunity. Someone he would love to see go down for it." Steffi savored the moment before adding, "And guess who he has in mind."

"Hammond, I've been trying to locate you all morning."

"Hey, Mason." He had got the message that Mason was looking for him, but had hoped to dodge him. He didn't have time for a meeting, however brief. "I've been awfully busy this morning. In fact, I'm on my way out now."

"Then I won't detain you."

"Thanks," Hammond said, continuing on his way toward the exit. "I'll catch up with you later."

"Just be sure you're free at five o'clock this afternoon."

Hammond stopped, turned. "What happens then?"

"A press conference. All the local stations are broadcasting it live."

"Today? Five o'clock?"

"City hall. I've decided to formally announce my retirement and endorse you as my successor. I see no reason to postpone it. Everybody knows already anyway. Come the November election, your name will be on the ballot." He beamed a smile on his protégé and proudly rocked back on his heels.

Hammond felt like he had just been slam-dunked, head first. "I . . . I don't know what to say," he stammered.

"No need to say anything to me," Mason boomed. "Save your remarks for this afternoon."

"But—"

"I've notified your father. Both he and Amelia plan to be there."

*Christ.* "You know, Mason, that I'm right in the middle of this Pettijohn thing."

"What better time? When you're already in the public eye. This is a great opportunity to make your name a Charleston household word."

The statement harkened back to a recent conversation. Hammond closed his eyes briefly and shook his head. "Dad put you up to this, didn't he?"

Mason chuckled. "He bought a few rounds last night at our club. I don't have to tell you how persuasive he can be."

"No, you don't have to tell me," Hammond said in a angry mutter.

Preston never sat back and let the cards fall as they may. He always stacked the deck in his favor. His philanthropy on Speckle Island had disarmed Hammond and practically assured that he would not be held accountable for any wrongdoing that had taken place on the sea island. But just in case Hammond had in mind to continue pursuing it, Preston had upped the ante, raised the stakes, and increased the pressure.

"Look, Mason, I've got to run. Lots going on today."

"Fine. Just remember five o'clock."

"No. I won't forget."

## CHAPTER 37

Loretta swished her feet in the tub of cool water where she'd been soaking them for almost half an hour.

Bev came down the hallway, yawning and stretching. "Mom? You're already up? You didn't sleep long."

"Too much on my mind," she said absently. Then, looking up at Bev, she asked, "Are you sure you checked for messages when you came in this morning? I hope nothing's wrong with our voice mail."

"There's nothing wrong with it, Mom." Bev turned toward her, a guilty look on her face. "You did have a message from Mr. Cross. I just didn't want to give it to you."

"How come? What did he say?"

"He said never mind about the guy from the fair."

Loretta looked at her with patent disbelief. "Are you sure?"

"I thought he said 'the fair.' "

"No, are you sure he said never mind about him?"

"I'm certain of that part. Pissed me off. After all the hard work—Careful, Mom, you're sloshing water on the floor."

Loretta was on her feet, hands planted solidly on her hips. "*Has he gone crazy?*"

\*   \*   \*

Bobby Trimble hadn't counted on jail. Jail stunk. Jail was for losers. Jail was for the old Bobby, maybe, but not for the one he had become.

He had spent the night sharing a cell with a drunk who had snored and farted with equal exuberance throughout the night. He'd been promised that he would be released first thing this morning, as soon as he could be processed out. That was part of the deal he'd struck with Detective Smilow and the bitch from the D.A.'s office—no more than one night of incarceration.

But come this morning, they were taking their sweet time. They served breakfast. At the smell of food, his cell mate rolled off the top bunk barely in time to make it to the open toilet, where he puked for five full minutes. When he was finally empty, he climbed back into the top bunk and passed out again, but not before stumbling into Bobby and soiling his clothes so that he, too, smelled like vomit.

Of course, Bobby didn't take any of this mistreatment quietly. He voiced his complaints loudly and frequently. He ranted and raved, but to no avail. He paced the cell. As the hours crawled by, he sank into a deep funk. Pessimism set in with a vengeance.

It seemed he couldn't buy a break.

Things had been going from sugar to shit ever since Pettijohn got killed. That hadn't been in Bobby's game plan. He was no saint, but he wanted no part of a murder rap. If painting Alex guilty—and who knew? maybe she was—would get him off the hook, that's what he would do. But in the meantime, he would be on a short leash. Until after her trial, his ass belonged to Charleston County. No partying. No women. No drugs. No fun.

Nor was he a hundred thousand dollars richer, as he had expected to be. He had never collected the blackmail money. It remained unknown whether or not Alex had collected the cash from Pettijohn, but that was a moot point. *He* didn't have it.

His future was looking bleak and uncertain, the only surety being that he was going nowhere fast as long as he remained cooped up in here.

Coming off his bunk, he pressed himself against the bars. "What's taking so freaking long?"

His questions were ignored. The guards were impervious to his demands.

"You don't understand. I'm not an ordinary prisoner," he told a guard as he ambled past his cell. "I'm not supposed to be here."

"Wish I had a nickel for every time I've heard that one, Bobby."

Bobby whipped his head around. A newcomer, escorted by another guard, wore a lightweight summer suit and necktie. He was clean-shaven, but he still looked a little ragged, probably because of the sling supporting his right arm. He introduced himself as Hammond Cross.

"I've heard of you. D.A.'s office, right?"

"Special assistant solicitor for Charleston County."

"I'm impressed," Bobby said, resuming his modulated voice. "Frankly, I don't care if you're Tinkerbell, so long as you came to escort me out of here."

"That was the deal, wasn't it?"

Cross was a smooth customer. Bobby immediately resented the sophistication that came naturally to him.

He motioned for the guard to open Bobby's cell, but then he was ushered into a room reserved for prisoner/solicitor conferences. "I don't consider this release, Mr. Cross. I made a deal yesterday. Or have you conveniently forgotten?"

"I'm aware of the deal, Bobby."

"Well, fine! Then do what you've got to do to set wheels into motion."

"Not until we've talked."

"If I'm talking to you, I want a lawyer present."

"I'm a lawyer."

"But you're—"

"Sit down and shut up, Bobby."

He was fit, but not all that beefy, this Hammond Cross. Besides that, he was the walking wounded. Arrogantly, Bobby rolled his shoulders. "Harsh words coming from a man with his arm in a sling."

Cross's eyes took on a glint almost as hard and cold as Smilow's. While it didn't frighten Bobby, exactly, it intimidated him enough to sit down. He glared up at Cross. "Okay, I'm sitting. What?"

"You can't possibly appreciate how much I would love to beat the shit out of you."

Bobby gaped at him, speechless.

Cross's lips had barely moved, and his voice was soft, but the hostility behind his statement made the hair on the back of Bobby's neck stand on end. That and the fact that every muscle in Cross's body was flexed as though about to split open his skin.

"Look, I don't know what your beef is, but I made a deal."

"And I made another one," Cross said blandly. "With one of the investors—make that a former investor—in the Speckle Island project."

He let that sink in a moment. Bobby tried hard not to squirm in his chair.

"This individual is willing to testify against you in exchange for clemency. We've got a laundry list of charges for your activities on Speckle Island that are irrelevant to the deal you made yesterday. It would probably bore you for me to list them all, but taking them in alphabetical order, arson would be first."

Bobby's palms were sweating. He wiped them on his pants legs. "Listen, I'll tell you anything you want to know about my sister."

"Useless," Cross said with a wave of dismissal. "She didn't kill Pettijohn."

"But your own people—"

"She didn't do it," he repeated. Then he smiled, but it wasn't friendly. "You're out of chips, Bobby. You've got nothing to bargain with. You're going to be in one of our jails for a while. And when South Carolina gets tired of housing and feeding you, the authorities down in Florida can't wait to have a crack at you."

"Fuck that! And fuck you," Bobby shouted, lunging from his chair. "I want to talk to my lawyer."

He took two steps forward before Cross placed his left palm against his sternum and shoved him back into the chair with so much impetus it almost tipped over with him. Then Cross leaned over him so closely that Bobby had to angle his head back until it strained his neck.

Cross whispered, "One final thing, Bobby. If you go near Alex again—ever—I'll break your neck. And then I'll mess up that pretty face of yours until you're no longer recognizable. Your days as a ladies' man will be over. The only looks you'll get from women are ones of pity and revulsion."

Bobby was stunned. But only for a few seconds. Then it all came together—the threat, the prosecutor's insistence that Alex was innocent. He began to laugh. "Now I get it. Your cock's twitching for my baby sister!"

Playfully he poked Hammond in the chest. "Am I right? Never mind, I know I am. I can read the signs. Tell you what, Mr. Special Assistant whatever the hell you call yourself. Whenever you want to fuck her, you come and see me. Any way you like it, backward, forward or sideways, I can set it up."

The chair was uprooted, and Bobby was sent flying backward along with it. Rockets of pain were launched from the point of contact on his cheekbone. They detonated inside his skull. His ribs snapped as a fist with the force of a piston slammed into them.

"Mr. Cross?"

Bobby heard running footsteps and the voices of the guards. The sounds wafted toward him through a vast and hollow darkness.

"Everything all right in here, Mr. Cross?"

"I'm fine, thanks. But I'm afraid the prisoner needs some assistance."

## CHAPTER 38

THIS IS INTERESTING."

Steffi cradled the receiver of her desk phone between her ear and shoulder. "Hammond? Where are you?"

"I just left the jail. Bobby Trimble is ours for a while."

"What about our deal with him?"

"His crimes on Speckle Island superseded that. I'll fill you in later."

"OK. So what's interesting?"

"Basset," he said. "Glenn Basset? The sergeant who oversees the evidence warehouse?"

"Okay. I know him, vaguely. Mustache?"

"That's him. He has a sixteen-year-old daughter who was arrested for drug possession last year. First arrest. Basically a good kid, but had gotten in with the wrong crowd at school. Peer pressure. Isolated—"

"I got it. What does this have to do with anything?"

"Basset went to Smilow for counsel and help. Smilow intervened with our office on behalf of Basset's daughter."

"They swapped favors."

"That's my guess," Hammond said.

"Only a guess?"

"So far it's just rumor and innuendo. I've been nosing around. Cops are reluctant to talk about other cops, and I haven't approached Basset with it yet."

"I'd like to be there when you do, Hammond. What's next?"

"I've got one more stop to make, then I'm going over to the Charles Towne."

"What for?"

"Remember the robes?"

"That people wear to and from the spa? White fluffy things that make everybody look like a polar bear?"

"Where was Pettijohn's?" he asked.

"What? I'm not—"

"He got a massage early that afternoon. He showered in the spa, but he didn't dress. I asked the masseur. He came in wearing a robe, and he left wearing it. There should have been a used robe and slippers in his room. They weren't among the evidence collected. So what happened to them?"

"Good question," she said slowly.

"Here's an even better one. Did you know that Smilow gets routine manicures in the spa? Get it? No one would think twice about seeing him wearing one of those robes. I'm going to check the suite again, see if we've missed anything. Just wanted to keep you posted. By the way, have you seen him today?"

"Smilow?" She hesitated, then said, "No."

"If you do, keep him busy so I'm free to operate."

"Sure. Let me know what turns up."

"You'll be the first."

"Thanks for meeting me, Hammond."

He slid into the booth opposite Davee. "What's up? You said urgent."

"Would you like some lunch?"

"No, thanks, I can't. Busy day. I'll have a club soda," he told the waiter, who withdrew to fill his order. He fanned smoke away from his face. "When did you start smoking again?"

"An hour ago."

"What's going on, Davee? You seem upset."

She took a sip of her drink, which Hammond guessed correctly wasn't her first, and it wasn't club soda. He had responded to her page, surprised when she asked him to meet her at a restaurant downtown. He was headed that way anyway, which, given his tight schedule, was the only reason he had agreed to the spontaneous invitation.

"Rory called me last night. We had a rendezvous. Not of the romantic sort," she clarified.

"Then what sort?"

"He asked me all kinds of questions about you and Lute's murder investigation." She waited until the waiter delivered his club soda before continuing. "He knows that you met with Lute last Saturday, Hammond. But I didn't tell him. I swear I didn't."

"I believe you."

"He said you were seen in the hotel. He's guessing about your appointment with Lute, but as we know, he's a damn good guesser."

"It's a harmless guess."

"Maybe not, because there's something else you should know." Her hand was shaking as she lifted the cigarette to her lips. Hammond took it from her and ground it out in the ashtray.

"Go ahead."

"I know about you and Alex Ladd."

He considered playing dumb but realized that Davee of all people would see through the act. "How?"

He listened as she told him about Alex's visit to her house that morning. "I don't know the details of how you met, or when, or where. I didn't ask for any insider information, and she didn't volunteer any. And by the way, she's lovely."

"Yes," he said thickly. "She is."

"As I'm sure you're aware," she continued, "this love affair is ill-timed and most inappropriate."

"Very aware."

"Of all the women in Charleston who're hot for you, why—"

"I have a pressing schedule today, Davee. I haven't got time for a lecture. I didn't plan on falling in love with Alex this week. It just happened that way. And by the way, you're a fine one to be preaching sermons about indiscretions."

"I'm only warning you to be careful. I haven't even been in the same room with the two of you, but it was evident to me just by the way she spoke your name that she's in love with you.

"Anyone who *has* been with you when you're together is bound to sense those undercurrents. Even someone as romantically disinclined as Rory. That's why I called you." Tears filled her eyes, and that alarmed him, because Davee never cried. "I'm afraid for you, Hammond. And for her."

"Why, Davee? What are you afraid of?"

"I'm afraid that Rory killed Lute, and that he might kill someone else to cover it up."

He looked at her for a long moment, then smiled softly. "Thanks, Davee."

"For what?"

"For caring about me. I love you for it. I love you even more for caring about Alex. I hope you become best friends." He slid out of the booth, leaned down, and kissed the top of her head. "You've got nothing to worry about."

"Hammond?" she cried after him as he rushed from the booth.

"I'm on top of it," he called back to her. "I promise."

He jogged from the restaurant to his car. As he drove toward the hotel, he dialed Alex's home number.

The lock on the kitchen door was still broken. It was careless of her not to have had it repaired by now. As he remembered from before, the kitchen was cozy and neat, although the faucet in the sink had developed a drip.

He was moving past the telephone when it rang, startling him. She answered it in another room on the second ring. Her voice drifted down the hallway toward him.

"Hammond, are you all right?"

She was in her office, her back to the door opening into the hall. He could smell the clove-spiked oranges in the bowl on the console table. She was seated in an armchair with what appeared to be patients' files stacked on the end table at her elbow. One folder lay open in her lap along with a palm-size tape recorder. Sunlight streamed in through the tall windows. Her hair attracted it like a magnet.

"Don't worry about me, I'm fine. . . . What about Sergeant Basset? . . . So, you were right. In a way I feel sorry for him. There's no telling what threats were used to get him to cooperate. . . . Yes, I will. Please call me as soon as you can."

She ended her call and set the cordless phone on the table. Catching movement out of the corner of her eye, she turned toward him suddenly. The open file folder slid off her lap onto the floor, scattering its contents across the Oriental rug. The recorder landed at her feet with a thud. Clearly, she had thought she was alone.

Her voice a near gasp, she said, "Detective Smilow, you startled me."

Smitty had someone in his chair when Hammond walked past on his way to the elevators. "Hi, Smitty. Have you seen Detective Smilow today?"

"No, sir, Mr. Cross. I surely haven't."

Usually gregarious, Smitty didn't look up and never broke his rhythm as he alternately whisked the brushes across the toe of his customer's shoe. Hammond didn't dwell on it. He was preoccupied with getting to the fifth-floor penthouse suite.

The yellow tape still formed an X across the door. Having obtained a key from the manager last night, he stepped through the tape and went inside, leaving the door slightly ajar.

The drapes were drawn, so the room was dim. He made a routine check of the parlor where the bloodstain in the carpet showed up almost black. As he understood it from the housekeeping staff, replacement carpet had been ordered.

Standing over the stain, he tried to work up some feelings of remorse for Pettijohn's death, but he couldn't garner any. He'd been a bastard in life. Even in death, he was still wreaking havoc on people's lives.

Hammond moved into the bedroom and went straight to the closet. He gazed at the robe, hanging with the belt tied at the waist. It matched the one Lute had worn down to the spa. He had left his clothes here in the suite, showered in the spa, then exchanged the robe for his clothes when he returned.

"I might never have thought of it if you hadn't mentioned it that afternoon we had drinks in the lobby bar," he said.

Turning, he faced Steffi, who had thought she was sneaking up behind him. Actually he'd been expecting her.

He continued, "Rhetorically you asked if I could imagine Lute strutting around in one of the spa robes. I couldn't. I didn't. Until last night. And when I imagined it, it caused me to wonder how you knew he had been strutting around in a spa robe that day. I then went on to wonder where the used robe was." He gazed at her thoughtfully. "What I surmise is that you wore that robe out of the suite over your clothes."

"Workout clothes. Which I had thought were a good idea. Who goes to a murder dressed like that? But the robe was even better."

"You dropped it at the spa."

"Along with the towel Pettijohn must have carried from the spa. I wrapped it turban-style around my head. Put on sunglasses. I was virtually unidentifiable. I dropped off the paraphernalia at the spa—there were a lot of people bringing robes and towels in from the gym and pool. No one paid me any attention. I ran a few miles, and by the time I got back, the body had been discovered and the investigation was under way."

"Very clever."

"I thought so," she said with a cheeky smile.

He nodded down at the revolver she had aimed at him. "Is that it?"

"Of course not. Do you think I would be so stupid as to use the same gun twice? When I returned the one I used to shoot Pettijohn, I pilfered another. Just in case."

"As we speak, Basset is spilling his guts. He's a repentant man with a guilty conscience."

"It'll be my word against his. They'll never trace these weapons to me. I didn't sign the log and neither did he. Basset could be making up wicked stories about me because he holds a grudge."

"Smilow asked you to go easy on Basset's daughter."

"And I did the first time. It's not my fault she was busted again. Her hearing is scheduled in a few weeks."

"What did you promise Basset?"

"That I'd be lenient in my recommendation to the judge."

"Or?"

"Or sweet Amanda would get the book thrown at her. It was up to him."

"You drive a hard bargain."

"When I'm forced."

"And you felt forced to kill Pettijohn?"

"He double-crossed me!" she exclaimed in a shrill voice that Hammond had never heard before. Steffi had lost touch with reality.

"I spied for him," she was saying. "Counseled him on legal maneuvers that would snare his rivals but leave him inside the law. Barely, but inside nonetheless. He told me he was going to use the goods on Preston to ruin both of you. Get you out of there completely and install me in the top seat. But then he reneged."

Her eyes turned hard. "He saw a better use for Preston's involvement, and that was to coerce you. He thought he could use that as leverage to get you to come around to his way of thinking. He thanked me for my time and trouble, but asked why he should settle for second best, when he could get *the* best lawyer on his side."

"So you came here that afternoon to kill him."

"I was out of options, Hammond. I had played by the rules and they weren't working for me. Since joining the office, I had worked the hardest, strived the hardest, but you were going to get the job, just as you'd gotten the last one.

"Pettijohn came along and offered me an advantage. For once, I would be the one with the edge. Then, when the reward was in sight, the son of a bitch yanked his support out from under me.

"I had experienced disappointments before, but none that crushing. Every time I looked at him, I would be reminded of what a chump I'd been. A gullible female, which is probably how he saw me. I couldn't tolerate being that susceptible and having him lord it over me. Something inside me snapped, I guess you could say. I simply couldn't let him get away with it.

"He broke the news to me over the telephone, but I insisted on a face-to-face meeting. I showed up a few minutes early for our appointment, and when I saw him sprawled on the floor, my first thought was that someone had robbed me of the pleasure."

"Alex, maybe."

"I didn't know anything about Alex Ladd. Not until that Daniels character gave us her description—and I was sweating bullets when I faced him in that hospital room. I was afraid he'd finger me to Smilow. I hadn't seen him in the hotel, but I couldn't be certain that he hadn't seen me. Anyway, when he described Ladd, I couldn't believe my good fortune. There was actually a suspect. And then when Trimble turned up, I started believing in guardian angels," she said with a laugh.

"You made the attempt on her life."

"That was a mistake. I shouldn't have trusted anyone else with the job."

"Who was he?"

"Someone who drifted through the justice system a few months ago. I had him on an assault and battery. His lawyer pleaded him out. I thought that having someone like him on standby might prove useful one day—maybe I had a premonition that my alliance with Pettijohn might end badly." She shrugged.

"Anyway, I let the guy plead out of incarceration. But I kept track of him. He was willing to slit her throat for a measly hundred dollars. But he blew it. Skipped town with the fifty I gave him as a down payment. He didn't even report in to me that night."

She slapped her forehead with her palm. "Silly me. I didn't connect your mugger with my assassin until I discovered that Alex Ladd was alive and well."

"You were afraid she had seen you Saturday afternoon in Pettijohn's suite."

"I thought it was a distinct possibility. From that first interrogation, I sensed she was holding something back, and was afraid that she had recognized me and was waiting for the perfect moment to spring her secret knowledge. I must admit I was rather taken aback to discover that the secret she was harboring was you. When did you meet her?"

He refused to answer.

"Oh, well." She sighed softly. "You're right. I suppose it doesn't matter, although it shattered my ego to know that you could so easily move from my bed to hers. And, of course, I understand her attraction to you. It wasn't hardship duty to sleep with you. I would have even if Pettijohn hadn't suggested pillow talk as a good source of information."

She hefted the pistol. "I don't hate you, Hammond, although I'd be less than honest if I said I didn't resent your achievements and the ease with which you come by them. It's just that, now I've come this far, you're the last obstacle. I'm sorry."

"Steffi—"

She fired the pistol into his chest.

Steffi turned and hurried across the parlor. She pulled open the door. On the other side of it stood Detective Mike Collins and two uniformed policemen, pistols drawn.

"Hand over the weapon, Ms. Mundell," Collins said. There was no underlying joke in his voice now. One of the policemen stepped forward and took the pistol from her loose grasp. "You okay?" Collins asked.

Hammond was watching her face when she turned her head, her mouth going slack with astonishment. Kevlar had saved him, although he was going to have a bitch of a bruise to go along with the other injuries he had sustained this week.

"You tricked me?"

Collins was reciting her rights, but her attention was on Hammond.

"I figured it out last night. Smilow and I had a conference before daylight. I told him everything. Everything. So we staged all this. I was pretending to gather evidence against him, but actually he and I have been working together today. He's the one who suggested you might get worried when I shared leads with you, leads that pointed to you. He urged me to wear a wire. Also the vest. On both counts I'm glad I took his advice."

She was practically bristling with hatred. He found it hard to believe he'd ever been lovers with her. But it was with a degree of sadness that he said, "I knew you regarded me as your rival, Steffi, but I didn't think you would try to kill me."

"You've always underestimated me, Hammond. You've never given me enough credit. You never thought I was as smart as you."

"Well, apparently you're not."

"I'm smart enough to know about your affair with Alex Ladd," she shouted. "Don't even attempt denying it, because I've got proof of your being in her bed this week!"

Hammond hitched his chin at Collins, who turned her around and nudged her through the open door. Turning her head, she yelled at him over her shoulder, "That's what I'll beat you with, Hammond. Your affair with this woman. Talk about poetic justice!"

There was a soft laugh of self-deprecation behind Alex's voice. "I was expecting you, but I didn't hear you come in, Detective."

"We don't know who or when Steffi might strike. I checked the back of the house and came in through the rear door. That lock still isn't fixed. You should have it repaired immediately."

"I've had more pressing matters on my mind this week."

"Hell of a week."

"To say the least."

He knelt to help her pick up the scattered papers. She thanked him as she gathered the materials back into the folder.

"I couldn't help but overhear," he said. "Hammond told you about Basset?"

"Yes."

"Pretty damn smart of Hammond to figure it out."

"But not long before you did. He told me that when he shared his suspicion with you early this morning, you admitted that it had crossed your mind that Steffi might be involved."

"It had, but I didn't follow up. Frankly because I was so glad Pettijohn was dead." He looked her in the eye. "Dr. Ladd, I never really thought you were the killer. I'm sorry about some of the questions."

She accepted the apology with a small nod. "It's hard for us to back down once we've taken a stand. I was a viable suspect, and you didn't want to be wrong."

"More than that. I didn't want Hammond to be right."

An awkward silence fell between them. It was relieved when his cell phone chirped. "Smilow."

He listened. His face remained expressionless. "I'm on my way." He disconnected. "Steffi shot Hammond. He's okay," he said quickly. "But he got her to admit on the wire that she killed Pettijohn. She's in custody."

Alex didn't realize how anxious she had been until pent-up tension ebbed out of her and she sank into a chair. "Hammond's all right?"

"Perfectly."

"So it's over," she said softly.

"Not quite. He's holding a press conference in half an hour. Can I offer you a lift?"

## CHAPTER 39

Because the temporary Charleston County Judicial Building had such limited space, Monroe Mason had asked if his press conference could be held downtown in city hall. His request had been graciously granted.

Out of respect for the man who had served the community so well for so long, many, who typically rushed headlong toward the weekend at five o'clock on Friday afternoon, had congregated to hear the formal announcement of his retirement.

That's what they had come to hear.

They got more than they bargained for. A head start on the weekend didn't seem such a sacrifice when rumors began to circulate about what had transpired in the same hotel suite where Lute Pettijohn had been found dead less than a week ago. One of the solicitor's own staff had been arrested for the murder.

The room was already crowded when Hammond entered behind Mason and the rank and file of the County Solicitor's Office. Even Deputy Solicitor Wallis, looking gray and ravaged by chemotherapy, had found the strength to attend. Only Stefanie Mundell was absent as they took seats on the dais.

The first row of spectator seats was occupied by reporters and cameramen. Behind them were three rows reserved for city, county, and state officials, invited clergymen, and assorted dignitaries. The remainder of the folding chairs were for guests.

Among them were Hammond's parents. His mother returned his hello nod with a cheerful little wave. Hammond also acknowledged his father, but Preston's visage remained as stony as those gracing Mount Rushmore.

That morning, Hammond had called Preston with the deal he had referenced to Bobby Trimble. It was this: He would recommend to the attorney general that no charges be brought against his father if Preston would testify against Trimble.

Of course that was tantamount to Preston's admitting to his own knowledge of the terrorist activities that had taken place on Speckle Island. He had separated himself from the venture, but not in time to relieve him of culpability.

"That's the deal, Father. Take it or leave it."

"Don't issue me an ultimatum."

"You admit your wrongdoing, or you go to jail denying it," Hammond had stated with resolve. "Take the deal."

Hammond had given him seventy-two hours to think it over and discuss it with his solicitor. He was betting that his father would agree to his terms, an intuition strengthened when Preston's hard stare wavered and he looked away first.

Was it too much to hope that his father was experiencing a twinge of conscience? Although there would always be chasms they couldn't cross, he hoped they could find reconciliation on some level. He wanted to be able to call him Dad again.

Davee was also there, looking like a movie star. She blew him a kiss, but when a reporter poked a microphone at her and asked for a comment, Hammond saw her tell him to fuck off. In those words. But smiling sweetly.

He was watching the rear door when Smilow escorted Alex in. Their gazes locked and held, gobbling up each other. They had spoken on their cell phones while en route, but that wasn't as satisfactory as seeing for himself that she was, finally, safe. From prosecution. From Steffi. From Bobby.

Smilow motioned her toward an empty chair next to one in which Frank Perkins was seated. The lawyer stood and hugged her warmly. Smilow relinquished her to Perkins, then moved down the outer aisle toward the dais. He motioned Hammond over. Nonplussed, Hammond excused himself and stepped down from the temporary platform.

"Good work," Smilow told him.

Knowing the pride that the compliment must have cost the detective, Hammond said, "I just showed up and did what you advised me to do. If you hadn't coordinated it, it wouldn't have worked." He paused a moment. "I still can't believe she came after me. I would have expected a surrender and confession first."

"Then you don't know her very well."

"I came to realize that. Almost too late. Thanks for all you did."

"You're welcome." Smilow glanced toward Davee and caught her looking at him. Unless Hammond's eyes were deceiving him, the detective actually blushed. Quickly he returned his attention back to Hammond. "This is for you." He extended a manila envelope toward Hammond.

"What is it?"

"A lab report. Steffi gave it to me this morning. It matches your blood to that found on Dr. Ladd's sheets." Hammond's lips parted, but Smilow shook his head sternly. "Don't say anything. Just take it and destroy it. Without this, any allegations Steffi makes about you sleeping with a suspect will be unsubstantiated. Of course, since Dr. Ladd turned out not to be the culprit, it's really only a technicality."

Hammond looked at the deceptively innocuous envelope. If he accepted it, he would be as guilty as Smilow had been in the *State v. Vincent Anthony Barlow* case. Barlow was guilty as sin of murdering his seventeen-year-old girlfriend and the fetus she was carrying, but Smilow had fudged some exculpatory evidence which Hammond was obligated by law to disclose.

It wasn't until after he had won a conviction that he learned of Smilow's alleged mishandling of the case. He could never prove that Smilow had deliberately excluded the mitigating evidence in his discovery, so an investigation into malfeasance was never conducted. Barlow, now serving a life sentence, had filed an appeal. It had been granted. The young man would get another trial, to which he was entitled no matter how guilty he was.

But Hammond had never forgiven Smilow for making him an unwitting participant in this miscarriage of justice.

"Don't be a Boy Scout," the detective said now in an undertone. "Haven't you earned all the badges you need?"

"It's wrong."

Smilow lowered his voice even more. "We don't like each other, and we both know why. We operate differently, but we're working the same side. I need a tough prosecutor and trial attorney like you over there in the solicitor's office, not a glad-handing politician like Mason. You'll do far more good by serving this county as the top law officer than you would by making a confession of sexual misconduct, which nobody gives a damn about anyway. Think about it, Hammond."

"Hammond?"

He was being summoned back up onto the dais so they could begin. Without turning, he said, "Coming."

"Sometimes we have to bend the rules to do a better job," Smilow said, staring hard at him.

It was a persuasive argument. Hammond took the envelope.

Mason was drawing his speech to a close. The reporters' eyes were beginning to glaze. Some of the cameramen had lowered their cameras from their shoulders. The account of Steffi's attempt on Hammond's life and subsequent arrest had held them spellbound, but this portion of Mason's address had caused their interest to wane.

"While it pains me that someone in our office is presently in police custody, soon to be charged with a serious crime, I'm equally proud that Special Assistant County Solicitor Hammond Cross was instrumental in her capture. He demonstrated extraordinary bravery today. That's only one of the reasons why I'm endorsing him as my successor."

That received a thunderous round of applause. Hammond stared at Mason's profile while his mentor extolled his talent, dedication, and integrity. The envelope with the incriminating lab report was resting on his knees. He imagined it to be radiating an angry red aura that belied Mason's accolades.

"I won't bore you any longer," Mason boomed in the good-natured, straightforward manner that had endeared him to the media. "Allow me to introduce the hero of the hour." He turned and motioned for Hammond to join him.

The cameramen repositioned their video recorders on their shoulders. The newspaper reporters perked up and almost in unison clicked their ballpoints.

Hammond laid the envelope on the slanted tray of the lectern. He cleared his throat. After thanking Mason for his remarks, as well as for the confidence he had placed in him, he said, "This has been a remarkable week. In many ways it seems like much more time than that has passed since I learned that Lute Pettijohn had been murdered.

"Actually, I don't consider myself a hero, or derive any pleasure from knowing that my colleague, Steffi Mundell, is to be charged with that murder. I believe the evidence against her is compelling. As one familiar with the case—"

Loretta Boothe rushed into the room.

Hammond's heart lurched; his speech faltered and died.

Only those standing near the door noticed her at first. But when Hammond stopped speaking, all heads turned to see who had caused the interruption. Impervious to the stir she had created, Loretta was frantically motioning him toward her.

With all the other events unfolding so rapidly today, he hadn't had time to call and tell her that Alex was no longer a suspect, therefore her whereabouts last Saturday evening were irrelevant.

But Loretta was here, with one of the brawny marines from the fair in tow, and there was no way he could avoid her. "Excuse me a moment."

Despite the murmur of puzzlement that rippled through the crowd, he stepped off the dais and made his way to the back of the room. As he went, he thought of all the people the next few moments would inevitably embarrass. Monroe Mason. Smilow. Frank Perkins. Himself. Alex. When he passed her, his glance silently apologized for what was about to happen.

"You wanted to speak to me, Loretta?"

She didn't even try to mask her irritation. "For almost twenty-four hours."

"I've been busy."

"Well, so have I." She stepped back through the door and spoke to someone who had been left standing out in the hallway. "Come on in here."

Hammond waited expectantly, wondering how he was going to explain himself when the marine gaped at him and declared, "He's the one! He's the one that was dancing with Alex Ladd."

But it wasn't a fresh recruit who came through the door. Instead, looking self-conscious and miserable, a slight black man with wire-rimmed spectacles stepped into the room.

Hammond released a short laugh of pure astonishment. "Smitty?" he exclaimed, realizing that he didn't even know the man's last name.

"How're you doing, Mr. Cross? I told her we shouldn't interrupt, but she wouldn't pay me any mind."

Hammond looked from the shoeshine man to Loretta. "I thought you went to the fair," he heard himself say stupidly. "That's what your messages said."

"I did. I bumped into Smitty there. He was sitting in the pavilion all by himself, listening to the music. We started chatting and the subject of the Pettijohn case came up. He's moved his business to the Charles Towne Plaza."

"I saw him there today."

"I'm sorry I didn't talk to you, Mr. Cross. I guess I was feeling sort of ashamed."

"For what?"

"For not telling you about Steffi Mundell's switcheroo last Saturday," Loretta cut in. "First he sees her in jogging getup, then in one of the hotel robes, then in jogging clothes again. All very strange."

"I didn't make much of it, Mr. Cross, until I saw her on the TV yesterday, and it reminded me."

"He was reluctant to get anyone into trouble, so he didn't say anything to anyone except Smilow."

"Smilow?"

The detective, who had moved up beside Hammond, addressed Smitty.

"When you referred to the lawyer you saw on TV, I thought you were talking about Mr. Cross."

"No sir, the lady lawyer," the older man explained. "I'm sorry if I caused y'all any trouble."

Hammond laid his hand on Smitty's shoulder. "Thank you for coming forward now. We'll get your statement later." To Loretta he said, "Thank you."

She frowned, grumbling. "You got her without my help, but you still owe me a foot rub and a drink. A double."

Hammond turned back into the room. The cameras were whirring now. Lights nearly blinded him as he made his way back to the dais. He could have skipped like a kid. The bands of tension around his chest had been snipped loose. He was breathing normally.

Nobody knew about him and Alex. There wasn't going to be any surprise witness who had seen Alex and him together last Saturday. Nobody knew except her. Frank Perkins. Rory Smilow. Davee.

Well . . . and him.

He knew.

Suddenly he didn't feel like skipping anymore.

He resumed his place behind the lectern. As he did so, Monroe Mason gave him a wink and a thumbs-up. He glanced at his father. Preston, for once, was nodding his wholehearted approval. He would agree with Smilow. Let it drop. Accept the job. Do good work and the misbehavior would be justified.

He was a shoo-in. He would win the election in a landslide. He probably wouldn't even have an opponent. But was the job, any job, worth sacrificing his self-respect?

Wouldn't he rather tell the truth and have it cost him the election than keep a secret? The longer the secret was kept, the dirtier it would become. He didn't want the memory of his first night with Alex to be sullied by secrecy.

His gaze fastened on hers, and he knew in an instant, by the soft expression in her eyes, that she knew exactly what he was thinking. She was the *only* one who knew what he was thinking. She was the only one who would understand why he was thinking it. She gave him an intensely private, extremely intimate smile of encouragement.

In that moment, he loved her more than he had ever thought it possible to love.

"Before I proceed . . . I want to address an individual whose life has been unforgivably upended this week. Dr. Alex Ladd cooperated with the Charleston Police Department and my office at the sacrifice of her practice, her time, and most importantly her dignity. She has endured immeasurable embarrassment. I apologize to her on behalf of this county.

"I also owe her a personal apology. Because . . . because I knew from the start that she had not murdered Lute Pettijohn. She admits to seeing him that afternoon, but well before the time of his death. Certain material elements indicated that she might have had motive. But I knew, even while she was being subjected to humiliating interrogations, that she couldn't have killed Lute Pettijohn. Because she had an alibi."

*Nobody knows. Really only a technicality. Why be a Boy Scout? You'll do far more good . . . Nobody gives a damn anyway.*

Hammond paused and took a deep breath, not of anxiety, but relief.

"*I* was her alibi."